Golden Seeds

Y.A. Picker
&
Rand Soler

Publisher: Archean Enterprises, LLC

Y. A. Picker & Rand Soler

Golden Seeds

Published by: Archean Enterprises, LLC

Suite #3173, 1321 Upland Drive
Houston TX 77043
United States

Cover Design by: By ArcheanArt

ISBN: 9780999281772 (Paperback Edition)
ISBN: 9780999281789 (Ebook Edition)

Contents

Foreward

Humanity has always been on a collision course with evolution. A single species cannot ravage the biosphere without consequences, and Homo sapiens may have become the masters of their own demise. The single lesson flowing from the biosphere's four billion years of history is evolve or sink into the void of extinction. Life is kinetic, and those who can't change must crumble like dust in the winds of time.

After Mark and Mat unexpectedly stumble upon the exotic origin of the Strings of Life in their previous adventure, the world begins shifting around them. Time runs short as a deadly new strain of Ebola lays waste to an unwary planet. They hold in their hands the unlikely genetic secrets for a cure. But outrunning a rapidly spreading virus proves difficult when the price for life requires alterations to the human genome. In a world of myopic humans, unable to envision the next stage of human evolution, some will live, but most will perish.

Mat Dover and Mark Baret Novels

The Strings of Life

Golden Seeds

Night Parrot

The GippsAero GA8 Airvan 8 smoothly left the ground on a westbound trek, leaving behind Esperance, Australia. It banked northward. The patchwork of farms below displayed a mixed bag of crops, mainly wheat, but also a smattering of sorghum, barley, hay, oats, vetch seed, maize, canola, mung beans, soybeans, cottonseed, millet, triticale, and chickpeas. Fifteen minutes later, the plane reached 3,000 meters and leveled off.

The scenery below changed dramatically as it left farmland and entered the Dundas Nature Reserve. The change was indicative of desert terrain, which continued northward 2,100 klicks to Ninety Mile Beach on the north coast. Miles of undisturbed white sand beaches along the Indian Ocean awaited. Upon arrival, a cold brew and grub could be had at the Pardoo Roadhouse & Tavern. In between lies some of the most inhospitable real estate on the planet. But the plane would stop short of there, traveling only 750 kilometers or so to Duketon Airport.

The three-bladed prop turned by a 320 HP Lycoming TIO-540-AH1A Turbocharged Fuel Injected Engine pushed air over the wings providing lift. It moved the plane through the air at a steady 200 kilometers per hour, slightly below its typical cruising speed. The captain and first mate were not in a hurry, and ultimately, they would meander a bit from the straight-line flight path several times. The plane could be fitted with seven rear seats but was not. Instead, the space was tightly loaded with 900 kilograms of various containers, packages, mail, and the like, along with small motors, parts for vehicles and mining implements, mail, liquor, and beer.

Its rugged, boxy design made the plane perfect for this type of operation. Wide-view bubbled windows provided an open feeling from front to rear, making the aircraft like a flying van. Pilots described the plane as being very forgiving. It could be landed on short stretches of outback tracks as well as conventional surfaces like paved runways. Everything on this run was being dropped off at the Moolart Well Gold Mine, located just east of the airport. The run was made on an as-needed basis and was sometimes combined with other stops as well.

Jillora Bindi was the pilot on this trip, and her husband Tom was riding shotgun. Both had been flying just shy of forever, and this trip was one they sometimes made together. Tom had business at the mine. He had been in the mining business longer than he had been flying, and one of his cousins was the manager of the Moolart Well operation. Tom ran or oversaw the operations at several mines spread across most of the country's western half. He had cousins or close friends mixed up in multiple businesses, mostly legal, across Western Australia.

Mining occupied most of his time when he wasn't fishing off the coasts or occupying a prominent seat at a local roadhouse or pub. He was somewhat of a legend for his ready smile, instant generosity, and the ability to dispatch a man in a piece of a second, if necessary, even though he had slowed a bit with age. Old folks spoke in hushed tones about what a true badass he was in his early days. Tom wisely allowed the legend to grow without disputing the stories.

Jillora had learned how to mostly keep Tom in line over the years, but she had other business to attend to on this trip. They had been together since first laying eyes on each other many moons ago. They owned a small place on the Esplanade just up from the Esperance Yacht Club. Tom kept a Jet Black 6-meter Northbank 600 Cuddy Cabin equipped with a 200hp Suzuki 4-stroke parked at the Club for the occasional outing. They actually owned several properties on the south, west, and north coasts, as well as a ranch in the interior. The homes were all fully equipped and stocked. Their main home on the beach in Mandurah was filled with an amazing array of all that is Australia.

They liked to hang out on the beach or smack golf balls around the Mandurah Country Club occasionally when they were home. The other properties were regularly made available to various non-profits, conservation groups, and, of course, scientific research entities. Open accounts with local grocers, restaurants and various vendors made the stay painless and free for those lucky enough to reach the top of the waiting list.

She banked the plane a bit east, dropped to 1,000 meters, and together they viewed the Precambrian granite outcrops and boulders, sand and pebbles, and the utter devastation left by one of the hundreds of massive fires that ravaged the country several summers ago. An estimated three billion animals died during those fires, wiping out entire populations and putting some endangered species on the extinct list.

She was sickened that many people still denied the apparent truth about atmospheric warming, as backed by countless scientific studies. Sometimes she felt like pummeling someone or something to get the attention of the moronic drumbeats of the climate-change deniers. Her thoughts ran from what's wrong with you people to fuck all of you who helped wreak this havoc on Mother Earth and her children. Tom wasn't nearly as timid with his opinions.

A tear coursed its way down Jillora's cheek as she viewed the devastation and relived earlier times hiking through the area enthralled with the unique desert scenery and glimpses of the now-departed residents, both large and small. Tom gave her a bit of a pat on her thigh as he surreptitiously wiped a tear from his eye. Real jacks don't cry.

Jillora brought the plane back up to cruising altitude and speed and continued the journey north. She retrieved a marble-sized crystal from the breast pocket of her camp shirt and gently rubbed it in her hand as she flew high above the desert toward the mine. Tom naturally took command of the aircraft without being asked, and they cruised on.

After a while, she opened her eyes and returned the crystal to her pocket, looked over at Tom, and said, "Hard times are coming, but I may be able to help." Tom nodded.

They circled Laverton and the airport twice at 500 meters, wing-wagging, and waving. Between them, they were related to about half of the 340 or so folks who called this thriving metropolis home. The locals always stopped what they were doing to wave at the very limited number of low-flying aircraft that came by every so often.

Later they dropped out of the sky onto the 1,200-meter black tarmac that was Duketon Airport. The airport was there strictly in support of the Moolart Well Gold Mine. Even though the Airvan had an additional fuel tank for extended range, they would still top off both tanks before departing. A general rule in any outback worldwide is, if there is a facility, use it.

An old duce and a half and an even older Landcruiser were off to the side of the runway. Two rugged young men greeted Uncle Tom and Ngangkari Jillora. She was a medicine woman indeed, and much more. Jillora Bindi means Ball Girl, and she was actually the 1,111th daughter descending from the first Jillora Bindi, some 20,000 years ago.

The original plan was for Tom to finish up business, and then they would fly over to Leinster for dinner at the Leinster Tavern Gold n Nickel Bar & Bistro. Their favorite was the Whole Chicken & Chips meal for $50 with a pint or two on the side. They would sack out with friends overlooking the bit of blue water in the middle of town and head back toward Perth the following day.

Jillora changed those plans, meaning Tom would spend a night, or maybe two, in a tiny but adequate mobile apartment at the mine. But an evening or two of cards and pints with the boys suited him just fine. Jillora was going to take the Landcruiser and trek a bit. Tom and Jillora loaded their personal gear into the Landcruiser.

Once the remaining cargo was offloaded and secured in the duce and a half, the boys drove it away. Jillora drove the Landcruiser with Tom riding shotgun. Upon arriving at the mine, pleasantries were quickly exchanged. Tom removed his gear, and Jillora climbed back into the Landcruiser, heading out across the desert on a northeasterly track that soon petered out. From there on, it was never clear whether she was on an established track or breaking new ground.

She was in the general vicinity of the De La Poer Range Nature Preserve, but that was irrelevant. She was headed to a place where time and boundaries were for others. The red-hewed sand and gravel desert floor gave way in places to low broken ledges and boulders. Small hills appeared on the horizon. The landscape was dotted with small to medium-sized trees, including Desert Oaks, Boabs, and Mulgas. A wide variety of grasses were scattered in clumps and small communal patches. These included kangaroo, pulchellus, couch, spinifex, and more. Spinifex would become the center of her attention before the day was done.

The air was very dry, but the temperature was a comfortable 25C with variable breezes blowing generally westward. The elevation was around 500 meters, and annual rainfall hovered at 225 millimeters, making this geographical area, by definition, a desert. However, the low hills displayed significant erosion features because the rain, when it came at all in a particular spot, usually came down all at once, inundating the land.

This particular day the sky was its usual brilliant blue with a smattering of cumulus clouds in the distance. The occasional red kangaroo avoided the slow-moving vehicle. A caravan of feral camels crossed her path a klick or so to the north and disappeared over the horizon. Though non-native, escaped camels infest much of the country. Originally brought to Australia in the 1840s, they now number over a million.

Jillora was both a shaman and a Ngangkari. Further, being the direct descendant of the first Jillora Bindi, she was revered for her place in Dreamtime. The Aboriginal healers known as Ngangkari use a combination of talking, questioning, and touching as a holistic way to provide comfort and relief. Shamans apply these techniques as part of their regimen and also use a wide variety of herbs, minerals, and certain other things found in nature that don't neatly fit into a

11

particular category. Jillora was looking for one of these 'other things.' Known mainly through legend, she felt a calling to seek out the ancient cure.

Tom had recently helped an American team recover a marble-shaped crystal from where it had lain for 20,000 years in the cave-like home of her ancestor, the original Jillora Bindi. The cave was currently submerged near Esperance along the ocean shoreline.

The crystal was rare but not unique. Jillora was the current holder of a similar crystal marble passed from mother to daughter for as far back as she knew, a shaman secret shared only by descendants of the original Ball Girl. She would pass it on to her own daughter when the time was right.

One of the American's involved in Tom's last adventure was a geologist named Mat Dover. She was sure his fiancé Jenara Solido possessed another similar crystal. The women had only spoken once on the phone, but the connection was electric. They both instantly felt the bonding, and Jillora was sure the two had some unfinished business together. This certainty was one of the reasons she was now deep in the outback wilderness.

Vague ghost-like thoughts and visions of late led Jillora to also believe there were other crystals on Earth possessed by souls of a similar nature to her and Jenara. The feeling she experienced while flying to the mine convinced her a crisis was coming, and she had a part to play.

Jillora continued her north-northeasterly trek heading to a place unvisited by anyone other than herself for thousands of years. She maneuvered the old Landcruiser up an erosion feature into the heart of a low escarpment until the walls closed in, and from there on she had to hoof it. Jillora wore Salomon XA Pro 3D GTX hiking boots over Bridgedale Hike Midweight socks, double-canvas cargo khaki pants, imported Turtleskin SnakeArmor Gaiters, an old long-sleeved fishing shirt, and an even older fishing vest.

Her well-worn day pack was strapped across her back. It contained two gallons of water, light provisions for two days, and various useful odds and ends. She carried an ultrathin tarp and a bedroll strapped onto the pack and suspended from her custom kangaroo-hide belt were a canteen, sheath knife, and a Glock 19 Gen 5 G34 Competition 9x19mm pistol. The pistol was a bit larger than a female would normally carry, but it was her favorite.

She could shoot the nuts off of a gnat at thirty paces with it. And it could reach out beyond a hundred meters with devastating accuracy. The chances of encountering anyone were small, but there were more than a few totally off-the-grid folks traipsing around the desert. Tom had encountered more than his share of questionable and potentially dangerous strangers during his years in the outback. The sidearm was a must.

Tom had learned years ago that buying Jillora clothes and accessories was a waste of time and money. When she needed something, she bought it. If it was comfortable and functional, she would wear it out. She trekked now with a pair of Leki Makalu Lite Cor-Tec telescoping walking poles. The tarp was large enough to act as a ground cover and a shelter, and there were grommets fitted with small bungee cords for the walking poles to act as supports. Simple but effective.

The snake leathers had been useful over the years. She was hit by a Western brown snake and a Mulga several years ago. The venom from either bite would have proven fatal given that she was hours, perhaps days, from a medical facility. Even her knowledge was not sufficient to survive any of the many venomous snakes she could cross paths with. Fortunately, none of them were plentiful, and her seasoned eyes always scanned the area ahead well before she traversed it. Same as all experienced trekkers, she used her walking poles to prod brush or explore crevasses before she put her hands there.

A shadow passed by, making her look up. The culprit was a Wedge-tailed eagle. The majestic bird at the top of the food chain made her think of the amazing desert ecosystem she was traveling across. Deserts are relatively easy to study from a systems-analysis perspective. She and Tom had casually participated in many such studies over the years. Researchers were grateful for their contributions. There are many inhabitants in the desert, from the smallest microbe to the largest mammal. The scarcity of vegetation makes the desert much easier to study than, say, the Amazon.

Jillora continued her very gradual ascent. The terrain slowly leveled off, and the vegetation increased around her. Another winding two klicks found her in a fairly dense copse consisting mainly of Desert Oaks and Spinifex. She climbed the small ledge she remembered and eased her way into the cavity that had been there for millennia. The cavity, basically a room, measured about two meters high by three meters wide by six meters deep.

The ceiling and upper outer face were slightly smoke-tinged from fires burned just inside the entrance eons ago. Jillora decided she would add a bit of soot to the entrance that night to ward off snakes and the like. The interior was covered in a rich panorama of drawings and carvings in the stone. Prominent among the various depictions were the Southern Cross and the constellation depicting the Ball Girl. This theme, the Ball Girl, was found in many such grottos all across Australia.

She unpacked half of the water, bedroll, and tarp and placed them against the south wall. Then she sat on the shallow ledge and gazed out through the thin canopy of vegetation at her surroundings. The sun was perhaps fifteen degrees above the horizon in the west, so she climbed down and gathered bits of dried grass and sticks.

The fire would be relatively meager but satisfactory. She found one larger dead limb and built a fire on either side of it in the shallow pit that had seen countless fires. In reality, it was the same fire used by her and her ancestors across time and space from the days when our distant ancestors had first learned to harness fire.

Her substantial medicine kit at home contained only one item she herself had not collected. It was a small, ancient, hollowed-out humerus bone from, as best as she could tell, a bird roughly the size of a crested pigeon. The end of the bone was stoppered with a tiny stub of a twig. She had inherited the bone and, according to her mother, its origin was from Jillora Bendi number one.

Inside the bone was the vaguest hint of the remains of a dried herb. She had never used it. She had no way of knowing if any of her ancestors had ever used it. She did know, however, the singular smell of the herb. She also knew it was unknown to science. She only had knowledge of its potential use from stories passed down through the ages from mother to daughter. Watching the sun slip westward, she knew, without proof, that Jenara was in search of an ancient remedy also.

The legend handed down, and the hypothesis she was about to test, was that the herb could be found in only one place in the world, Australia, near where she was, in the nest of a Night Parrot. The information handed down to her seemed to indicate the Night Parrot would ingest an incredibly rare seed or seeds along with everything else it ate.

An unknown chemical process in the digestive tract stripped the seed of its outer structural covering and allowed it to germinate in the small pile of poop that was shoved to the back of the nest. None of this had ever been described by science. Nonetheless, Jillora was on a mission to see if the tale passed down to her had substance.

Jillora was not deterred by the fact the Night Parrot was, in all likelihood, extinct. The bird was indeed thought to have been extinct for many years until a single specimen was captured, radio-tagged, and released several years ago. The specific location of this event was a closely held secret, but she surmised it was probably on the west side of Lake Eyre. The area had been incinerated recently, along with large swaths of Australia. A team of researchers she and Tom sponsored a few years ago found a single weathered feather they were fairly sure belonged to a Night Parrot. She was now within 200 kilometers of their find.

Spinifex grass sprouts and grows straight upward to perhaps a meter. During periods of drought, it then lays down in a circular fashion. It depends on its three-meter-deep root system for sustenance. If the old tales were true, the Night Parrot essentially burrowed into these donut-shaped havens and made a nest. She could count perhaps a thousand or more possibilities from her perch three meters above the rest of the landscape. And all were within a half a klick. Beyond that, in all directions were countless possibilities.

So, her job was to find a needle in a haystack the size of Western Australia. As the old saying goes, a journey of ten thousand kilometers begins with the first step. She came off of her perch and began traversing the immediate area. She used the walking poles to poke and prod a bit into patches of spinifex.

The red ball called the sun was setting westward as usual, and a three-quarter moon poked itself up over the eastern horizon. Jillora stepped more cautiously as the day sank into evening. Darkness came quickly in the flat desert. The clear skies began to fill with stars. She stood still for a while, taking in the deepening darkness and the rich desert scents on the easterly breeze. She began moving again and traversed an arc of perhaps a kilometer or so. She then repeated the stand and listen and soak in her surroundings routine. She admired the Southern Cross and, off to the side, Jillora Bindi, her favorite constellation.

The desert was alive with the tiny sounds of creatures small and not so small hunting and being hunted. Well after midnight, by her reckoning, she caught a shadow out of the corner of her eye—a shadow in flight. She shifted slightly and watched the bird continue eastward into the moonshine. Although darkness was around her, she was sure she had seen half-black wings and the half-black tail of a Night Parrot. So, there was at least one still roaming in the wild spaces. She held her ground for a while and continued to absorb her surroundings. This time when she moved, it was deliberate. She had seen the parrot return along the outbound line of flight. It disappeared beneath the horizon no more than 100 meters away. Hopefully, it had headed home.

She stepped lightly, alternating her gaze from the ground below back up to where she hoped to find a nest. Another stop and go, then another as she progressed. All of a sudden, it hit her. Subtle as a hummingbird feather, but there just the same. A unique scent coming down the breeze from the east. A scent that existed only in her relic hollow bone. A scent she had never known outside of her realm. The scent of a plant unknown to science. But a plant only known to those who came before her and perhaps a handful of her fellow shaman.

She moved and gently prodded the clumps of spinifex, constantly sniffing the breeze as she moved eastward. Suddenly a quiet explosion occurred right under her feet as a bird, most definitely a Night Parrot, emerged from a patch of spinifex grass and fled low across the horizon. With it came the unmistakable scent she had been following. She paused a minute to regain her wits. Quiet explosions in the desert in the middle of the night in the middle of way-far-away could be somewhat unnerving.

Jillora lowered herself to the ground. From one of the vest pockets, she pulled a small black Olight Baton Pro rechargeable LED torch. She found the camouflaged opening and slowly and gently eased her right hand inside. At elbow depth, she felt the edge of what was, hopefully, a nest. A dozen centimeters more, and she felt wetness, probably poo, and then a soft, cottony lichen-like material. Gently she prodded the plant out of its niche and then into the soft light of the torch.

The scent was powerful but not unpleasant at all. The entirety of the plant filled a tiny glass vile she had brought just in case. She reached in again, but only the nest and some poo remained. The vile went into a Velcro-sealed breast pocket on the vest. Shaking a bit, she stood and gathered herself. She took in the position of the moon, the Southern Cross, and Jillora Bindi and headed westward and a bit south. She figured she would be back at the cave in ten minutes or so. She was correct.

A pair of bilbies were grubbing around her bedroll. The pointy-eared cuties were not shy, so she had to shoo them out. Jillora stirred the ashes of the fire and added some grass and small sticks. She nibbled a nutritious snack, listened to dingoes' howl, rolled out her tarp and bedroll, and slept until the first vague tendrils of dawn crept through the branches and into the cave. Perched on the ledge, she performed her morning rituals, including rubbing the crystal in her hands for several minutes.

Almost immediately, she felt connected to the cosmos and felt Jenara's presence in the ether. She smiled. Maybe they could make a difference. A few moments later, she was about to put the crystal away when a different feeling crossed her palms. She had never felt it before. It was fleeting but, in her mind, it felt a bit sinister.

The hike out and the ride back to the mine were uneventful. Tom came out to greet his beautiful bride. She was his whole world and always delivered a huge grin to his face. She brought him up to speed. They decided it was best to head directly back to Perth. In the event international travel was necessary, Perth would be the starting point. Same in reverse if there were incoming travelers.

Tom let the materials foreman know about the change in plans. He and two other lads jumped into the duce and a half and drove to the airstrip. They had finished offloading the plane and refilled it with items headed to Perth by the time Tom and Jillora arrived.

Jillora completed the preflight routine and spun up the prop, turned the plane onto the runway, and they were at cruising altitude fifteen minutes later. The 700 kilometer ride would take about four hours. Tom tried to raise Mat on his satphone but was met with dead air. Same with Mark. The satphone was originally provided by John early on during the events surrounding the recovery of the crystal from the ancient cave. Tom found it to be too useful to return, so he kept it. And as long as he never got a phone bill, he was damn sure gonna keep it. He rang up John. The call was answered on the first ring.

"Good day Mr. Tom!" John exclaimed. "How may I be of service?" John was actually artificial intelligence (AI) so Tom was speaking to a computer with an Aussie accent.

"Excellent, John. I hope you are well." Tom actually said that even knowing what he knew.

"I have a bit of hay fever, sir, but it will pass. Thank you for asking." The computer had hay fever. If Mark heard this conversation, he would probably shoot something. John actually existed because of an earlier business investment Mark had been involved in. Despite the venture's success, dealing with a smartass computer pissed him off way more than it should have. Something going back to his college days and a computer program named Fortran.

"John, I wonder if you can lend a hand. I've tried Mat and Mark on the satphone to no avail. I have a bit of news they may find useful." Tom's demeanor would lead one to believe he was simply ordering another pint at the Leinster Tavern. In his early days, this trait in a grizzly bear-sized guy was unusual. It also somewhat lulled those that chose to mess with him into a false sense of power. A visit to the local hospital was sometimes the result of such complacency.

"Yes sir, I can make sure they know you require a call. Mr. Mark is on a walkabout, whereabouts unknown, or so he thinks. If necessary, I can send a bear or mountain lion to retrieve him. Mat is airborne at the moment and requires stealth for somewhat secretive reasons. Is there anything else I can help you with at the moment?" John could probably make the Earth spin backward, but Tom did not ask him to.

"Good for now! I'll listen for the return call." Tom almost clicked off.

"Give my best regards to Ms. Jillora for me, please. Cheers." John did click off.

Tom keyed his headset mike and said, "Now how did he know that you were with me?"

"You silly man. John probably watches us have sex if he wants to." Jillora said with a sly grin.

Mark would say "damn machines" and hit something. Or shoot something. Or, perhaps, run over something. Probably a good thing he was whereabouts unknown.

They flew over the massive salt flat known as Lake Barlee, then the beautiful Karroun Hill Nature Preserve, before crossing into farming country. Jillora wagged the wings to folks below in Beacon. Shortly after crossing the hills that comprised Youraling State Forest, they touched down at the Murrayfield Aerodrome. The cargo was offloaded, and the plane was refueled and tied down.

17

Tom helped Jillora up into the shotgun seat on his new Toyota Landcruiser. It was raised and modified for unfettered outback travel. He was like a kid with a new toy every time he climbed aboard. He had it special-ordered after narrowly escaping some very bad guys not that long ago in his old truck.

Back home, Jillora carefully examined her new treasure and made certain preparations. Tom sat on the deck, watched the ocean, and sipped an Otherside IPA. It was so good he had another one while watching the world turn. Mat or Mark would call when they got his message.

Go With the Hunch (Mat)

I rolled over and looked at the clock. The blueish display read 4:23 am. I could feel Jenara's side of the bed was empty, and the covers had lost their warmth. She must have been up for a while. I laid on my back for a few minutes collecting my thoughts and letting the fog of sleep lift. Before I got out of bed, I checked my phone and saw Joseph had left a message. He was in Luanda on personal business but had promised to fly out via South Africa and check on some geological fieldwork I was sponsoring.

Susan Calder, a graduate student I mentor, had proposed the fieldwork to me as part of a larger project. After discussions with Jason Sing, her advisor, we put together a team to work on the Kaapvaal Craton in South Africa. Geologists use the name craton to designate the geological core or nucleus of a continent. The term refers to a large, stable segment of the earth's crust around which a continent forms. The North American Craton is a great example. It encompasses much of the eastern, midcontinent, and western portions of the USA. Then it goes northward into Canada and on to Greenland. But Oregon, Washington, and California are not part of the North American Craton. They were glued onto the craton later while tectonic plates drifted around the planet smacking into each other.

The Kaapvaal Craton, where Susan was currently working, occupies the northeastern third of South Africa. It also spills over into Botswana, the southern edge of Zimbabwe, and Mozambique's southwestern-most fringe. This craton formed during the Archean Eon between 3.6 and 2.7 billion years ago. The oldest rocks of the Kaapvaal Craton outcrop in the Barberton Greenstone Belt along the eastern edge of the craton in the Makhonjwa Mountains.

Susan's project focused on the Barberton Greenstone Belt. Since greenstone belts are widely interpreted to represent the remains of ancient oceans, they are a great place to search for signs of early life on earth. Susan and her associates were in South Africa looking for traces of life in the Barberton greenstones. Joseph's company managed logistics for the team, but he was also an advisor on the project. He worked extensively on these same rocks for one of his undergraduate projects at Laurentian University. His expertise had been critical in setting up the project.

Several months ago, following the unexpected discovery of alien technology in Greenland, Susan became a bit of a celebrity because she was the field geologist uncovering the artifacts. Her new work in South Africa focused on rocks believed to be younger than the four billion old Greenland rocks but testing this hypothesis about their age was one of her goals.

I dragged myself out of bed and grabbed my robe from the back of a rusty-red armchair. It was October in Portland, but the summer had mercifully lingered on, with warm sunny days and cool evenings. I made my way to the balcony and silently slipped into the lounge chair next to Jenara. We sat perched 21 stories above the streets of Portland's Pearl District, with an unobstructed view of the city. She said nothing, so I reclined and enjoyed the early morning view looking north over the river. She would talk when she was ready.

Lights reflected off the waters of the Willamette River as it wound its way through the city. Headlights from truckers and early morning commuters flowed northward and southward across the city's famous bridges. I thought about the last several months. We were involved in a wild and weird piece of business last July, and it had taken a couple of months for things to settle down.

Through a string of unusual events, Jenara and I found ourselves waist-deep in the unlikely pursuit of four-billion-year-old artifacts. It was an adventure that emerged from one of the field projects I was funding. Susan was the lead on that project, and she turned up a manufactured object embedded in old Archean rocks. These rocks were in Greenland, where she was investigating the Isua Greenstone Belt. She initially found several objects, but one was unique, and I could only liken it to the philosophers' stone of life.

Governments, corporate entities, and privately funded religious groups worked against us to keep the newly discovered artifacts from public view. They almost succeeded, but my friend Mark and a team he assembled in Australia did an end-run around everyone at the last moment. They procured an essential component from the artifact, allowing us to decipher the history of the object.

The ramifications of these discoveries were huge and still reverberated through the worlds of research, business, religion, and social media. The artifact Susan found was a black orb constructed from an ultra-dense metal-graphene composite material. The material represented an unknown technology, something not manufactured on earth. Inside the container was DNA preserved in some type of chemical gel. Also found inside was a small one-inch diameter crystal sphere, which later proved to be a crystal-lattice memory storage device.

One of the key roles we played in this saga was ensuring researchers worldwide had access to the DNA. When we originally sequenced the DNA, the research community referred to it as "stem-cell DNA" and lauded its potential for medical advances. This original assessment appeared correct based on my recent contacts with several research teams still working with this DNA.

The crystal lattice memory device was not as straightforward as the DNA. Originally, we recovered two separate storage crystals during our work, and I knew of two more in private hands. The government relieved me of one of these units under the pretense of national security. The second, however, was recovered from Australia by Mark and surreptitiously passed on to me.

I, in turn, left the memory storage device with Carl Jennings, the CEO of Three Rock Inc. His company is a private venture I helped finance. They specialized in developing crystal-lattice memory technology. Their possession of this artifact was not public knowledge and, as far as I knew, not government knowledge either. Thus far, Three Rock had filed about 20 patents pertaining to new technological breakthroughs in the crystal memory field. I suspected the government was now casting a suspicious eye in their direction.

The only immediately readable part of the crystal lattice memory was a simple visual message from four billion years in the past. A message from our genetic benefactors about the intimate nature of life and the planet on which they once existed. A warning that you have but one planet, live in balance with it, or you will cease to live. I had managed to get this message circulated around the world via social media.

However, terabytes of data still needed deciphering. As a member of the Three Rock Board of Directors, I supported Carl in starting a corporate division dedicated solely to retrieving data from the crystal sphere. I was particularly interested in a bit of the message they left for us regarding a string of pandemics, which had almost wiped out their species at one point in time. Evidently, after the pandemics, they had poured the civilization's remaining resources into medical advancement. No pandemics appeared in their history after the first disaster. Hopefully, some of the medical knowledge on pandemic control resided in the memory sphere's undeciphered information.

Jack, the head of research at Three Rock, told me that about half of the memory storage space contained information in binary code, and this data was the first subject of investigation. The remaining information was in a format they did not yet understand. He recently hired an MIT graduate with PHDs in quantum physics and mathematics to work on the non-binary data sets. The new hire had been part of a university research team making significant breakthroughs in linear algebra applications for quantum computing. Jack claimed this kid was the creative driver for the breakthroughs. I was hopeful the new guy, Dan Rohden, would make some quick progress.

Jenara stirred in the chair beside me and brought me back to the present. She sat silhouetted against the soft glow of night lights surrounding a hot tub off to her right. When she turned her head slightly, I could see the glint of tears in her eyes. I reached over, rubbed her forearm, and took her hand. Maria, her grandmother, passed away a month ago. Jenara had traveled to São Paulo for the funeral and returned with some closure. Maria had kept her alive and sane when Louisa, her mother, was killed in a robbery gone wrong. She was both mother and grandmother to Jenara.

But I also knew there was more on her mind. Jenara's research into the Rohodi tribe of southwestern Brazil was a signature piece of her anthropological work. The work started when she was a graduate student, and she continued building on that foundation over the years. Her current position as a professor in the anthropology department of Portland State University allowed her the freedom to make annual trips to the jungles of far western Brazil. Recently she had alluded to issues facing her "Rohodi family," but she avoided delving into specifics. She traveled to Texas just two weeks ago to meet with Amber Lee and given Amber Lee's background as a biologist and environmentalist, I suspected the trip was more than just a social visit with a newly acquired friend.

Jenara and Amber Lee originally met this past summer when we were involved with the ancient artifacts. Amber Lee was part of Mark's team in the retrieval of the Australian crystal sphere. She performed the actual underwater retrieval in a specialized sub. She's a smart woman with computer-like knowledge about biology and Anthropocene species extinction. Show her a plant, and she can not only tell you what it is, but she can divulge its evolutionary history and genetic affiliations. I could only guess that whatever was on Jenara's mind had to do with the Brazilian Rain Forest's ongoing exploitation and protecting her Rohodi family. After years of living with them, she considered herself to be personally responsible for their wellbeing.

She finally spoke. "Mat, I received a letter several weeks ago from Hoshikay. There has been a lot of trouble for the tribe recently. More issues with the loggers, but now, groups of people asking about various traditional medicinal cures are sniffing around. I think pharmaceutical companies are backing these inquiries. Some of them have been pretty aggressive, and there was a recent blow-up where one of the tribe's men was seriously hurt. She says I am needed."

"That's a big ask," I said.

Jenara collected her thoughts and went on, "She has never really asked anything of me except when I am there with the tribe. But this time is different. Her message said: Gavião, this is your time; I cannot do this alone."

Gavião was the private name that Hoshikay used for Jenara. The harpy eagle, or Gavião-real in Portuguese, is one of the alter-egos of South American shamans. Transformation into a harpy eagle's body allows the shaman to traverse a journey between the celestial domain and our earthbound human existence.

Most of the Rohodi tribe viewed Jenara as a shaman-like figure and privately caller her La Bruxa, the witch. At first, this name reflected fear, but after returning year after year, the name developed an affectionate context. Her original acceptance into the tribe was only because of Hoshikay, who, at the time, told the elders, "the woman must stay."

"I debated back and forth on the trip until last week when there was an incident at my office," she said.

My sixth sense went off like an alarm bell. She had mentioned nothing of this to me last week. But I kept my curiosity in check and simply asked, "What happened?"

"Someone broke into my office Tuesday evening," she continued. "Nothing was taken, but whoever it was, had meticulously looked through all of my medicinal herbs."

Jenara had a complex background with natural healing. Her late grandmother, Maria, was skilled in natural remedies and trusted by her local community. A trust not given to the local medical establishment in the area. She passed her knowledge on to Jenara over the years, so by the time Jenara started her work . with the Rohodi tribe, she was already steeped in the world of medicinal herbs and plants. Once Hoshikay, a Rohodi shaman, took Jenara under her wing, her knowledge of medicinal rainforest plants exponentially increased.

Jenara had cabinets of leaves, powders, and extracts at her work offices. Still, it was odd someone broke in and took nothing. I remembered the Ebola incident and wondered if there was a connection. I was set to travel to West Africa during one of the Ebola outbreaks, and before I left, she prepared some sort of herbal tea and insisted I drink it. I tasted like cat pee mixed with ants. When I complained, she told me to quit being a child and take my medicine.

I did as I was told and then got on a plane to Luanda, where I joined Joseph. Things quickly went to hell in a handbasket once we got into the field. In the process of avoiding warring rebel groups, we got separated, and I ended up in a remote village, devastated by an Ebola outbreak. It was four days before Joseph could get to me with some backup. I helped where I could and tried to avoid contamination, but with no protective gear, I figured my chances of ending up in the dead-body pile were good.

Joseph finally arrived with some medical help. At that point, over 70 percent of the village was infected, and his backup team came with full hazmat gear. They kept me in isolation until it was clear I didn't have the disease, and then they marveled at my good luck. The odd thing was, when I returned to Portland, I went to a private clinic and had them run ELISA tests, which identified Ebola-specific antibodies in my system.

When I told Jenara about the positive antibody test and mentioned the herbal tea, she just said, "Hum… good fortune, I suppose." She clearly wasn't going to say more, so I let the matter go.

On a hunch, I made a flat statement. "They looked through almost all of your medicines, but they didn't get the prize they wanted because you keep that well-hidden."

She gave me a half-amused but also annoyed look and said, "You and your damn hunches. They're going to get you into trouble—again." I turned my head to the left as I reached for a glass of water, keeping my smile to myself.

We sat in silence as the eastern sky brightened. Sunrise was slightly southeast of Mount Hood, and it lit up the southern side of the mountain with a pinkish glow. Jenara shifted around in her chair and said, "I have to leave for Brazil this week, and Amber Lee is meeting me in Rio."

"I wondered about your visit to Texas the other week," I remarked. "But I think what you meant to say was that we have to leave for Brazil soon, and Amber Lee is meeting us in Rio. I will make the arrangements to leave tonight and get Joseph to organize transport logistics from Rio to the Western Jungle."

"You don't have to come, Mat. But I also know there is no use trying to stop you now that you have some delusionary ideas from this hunch of yours."

We fixed an early breakfast of poached eggs, fruit, and yogurt. At about nine o'clock, Jenara left for her office to collect some items. I was spooked by the break-in and called Marcelle Fabre. Marcelle is the head of the firm providing security for me. Normally it is routine things like home security systems or hardening my cybersecurity. I asked her to send a person around to Jenara's office to keep an eye on things and set up security cameras when Jenara finished.

I also asked her to make security arrangements for our Rio stay. She didn't actually have an office in Brazil, but I knew she would have contacts we could trust.

My next call was to Jennifer. Jennifer can only be described as my office manager. I don't have an actual office, and she works from her home south of Portland on a vineyard in the Willamette Valley. Jennifer keeps my appointment books and runs reception for inquiries, both personal and business. She keeps me organized and on schedule when I travel, booking most of my flights, ground transport, and lodging. I had her book us on a flight to Rio that evening and asked her to arrange a good hotel. I also let her know to coordinate with Marcelle on transport and security logistics.

Joseph was next on the list, and I got him on the first ring. "Joseph, are you in Johannesburg yet?" I asked.

"Just landed about an hour ago," he replied. "I will be checking in with Susan tomorrow."

"Was your trip to Luanda successful?" I inquired. He gave a curt "Yup," but didn't volunteer more information, so I didn't ask.

"Listen," I said. "I need you or one of your guys to arrange some logistics for me in Brazil. Jenara and I are leaving this evening for Rio, and from there, we need to travel west to Rohodi land." Joseph was familiar with Jenara's work, and he had actually pulled her out of the jungle on short notice several years ago. "We will need to chopper in and out as usual, and have the service on call for the duration. I have no idea how long we will be in the jungle or exactly where we might travel to, so we will need sat-phones and also some independent GPS trackers."

"Mat, you know you can't always get full coverage that far out."

"I understand," I replied. "But we will have to make do with what's available. We will also need all the usual for hiking and camping where necessary. I do need a couple of specialty items. You know I'm not much of a gun guy, but I would like a light-weight long gun that can be packed down and a short barrel shotgun. The long gun needs a good scope with night vision. Ammo for both also."

There was a long pause at the other end of the line. "You can't seem to stay out of trouble, can you, my friend? I have the connections to get those weapons on-site for you, but it's all below board."

"I'm OK with that, Joseph. We will be in the middle of frigging nowhere, so I suspect no one will care. Hey, also make sure they pack in my favorite pocketknife, so I don't have to ship one through customs." I rarely went into the field without my favorite tool, the Oregon Benchmade Freek 560. The M4 steel was hard and durable, and the blade's serrated bottom segment had gotten me out of trouble more than once. "In fact, send me a dozen of them. I might need to be bearing gifts on this trip."

"Do you need someone on the ground with you?" he asked.

"Jenara can get herself in and out of the tribe's territory, but let's get one guide to take us in and help carry some of the gear," I responded. "He can return the next day."

"I'm on it, Mat, but you are getting too old to be running around the jungle like a mad man."

"I hear you, buddy, but I'm doing it anyway. Say Hi to Susan, and I will keep you posted." I hung up.

Jenara had returned by the time I finished my calls. We had some lunch and then packed a couple of light bags for the trip. Most of what we needed would be in-country when we got there. I checked my watch and noted 20 minutes until the driver would arrive to take us to PDX. I had one last call to make.

Mark picked up, and I could tell from the background noise he was in his Toyota. "You headed my way, old friend?"

"I'm a couple of hours out," he replied.

"Since you are generally a trustworthy person," I said, "I'm leaving you to guard my Scotch collection. Jenara and I are headed to PDX in 20 minutes to catch a plane to Rio. Her Rohodi tribe evidently needs her. Some sort of weird shit is going on, and it makes me nervous. I am sticking with her until we know what it is. She's told me Amber Lee is gonna hang with us on this little adventure. Marcelle is doing Rio security, and Joseph is arranging logistics for the trip west."

"Yea," he said. "Joseph called me and said you were already in way over your head for an old man." He paused for a moment. "Oh, and you can stop flipping your middle finger at the phone."

I stopped.

He continued. "I would say that the trip is probably all routine, but I know that never happens with you. At any rate, I will take good care of that Scotch. Oh, and I gave Joseph some ideas on that hardware you ordered. You know where I am, so call me when you are waist-deep in shit and need someone to hold your hand."

"Roger that good buddy. Stay safe and talk to Marcelle about the break-in at Jenara's office." I hung up, thinking that would give him a bone to chew on.

Houston

The view from the thirteenth floor of a non-descript high rise off of Sage Avenue was unimpressive. A light rain limited visibility and fell on traffic in the Galleria area of Houston. Cars crawled around below like blood cells in a network of clogged veins. Houston is flat, and the horizon is a straight line when you can see it. But the thirteenth floor was not that far up, and other buildings occupied much of the drab view.

Donald Faillen sat facing his office window, gazing at a gray cloud-laden sky, his feet propped up on an expensive teak desk. A polished, black stone lay snuggled in the palm of his right hand, and he was rubbing it with his thumb. He liked stroking his "worry stone" when he was thinking about a problem. The solution to his current problem had vanished, but the problem remained.

Donald was the owner and CEO of a firm called Fourth Wing Corporate Solutions, specializing in industry intelligence. The majority of his clients were pharmaceutical companies, and they kept the money flowing. His company maintained a low profile and generally relied on word-of-mouth advertising to generate new business. His services were in high demand but rarely discussed in open offices and never discussed in corporate board rooms. Fourth Wing often delivered certain information that was difficult to obtain, and as a rule, his clients never asked how he acquired such information. For Donald, industry intelligence generally boiled down to theft or blackmail.

His current problem involved theft, or lack thereof in this particular case. He was pissed off with Eric for botching the acquisition and then sending a red flag up the pole by leaving signs he had been there. Even as he sat thinking, he knew upgraded security equipment was being installed in the target office.

The heightened security would make it more difficult to gain access and have a second look.

Fourth Wing employed a variety of people, including some ex-military types who found themselves out of work as the USA backed out of various wars in the Middle East, and tighter military budgets eliminated private security contractors. The people were good, but all expendable in Donald's view. He worked on a simple principle: people were pawns to be used in his game of survival and ascendance. Non-disclosure agreements kept his employees tightly bound, and in most cases, he also had some private files on them for extra leverage. He wasn't in a real squeeze right now but still wondered if he should fire Eric as an example.

He put that thought on hold and returned to the core problem. His eyes drifted over the documents provided by one of his clients as part of a background brief. The client understood the issues but didn't have any real appreciation for the task at hand. But this type of ignorance was normal in his experience. The acquisition of physical objects was always inherently riskier than acquiring information from cyber theft.

Initially, he had put his cyber investigations team on the problem. They were all brilliant hackers but managing them was like herding cats. The first problem he ran into was cyber-hardened computer systems on the woman's private network. This level of security was very unusual for a college professor, so he had done a little digging and traced the security back to a Portland-based firm. It had taken them several weeks to finally make the connections tying the Portland security firm to the woman's boyfriend, some rich, nerdy geologist. His people couldn't budge through the firewalls, so they had to move on to the next stage without the background intelligence Donald wanted. It made the whole process riskier, and he was careful to keep no records of their plans. Email, text messages, voice mails, etc., none of it was allowed. Plausible deniability was a cornerstone of his survival strategy.

He picked up the documents from the brief and sifted through to the one that held his interest. It was about 15 years old, and the brief contained copies made from an obscure set of notes on file at Portland State University's library. Anthropology, he thought, was another useless waste of time. He understood the careful study of people, but his observations were practical and focused on wealth acquisition. Deceiving people required an intimate knowledge of their weaknesses and vanities. Tell people whatever it takes to get the job done was another one of his cornerstone philosophies.

The notes he pulled from the stack of papers covered a full two years, and they related specifically to the medicinal practices of an Amazon tribe. Donald was keenly aware of the importance of Amazon plants in modern medicine. He knew that somewhere around 25 percent of the drugs available on the market today had their origins in Amazon plants. The jungles were a goldmine for cancer researchers since 70 percent of all the known plants with anti-cancer properties came from the Amazon rainforest. Not only did they originate there, but they were also unique to the Amazon and found nowhere else on the planet. People in the pharma industry referred to the Amazon as the "world's rainforest pharmacy."

Researchers working for Donald's client originally dug up the notes as part of a larger investigation. There were probably fifty pages of material, but the crux of their interest was captured in three separate entries. The earliest of these entries occurred during the professor's first six-month stay with some tribe in western Brazil. The first entry of interest was proceeded by twenty pages of notes on a wide variety of plants used by indigenous people for everything from cuts and scrapes to religious rituals. Donald was unfamiliar with the plants and their biological classifications, and it was irrelevant to him. The client had assured him the uses of compounds from those plants were already well known.

He leaned back in his chair and started reading:

Today about mid-morning, I returned to the hut and found Hoshikay working in a patch of sunlight near her medicine storage shelves. She didn't immediately see me come in since her back was to the entrance. From my angle, I could see her dropping pea-sized, dried seeds into a small, light-gray stone mortar and slowly crushing them with a pestle. The seeds were a strikingly golden color and were utterly unknown to me. She was collecting the powder from the crushed seeds and placing it in a separate container. Once she realized I was there, she quickly put the seeds out of sight in a box on the bottom shelf and refused to discuss them when I asked about their purpose. This reluctance was unusual because she usually went to great lengths to explain the origin and use of the various herbs, medicines, and powder mixes she kept.

My assumption was, her potions had something to do with the news we received yesterday when a hunting party returned. A sickness was passing through tribes to the north, resulting in some deaths. It was rumored to have originally been spread by loggers in the area. The illness appears to be a viral infection of some sort. Historically these can be devastating to the indigenous people since they lack many of the common immunities we have in modern society.

Hoshikay shooed me out of her hut and went back to work. She must have made some sort of infusion with the powdered seeds, and that evening she insisted that everyone, including me, drink a cup of the medicine she had prepared.

Donald sifted forward through the pages to the second entry of interest, occurring a year later during a return visit to the tribe.

My second evening back with the tribe provided me time to catch up with Hoshikay. I was curious about the health of the people. It was only after I returned from my trip last year that I understood the full impact of the viral contagion on the Amazon tribes. The reports I had been able to gather reported up to 15 percent death rates for some tribes. Because of the nature of the virus, it was widespread due to a long incubation time when the carrier was infectious but not symptomatic. I knew tribes to the north and south of the Rohodi had been devastated, but I had heard nothing about the tribes in the area of the Parque Nacional da Serra do Divisor, the Rohodi homeland.

I was shocked when she told me there had been no sickness or death. The disease had traveled along trade and hunting routes, starting in the north and moving south. But it had seemingly passed through the Rohodi area with no effect. When I asked Hoshikay about how she had protected her people, she was evasive and essentially said, "perhaps later." I tried to push the conversation back to the infusion she made with the powered golden seeds, but she wouldn't go there.

The last of the entries occurred another eight months on.

The night before I was due to leave, Hoshikay took me aside and entered into a vague conversation about secrets I needed to know. She said, when I returned next year, we would collect the golden seeds together. I must have looked confused because she reached into a box on her medicine shelf and showed me a hand full of the golden-colored seeds I had asked about numerous times. Something fundamental had changed, and I seemed to have passed from researcher to shaman apprentice.

The curious part of these notes was that the golden seeds were never mentioned again in the many reports and papers the professor had since published. His client believed the Solido woman knew something of extreme medicinal value, which she kept hidden for reasons unknown. It was this information Fourth Wing was hired to find.

Donald mulled it over for a few more minutes before he made a decision. Janera Solido and her partner had flown to Rio, and he didn't have the infrastructure to pursue them around Brazil. However, he knew someone who did. But he'd be damned if he wanted to do business with Carlos again. The fucker had double-crossed him and almost killed him last time they worked together. He couldn't find another option, though.

His first call was to his client, explaining how the professor had unexpectedly traveled to Brazil. He lied and said his operations had uncovered evidence she was in the country specifically to retrieve samples of the plant his client so desperately wanted. Just enough of a lie to extract the extra funding he needed, but he inflated the cost to cut at least forty percent off the top for himself. He would shuffle that into his private offshore accounts, not the company accounts. The client was already hooked, and he had no problem getting the extra funding.

His next call was to Carlos Mattes. Carlos also claimed to offer corporate security and intelligence services, but in reality, he made his money from blackmail, theft, and kidnapping. Donald was keenly aware of the danger. Carlos was a clever psychopath and was quick to eliminate people who were a threat to him. Donald hoped he wouldn't need to be in-country for this operation. He would need feet on the ground, but he would send his employees.

He had to speak with two intermediaries before reaching Carlos, but he waited patiently. "Carlos, it is good to speak with you again," he lied. "I've got a piece of business that has spilled onto your turf and thought you might be interested."

"Donald, my good friend, it has been too long since we did business together. I still cherish the memories of our last venture. The profits were most excellent."

Carlos was right about the profits, but the rest was psychopathic bullshit. But Donald knew the game and played along. "Indeed, the profits put a smile on my face. It was a pleasure doing business with someone as efficient as yourself. Your final financial transfers were a stroke of genius," Donald replied. Carlos had cheated him out of 15 percent of his take, but that fact could slide for now. The current business could be even more lucrative, and Donald would be steering the financial transactions.

Donald continued, but he didn't want to reveal too much, "My client is very interested in a woman traveling to Rio with her fiancé. She has information regarding certain pharmaceutical products. She's dual citizenship, Brazilian and American. I need her to be isolated where my people can question her. Her fiancé is wealthy enough to hire private security, and I suspect he will hire the best in Rio."

Carlos interrupted, "Then he probably has engaged Antonio Torres. Fortunately, I have a contact there, so I am sure we can help you with this matter."

"Excellent," Donald continued. "I have their flight details, and I will send the usual information along with photos. I am sending a man down to retrieve the information we need once you detain her. Oh, I'm also sending a third dossier on a woman who will be joining them. A biologist of some sort."

Donald let the conversation pause for a moment before he continued. "Payment is the usual $40,000 with half upfront and half on delivery."

"What you are asking carries some risk, my friend," Carlos retorted. "I like you, but it's going to take more money to pull this off without collateral damage. I am assuming you want all involved to walk out alive. For $70,000 I can make sure that your three targets walk away unharmed but also completely in the dark about who took them." He knew that Donald's firm had a reputation of not crossing the line of torture or murder in their operations. That kind of publicity would drive off potential clients.

After some haggling, they reached an arrangement for payment of $60,000 with 25 percent upfront and the rest on delivery. Donald smiled since this left him with $40,000 to slip into his offshore accounts. He had accumulated about four million untaxed dollars this way over the past three years.

Donald hung up the phone, propped his feet up and continued rubbing his worry stone while he thought through the plan again. There were uncertainties, of course, but finding and detaining a bunch of academic geeks should be a walk in the park for the likes of Carlos. His man could play off the Solido woman against her fear for the safety of her fiancé. Once they found out where she kept the medicinal seeds in question, he was sure his men could acquire them.

Specter of Evil (Mark)

I drove through Plymouth, Washington, crossed the Columbia River, and passed into and through Umatilla, Oregon. In a few miles, I-82 southbound ended, and I headed west on I-84. I had spent the last month or three on the East Fork of the Yaak River. My Landcruiser was limping a bit from that trek. I had run over trees that were larger than I thought and straddled rocks much higher than they looked.

On my way out of the wilderness, my eyes stayed towards an impressive bull elk standing in the river below me. The gaze lasted a bit too long and my rig slid off the goat path I was on, sending me and the rig down to the elk. Once I collected my wits and realized I was not upside down but upright in the river, I stared out the windshield at the elk. Quite impressive, I thought.

What a dumbass, the elk probably thought. He snorted, stomped a hoof with a splash, then casually walked upstream and disappeared into a small feeder creek. I winched the rig downstream and finally clear of the rocks, then up through the thickets to the dirt road—probably four hours lost in total. There were now more parts needing replacement, dents to bend out, and the like. But it still ran, so I was back on the road to civilization.

I had anticipated needing a new ride before my latest trip to whereabouts unknown. Truthfully, I had wanted something a bit larger and perhaps more rugged for a while now. I called a guy named Lefty, who lived just outside of Ghost Ranch, New Mexico. Lefty had provided me with my current modified Landcruiser several years ago. I told him about a rig I discovered one night when my MacBook had some weak connectivity to the outside world.

It was an orange Russian-made Ural Next. Orange in case rescue choppers needed to find me. I did not specifically want a Ural, just a rig of similar size and off-road performance. His email message from a few weeks ago said it was ready to be shipped, but I decided to pick it up in person.

First, though, since I was damn near in Portland when Mat called to say he was not home, I was going to grab a shower and a bed anyway. I had called Sirocco once I hit pavement, and she was headed back home to Dallas the next day. She said she couldn't wait to get me into the sunset Jacuzzi. We talked a while, and she described what Marcelle had told her about Jenara's office break-in. It was a bit curious that nothing was taken. Things had been sifted through, but nothing was missing.

When someone trespasses on Jenara, they trespass on Mat and hence on me. Details would come later. I told Sirocco I'd let her know my ETA once John secured my ride.

I rang John next. He answered on the first ring. I told him where I was and where I was heading.

"Yes sir, I know, sir. How may I help you?" John is the result of one of the better moves in my life. The result of my semi-scientific mind jumping from three to ten and funding a five-million-dollar startup overnight. John is basically a glorified AI travel agent. John also knows where I am, even if I don't know exactly where I am. The fact that he does know has saved my ass more than once. On the other hand, the fact a computer knows where I am all the time just plain pisses me off.

"I need a crew of two to pick up my Landcruiser from Mat's today. I'll park it in the underground deck, keys in the ignition, by 2 pm. The drivers need to take it straight through to Sirocco's in Dallas."

"Yes sir, I know where the incomparable Ms. Sirocco lives." Damn sarcastic computer. I felt like stopping in the middle of the Interstate and shooting holes in a sign with my Desert Eagle .50 cal. But I just continued westward.

"Get me an early flight tomorrow from Portland to Santa Fe, deadhead me on someone's Lear if you can find one going that way or charter jet if you can't. I need to be in Dallas no later than first thing the day after tomorrow."

I originally planned to drive my dented rig from Portland to Santa Fe, swap it out for my new one, and then head to Dallas. There are as many beautiful things to see on that ride as there are grains of sand on all the beaches of the seven oceans. But my conversation with Mat led me to believe I may be needed in South America to pull his worthless ass out of whatever jam he was getting himself into. Hence my accelerated pace.

"Have the crew update me on their timing. I want to transfer all of my crap to the new rig quickly. Once I'm done, they will drive the Landcruiser over to Lefty. Then send them on their way."

"Yes sir. While you have been expounding in your long-winded way, I have made your flight arrangements. A car will pick you up at 5 am sharp tomorrow at Mat's. A friend of mine was gracious enough to offer you the airlift."

"Drivers will meet you in the deck at Mat's. They'll be there in a little while and await your arrival. I've also arranged the delivery of fresh flowers and mesquite firewood to Ms. Sirocco from her usual supplier in Leakey. I even put your name on the delivery instead of mine because I am thoughtful, unlike you." I considered whether it was possible to strangle a computer.

"Have Lefty meet me at Santa Fe Regional. Pay him with your black card, payment untraceable to him, same as cash."

"I already did, sir. I paid him as soon as he let me know the truck was ready. Some folks cannot wait months to collect payment while their wealthy clients lollygag around in the woods chasing ferns and whatnot. Presuming you would be late, I also included a 15% storage surcharge. Oh, I almost forgot. Mr. Tom would appreciate a call from you." The machine didn't forget anything. He was just pretending to be human again.

I wondered what Tom wanted to discuss. I hadn't had the pleasure since Sirocco, Amber Lee, and I flew out of Esperance Airport a few months ago with the crystal Mat needed. So, I rang him up on the satphone.

Naturally, he picked up on the first ring. "Mark, how the hell are you! Long time no see! Cheers, my friend!"

"Amazing and well met my friend! Tell me Ms. Jillora is splendid also!" We both were grinning ear to ear about ten thousand miles away from each other. The shared experience of recycling a body or two makes the heart grow fonder. Not to mention it was probably past his bedtime.

"She is indeed. The love of my life! And also the purpose of my call. It seems she has acquired a product of interest to Ms. Jenara. Don't ask me what scheme they're up to because I never question a shaman as I wish not to be turned to stone!" He chuckled.

"Tom, hang with me." I clicked up John.

"And how may I be of assistance, sir?" The machine was doing his Aussie accent. I wanted to finish wrecking my truck.

"Secure Tom and me on both ends. I know we're secure on both ends but double-check just to appease this old derelict." I probably annoyed the computer—hopefully.

"Done, sir, anything else? And I hope you are having a marvelous day Mr. Tom." More Aussie.

"Splendid John. Thanks for asking!" Tom was like that.

"John, can anyone hear us besides you?" I'm definitely paranoid when it comes to talking out loud across the globe.

"None sir. Your conversation is transferred from one satellite to a different one many times each second. Most of the satellites are secret military fliers, and I'm using a master key to the back door. That is to say, we have absolute security and also free airtime. I could provide you with more detail, but I fear it would only be a waste of time." Good, I'm thinking. It probably saves me about a million dollars a month. And, yea, the computer just insinuated I was a dumbass.

"Anything else I can help you with, sir?" I replied no, and he rang off.

"OK, Tom. Tell me about it."

"We were flying from Esperance up to one of the mines on a semi-regular run. But when we got there, she went walkabout for the rest of the day and night, returning with something looking like salad greens. We returned home to Perth, and I called John since I could not raise either you or Mat." Tom drew a breath, and it sounded as if he took a sip or two. Probably medicinal.

"Since I called you gents, Jillora has informed me that her pharmacopeia has been touched by an intruder. You see, she leaves otherwise invisible markers around her things. She has done so ever since I smoked some of her stuff while a bit intoxicated many years ago. Only she knows what I smoked and, since I completely lost four days on the endeavor, she does not really need the precautions. But she uses them anyway. A bit strange, but nothing was missing. And, to add to the mystery, there was nothing on the cameras. Nothing. Nobody, no anything."

"She said it felt strangely like a specter of evil had come and gone. I'm sure you remember that the girl I love is Ngangkari, Shaman, and the 1,111th in a line of daughters from the first Jillora Bindi, dating back some 20,000 years or so. So, when she utters such words, this old boomer perks up and takes note." Tom seemed a bit perplexed.

"Tom, apparently a similar incident occurred with Jenara. Let me ask you this without you divulging any secrets. Did Ms. Jillora have her, I'll call them valuables, with her on her walkabout instead of at home?"

I felt I needed to tread lightly. And, in spite of John's assurances about privacy, I was still reserved.

"Naturally there are certain things that are always with her." Tom was a bit cagey too. I did not blame him.

"Mat, Jenara, and Amber Lee are headed to somewhere in the outback of Brazil. I get the feeling I may be there sooner rather than later. I'll be in Dallas late tomorrow or very early the next day, at Sirocco's. I'll touch base with you then, if not sooner. Hopefully, I can catch up with Mat for an update. Tom, in the meantime, I recommend ya'll take extra care. I don't know what's up, but it doesn't feel right."

"Will do Mark. I'll have a few of the lads hang out nearby. I'll also see what Croc is up to these days. Not a bad guy to have hereabouts. Cheers mate!" Tom clicked off.

I had one more call to make, but I wanted a sip of something old and smoky before I made that call. I pulled into Mat's underground parking deck and stopped in the common area. Two fairly seasoned-looking young men met me there. Brief words were spoken before they pulled my rig back out of the garage and headed for Dallas. They had a 2,000-mile trip and a head start on me, but I'd fly all but about 650 miles of it.

I stood at the elevator. Mat had informed me I had to gaze into a hole and place my hand on a piece of glass. I did both and swoosh the elevator doors opened. I climbed aboard, the doors closed, and I was whisked upward nonstop to the penthouse. The doors opened again, and I stepped into Mat's private residence.

Big, open, and airy best described his current digs. The latest and greatest burners, refrigerators, ovens, coolers, pots and pans, and a bunch of other paraphernalia made up the central kitchen area. The rest of the place, bedrooms, and such, were recessed. I never felt like exploring the back areas, but I figured 15-20 folks could live comfortably based on the central interior arrangements.

A variety of good and not-so-good art hung on rich wood-paneled walls. Sculpture, pottery, and trinkets from around the world were strategically placed around the huge living spaces. I knew they were all artisan crafts he knowingly paid dearly for. The proceeds helped the artisans survive and feed their families and villages. I often made similar purchases but never seemed to actually take procession—only so much room in the Landcruiser. Maybe my new rig would allow room for some necklaces or bracelets or whatever. Nonetheless, it felt good being able to contribute to the common cause we call Earth.

John has a network of philanthropists as clients. He could spend a million or so without asking. He could typically get ten million or more for special projects. The generous folks involved neither asked for nor received a receipt, and they remained anonymous. A smart person understands that split seconds here and there separate them from homelessness or eternity.

All of this was nice, but the only reason I came here, instead of sleeping on a bench at PDX, was the liquor cabinet. There was older and much more expensive Scotch, but I pulled out a bottle of Lagavulin 16, placed it on a counter, pulled the tab, and then the cork. I found a Glencairn glass and poured myself a dram, probably more like two. The smoky, complicated elixir filled my senses as I sipped a bit. I rolled it around my gums and allowed it to slip down the hatch. I decided the inconvenience of hanging around Mat's condo was worth it.

Time for the call I had been avoiding. I'm not complaining, but the lady I was calling could be downright bitchy. I had been down that road once or twice before. I'm too damn old for it anymore. I had another sip, walked out on the deck, and took in the Portland skyline. I punched in a number on my satphone. It was answered on the first ring.

"Mark, about time. Mat said you would call hours ago." The dear lady on the other end of the line was part of Mat's security setup. She was and would remain eternally pissed at me for a slight mishap a few years ago. Shit happens.

"The pleasure is all mine, Marcelle. I hope this crazy world is treating you as it should." A blindingly nice way for me to say fuck off. "Mat recommended I contact you about an incursion at Jenara's office. Can you enlighten me, please?"

"Yes. Naturally, normal surveillance equipment was in place, cameras, and such. We know the break-in occurred, but there is no traceable lapse or break in the surveillance and no one on the film. I've seen this type of activity before, and it is very sophisticated. Very fucking sophisticated. I'm pissed because I never anticipated it."

"Damn. Either government or, possibly, government, huh?" I was jumping ahead at light speed again.

"Maybe, but there are private groups who could pull this off. Anyway, I've installed a much more sophisticated system at her office, and I've upgraded Mat's home system as well. You need a haircut and a shave, by the way. And Lagavulin tastes like elephant piss." I grinned at the image of her firing down a dram or two of elephant piss. I actually laughed out loud and raised my glass and said cheers. I don't know if she got the last part because she had clicked off.

I found a shower in one of the suites. I walked into the glass-enclosed single-car garage-sized booth and turned the water on to hotter than hell—a clear mistake. I was hit from the front, behind, low, and high with scalding spray. I leaped back through the still-open door and promptly slipped and landed flat on my ass. I presumed Marcelle had the entire episode on film. I also presumed the film would eventually end up on youtube so a million people could view me busting my skinny old ass. I pushed up off the tile floor and steadied myself on one of the vanities.

Most of a season, whereabouts unknown, without a booboo. Ten minutes in Mat's, and I almost died trying to take a shower. Maybe I should have settled for the bench at PDX. Anyway, I finally figured out the shower arrangement, scalded myself for a few minutes or an hour or so. I tiptoed out to the kitchen a couple of times in the middle of my watery bliss without further calamity. I refilled my tumbler and also found two cans of Sweetwater 420 Strain G13 IPA.

An enjoyable libation with a distinctly pot-like noise in the background from the most pot unfriendly state of Georgia.

Later I slipped into some tactical khakis and an old fishing shirt. I found fresh prawns in the fridge. Mat must have really been in a hurry. I peeled a few, putting the rest into a ziplock, and stuck them in the freezer. I found the cookware I wanted for cooking the shrimp and tossing a salad—Chalula, crackers, and, yes, two dozen fresh Olympia oysters. I cracked the oysters and laid them on the half-shells. I carried the entire meal onto the deck and laid it out on the four-seat table. I was very happy that Mat was not home, and I grinned throughout the superb meal. He never shared very well.

After cleaning up, I settled back in a comfortable chair with my phone and punched in Mat, but he didn't answer. He'd know I called and ring me when it suited him. If I got worried, John could pinpoint his location—I hoped. Brazil is just a tad smaller than the U.S., and it has a lot more jungle

I closed my peepers for a few minutes. I wasn't really tired, just pensive. My bright and not so bright friends in the evening sky came out, and I drifted a bit.

Bull elk and bear and trout crossed my field of view. I imagined four billion years ago a dying civilization firing off a gazillion orbs full of DNA and encapsulated crystalized information across the universe. Wanna feel small? Just try to understand that we were apparently spawned from a very sophisticated bio-chemical-quantum-mechanical civilization a few billion years ago during the infancy of our planet. They sent us a note telling us not to be fucking dumbasses. One thing I have learned, though, is that you cannot fix stupid. Just look around. So it goes.

While I was half-awake, I gave more consideration to Mat and Jenara. Joseph had called and asked what to stock in the way of armaments for their little hike. Mat had ordered a bunch of pocketknives for the locals. The Benchmade Freek 560 is a good thing to have if you need to unstick a bit of meat from your teeth or clean under your nails. I left that part of the order alone anyway—no need to hurt his feelings. Besides, they were good trinkets.

I added a half dozen Ka-Bar KA1214 BRK USA Fighting Knives. Hard to argue with the USMC blade of choice. Mat would probably just cut himself with a knife anyway. I might as well give him one that would require stitches. They needed sidearms even though Mat had not mentioned them. I recommended Glock 19 Gen 5 G34 Competition 9x19mm pistols. A hefty semi, but handy if the range extends out to 80 yards or so. Also, an excellent and reliable friend to have closer in. Included were a few standard 17 shot magazines per gun, loaded with Federal Premium 124gr HST JUP rounds. Close in, point and shoot, find another target.

The long gun was a little more complicated. Normally they would be useless in a jungle dogfight, fine for savanna, maybe. So, I compromised and said get Wilson Ultralite Ranger .243's fitted with Ranger 1-8x24i Rifle Scopes. Twenty round clips fleshed out this well-appointed, lightweight, and extremely portable choice.

Excellent for clearing out tight spots, fair to good at 300 yards. Much over that distance requires lots of practice. Mat was not going to have lots of practice. Actually, Mat was not going to have any practice. Besides, 300 yards is a long way, and running away is probably a better bet than a firefight when possible. I added a few boxes of Seller & Bellot ammo, and they were set for rifles.

Rounding out the list was a pair of JTS M12AR 12 Gauge Semiauto Shotguns. The five-round clips would be stacked with Federal LE Tactical with FliteControl 12-gauge 00 Buckshot. Nine pellets per shell. Good for knocking down trees at close range. A handful of boxes of 25 shells should do. This entire inventory was probably 99% unnecessary because they had a chopper in and out—hopefully. Otherwise, most of this shit would rot in the jungle in a few years.

I sipped some more Scotch and drifted off with a light breeze blowing across my face. My internal clock woke me at 4 am. I fixed a cup of Mat's coffee using the squatty little machine and plastic inserts. A mystery to me, but it was dark and hot. I grabbed a shower and was downstairs before my ride arrived.

Ready to Launch (Mark)

I stopped in the Lobby Level of Mat's building and chatted with the security guy for a few minutes while waiting for my ride to PDX. I recognized his face, but I am shit for remembering names. His nameplate read Mr. Jones, so I was not embarrassed. He called me Mark, but even though he recognized me and knew my relative standing up the food chain, he gave away zero on the recently upgraded security measures.

Instead, we talked about the weather, both agreeing there was indeed weather. My ride arrived; I said cheers to Mr. Jones and left. I made a note to mention Mr. Jones to Mat. Time to upgrade the man's pay rate. Seymour R. Goff created a poster for the War Advertising Council early in World War II. The US Office of War Information used his poster to remind people that "Loose Lips Sink Ships." Enough said.

The tall, jacked young driver put my bag in the back of the Explorer, and I climbed in as shotgun. Per my request, he had picked up Starbucks venti Americanos for both of us. In exchange, he reluctantly accepted a Starbucks card loaded with $100. I drank mine on the fifteen-minute ride. He dropped me at the foot of a Cessna Citation Mustang in the private area of the airport.

Captain Melissa Gold, the pilot, greeted me. By my estimation, Ms. Gold looked to be about nineteen years old, but half the world looks nineteen years old when you get to my age. She said we were set to depart. The owner had backed out of the trip at the last minute, so it was just the two of us. She parked my lanky butt in the right-hand front seat and pointed at a Starbucks venti Americano in the cupholder. Her choice was a venti latte. After weaving through the morning traffic, we were airborne headed south southeast in fifteen minutes.

She asked if I could fly. I had been at the controls of a variety of aircraft over the years, but I kept that information to myself. She laughed when I replied I couldn't fly a paper airplane. Ms. Gold had an infectious laugh and a brilliant smile, and I kept my hands firmly clasped in my lap for the thousand-mile flight. We flew at 30,000 feet, and I recollected the various times in my life I had driven across much of the stunning terrain we were passing over. Hell, Mat and I had hitchhiked much of it as kids in some of our unconventional adventures.

The skies were clear for the entire trip, and there was only minor turbulence. Eventually, we came in over Bandelier National Monument, then the Rio Grande Gorge, and touched down in Santa Fe. The flight was more than excellent. I handed her a black Starbucks card as I climbed down and out. Free Starbucks for life. I hoped she lived until she was a hundred.

Lefty was off to the side of the tarmac in an oversized golf cart. He grabbed my bag, and we exited through the fence to Reserved Parking. I was pleased to see my new rig took up five spaces diagonally.

"Mr. Mark, meet your new Mercedes' Zetros platform 428 hp 12-liter diesel 16 forward/2 reverse auto/manual shifting 4X4 monster truck. The 25-inch off-road tires should take you anywhere, including all the way to the end of nowhere. I hope you like it. The Russian rig was good quality, but if something broke, it would stay broken for months waiting on parts. I decided on Benz for the top-end quality and the fact that parts are obtainable."

I got the grand ten-minute tour. Lefty had transformed the already-huge vehicle into a hulking massif. Even though I had loved my Landcruiser just one day ago, I now couldn't remember what color it was. He had added a battery option, which charged via socket or a built-in solar array when parked or by a massive alternator when in motion. This option, plus additional fuel tanks, gave me coast-to-coast capability. Most importantly, it held a full-sized shower and head. God, I was getting soft in my old age.

Small to very large, self-locking storage bins were located with some interior access and some exterior access. Two refrigerators, one dorm size and one full size, and a freezer gave me ample room for fish, tators, greens, and beer. The roof rack was multi-faceted and adaptable with quick pull-and-release connections. There was a built-in ladder for access.

I settled into the cockpit and looked around. It held the driver and a shotgun rider up front, along with two in the crew area. The seats were cowhide and adjustable in approximately one million different ways, warming or cooling depending on your preference. The arrangement was a cross between the Cessna I just left and a Hatteras 65' platform.

John had helped Lefty procure some interesting electronics and communication equipment—stuff not available on the streets. Hell, by the looks of some of it, 'not readily available outside' meant top secret. The crew seats could fold flat and offered a platform directly into the living area. Perhaps the best part was something Lefty invented.

The flick of a switch caused a king-size interlocking platform to magically appear from the interior roof area. It descended, supported by various built-ins. An ultrathin self-inflating mattress, extra firm, populated the top of the platform. There was ample headroom for a romp and multiple recessed lights providing dusk-to-daylight as needed. For the first time in years, I had a real bed!

Above the bed was the solar panel array. It was deployed through slats on either side of the rig just below the roofline. Fully extended, the panels covered 100 sqft and offered a handy 30% efficiency. An oven/microwave oven assembly was situated next to a small double sink. Embedded into the walls were two flat-screen TVs. One was ideally situated for watching from the bed, the other for 'living room' viewing.

Lefty laughed when he showed me the controls for the TVs and said to call him for instructions if I ever decided to use one of them. Lefty was aware of my aversion to the idiot box. He thought the TVs added to the resale value. I didn't tell him it was much more likely that I'd end up smashed and dead inside the rig at the bottom of some unnamed canyon than putting it on sale.

The ample glass up front, on the sides, rear-facing, over the cab and part of the roof was tempered and doubled. Not bazooka-proof, but it would stop most small arms fire.

There were two 12,000-pound Drive Recovery winches, one forward and one aft, just in case. Just-in-case is a place I seem to find myself in on occasion. I am a natural-born non-salesman, but I do believe I could sell somebody one of these rigs.

The Landcruiser had been my home for years, but this was my new home. I climbed into the left-side cab area, waved Lefty off, and proceeded out of the airport, hung an east on northbound I-25 for a few miles, then hung a right on SR 285 down to I-40. I left I-40 east of Amarillo, took SR 287 on into Fort Worth, and the signs took me from there to downtown Dallas.

With the two-hour time change from Portland, I rolled into the interior parking deck loading area under Sirocco's building around 11 pm. Sirocco arranged parking in the loading area since the rig would not pass under the hanging white PVC pipe warning devices. The boys were there with my Landcruiser.

I started transferring my crap from the Landcruiser to my new ride. For the time being, I pretty much just shoved everything into the huge rear living area. In went a variety of weaponry, including handguns, long rifles, semi-automatics, and some not so semi. I stowed my Desert Eagle in its own compartment. In went my camp stove and table, fishing gear, my 1985 Yairi Alvarez box guitar in a hard-shell case, some knives, clothes, boots, tennis shoes, several bottles of Scotch, and three IPAs. Only three IPAs left! Boy, was that a close call up on the Yaak River!

Sirocco knew I had arrived but stayed at the top of the building, knowing this was a job for me alone. Sometime after midnight, I did the look-in-the-hole thing and placed my hand on the glass plate beside the elevator. I had a small Filson bag as my only companion. The elevator took me straight up to her place. Same as Mat's elevator.

She greeted me like we had not seen each other in months because we hadn't. Then she stood back, looking me over from head to toe, and headed for the kitchen. She handed me a cut glass half full of 30-year-old Balvenie and sent me packing to the showers. A half-hour later, I found her in the west end lounging in the oversized Jacuzzi, sipping something, and watching the moon heading down to the horizon, somewhere past Midland.

A tray with meats, cheeses, fruit, veggies, and crackers sat on the ledge. I ditched my robe and descended into heaven. We had nothing to do tomorrow, actually today, so time did not matter. Her long straight black hair shone wet across her mocha skin. The word beautiful was a waste. She updated me on all that had been going on since I went walkabout. She had been busy, indeed.

Amber Lee had called Sirocco just before she left for Brazil to ensure work would continue on their current project involving plastic pollution on Antarctica's shores. Several floors below where we were lounging, Sirocco had a lab where she employed scientists and techs to analyze what, where, when, and how on everything collected. A typical scientific look-see at something of interest. Ocean currents were mostly the culprit of transport, although some micro-particulate deposition inland was definitely wind-related. They were trying to separate out the two and determine if the windborne contamination was from beach debris or carried long distances from other continents.

This exceptional North African woman had been adopted and brought to the States as a youth. She earned her PhD in Astrophysics from MIT at the ripe old age of 22, and now she was involved in projects across the globe covering, basically, an orgy-of-the-ologies. If it appeared to benefit humankind, she was likely to be on the forefront, or behind the scenes, as appropriate.

"I just glanced around on the way from the elevator, and it looks like you have finished redecorating." Her penthouse had been all but destroyed during a dust-up with federal agents while Mat was pursuing the crystal memory sphere. One of my team, Hunter, activated the penthouse's custom "defense system" when he had to implement an emergency evacuation. So, the system swung into action when agents entered her penthouse, probably sending several to the hospital. Unfortunately, much of her furniture and artwork was damaged beyond salvage.

"I had my interior decorator visit, but he quit on the spot. Too much blood, I guess. So John found me someone with a stronger stomach. She recovered what she could and worked with John to make selected art purchases. You know my penchant for indigenous tribal art, so ultimately, many deserving but unrecognized artists benefited from my remodeling project. It makes me feel good to help."

Sirocco selected a bite of cheese and a cracker and fed it to me. I reciprocated. A sip of something very tasty led to swapping sips, which led to a curtailment of conversation for some time. Sirocco came up for air and laughed softly. Shit, my manhood had become a laughingstock. Again.

"Did I tell you about Hunter and the pony car he took when he evacuated?" she asked. "No? He almost got to stay in Post, Texas, free of charge for a year or two—running 204 in a 55-mph zone. John fixed his bail and contributed a non-trivial cash sum to the Sheriff's favorite charity—himself. Hunter was released but given clear instructions. There is now a permanent shoot to kill order on his head in Post."

She punched in a sequence on her sat phone and handed it to me. "Watch this short clip."

I was watching through the front windscreen of the '67 Mustang. The screen was split between a view of the highway and the instrument panel. There was the classic set of gauges and an electronic speedometer as well. The original dial speedometer was pegged at 120 mph. Mr. Selby himself had hit 170 in his original '67' ride. Sirocco's car was somewhat modified. The electronic gauge was showing 197 and climbing.

Hunter was narrating, just a word or two at a time. He was on two-lane SR 70 headed eastward downhill from Ruidoso Downs toward San Patricio. The straight stretch ahead was clear. The rebel yell was probably heard down in Hondo when the digital speed hit 209. He managed to get it back under a hundred as the road veered slightly to the right going through San Patricio.

"Holy shit. What did you say when you talked to him?" I asked.

"I told him the record is his and the car title too!"

"I'm getting too old for the high-speed shit anyway," she continued. "I'd end up dead trying to beat him, so I capitulated. He owns the fastest '67 Shelby GT 500 on Earth, and I get to live. Life is good."

"What did your neighbors think about the whole unfortunate episode," I inquired.

"After the noisy foray, my five other tenants occupying floors twenty and down approached me with requests to get out of their leases—very private, very wealthy tenants. Police and fire units blazing red and blue lights and blaring sirens were not what they signed on for. I released them from their leases immediately. The last one made their final exit last week, so I have the entire building to myself now. Amber Lee is completing her lab space on three of the floors. She has TEM's, SEM's, MRI's and a variety of other instruments related to gene sequencing and genetic research. Evidently, she thinks it will assist Jenara and Jillora in whatever venture they have set up. That's why she traveled to Rio with Jenara and Mat.

As we spoke, we quickly realized neither she nor I knew the full extent of what Jenara and Jillora were up to, but we both knew Jenara didn't have to coax Mat into heading down to Brazil. If she needed to go, he would go. And if he needed to go, that meant I would end up going. Now Mat was versed in a variety of both popular and virtually unknown martial arts. He could kick the shit out of a dummy in the gym. But in a street fight or a jungle shit show, he'd probably get his clock cleaned in a New York second, and Jenara would be on her own.

I told Sirocco about my conversation with Marcelle concerning the break-in at Jenara's. Then I added the information from Down Under relayed from Tom about the same type of incursion into Jillora Bindi's personal space. I repeated the words 'specter of evil' Jillora Bindi used to describe the feeling the discovery gave her. I could see the change of expression on Sirocco's face as she felt the hackles rise on the back of her neck.

"It's disturbing, but that's a mystery for another time," she said. "For now, we need a plan."

Sirocco pulled herself out of the Jacuzzi, reached for my hand, and dragged me out too. The night air had a slight chill, so she pulled on a petite red and black Filson Alaskan Guide robe and tossed me an otter-green-and-black extra-large.

Inside, she used her voice to conjure up a huge screen on the wall above a vintage pinball game. She asked for the Google map and narrowed it to the 100-mile scale. Lima, Peru up to Guayaquil, Ecuador on the left side of the screen, and Rondonia to Manaus, Brazil on the right.

"OK. Deep in the heart of the western Brazilian rainforest, I see three potential airports: Tabatinga to the north, Rio Branco to the south, and Manaus to the east. I know Manaus is the third largest airport in the country, so it should have anything we may need." She voice-pulled up the other two airports.

"While full-sized jets can land, there seems to be a high probability of having to pack in everything we might need, including fuel for my Bell 505 Jet Ranger X helicopter." Sirocco was fully engaged.

"You anticipate us both heading south together, beautiful woman?"

"Naturally. We sure as hell aren't going to let those three have all the fun. What do you think?"

"I already put Hunter on notice," I replied.

"You old dog. Ahead of the game, as always." She picked up her sat phone from a glass-top driftwood table and punched in John. He answered on the first ring.

"Good early morning to you, Ms. Sirocco! How may I be of assistance?"

"John, Mark is here with me."

"Yes, ma'am. I know." Damn computer, I thought.

"We may need to set up the delivery of my bird to one of three airports in western Brazil. Or perhaps northeastern Peru."

"Manau, Rio Blanco, and Tabatinga seem to be viable candidates Ms. Sirocco. Coronel FAP Francisoc Secada Vignetta International in Iquitos, Peru also." The computer purposely ignored me. "Manau has full services, but the other three are a bit sketchy on supplies and services. I'll scramble up an Airbus A400M or similar. Will you fly from Love or DFW?"

"Either airport is fine."

"Departure date/time, ma'am?"

"Have us ready to go by dawn tomorrow since it's almost dawn today here. Our destination will be decided by then. Have the pilots forward flight plans. We'll also need guides."

"Anything else, Ms. Sirocco?"

"John, any word from Mat?" I asked.

"They arrived and departed Rio de Janeiro is about all I can say, sir. Military satellite coverage is very spotty, especially in the western jungle regions. Some global weather services continue to overview the massive destruction of the rain forests, but there are limitations in my ability to use them for communication, unlike the military satellites. They are designed for photography, not comms. His sat phone is apparently either off or malfunctioning. Same with Ms. Amber Lee's."

"Shit. OK John, let us know about our flight." Sirocco clicked off. She had a wary look in her eyes and was poised like a top-of-the-food-chain cat ready to pounce.

I found my sat phone and punched up Joseph. He answered on the first ring.

"How are you, my friend, and how may I help you?" Joseph was always positive and ready for action.

"Excellent, and I hope the same for you. Sorry to wake you if I did. Do you have a minute?"

"Absolutely. You have my undivided attention."

"Sirocco and I will probably leave for Brazil around dawn tomorrow. Since you already ordered armament, can you simply add on two of everything, except for the pocketknives, and have the parcel delivered to Ms. Sirocco's by late this evening?"

"Mark, everything should be arriving before 10:30 am this morning. I anticipated you and Ms. Sirocco would take up the chase as a rearguard, so I added the additional items to the original order and had them shipped to Ms. Sirocco's. Sorry but I included Mat's pocket cutlery in your order as well. Didn't want to hurt his feelings."

"Joseph, you're the best. We'll keep you informed. Cheers." I clicked off.

Sirocco grabbed two Braindead Brewing IPAs from the ice and popped the tops.

"Let's finish what we were doing before we so rudely interrupted ourselves, sleep a bit, and then plan for our jungle holiday." She dropped her robe. It don't get much better than this.

Rio (Mat)

The trip to Rio was a bitch. A missed flight led to an unplanned night in Miami, followed by a delayed departure the next day. We stayed in South Beach with a great view of the ocean, and I sat out on the balcony that evening, pondering life at zero feet elevation. When you live at sea level, the future only holds two paths. You will either have more land or less land on which to live. Sea level will rise or fall depending on whether ice is accumulating or melting at the poles. If sea level falls, then you get more land to live on as the ocean recedes. Unfortunately for Miami, the city is on the losing end of the climate change proposition since global sea levels are rising. The city will gradually move from having less dry land to no land.

Citizens and politicians don't seem too bothered by this wet future. Of course, most people can't plan beyond tomorrow, so I'm not surprised. Perhaps the wealthy will turn South Beach into an elevated luxury retreat only accessible by boat or helicopter. Tough luck for those living in cinderblock ranch homes.

Despite Miami's somewhat bleak future, feeling a warm nighttime sea breeze, sharing a bottle of chardonnay with Jenara, and listening to the waves had its charms. I hoped Mark was enjoying my scotch in Portland.

I squeezed in a bit of light sleep on the flight to Rio the next day, so I wasn't a walking zombie by the time we got to immigration and customs. I thought I was fast-tracked through, but something went wrong. Jenara breezed through on her Brazilian passport, but I got pulled aside and given the third degree. I soon realized there was more going on than just a random check. The officers had questions about several of the last international entries in my passport, what kind of work I did, and why I was traveling, etc.; the list went on. But after about twenty minutes of useless questions and answers, they tipped their hand. They asked me whether I was transporting any medicinal plants and if I intended to take any out of the country. I replied no to both, but the connection between the break-in at Jenara's office and our trip to western Brazil was on my mind.

My answers still seemed to be unsatisfactory, and the interrogation turned to our specific travel plans within the country. I kept it as vague as possible and stuck to the story—I was accompanying my fiancée on a trip related to her professional anthropological studies. Before the conversation was over, I gleaned that they already knew we had a booking on Ipanema beach at the Fasano Hotel. This realization raised a red flag for me. These guys were being paid to pump me for information.

By the time immigration finally stamped my passport, dusk was settling over the city. Jenara had already located our driver, Marco, and the two of them were waiting as I exited customs with a long line of recent arrivals from London Heathrow. We were packed light with carry-ons and headed directly outside.

It turned out that Marco wasn't the driver. He opened the backdoor of the limo for us and then took the shotgun seat. The dark glass center panel of the window to the front slid down with a high-pitched hum, and Marco's face appeared. "Anita is our driver this evening. I'm along for the ride and a little extra support if needed. Make yourself comfortable. You have a well-stocked bar back there, so help yourself, and there are bottles of cold water in there also. Relax, it will be a bit of a drive to Ipanema."

"Thanks, Marco," I said, "I think we are good-to-go. Anita, good to meet you."

"The pleasure is mine Mr. Dover, and welcome to Rio," came the response from my unseen driver.

The opened window section was only a small center panel, and I was seated behind the driver, so my view of her was blocked. Jenara, who had a view of the driver's side, carried on a rapid back and forth conversation in Portuguese with Anita as she put the car in gear and pulled out into traffic. I couldn't pick up much of it, but the conversation stopped once Anita's attention turned to the road. The window slid smoothly back into place, and I poured a glass of Dalwhinnie single malt. Jenara settled for a glass of red wine.

It had been a while since I was in Rio, but the magnificent scenery had not changed. Wide white-sand beaches, like Copacabana and Ipanema, rimmed the Atlantic shoreline. Rising behind them were peaks of granite jutting out of the ground like pagan monoliths. These were the remnants of a violent and volatile episode in earth's history over 100 million years ago during the Cretaceous period. The planet was in transition, driven by forces deep below its crustal layer. The continents of Africa and South America split apart as plate tectonics birthed the nascent Atlantic Ocean.

Magma from the earth's mantle rose to fill the voids as the crust fractured and tore open. Massive chambers of molten rock developed below the surface, and volcanos spewed lava above ground. The chambers of hot rock cooled with time to become granite batholiths. Then over the eons, wind, rain, and ice slowly ground the land into what exists today. The granite pinnacles that decorate Rio today were the most durable parts of the batholiths and resisted weathering. They didn't rise from the ground; the ground had fallen away from them.

I took in the views for a few minutes, then reclined my head and shut my eyes to rest while my mind slipped back to a time before Jenara, before wealth, and before college. The American west spread out in front of me like a surreal panoramic landscape. Mark was riding shotgun, and I was driving a beat-up blue ford station wagon. Judy was asleep in the back seat. The car belonged to Judy, and Mark and I were just hitchhikers seeing America's vast, glorious spaces for the first time.

We had crossed the Colorado-Utah border not long ago, and the sun was getting low on the horizon. It is in that low light of the evening where a bit of magic happens. We had burned a few on the way across Colorado, and I had a smooth, relaxed buzz going as we blasted westward on Interstate 70. The shadows deepened until crevasses on the hillsides became black pits. But where the light did strike the cliff faces, it impinged at an angle close to perpendicular. This low angle enhanced color in the rock strata, with each layer glowing in a slightly different hue.

The operative word for geology in this part of the world was "Flat." One layer of rock stacked flat on another, so the only way you could see them was when a river cut down through the layers exposing the whole stack.

Judy was running from an abusive biker husband in Nebraska. Mark and I were just running, and it wasn't clear to me if we were running from something or to something. I didn't ponder the question too long because it took the edge off of our adventure.

We turned a little later on SR 191 and headed south to Moab. Judy's goal was California, but she was asleep, and we were doing a bit of sightseeing. Arches National Park and Canyonlands were in front of us now. We parked the car on a pull-over just south of the Arches entrance and leaned back in the seats to get some shut-eye.

Judy took the detour news well when we woke up the next morning. We sat on the hood of the Ford enjoying egg salad sandwiches for breakfast. They were left over from yesterday afternoon but still smelled okay, and we were hungry. One thing led to another, and eventually, Jack appeared. He stopped because of his misconception that we had broken down by the road and needed assistance.

He was in his late fifties or early sixties and lived in a self-built yurt in the desert outside of Moab. It seemed his father had owned a few acres in the middle of nowhere and passed it on to Jack along with a modest inheritance. Jack said he thought about it for a full three seconds before he quit his job in Chicago and moved to Moab ten years ago.

He worked as a river guide for tourists during the summers and managed the winters by living off his investments. This idea of living off investments was the first time I ever realized that a person could live a good life and not have a real job. Jack was a bit of a philosopher, though, and he said something to me one day that blew my mind and set me on a course to my present situation.

We only hung with Jack for about a week, camping out beside his yurt. However, Judy shared the bed with him and stayed inside, living in a bit more civilized fashion. One morning Jack and I sat on some boulders about a hundred yards behind his yurt, soaking in the sun and chewing on a few peyote buttons. Judy and Mark shared a joint or two since she couldn't stand the peyote's taste, and Mark said it just made him want to sleep. Everybody's metabolism is different, and each to his own isn't a bad way to start the day.

That afternoon we drove out to Dead Horse Point. By the time we arrived, the mescaline had kicked in. Judy and Mark took a walk-around while Jack and I sat on the highest vantage point we could find, taking in the views. Off in the disance, the Colorado River was snaking around. After millions of years of snaking, it had created a most magnificent array of mesas, canyons, and cliff faces exposing layer after layer of earth, almost like a geological history book.

The sky was a cloudless, chemically enhanced blue, and the multicolored cliffs glowed. Jack and I spent the afternoon discussing the classic beat-generation book "On the Road," written in 1957 by his namesake Jack Kerouac. After a silent pause where we reflected on the world around us, Jack said, "You know, it's all a bit of fantasy when we say we are going somewhere. Like when you told me you are going to California. Hell, we don't know. The truth of the matter is, as travelers on the road of life, we can only do one thing. We can only go where the road takes us."

Bingo, I thought. I didn't have much to say the rest of the day while I pondered Jack's bit of philosophical wisdom. By the end of the day, I had decided that the road took me to geology, so I would look into it when I headed back to college.

I must have dozed off on our trip to Ipanema because when I open my eyes, the entire panel between us and the front was down, not just the center panel, and Marcos was telling us to buckle up. "We have someone tailing us, and there is a narrow stretch ahead between two favelas where we could be cut off and trapped. We are breaking the scheduled routine and taking an alternate route that gives us more maneuvering room to buy time. It may be nothing but stay buckled."

I gave him a thumbs-up, and Jenara nodded. Marcos left the glass partition down and placed a call, presumably to his headquarters for backup. It was dark by now, but I could see the action unfold from my position in the back seat. Judging by the headlights in the rear window, the tail behind us got a little closer. Anita took two quick turns to the right and then to the left. As we swung around the second turn, I saw the headlights from another car about three blocks away. We were both pushed back into the soft leather cushioned seats as Anita accelerated. She rapidly covered two blocks in the time the oncoming car covered one, and then she took a sharp right through the gates of an abandoned storage yard.

She circled to the right around the yard and slowed slightly near a junked truck. Marcos opened the door and rolled out of the car, disappearing into the shadows of the truck. There was street lighting at the front of the yard, but the back was only dense shadows. Anita skidded to a stop by a twelve-foot-high granite ledge and said, "get out on the cliff side and keep your heads down. We have the buy ourselves ten minutes."

By the time we were out, Anita had a pistol in her right hand and handed us each a gas mask. I peeked over the top of the car and saw two vehicles blocking the gate we just came through and about eight men silhouetted against the streetlight glare. I knew they couldn't see anything at the back of the lot.

"Head down," Anita said, a hushed, annoyed voice. Jenara said something in Portuguese as I ducked back down. My Portuguese is barely passable, but as far as I could make out, it was, "He never listens to good advice."

Anita was talking softly over her headset to Marcos. I could hear her counting down before firing a shot into the air. At the same time, one of our pursuers cried out, and about six shots came our way. Only four of them managed to hit the car, but no one fired towards Marco. He remained our ace-in-the-hole. I peeked again, and they were all scrambling behind their cars, dragging one guy who was clutching his right leg.

It took about two minutes for them to reorganize. Anita was peering into the dark wearing night-vision goggles, and I assumed Marco had a pair also. Anita spoke low into the mic, barely at a whisper. "Two of them just split off, moving around the edge of the yard towards you." She spoke in English, so I was intentionally included in the conversation. While she listened to Marco's reply, I looked around the car's front bumper and could see the occasional flicker of the two men's shadows against some distant streetlights.

Jenara tapped me on the left shoulder and motioned with her finger at my gas mask. Hers was already on, and I could see Anita pulling one over her head. As I slipped mine on, Anita extracted a tear gas canister from the bag at her feet and made a superb lob placing the canister directly between the two attackers and the rest of their group. Smoke was pouring out by the time it came to rest. The sea breeze carried the gas directly toward the cars at the front gate.

About the time the canister hit the ground, I heard two thumps from Marco's direction. These were immediately followed by a shrill scream, a grunt, and mixed cursing in English and Portuguese. One of the men was limping into the gas towards the cars, holding a tee-shirt over his face. The other seemed immobilized.

I could see several pairs of headlights about four blocks away and headed in our direction—the cavalry, I presumed. The crew blocking the gates had realized the game was up, and they were piling back into their cars. They blew out of there as the oncoming cars covered the last block.

Marcelle told me that Antonio Torres ran a slick operation, and I believed her now. The new cars, three in total, waited until the tear gas had cleared the area before entering. Two of the cars parked just inside the gates, and the third one circled the yard, pulling up beside Anita's limo. It was a black SUV with an after-market fitting of bullet-proof glass and some side armor, not quite a tank but getting there. Anita hustled us to the rear door and made us both slip in from the side away from the street.

A male driver partially turned around and introduced himself as Luis. "You can ditch those gas masks now; just leave them on the floor." He had a U.S. West Coast Accent and was wearing a lightweight mahogany-brown leather jacket with an aviator cut. "Sorry, I'm dressed down a bit for this driver detail, but Mr. Torres called me in on short notice from a personal engagement.

"I'm sure she was disappointed," said Jenara with a smile as she removed the gas mask. She couldn't help but notice the classic Latin good looks of the man. Hell, even I noticed them.

He smiled back and said, "You two look relaxed for a near-miss kidnapping."

"They never stood a chance," I said. "My impression of Anita was that she could have done the job without Marco if needed."

He smiled again. "You don't want to get on the wrong side of that woman." His tone of voice hinted he had been on that wrong side before. He cranked the engine and continued, "Let's get you to the hotel. Mr. Torres is waiting for you there."

As we rolled into Ipanema, memories flooded back of a great time spent in Rio several years ago. I had requested the Fasanoon this trip because of my pleasant previous stay. The hotel is located on the corner of Av. Viera Suoto and Rua Joaquim Nabuco and occupies some prime beachfront property at the east end of Ipanema.

Philippe Starck originally designed the building, and the interior decorations took inspiration from the golden age of bossa nova. I still had fond memories of enjoying the infinity pool on the roof and gazing out over the Atlantic. We reserved a large oceanfront suite for this trip, and I was hoping we would have some time to enjoy the amenities. Comfort would not be high on the list once we left for western Brazil.

Luis dropped us off at the front entrance, and the concierge personally escorted us up to our suite. Antonio Torres was waiting for us when we arrived. He was in his fifties but looked younger with just the slightest touch of gray around the temples. He was clearly a man who kept himself fit. A lightweight charcoal gray suit, probably custom-tailored in London, gave him the look of a man at ease with himself and his position. "Mr. Dover and Ms. Solido, welcome to Rio." He placed a light kiss on Jenara's hand and gave me a firm shake. "I apologize for the inconvenience earlier this evening. It is embarrassing for me to have to admit that my organization has a leak. Your travel route appears to have been known in advance by the thugs who tried to intercept you. Marco kindly arranged for one of them to remain alive but immobilized, and we have already determined from some light interrogation that Carlos Mattes organized the kidnapping operation."

"Not a name known to me," I replied with a bit of interest.

"He's well known in the wrong sort of circles here, and we suspect his attack tonight has connections to a group in Houston. Marcelle is investigating. Undoubtedly, we will flush out the leak in my organization and probably get a bit more information. In the meantime, I am assigning Luis to you full-time. By the way, we took the liberty of cleaning your room and found three bugs. They are gone now, and your privacy is intact, but use some caution. Mattes mounted a large operation tonight, which means that significant money is involved, and he won't give up easily."

Luis came through the door as soon as Antonio had finished speaking. It was the first time I had a good look at him. Luis was about my height, but the similarities ended there. He had an extra 40 pounds over me, and it was all muscle. He appeared to be in his mid-twenties and had the looks of a male fashion model.

Antonio beaconed him over for a formal introduction. "Mr. Dover, Ms. Solido, this is Luis Duyo. He will be watching over you during your visit. You have some people whispering in my ear who are quite interested in your welfare. Marcelle filled me in, of course, but then I received a call from your friend Mark. He mentioned that you had a knack for attracting trouble and needed someone to 'watch your back,' as he put it. I worked with Mark several years ago, and he has good instincts."

I interrupted, "I didn't know there was a connection between you two."

"I had some unusual problems at the time, and Marcelle recommended him." I raised my eyebrows, but he continued. "Yes, yes, Marcelle told me of her reservations about the man and the little dust-up between them. But she thought he was the right fit for the task at hand. He told me one time that he could shoot the nuts off a gnat at 100 yards. I told him that that qualification was adequate but that Luis, who was with us at the time, could do the same, except Luis would let you pick whether it was the left one or the right."

I smiled, 'adequate' was not a word Mark would have appreciated. "Well, I'm glad to know that he is taking an active interest and not just sitting around my condo drinking my thirty-year-old scotch."

He caught me off guard with his next request. "I would like you to consider taking Luis with you to western Brazil. He is familiar with operations in the jungle, and I am concerned that Carlos is tracking you. He is an unpredictable psychopath and a very clever one at that. He will figure out where you are going and come after you again. We can keep a tight circle around you here, but the open jungle is a different matter."

He was looking me in the eye when he spoke, and Jenara remained silent. I paused before I spoke, "it's not my call. I am just along for the ride. It's Jenara's decision." I passed the ball to her.

"Mr. Torres, it's a generous offer, but the tribe we will be visiting is very shy of outsiders and strangers."

Luis spoke up, but not in words I could understand. He and Jenara then proceeded to carry on a two-minute conversation. I could see that Antonio was in the dark also, but not surprised. When the conversation was over, Jenara turned to Antonio. "I spoke too quickly. We will take you up on your offer."

It turned out that Luis had spent several years working in the jungles of the Parque Nacional da Serra do Divisor. He worked for an NGO collecting data on the indigenous people and criminal intrusions into their territories. Luis picked up the Rohodi language during that work and could speak it well enough to impress Jenara. He had even heard of Hoshikay from one of the other tribes in the area. I was personally glad Janera made the call to bring Luis along because I was starting to think we were into something deeper than I originally anticipated.

The next day and a half were filled with handling the logistics for our next leg of the journey. Luis turned out to be a resourceful addition to the team, and several times he tweaked the arrangements to improve security. We were leaving the next morning via private plane to Cruzeiro do Sul, and Amber Lee was arriving late afternoon and joining us at the hotel. She had not yet arrived, so Jenara and I propped our feet up on the front balcony to relax and enjoy the sea breeze and ocean views.

At about five o'clock, Luis knocked on the door and joined us on the balcony. He was tense, and we both could tell there was a problem.

Amber Lee had disappeared at the airport. Computer records showed she arrived on the plane, and her passport was stamped by immigration. But she never showed up in the airport reception area outside of international arrivals. Antonio and Luis both knew about my experience entering the country, and they were sure that Carlos had some airport security on his payroll. Their working hypothesis was that she had been snatched by security personnel and delivered to Carlos.

"I need to let Mark know," I said while pulling the phone from the pocket of my wrangler jeans.

Luis placed a hand on my arm. "Antonio has already contacted both Mark and Marcelle. Everything that can be done is being done, and we will get her back. But there is nothing you can personally do here. The best bet is to depart on time tomorrow and force Carlos to deploy some of his resources out of the city. That in itself may provide some valuable information to help track her down. If we can locate one weak link in the chain, it may help us close the net tighter."

I looked at Jenara and she simply nodded. Above all, she was always calm and practical under stress. I sent a text to Mark, "The shit is already past waist deep."

Brown Paper Bags (Mark)

The equipment Joseph sent us did arrive before 10:30 am. We sorted, packed, repacked, and got the gear stowed into the bird on the roof. John had the transport crew all set, and now we were waiting on word from Mat. Per John, they were in Rio. Their plan was apparently to head inland toward the far western end of the rain forests. Sirocco had unpacked and repacked her jungle bag, and I stowed my usual shit since it was all I had and it was all I wanted.

We spent the day poring over maps with lots of unmapped territories and, truth be known, just taking it easy. Seldom does the opportunity arise for Sirocco to take a day off. As for me, I'm always technically off, period. She told me a tale or two about some of the new furnishings. The art ranged from primitive baskets to exquisite stone carvings. A 21-string kora naturally caught my eye. The gourd-like West African instrument was astonishing in its craftsmanship. A bolon, an ancient musical instrument used by hunters, brought a wow from my lips.

Several drums of the djembe style stood on stands, ready for someone with rhythm to climb on board. I've been a guitar picker for 50 years but have never been accused of having rhythm. A long didgeridoo with ornate carvings stood in a corner. A painting of a Springbok, rendered on stretched skin and framed with antlers, took me back about 35 years or so to a walk I took on a twenty-section ranch about halfway between Iraan and Big Lake, out in West Texas.

The terrain I walked consisted of broken mesas and small, narrow box canyons. Top to bottom, you gain or lose 300 feet or so. A blue norther was blowing down from Canada, and across the Llano Estacado, so it was windy and almost too cold to adventure out, but I did anyway. Sugar, my old manly-man cockapoo dog, opted out of the walk and stayed where it was warm—having a dog smarter than you is OK.

I was layered up with a pea coat over my coveralls over a flannel shirt over a tee shirt. The hood was pulled up over an old wool stocking cap. Two pairs of wool socks were nestled inside my roughout boots to keep my toes warm. Wool inserts inside worn rawhide work gloves completed the show. I looked the part of being part of the scenery.

I had just dropped down to the bottom of a very narrow slot canyon and stepped out onto a bit of flat terrain. Mesquite, sage, creosote bushes, cholla, and prickly pear cactus were scattered about in no particular order. The footing ranged from intact to broken Cretaceous sedimentary rock, gravel, and sand. The land slipped a bit downward and opened up southwestward.

I had the old song 'High Hill Country Rain' by Jerry Jeff Walker running through my head. But I damn sure was not going to be running naked today.

I came out of the end of a very narrow and shallow canyon, stopped, and checked a full 360 degrees, then did so again. On the first sweep, I covered the mouth of the next slot canyon to the north, passing my gaze on further westward. The second time I checked to my right, I watched a band of pronghorns, consisting of an old buck, five does, and several yearlings and fawns, walk out into the open. I was south of them about seventy yards. The norther moved my scent away from their vantage point.

Family: Antilocapridae, species: Antilocapra Americana—the only such critter in the New World. They have been here well over one million years. Beautiful beyond words, agile, and only slightly slower than a cheetah for short distances, but faster than the cheetah for longer distances because cheetahs get winded very quickly. The pronghorn can cruise a half-mile at 55 mph. They can traverse much longer distances at slightly slower speeds.

The old buck weighed in around 100, maybe 110, pounds and stood about four and a half feet high at the tips of his magnificent horns. I did my best to blend in with the landscape, but there was little I could do to hide the fact that a six-foot-three-inch guy had invaded their territory. So, the buck and the rest of my new little friends were a quarter-mile away in about twelve and one-half seconds.

I took that scant moment in time to partially break my silhouette by repositioning so some prickly pear was up to my waist in front of me, and a tilted old broken mesquite somewhat hid my upper body from their viewpoint. Why? Because my small friends are perhaps the most curious wild creatures around. They stopped, turned, and the old buck lined up at the point of a protective V formation formed by him, the females, and the younger animals. The youngest lined up inside the V for protection.

I pulled my faded blue bandana out of my back pocket and held it in my left hand. I stood stock-still and, since I didn't chase them, they apparently wanted to know why. I slowly waved the bandana in the wind, then lowered it and stopped. They edged forward fifteen yards or so. I waved the bandana again. I played this game for about five minutes until they were back within about fifty yards of me. By then, I was so damn cold that I had to move.

We played the same come-and-go game for another two hours or so until they had lured me about five klicks from the trailer. Sugar greeted me near dusk with that what's for supper look. Not pronghorn, I muttered. It took me the better part of an hour to thaw, but the playtime had been more than worth it. My love of the wild places is just a bit stronger than my dislike for being around most of humanity.

Sirocco brought me out of my reminiscing with a taste of Lagavulin and a sweet kiss. We still had not heard from Mat so I tried him again on my satphone. No luck. John answered on the first ring and had no update either. It was going to be hard to fly into a country as big as Brazil and just run around until we found a trio of folks without any information other than they were 'headed to Rio'. Fuck.

Sirocco and I seared some 21-25 count fresh shrimp with peppers and onions, steamed a pot of basmati brown rice, and crafted a simple salad. Our eyes feasted on the last vestiges of an amazing sunset, and we ate in companionable silence, sipping a credible 2014 Cakebread chard. The kitchen cleanup was simple; then Sirocco whipped my ass on the Playcraft Charles River 8' Chestnut Slate pool table playing nine-ball. It stands to reason that if you own a fine pool table, you can probably play.

Sirocco's phone required her attention, and she settled into her office to work out some issues half a world away. I settled my skinny ass onto an ornate bar stool and chocked up the first silver ball on an original 1973 Watergate Caper pinball machine built by Nutting Associates. A quarter bought three games. There was a point in my early life where I was known as the pinball wizard—not The Who guy but close. I still had the magic, and I played free games the rest of the time until my satphone chimed.

I picked it up on the first ring. It was Antonio Torres of all people. He told me Amber Lee had been kidnapped in Rio. A text came through at the same time from Mat. I tapped in John. He picked up on the first ring and, in his serious tone, told me he was working satellites, human resources on the ground, and other angles as well. He would determine where Amber Lee was.

"Good. Change our flight to Rio instead of the jungles. We'll still take the chopper but leave my truck here for now. There's no need for it in Rio since it's too big for the narrow streets and millions of cars and pedestrians. I'll let you know asap when we're ready. Get the pilots on standby as of now."

"All set on my end, sir. The plane is sitting on the edge at Addison Airport, about six miles north of Love. The pilots are napping aboard. Ms. Sirocco can land within fifty yards or so. Loading the bird will take about ten minutes. Take-off will be within ten minutes after ya'll are secured aboard." Even in his serious tone, John said ya'll. Fucking computer.

"We need to get into Rio without anyone knowing. Mat was already burned before he and Jenara arrived."

"Yes sir, already arranged. You will be landing at Jacarepaguá Airport. It is a small airport on the south side of the city. The plane will be using its own transponder number into RIOgaleao – Tom Jobim International. I've hacked both airport's computer systems. I will show you land there and park inside a rented hangar. Simultaneously I will assign a Brazilian transponder number showing the plane made a short in-country hop and landed at Jacarepaguá. No one will be the wiser. The plane is as common as bikinis around Rio." Too much information for me, but Sirocco would want to know.

Amber Lee had been kidnapped. Someone had a death wish. I collected my thoughts and went into Sirocco's inner sanctum on the eastern end of the circle. She was talking on the phone, but I caught her attention anyway. Highly unusual for me to interrupt someone, especially Sirocco, on the phone. She muted the sound and looked at me.

"Amber Lee has been kidnapped." How else do you break shit like that to someone? She looked at me, blinked slowly then quickly ended the call.

She stood and asked me where. I told her Rio. She told me to call John again and have him birddog for Hunter, wherever he was. She reached for her satphone and punched up Hunter. He answered on the third ring, and it turned out he was close by.

"Hunter, where are you?"

"Ah, honestly Ms. Sirocco, at the moment, I'm in the arms of an old friend's wife in the Presidential Suite at the Peabody Memphis." She almost grinned and realized why the delay in answering but came back to the moment.

"I need you to finish, have a smoke, pull on your Levi's and those old Lucchese's, tighten your leather belt up with that Lone Star buckle, and pull on that Big Daddy Zanes Bar T-shirt. Head west across the de Soto Bridge on I-40 and call me from your pony car. In five minutes." She clicked off.

Sirocco asks and Hunter makes it happen. In four minutes he rang her up.

"I just passed the Bass Pro Shop Ms. Sirocco, and I'm over the Mississippi westbound. What's up?"

"Amber Lee has been kidnapped in Rio de Janeiro." Sirocco did not waste time on niceties.

"Someone has a death wish. I'll be a participant in that party. Logistics?" Hunter was short on words but understood that a plan was required.

"Map." Sirocco called up a map on the LG Electronics 50-Inch UHD 4K HDR Smart LED TV on the wall above her.

"Saline County Airport is about a hundred fifty miles or so from you, off of I-30 west of Little Rock. I have a friend there. Name's Carolina. She can stow your car, and I can chopper in and out without anyone knowing.

"I'll be there in about an hour." Hunter rang off. He figured he'd be slowed down a bit from crossing the Mississippi, clearing the truck stops and junk food shops, and getting out of W. Memphis, Arkansas. After that, it was smooth sailing across the Mississippi delta country, home of the blues.

Sirocco punched in a code, and I heard the bird on the roof fire off. We were dressed for flight and headed up the spiral staircase to the roof in five minutes. We strapped in, Sirocco completed the preflight and dumped us off the roof. I'll never get used to essentially toppling from the top of a building in a chopper then waiting for it to gain loft. Never. Sirocco was in complete control, and her face was taut.

We cleared her building westbound, staying between several other buildings, then she brought the bird around east-northeast toward Little Rock. Sirocco was on the radio with her friend Carolina at the Saline County airport. I called John and told him to scan ahead of Hunter for Smokies. Naturally, he was already on it with Hunter. He would create some diversions for the local constables, keep them off of the Interstate. Why do I even bother?

"John, we should be back in Dallas with Hunter in less than four hours. There is some last-minute packing we need to do based on the change in circumstances."

"Yes sir. I'm working on having everyone secured at a suitable location in Rio. Mat and Jenara are still mobile at the moment. Obviously, they did not anticipate the change in plan."

Change in plan. Only a machine could call a kidnapping a change of plan. Hunter called, and I answered on the first ring.

"Talk to me." Hunter, a man of many words. I could hear the deep-throated roar of the '67 Shelby GT-500 in the background.

"Mat hired a security service of some sort. Guy named Antonio Torres. I know him. Not sure what went wrong, but it turned into a shit show."

"What happened is probably an asshole named Carlos Mattes. Promised myself I'd kill the fucker next time I was in Rio. Now it's gonna happen sooner than I thought, hopefully. Long story, but if it's extortion, drugs, prostitution, kidnapping, and the like, it's Carlos Mattes. I know Torres too. Mostly upright

62

guy. He needs to maintain some semblance of integrity in order to get the top-end business trade. Let me drive and think." Hunter clicked off as he cleared Proctor, Arkansas, waved at the Jacksons, and cruised westward on I-40 at one-sixty mph. John was his birddog.

I punched in Joe. "You up for some entertainment?"

"Yup."

"Where are you?"

"Panama. Fishing out of Los Suenos Marina. My roomatiz is acting up from boating so many dolphin. Ready for a change of scenery."

"Amber Lee has been kidnapped in Rio de Janeiro."

"Someone is gonna die. I'm one hundred percent sure of it."

"Roger that. Get with John. He'll arrange transport. I'm with Sirocco. We're en route to pick up Hunter outside of Little Rock. We depart Dallas later tonight. We have ample firepower and other essentials so just get your worthless ass to the meeting."

Sirocco set us down on the tarmac just outside of the small airport building at the Saline County Airport and spun the rotors down a bit. Hunter came out with a petite, blond-haired woman, presumably Carolina. They were holding hands, and she had Hunter's rucksack in her other hand. That gave me pause for thought as Sirocco and I climbed out and greeted them. Sirocco got a huge hug from Carolina. I relieved Hunter of the two large brown paper bags he was holding. I told him to climb into the bird; we needed to go. He actually kissed Carolina, took his bag, and climbed in. Sirocco climbed back on board, did her check, wound up the rotors, waved at Carolina, and we were westbound headed back to Dallas.

It turned out that there were initially four large brown paper bags from Jordan's BBQ and Catfish. The restaurant was located just before the airport on SR 183. Hunter had called ahead and gotten two '8 or More Family Packs' for only $34.99 each. Two pounds of BBQ, two pints of beans, two pints of slaw, and twelve buns. He left one of the Family Packs with Carolina, so that probably explained their intimate moment.

Once he got settled, Hunter spooned chopped pig onto buns, added slaw and some sauce, and shoveled beans onto each plate. Nothing like health food to ease the suspense of not knowing where Amber Lee was. A six-pack of water bottles, three apple pies, plastic silverware, and a heap of napkins rounded out the feast. Sirocco and I switched off on the controls, and she ate first. Amazing that once in a while, a strict, healthy regimen is tossed to the wind. Sirocco finished off a third sandwich, beans, and her fried apple pie before reestablishing control of the bird. Hunter's feast was a stroke of genius because we probably would not eat for a while.

The roof-top catapult captured the landing skids, and Sirocco performed the shutdown while Hunter and I used the last of the napkins cleaning up various remnants from the meal. Sirocco punched in the roof hatch door code and we descended into her abode. Hunter continued down another level where Sirocco had directed him. There were clothes, shoes, boots, and accessories of various sizes and brands in an oversized walk-in closet. Hunter outfitted himself and put it all into a well-worn North Face Rolling Thunder 22" bag.

Sirocco and I had both done the same, so Hunter and I returned to the roof and stowed the bags. We were airborne five minutes later and landed at Addison ten minutes after that. The ground crew readied a rolling pallet, did the quick-release thing to the skids, set them aside, and laid the chopper on the pallet. It was quickly loaded and secured along with the skids. Once the rotor was secured, we strapped ourselves back into the chopper. We established comms with the flight crew and were airborne five minutes later southbound for Rio. Flight time was a little less than nine hours. Rio was two hours ahead, so we'd touch down before dawn.

Rio de Hunter (Mark)

Mat had texted, saying they would head inland as planned. I thought *good* because he'd only be in the way. He never did like to kill anything, which is okay, but he'd probably be like tits on a boar hog when lead started chipping mortar and brick all around his academic head. Carlos Mattes, or whoever was pulling the strings in Rio, was surely after Mat and Jenara anyway. Better for them to disappear into the jungle and be a waving bandana for the rest of us. The idea was to catch Mattes off-guard.

Sirocco and Hunter were attentive when I rang up Antonio Torres. I had the satphone on speaker.

"Mark, glad you called back. Where are you, my friend?" Torres was smooth as silk. Or the skin of an Australian Eastern brown snake. Mat seemed to trust him, but I count the folks I trust on one hand. I had worked with the guy once, but he was still not on my one hand, and he had a leak in his organization, which I didn't know if he had fixed.

"On a junker just clearing the Tanzania border headed for Cape Town, South Africa. I was with old friends in the Olduvai Gorge, searching for Lucy's brother. I'm probably three days out from you at best." I lied. "What can you tell me about the whereabouts of Amber Lee, my friend?"

"It seems a guy named Carlos Mattes is probably behind the kidnapping. He and I have had several unpleasant encounters over the years. He is a complete psychopath and not a person to be taken lightly— 'hijo de puta malo.' I will find out what I can, and then we can talk about a plan. By the way, Marcelle called and said she traced the break-in Ms. Solido's office to a man in Houston, Donald Faillen. It seems he worked with Mattes on some deal several years ago, so he may be tied to the current situation. At any rate, keep me updated on your travels. I look forward to seeing you." He clicked off.

"He has a gaping hole in his organization. We'll be in and out with Amber Lee while he draws up his plan." I was definitely not in the wait-and-see mood.

Hunter nodded his approval. "I just hope Mat knows what he's getting into in the rain forest."

"Jenara is not one to be taken lightly either. She will be in her element. She holds tremendous sway where they are headed in the western jungles of Brazil. Besides, she can blink, and men die. Remember that." Sirocco said this so casually an innocent bystander may have laughed out loud—and died. She was in no mood to be fucked with either. She and Amber Lee had been lovers and friends for a very long time.

I heard the bleep, and I answered my satphone on the first ring. It was John. I clicked it to speaker again and let John know he was on speaker.

"Yes, I know we're on speaker. Hello Ms. Sirocco and Mr. Hunter. Briefly, Carlos Mattes owns several properties throughout Brazil. His headquarters are situated on the west end of the Praia do Leblon at Mirante de Leblon. There are several commercial and residential properties, but essentially the whole thing is his compound."

"The Leblon Hotel, plaster over stone, French influence, is the ocean-side anchor. The hotel website shows it is always booked solid. Time-lapse photography shows very little foot traffic in or out. Virtually no taxi traffic. Typical of an overlord's abode. This land is one of the most expensive pieces of real estate in Brazil. Also, records indicate he is connected with everyone worth being connected to in the vast South American underworld."

"What else John?" Sirocco chimed in.

"I have as-built drawings of most of the compound, but they are probably outdated. Israeli government sat photos, updated a few minutes ago, show significant security measures in place—guns on the roof, rear perimeter razor wire, typical and as expected. Presuming we're in the right place and Amber Lee is being held there, it will be challenging to infiltrate just the outer perimeter. I'm working on schedule rotations, etc. Hopefully, I can find a backdoor. You have everything I have in your email as of now." John loved Amber Lee, plain and simple. Interesting for a machine to show emotion.

Sirocco popped open her Mac, tied it into the satphone link, and opened her email. We took in the sat photos. They were as John described.

"Can you pull up Google satellite?" Hunter was hunting.

Sirocco did and asked, "What do you see?"

"Rooftop guns, sandbags, lots of outward-looking cameras. The back lot has a handful of vehicles. Shit. A dove-gray Rolls Silver Cloud, what looks to be a

Lamborghini Veneno, a newer Ferrari, and, well damn, I'm officially jealous, an Aston Martin One-77. Okay, back to business. There, see the outflow canal to the right of Av. Niemeyer? There is a pipe crossing the canal just south of the bridge. Probably 48" or 60". Looks like it runs under the south edge of the hotel. It probably runs under what appears to be public restrooms or something similar on the opposite side of the canal."

I pulled John back up on my satphone, asked him to look into it, and we resumed scanning the satellite photos. We bounced back and forth on strategy—full frontal assault or stealth. Drop from Sirocco's bird or bale out of a taxi at the front door? One thing was for sure, the point of land due south of the compound had a turn-out parking lot convenient for tourists taking photos, and it would also be useful as an airborne escape route for armed-to-the-teeth hostage rescuers. So the escape route was settled. Everything else about the rescue mission was speculation. John rang me up.

"The pipe has been abandoned for several years, meaning it's empty. It was a water line but failed in several places elsewhere; hence it is out of service. There is an access hatch in a closet in the rest area pavilion on the canal's east side. And, based on the as-builts, there are two different access hatches in the basement of the Leblon Hotel."

"Mind you, this is not absolute, just a statement based on the as-builts. However, I strongly suspect the as-builts for the public works plumbing are correct, and the hatches exist. The place may have been renovated many times, but the basic plumbing would typically remain intact. Infrastructure drawings are almost always accurate. Otherwise, the contractor would not get to suck on the government contracting tit again. In the U.S., the access hatches would be bolted down. Standard specs in Brazil show a hinge and padlock affair."

"Stick with it John, we're about four hours out and need to have a workable plan before we land. Oh, find out what you can about a Donald Faillen in Houston. Marcelle seems to think he is the one behind the break-in at Jenara's office, and he may be in bed with Mattes." I clicked off.

"Recommend we pack." Hunter, aka Mr. Talkative, brought us back to the here and now.

Tactical packs were laid out and double-checked. Sirocco had grabbed some flashbangs, incendiaries, and similar devices during her packing in Dallas. We all grabbed a few and put them into easily accessible pockets. A fourth pack was assembled for Joe.

I strapped on a Ka-Bar KA1214 BRK USA Fighting Knife. Hunter did the same. Sirocco did not expect to have any close-in action. If she did, things had gone to total shit. I added one of the Glock 19 Gen 5 G34 Competition 9x19mm pistols to my belt and six 17 shot magazines, loaded with Federal Premium 124gr

HST JUP rounds, to the ammo pockets. We arranged the same set-up for Joe. Sirocco strapped down two Wilson Ultralite Ranger .243's fitted with Ranger 1-8x24i Rifle Scopes in the fore and aft of her bird; locked and loaded.

Extra clips of ammo were Velcroed down. Twenty-round clips fleshed out this well-appointed, lightweight, and extremely portable choice. Hunter handed me one as well and strapped one onto Joe's kit. Lastly, Sirocco tucked one of the JTS M12AR 12 Gauge Semiauto Shotguns onto the left floorboard by her door on the bird. The Federal LE Tactical with FliteControl 12-gauge 00 Buckshot, nine pellets per shell, rounded out the rig. Not much of a weapon past about 70 yards but, a devastating one close-up.

She arranged the winch-assisted spring-loaded fifty-foot rope ladder so she could deploy it out the right rear door from the left front seat. The ladder with positive grip handles was rated at 1,500 pounds. In the event it had to be deployed, it would have four riders weighing a total of about 700 pounds.

A bit later, Antonio Torres rang me up again. "Mr. Mattes sends his regards. He indeed has Ms. Lee under wraps. He says he means her no harm, and she is being treated well, but she is not free to go. He requests a meeting with you as soon as possible to resolve the situation. He suggests the Leblon Hotel. I told him you are approximately four days out, coming in from the northern reaches of Iceland. That will give us a day to plan."

"This asshole sounds like one of these guys who likes fancy cars." I tossed that one out softly. Did not want to spook the pronghorn.

"Ah, you guess correctly. He has several cars, each worth way north of one million American. His stock-in-trade, though, is his Rolls Royce Phantom. Anywhere he goes it is transported with him. It is his public persona."

"So, what is it, bright red or something?" I did my slightly agitated self. "Is the guy a pimp?"

"Oh no, the Phantom is dove gray. He likes to display his self-described sophistication."

"Tell him we will talk the minute I arrive, and Amber Lee better report to me she was treated like royalty; well fed, no bruises, no marks, no nothing!" I clicked off.

"We'll be knocking on the right door," said Hunter as he went back to securing his gear. He had that singular look in his eyes common to elite hunters around the world. Nothing to brag on, just a look that says the job will get done.

Sirocco clicked up the pilot and requested he put the peddle to the metal. The more darkness we had, the better. A few extra pounds of burned kerosene did not matter at this point. We continued to bounce around ideas until a basic plan was hatched.

Sirocco rang up John. "Yes Ms. Sirocco?"

"Find a bird similar to mine and have it sitting in the mouth of a hangar at the airport. Pilot to be airborne with a five-minute notice. Flightpath will be treetop and directly across Copacabana, the mouth of Guanabara Bay, and on toward Campos. Treetop level the entire flight and then disappear. Leave the disappearing part up to the pilot."

"Okay, while we've been talking, I have secured the bird. It is actually sitting in a hangar at Jacarepaguá Airport. The pilot required triple the going rate. I told him I was being robbed but accepted anyway. He understands the price of failure per our conversation." So John was talking to the pilot at the same time he was talking to us. A useful trick when time is of the essence.

"John, where is Joe?"

"He is five minutes from the hangar where the decoy chopper is parked."

"We need ground transport. SUV and discrete, not bright red."

"It is also at the hangar, sir. A rusty blue 2012 Chevy Trailblazer, Brazilian-made, ample room for the three of you." John was always just about an inch ahead of the storyline.

Joe, Hunter, and I would be in the Chevy.

"Sirocco is gonna do a bit of decoying on the landward end of the compound. Lights, wind from the rotor, a flashbang or three, maybe pop off a round or two into some of the second-rate ground transport in the compound. This effort will be timed as a diversion for our entrance through the water line into the hotel's basement. It's a fair assumption Amber Lee is being held in the basement. If not, we'll work our way upward." Hell of a plan.

We came out of the darkened sky, and the pilot kissed the tarmac just beyond 03, slowed, veered off the median ramp at the 30-degree angle midway down the runway, turned right to reverse course, and came to rest in front of the hangar John had reserved for them. The rear ramp dropped onto the concrete.

We descended, and Joe was waiting. He had on khaki shorts, a worn PFG fishing shirt, and a shredded fishing vest. The ground crew quickly unstrapped Sirocco's bird and rolled it down the ramp. The landing gear was attached, and she was in business.

"Ya'll got a plan?" Joe was the inquisitive guy.

"Yup. You're in the right rear seat of the Chevy since you have the shortest legs. Your gear is on the seat behind me. Strap on and up. Sirocco is solo in her bird."

"Perfect." Joe didn't need a lot of direction. He knew he'd hear the rest of the plan, if there was one, when it was time to hear it. He briefly hugged Sirocco and got a light kiss on the cheek in return, then climbed into the Chevy. Hunter jumped in shotgun, I drove.

Meanwhile, Sirocco spun up her bird and kept it at idle. The other pilot kept the jets warm and remained at the five-minute ready mark. She explained to him exactly what she wanted. He understood he was to hover at 500 feet above the eastern edge of Rocinha. At Sirocco's signal, he would proceed east and briefly hover directly over the hotel before continuing his flight eastward until he lost himself near Campos.

The plan was simple, KISS simple—Keep It Simple Stupid simple. We hit the ground two hours before dawn. Just before dawn is always the best time to kill someone like Mattes. Especially in his own fortress. It's the last place he would expect to be hit and the time when sleep is his worst enemy.

I drove the Chevy south then east on Av. das Americas until it became Elevado das Bandeira. Shortly thereafter, I veered off to the right onto Av. Niemeyer, drove by the Leblon Hotel on our left, crossed the bridge just above the abandoned water line, reversed course, and parked legally in the broad median—about 100 yards from the restroom. The trip of about five miles had taken ten minutes.

I clicked my sat phone twice, and Sirocco came back with three clicks. She was airborne one minute later. She stayed at treetop level southbound, crossed the beach, and skimmed the ocean, coming ashore again at the Gavea Golf and Country Club. She turned a bit north and cruised over Rochina, keeping the granite outcrop of Mirante do Morro Dois Irmaos to her right.

The bird climbed a bit to clear the low hills, buzzed Alice Moreau's mansion, and came to a hover slightly north of the compound. She clicked twice; I returned with three clicks.

Hunter headed straight to the restrooms. Joe walked under the trees due east for about 200 yards, cut over to the ocean, then walked on the beach to the restrooms. I cut inland one block, cut over one block then headed to the restrooms.

Hunter had cut the rusty padlock off the hasp, and the hatch was propped open. We verified all headphones were working. Hunter climbed down into the waterline. He was going to set a small charge on the first hatch inside the Leblon Hotel to break the padlock and hasp. I followed Hunter and Joe was close behind.

Hunter whispered he was at the hatch. Then he whispered that the hatch was open. Good. Better not to advertise our presence until absolutely necessary. Joe and I hustled forward and hovered under Hunter as he stood on the second rung of the access ladder and peered into a fairly large mechanical room. Hunter said to get Sirocco moving. I clicked twice. He climbed out and went to the only door. Joe and I climbed out of the pipe and hung back. Off to my left, I saw a steep set of rough-cut stairs leading upward. I pointed and left it at that.

Sirocco backed the bird off a little, armed some ordinance, tucked the nose forward and downward, and dropped her presents one at a time in about five seconds. She was nose up and back out over the ocean when all hell broke loose in the back lot. The Rolls erupted in a spectacular array of flames and flying debris. In seconds the entire yard was ablaze. She flew another mile, then hovered just above the water in the lee of Ponta Dois Irmaos.

Hunter, Joe, and I were standing by the door when the explosions started. I eased the door open and gazed down the sights of my Glock to the end of an empty hallway. We could hear raised voices penetrating the space from elsewhere in the building. Hunter hugged the wall moving forward fifteen paces to a connecting hallway on the left.

He glanced around the edge of the wall to see two guys in an animated discussion. One nodded, took off, and disappeared around a right turn. The other stood outside of a door and looked after his departed amigo. Hunter holstered his pistol and drew his knife.

The Ka-Bar knife used by the USMC is a heavy affair made for close-in work. It is not a particularly good throwing knife. Leave that to something like the Smith and Wesson SWTK10CP for a target more than a few paces out or a United Cutlery UC 2772 for longer range. Nonetheless, Hunter used his right hand and put the Ka-Bar squarely into the bad guy's right ear. It penetrated to the guard.

The guy dropped like a sack of wet cement. Mark and Joe covered as Hunter lightly ran down the hall to the guy. He placed his right tactical boot on the guy's neck and extracted the blade. Blood gutters are most useful to relieve the drag. He wiped the blade on the guy's shirt and returned it to its sheath and drew his pistol.

I approached as Hunter kicked in the door. It swung inward to the left and stopped abruptly at 90 degrees. Amber Lee was on the opposite side of the room, on her butt with her back against the wall. Her mouth was duct-taped, same as her hands and ankles. Her eyes instantly left Hunter and swung right.

Hunter swung his Glock up and left, and double-tapped through the door, stepped in and put a finishing round in the guy as he was going down. I reached Amber Lee in another second. Two shots from down the hall where Joe was were followed by a low grown of agony in the direction where the first guy ran off. I cut the bindings and pulled Amber Lee to her feet.

"You need me to carry you?" I asked.

She shook her head, walked over to the dead guy, and kicked him in the nuts.

"I'm tired of the room service in this dump; let's go." Texas Hill Country girls are as tough as square-cut nails.

Loud voices were now ringing down the hall. Evidently, there was a staircase leading upstairs. Hunter changed the pistol to his left hand as he peeked around the doorframe. Southpaws like Hunter and I are always ambidextrous. Two hombres came around the corner just about two feet too far before they skidded to a stop and hovered over their fallen compadre. Hunter swung his Glock 19 Gen 5 G34 up and knew to take the guy on the right as Joe double-tapped the guy on the left. Joe said "clear" into his mic. I said, "coming."

Amber Lee hung a left out of the door and sprinted toward Joe. I was right behind her. We went through the machine room door, and I touched Amber Lee's right shoulder. She veered right and then let me be first up the stairs since she was unarmed. Joe covered Hunter as he backtracked, and we were all up the stairs in another few seconds.

We found ourselves in a narrow back-hallway, probably used by staff. There were doors on the right side, and there was a wood-framed window on the left, ocean-side. Joe kicked the window square at the cross-bracing, and it shattered outward. Meanwhile, I clicked twice, and Sirocco came back with three clicks.

Sirocco called the other chopper pilot and said execute. She cleared the point, headed toward Mirante do Leblon, then toggled a switch, causing the rope ladder to descend its full 50-foot length. Hunter and Joe lagged a bit as Amber Lee and I sprinted away from the hotel directly toward the vantage point parking area and, hopefully, a rendezvous with a rope ladder.

Three guys came running out of the hotel's front doors, hung a right, and met 00 buckshot from both Joe and Hunter. The guys went down as Joe and Hunter turned and sprinted toward the point. Time was of the essence now.

Both guys swapped out the shotguns for their Wilson Ultralite Ranger .243's on the run. Sirocco brought her bird in, flared, and let the rope ladder drag the ground. Amber Lee pulled the ladder sideways between her legs and ascended. A rope ladder is climbed 90 degrees out from a fixed portable ladder. Otherwise, the climber will never make it up.

I did my best to hold the ladder stable in the downburst from the rotors. Joe arrived next and scrambled up double-time with Hunter right behind him. Shots rang out from the compound. Joe said hold into his mike, and he and Hunter emptied the rifle clips as a return favor. I wrapped myself into the ladder and said go.

At the same time Sirocco was pulling up on the yoke, the decoy chopper appeared. He was supposed to hover over the hotel, but evidently, one look at the scene below with a fire raging in the compound was too much for him. He was accelerating, climbing, and veering inland before he ever got to the hotel.

The roof gunners immediately opened fire on the bird as it was turning. We could see the chopper trailing smoke as it disappeared over the city.

The timing was near-perfect because anyone watching had eyes only for the chopper and live-fire coming off the roof. Sirocco headed back past Ponta Dois Irmaos, then slowed to a hover until everyone had climbed aboard. She dropped onto the tarmac five minutes later. The crew set the dolly in place, removed the skids, and had the chopper secured in less than five minutes. We were airborne five minutes later.

I tapped in John. He answered on the first ring. "Success?"

"Yup."

The noise of the afterburners was earsplitting in the rear of the cargo area. Nonetheless, everyone could hear John exclaim, "Oh, Ms. Amber Lee! I cannot tell you how happy I am!" The computer was happy. I was wondering what other emotions might be forthcoming.

"I watched the whole thing from a Chinese satellite. The decoy chopper made an emergency landing about 20 miles away. The pilot didn't hover over the hotel as I asked, so two-thirds of his payment won't arrive. Yes, he would have gotten his ass shot out of the sky if he had hovered, but a deal is a deal. He will probably have to leave Brazil anyway since I left a trail of breadcrumbs from his contract for Donald Faillen to find." John said.

"The pieces are sketchy, but Mr. Faillen appears to be in the business of stealing and selling industry secrets, primarily for pharmaceutical companies, and I know he was in contact with Mattes when Mat and Jenara traveled to Rio. Divide and conquer or wave a bandana—Mr. Mattes and Mr. Faillen will both be distracted by this apparent stain on their relationship." The name Faillen didn't ring a bell for me, but I liked the plan.

"John, you have the aviation records showing us headed toward Uruguay, correct?"

"Yes sir. As of now, your track north and west does not exist until I bring you back into the system in about 500 miles and then on into Rio Blanco." It is useful to be able to disappear and reappear at will—abracadabra.

I punched in Antonio Torres. He answered on the second ring. "Antonio, you probably already know Mattes' place has been hit. Amber Lee is free and currently headed State-side on a private Lear. Sorry for the end-run, but I didn't know if you had fixed the leak in your organization, so I went to plan B. Mattes will quickly find some evidence indicating the job was organized by his business partner Daniel Faillen. Marcelle can fill you in on Faillen, but some companies with deep pockets probably back him. Let us know if you get any hints on what they were up to."

"I already have a lead, Mark. We found the leak in my organization, and after some persuasion, he was kind enough to tell me Amber Lee was being held for questioning by Mattes' American Partner; Donald Faillen perhaps. He was sketchy on the rest, but it sounded like Mattes and Faillen are after information on rare herbal drugs. Their real target was Ms. Solido. They seem to believe she is the key. I haven't heard from Mat or my man Luis. All I know is they arrived without incident and then headed out on a two-day trek into the jungle. But I know at least five of Mattes' crew followed after them the next day."

"Also," he continued, "Mat's last message to me contained a note for you. Hold on, let me read it verbatim."

"I will assume you have bumbled around and managed to retrieve Amber Lee. Not bad for an old guy like you. If things go sideways for us, we may need a lift out of the jungle. Coordinates will follow."

I clicked off, grinned, said good job to everyone, stretched, and closed my eyes. He's right; I'm too old for this shit.

Luis

A black beetle slowly crept over the toe of Luis' left boot while he silently watched. The creature was cautious and momentarily stopped when Luis wiggled his toes. Its shell was sparkled with blue and green iridescence when the sunlight struck at certain angles. He was intently listening while he watched. He heard nothing except normal mid-day jungle sounds, but something wasn't right. He could feel it itching in the back of his head, and he trusted that instinct.

Luis looked up and glanced over at Mat, who was resting, propped up against the trunk of a large tree. Mat's right leg was stretched straight out and slightly elevated. Stains from draining pus and blood were visible on his pants—dark, wet-looking splotches, which seemed ominous in light of their present situation.

Luis turned his attention back to the jungle and contemplated a variety of security options. He knew the calm before the storm was the time to plan because when the storm came, action would replace contemplation, and the more thought-out options available to him, the greater his chance of survival. This sort of strategic thinking had permeated his world from a very early age. He took up martial arts before the age of five, and by the age of eighteen, he was one of the most prominent fighters on the international competition circuits. He had boxes of trophies in a rented storage container, but the only one he kept in his apartment was from a tournament at age seven when he defeated a boy twice his size. He didn't keep it because of the actual victory. Rather, the trophy served as a reminder of what his sensei told him as he prepared for the fight. The sensei had placed his finger lightly on the center of Luis' forehead and said, "Remember, you are the weapon. Hands and feet are simply the instruments available to you in this fight."

As his skills and reputation grew, he had earned the nickname of "Musashi." This title referenced the legendary Japanese swordsman Miyamoto Musashi, author of the Go Rin No Sho (The Book of Five Rings). Luis had studied the writings of Musashi early in his life and adopted the philosophy that a warrior must master the art of war. It is detrimental to favor one weapon over another. The warrior should be a master of every weapon, and all weapons must be the natural extension of a warrior's fighting technique. All of the deadly items that others considered "must-haves" in combat were simply useful tools for Luis.

After secondary school and four years at university, Luis joined the military and trained as part of the country's special forces— Comando de Operações Especiais. He excelled in tactical analysis and had few equals in active combat skills. His career in the military was all but guaranteed. However, following a long period of self-reflection, he exited the military after his second stint.

He found he enjoyed fighting but not killing, and increasingly the operations he was assigned seemed tinged with political motivations. Swift death was ordered when disabling the targets would have sufficed. Luis had obtained a degree in philosophy at college, and his studies led him to deep self-reflection about life and what it meant to be a human being. In the end, it wasn't the killing; it was the unnecessary killing that tipped the scales and sent him back to the civilian world.

Before joining Antonio's organization, Luis spent several years in the western jungles with NGOs focused on preserving the indigenous way of life for local tribes. This work allowed him to learn passable Rohodi dialects. This previous work was how he knew about the alcove they camped in last night. The shallow cave was located at the base of a rock formation along a foot trail commonly used by local hunters. One night there was an acceptable risk, but they couldn't return. If they were being hunted, the main foot trail was accessible to anyone who knew the area.

He glanced over at Mat again, checking to see if his eyes were still shut.

He liked Mat but thought it was odd that someone with his wealth was wandering around the jungle, waist-deep in affairs that could get him killed. Most clients with his means traveled with an entire security entourage, but here he was with Luis, Hoshikay, and Jenara. Never-the-less he related to Mat on some level. The two women, however, were opaque to him.

During his previous work in the western jungle, he encountered various tribal shamans, but Hoshikay was different and perhaps more dangerous than his previous encounters. He had occasionally heard her name spoken in hushed tones amongst other tribes he worked with. Jenara was in a class by herself, with the instincts of a big cat prowling the jungle under cover of darkness but the sophistication of a highly educated cosmopolitan traveler. Antonio had related to him the various whispered tales of the Solido women in Sao Paulo.

Antonio had also filled him in on the suspected roles Mat, Jenara, and Mark played several months ago in the explosive events around the discovery of alien technology. It was still all hearsay, and neither Mat nor Jenara would speak of it, but Luis suspected what he heard was true.

This day was the seventh since the group left Rio. Their trip had generally been uneventful until Mat's accident. After two nights in the Rohodi village, they hiked through the jungle for the next two days, guided by Hoshikay. Traveling mainly on hunting paths, but sometimes not, the group made their way due north along the edge of the flatlands where the land started to rise westward towards the Peruvian border.

All had gone smoothly until midday yesterday when Mat stirred up something from the jungle floor that left him with a nasty bite on his right calf. Mat wasn't worried, but Hoshikay was alarmed, and that was enough to make Luis alarmed. Hoshikay made them stop while she collected some plants and boiled them into a thick poultice. By the time she finished, the bite had turned to a mean-looking welt. She applied the concoction and insisted that they wait until it had partially dried before they continued traveling.

This morning the welt had an ugly pus-filled head that Mat lanced with his pocketknife. After a lot of blood and pus drained, he doused it with alcohol, and Hoshikay prepared and applied another poultice. A bit later Mat hiked up a mile or so into a narrow valley with Hoshikay leading the way. Mat managed but was limping by the time they arrived at their destination.

They were currently located about 400 meters uphill of the main path in a small forest opening with low ground cover and some wiry grass. Luis' position gave him a direct downhill view for about 300 meters before the jungle enveloped the open landscape. The women had left Mat and him about three hours ago and had seemingly disappeared into a cliff face. Luis inspected closer and found a two-meter-wide crevice in the rock, which opened into a narrow valley uphill, but he didn't follow them past there. He had returned to wait with Mat and provide cover if anyone followed.

At first, the sounds were soft but distinct; a group of people moving through the jungle below him. He tossed a pebble to arouse Mat and put his finger to his lips, beckoning him to remain quiet. Mat's eyes opened, and Luis pointed downhill as he squatted low and made his way to Mat's side. Quickly he unpacked one of the shotguns, loaded one five-round clip, gave it to Mat, and placed a second clip in Mat's vest. He took the Ultralite Ranger, mounted the scope, and attached a 20-round clip. Luis helped Mat ease down into a shallow depression behind the tree he had been resting against, and then he moved ten yards to the north, where he propped his rifle over a small rock ledge and started scanning the edge of the jungle below him.

It was not long before seven men filtered out of the shadows. They mustered half in and half out of the plant cover, scanning the upslope area. The rifle scope let him get a good look at the group, and he recognized two faces. The first one was Cristoble, one of Carlos Mattes' lieutenants. The second face caused his pulse rate to jump; Leon Scarez. Five years ago, Leon had beat one of Luis' cousins to death over a gang turf disagreement. Jorge, Luis' cousin, was no saint and mixed up in some ugly gang activity. But family is family, and Luis had Leon directly in his sights.

He caught a blurred movement over Leon's right shoulder and moved the scope slightly, peering into the deep shadows of the jungle floor. It took him a second to recognize the face of an indigenous hunter standing several yards behind the rest of the men. He recognized the man from his work in this area several years ago. He couldn't place a name, but he knew the hunter's tribe resided in a territory slightly north of their current location. The man was clearly a hired tracker, which meant Cristoble's team didn't follow them directly from the south but must have come from the north or northeast.

Luis found this disturbing since they must have already known the general area where Hoshikay was headed. The most likely vector for that information was the pilot who had originally flow them in. He recalled looking at maps with Jenara while on the chopper, and several times she roughly pointed to the area where she thought Hoshikay would lead the group. The information could have been bought from him or beaten out of him, but how they acquired it was irrelevant now. Mattes' men were here, and they probably came in from the northeast—these were the pertinent facts.

He ran several tactical scenarios through his head as he watched the group. Three of the men, including Leon, were in conversation, and Cristoble seemed to be the one in charge. The three of them stood in a row at the jungle's edge, pointing upward towards the cliffs. Cristoble was on the right and Leon on the left. He glanced in Mat's direction and saw Mat slowly moving undercover and dragging their packs and equipment in his direction but slightly upslope towards a tree line. The jungle edge off to Luis' left was about twenty meters away, and Mat would be there in a few minutes.

He returned his attention to the gang below, and they were still in conversation. Then Cristoble waved several of the others forward from the jungle. They were readying to move up the hill, and time had run out. He had Leon in his sights as he thought about Jorge. Family was family, and blood was blood, but Luis was more of a tactician than a family man, and his first shot shattered Cristoble's right shoulder. The second tap caught the middle guy directly in the chest and the last round, intended for Leon, only clipped his forearm as he dove back into the forest.

Now they had a handicapping liability. The unit's leader was seriously injured but alive, and everyone would have to compensate to keep him alive. Their chase, which would inevitably come, would be slowed down. Cristoble was the brother of Carlos Mattes' wife, and if they left him to die in the jungle, they would all be dead men when they returned. The middle guy was dead, so Cristoble would still be in charge, but Leon would have to execute the plan, and even though Leon was dangerously clever, he didn't have Cristoble's operational skills. They were all out of sight now except for the dead guy.

Luis rolled backward from his position and crawled to Mat. They stayed to the ground and cleared the tree line on the slope in about five minutes.

Jenara and Hoshikay appeared out of the trees like phantoms as Mat was catching his breath. He was sweating profusely, and Jenara conferred with Hoshikay after testing his temperature with the back of her hand. The two spoke rapidly, and Luis couldn't follow all that was said, but finally, Jenara turned and laid out a plan.

The valley where they had collected the herbal seeds was a dead-end feature and thus a trap. But the cliff face upslope from them could be followed along its base to the north. About two klicks away was a hilltop plateau that could only be accessed via a narrow, well-hidden set of open fractures in the cliff face. Another five klicks would bring them to the highest peak in the area, an optimal location to try and get satellite communications. Luis knew the optimal time for connecting was between 12:00 and 2:00 am, based on satellite orbital positions. It was mid-afternoon now, so they could probably reach the second peak by nightfall.

Luis told the two women about the tracker helping their pursuers. Hoshikay frowned a bit and said something to Jenara that made her smile. Everyone hoisted their backpacks, and the group made their way upslope to the cliff face. After about 500 meters of walking, Hoshikay had them stop. She and Jenara quickly constructed a small stone cairn, atop which they placed several types of plants and a bird feather Jenara extracted from a pouch in her backpack. The whole exercise took only 2 minutes, and Luis waited until they finished before asking what it was.

Jenara explained as they put their packs on. "The cairn is a traveler's marker, and the plants are poisonous, a symbol of death. The feather is from a harpy eagle, Gavião-real. It is a reminder that the eye of a shaman watches all travelers on this path. The tracker will understand the message; death is his companion if he walks this path. Our enemies may soon find themselves without a tracker."

The group continued northward. Luis looked over his shoulder at the cairn and smiled. Mat worked to keep up, but his leg was getting worse, and Luis eventually took most of the weight from Mat's pack and put it in his own.

By his best estimate, Luis figured Cristoble's group would be at least an hour behind them, probably two. Cristoble's shoulder would have to be bandaged, and their initial foray up the slope would be slow and cautious after one death and one serious injury. But, if he were in Cristoble's shoes, he would send Leon and three others ahead along with the tracker and then follow behind with the remaining person.

"How long will we need to get Mat secured?" Luis asked the women.

"Hoshikay says about a 20-minute climb through the crevices, 10 minutes to get Mat situated, and ten minutes to return. Only she and Mat can go up," Jenara replied.

Luis threw her a questioning look and then glanced at Mat.

"I can make it," Mat said.

Jenara paused before replying, "It's sacred ground where shaman's go on vision quests. You and I are not on such a quest."

Luis shrugged and let it go. Life was a mysterious experience, and while he didn't understand Hoshikay, he respected her and would not interfere with her world. By the time they arrived at the first location, Mat was limping badly, and his fever was up. Hoshikay shouldered his pack, and Mat took one of the shotguns with three extra clips in his vest. The two disappeared into a thin crevice, hidden ten meters off the path they were on.

Luis waited, listened, and marked their exact coordinates in his notebook. Hoshikay was back in 30 minutes and said Mat had expended most of his energy rapidly climbing through the crevices, so the rest of the group wouldn't be waiting on him. Luis was careful to cover any tracks or marks showing where someone left the main path. He hoped Hoshikay's cairn did its job and scared off the tracker. Even with his effort back-covering the deviation, he probably couldn't fool the local hunter. Thirty minutes were gone, so Luis assumed their pursuers were only half an hour behind them now.

The cliff face soon bowed out to the west, forming a long, curved arc. At the northern end of the arc, he had the group stop at a location where he could scale a tree and take in a view back from where they came. He had kept track of the time and landscape markers along the curved path, so as he viewed the route through his rifle scope, he spotted four of Cristoble's men about forty minutes behind him. As he had predicted, Leon was leading them.

He scrambled back down the tree and explained the situation to Jenara and Hoshikay. "Our pursuers have split into two teams. A group of four is about forty minutes behind us. The good news is they have passed by the path leading to Mat. The position of Cristoble, one of his men, and the tracker, if he is still with them, is unknown. We have about two kilometers to cover before we get to the second peak. I suggest we put as much distance as possible between them and us, so we have time to arrange some surprises should they decide to follow us up."

The group headed off at a hurried pace, but Luis could see Jenara was worried. None of them were aware that the warning cairn had not done its job. The indigenous hunter was visibly alarmed at the sight of the cairn, and Cristoble had noticed his fear. Cristoble warned the tracker he would be shot if he tried to abandon the group and made him walk in front of the two men so they could keep an eye on him.

The Dream (Mat)

Pain shot down my leg every time I put my full weight on it. Hoshikay was leading me upward through a set of interconnected, open fractures in the cliff face, and I was doing my best to keep up the pace so the rest of the team could move on to their next objective. My own carelessness got me into this situation. I should have had my hiking pants tucked into my boots, keeping unwanted insects out. A sloppy mistake on my part, and now I was paying the price.

The cliffs were composed of slightly metamorphosed sandstones. These quartzites exhibited a well-developed rhombohedral fracture pattern, and the crevices we were climbing through were the result of weathering along the intersecting fractures. Footholds and handholds were plentiful. My leg was the only problem. Hoshikay's care for the wound had helped slow down the infection, but slowly it was sapping my energy, and my fever was intensifying.

The climb took most of my remaining energy reserves, and I had to rest when we reached the summit. Hoshikay let me catch my breath, but not for long. She helped me traverse the flat rock surface to a small three-sided stone enclosure. It was big enough to sit or lay down but too low to stand up. The hut was constructed from angular slabs of quartzite collected from the cliff's base below, and the low roof consisted of several large slabs of stone supported by two sturdy wooden beams. The whole structure recessed about a meter from front to back and was two meters wide. Directly in front of the hut was a stone fire pit.

Hoshikay rolled out my sleeping bag and had me lay on top of it before she momentarily disappeared and returned with an arm full of dried wood, which she placed beside the fire pit. She also packed a small bit of dried grass in the bottom of the pit to get a fire going when necessary. Next, she pulled my pants leg up to inspect the wound, but she was not happy with what she saw. She asked for my Benchmade pocketknife and then reached into her side bag and pulled out several items. She poured a bit of alcohol over the blade and then gripped the handle between her teeth while she crushed up some dried leaves on the top of a flat stone and slowly mixed in a small amount of water.

I glanced into her side bag and saw something I recognized—a glass container filled with small golden seeds. They were what we had come for. She saw me looking and extracted the container, dumping three or four of them into her right hand. She gave them to me to chew raw and wash down with water. She then pulled the knife from her mouth, rinsed it again with alcohol, and gave me a stick to bite down on.

Her hands were steady and sure as she sliced open the skin over my wound with two quick cuts. I must have passed out for a moment because my next sensation was the intense burning of raw alcohol being poured into the open wound. She had cleaned up the pus and blood by that time, and despite the pain, it looked better. A handful of poultice from the dried leaves and water was packed over the wound before Hoshikay wrapped a clean elastic bandage around my leg, holding the poultice in place and applying pressure to keep the wound closed.

I was sweating profusely by the time she finished, and she placed a dried, gummy-looking fruit or seed in my upper vest pocket, with clear instructions to take it at nightfall and not before. My leg was still on fire as she made her way to the cliff edge and disappeared down through the fracture pathway. I could see the hut was constructed with a direct view of the single entrance to the flat-topped peak. I loaded a clip into the shotgun and positioned myself towards the cliff edge with a clear firing line.

Access to the flat, rock-floored hilltop required a person to be facing towards the cliff face and away from the hut as they made their final ascent onto the clifftop. Of course, this positioning required them to enter the area with their back to the hut where I was waiting. With my energy sapped, I was mentally drifting when I became aware of scraping sounds from a climber. The shape of the crevices amplified sounds, creating a natural alarm system. I rolled onto my belly and steadied the shotgun barrel on the rocks surrounding the firepit.

I didn't have to wait long before a head appeared, followed by shoulders and then a stocky body with a long gun strapped on his back. Once he cleared the crevice exit, he gained his feet in a squat and started rotating his body towards the hut. I only fired once, and the heavy-duty shot caught him in the side of his right knee. The whole leg was swept out towards the cliff edge, and I could see blood scattering in droplets across the rock. His body collapsed towards the cliff edge, and I heard the scream as he tumbled downward. At the same time, I heard the word "Stop!" shouted in Portuguese from below, and another shot echoed through the jungle. Then it was momentarily quiet except for the muffled moans of the climber.

Another three minutes passed before I heard a final shot and the moaning stopped. I pieced the scene below together in my mind. Cristoble, a companion, and the tracker lagged behind, and the rest of the crew moved as fast as possible to trail Jenara, Luis, and Hoshikay. They must have passed me by and not seen the tracks heading off toward the cliff path, something the native tracker would not have missed. Once my ascent was pointed out to Cristoble, he sent his companion to investigate since his own shoulder was badly damaged and he couldn't climb. During the confusion ensuing in the moments after I shot the climber, their tracker took the opportunity to slip away, hence Cristoble's shout to stop. I hoped I was right because Cristoble would have no option but to move on after the rest of his team. I was fading, and I knew a second attempt to take the hilltop would probably succeed.

I held my position in front of the hut but must have passed out because the sun was low in the western sky when I came to. My fever was raging, and I drank more than half my remaining water. I remained lying down, without the energy to rise, but started a small fire. The smoke was a hazard I would have to accept and assume the gang pursuing us was now four klicks to the north attempting to capture my friends. I chewed a small bit of dried meat for protein and remembered Hoshikay's instructions. Lodged in the top left pocket of my vest was the sticky wad of herbs she had placed there. The evening was upon me, and I started chewing the bitter medicine.

I passed out again and regained consciousness as twilight descended over the hills. The gummy wad of medicine was almost completely gone except for several acrid, woody bits, which I washed down with a sip of water. The back of my hand on my forehead told me the fever was still high, but I felt chilled even though sweat was soaking through my dark grey merino wool shirt. I stoked up the fire with my remaining wood and crawled into the recesses of the shelter, where I lay on my sleeping bag. My eyes weren't focusing properly, and I saw non-existent animals dancing in the flames. When I looked away from the fire, dim shapes sharpened like someone had placed night vision goggles over my eyes. Then the whole scene dissolved in front of me like colored paints melting and running off a canvass.

As the world returned into focus, I knew I was dreaming. I drifted downward in my dream, descending into a mist where only shadowy shapes and figures passed slowly by. The hilltop had disappeared, and I was on the semi-open floor of the rain forest. Despite the pitch-black blanket of the night hanging over the stygian jungle, I could see movement all around me. My sense of smell was intense. I smelled water from a running stream, and at a distance to my right, a capybara was huddled in fear. Overhead I smelled monkeys in the trees, and saliva thickened in my mouth.

As the mist started to lift, my vision cleared. I crouched low and looked around me, peering out from the body of a large cat. The dim outline of another jaguar appeared like a ghost about ten meters to my right. I could feel the visceral fear as she growled at me. But there was no aggression, only the stare of the beyond. Slowly she moved forward until whe was in front of me, where she crouched and peered back over her left shoulder. As she moved forward again, I followed.

I knew from Jenara that indigenous shamans saw the jaguar as a symbol of life in many forms. The native Rohodi term for shaman was even derived from the jaguar's name. Both jaguar and shaman share a deep, fluid connection that reaches past our world and into the metaphysical realm. The shaman is believed to be able to occupy the body of a jaguar, ascending the mystical tree of life, traversing the axis between our world and the next.

Slowly and silently, we glided along the forest floor like two spirits crossing the threshold into a fantasy world. The other cat kept pausing and waiting for me. I was weak and couldn't keep up the pace for long periods of time. Through breaks in the forest, I could see hills rising to our left and realized we were traversing a path at the base of the same cliffs we fled along just hours ago.

Eventually, we stopped beneath an impossibly tall tree with a trunk over twelve meters in diameter. My companion leaped onto the lowest branch, and I followed. Up we climbed, moving from branch to branch and ascending into the heavens. The leaves on the tree were a luminescent green, and the black skies above me shifted to a deep, translucent blue.

We sat at the top of the tree, towering over jungles to the east and hills to the west. Farther to the west, the top of the Andes gleamed. I looked back to the southwest and could see the dying fire in front of my hut. Below me, in the steepest portions of the hills, dim figures dodged in and out of sight on the flanks of a slope leading to a hilltop where two figures crouched. The faint sounds of occasional gunfire reached my ears. The jaguar beside me sprung outward, hurtling towards earth in a long arc and disappearing beneath the top of the tree canopy below.

She became a yellowish blur streaking across the forest floor towards the ensuing battle. I heard the rip, like a jagged clap of thunder, before I saw the sky open up above me. The luminescent blue sky gave way to utter blackness where light was sucked away into nothingness. Into this void floated the bodies of the dead, bloated with disease, blood oozing from their eyes and ears, and pus-filled boils covering their bodies. The skies above me filled with these bodies, and as some disappeared into the distance, others took their place. The devastation was complete, and the purview of death coiled through my soul.

Into the bleakness flew a bird, entering my view from the east and gliding westward. It was marked by a yellowish breast, a greenish upper body, black spotting and marking, and distinctive half-black wings and a half-black tail. Its claws securely held a clutch of golden seeds, like the ones Hoshikay gave me to swallow. As the bird passed over, the dead bodies morphed into arrays of bright green zeros and ones until the bird was flying against a background of computer code. Before the bird exited my vision, the numbers melted and dripped from the sky, leaving only the small parrot-like bird alone in an eternal void.

Everything faded from my vision, and I was enveloped in a world of grey mist and fog. But somewhere in the background, I could hear a steady rapid thumping. It was so faint, I wondered if it was real. The chopping sound was juxtaposed to the slow rhythm of my heart ringing in my ears with each beat. I wanted to sit up and open my eyes, but I couldn't. The invisible strings of sleep kept me bound in a netherworld. I struggled for what seemed an eternity in my dream world before my eyes popped open.

The eastern sun's first morning rays lit up the tips of the hills around me. The chopping sound was louder, and I saw a helicopter approaching from the northwest, clinging almost to the treetops. I rolled onto my left side and froze. Curled up meters away from me was a Jaguar, staring me in the eyes. The cat issued a low growl and leaped to her feet before pacing back and forth across the flat rock surface, constantly viewing me from different angles. She kept her distance, and I saw blood on her front paws.

As the chopper closed in on my position, the cat glanced over its left shoulder, eying the aircraft. In an instant, she took two bounds and landed at the top of the crevice exit. I took a quick glance at the helicopter, and when I looked back, I was taken by surprise to see the illusion of Hoshikay's face disappearing over the cliff edge and into the crevice pathway. I could hear the scraping sound of the cat descending through the fractures, but it sounded more like a person climbing down.

My attention returned to the helicopter, and it was clear the pilot would land on my hilltop. The back of my hand told me the fever was now low. When I felt the wound on my leg, it was sore but not inflamed. I felt no sixth sense warning but kept the shotgun by my side, although I doubted I had the strength to fire it accurately. I wondered about my dream. There was no fuzziness around the vision like most dreams once we awake. It was crisp and fresh, with every color, sound, and smell indelibly etched in my brain.

Jenara

Only minutes after Luis spotted the men in pursuit, Jenara heard a gunshot echoing from behind them, followed by an second shot and two minutes later a third. They all stopped, and she waited while Luis listened. He kept listening for a full five minutes before speaking. "The first weapon was a shotgun, and only one shot was fired, so the first shot did its job. If I'm right, Cristobal is alone and trailing behind. Cristobal's shoulder is useless, and he would have sent his extra man to climb up through the fractures after Mat. If the tracker is still with him, it is probably under duress, so he wouldn't have sent him. The most likely case is Cristobal is on his own now and following the rest of his crew. They are probably more interested in what Hoshikay is carrying than Mat. We need to press on and gain the peak before they get closer."

Jenara simply nodded her head and continued walking towards their destination. She was afraid for Mat at this point but knew there was no point in giving way to the fear. She also agreed with Luis's analysis. But she realized it was not a fact, merely a hypothesis. Hoshikay was unreadable and said nothing.

An hour later, they paused at the base of a steep slope, and Luis consulted his paper map and a GPS tracking device. The sun was settling into the west, and shadows around them deepened. Luis used his machete to cut two walking sticks for the women, and they headed northwest up the slope. The climbing was tough, and they didn't bother to cover their tracks. The key objective now was gaining the high ground ahead of Leon and his men.

More than once, Luis scrambled ahead and secured ropes to upslope trees to haul up Jenara's and Hoshikay's packs over steep terrain. At a point where their path bent around a large boulder, Luis paused and cut a medium-size sapling down. He jammed one end securely in a crevice between two boulders and strapped the Benchmade pocketknife Mat had given him to the other end—blade locked open and positioned to strike at chest level. He bent the whole mechanism backward and secured it with a trip string. Jenara was impressed. The entire process took him less than two minutes. They continued the trek upward.

Daylight was failing by the time they reached the peak. Luis moved about twenty large stones to construct a low wall between their position and the most accessible slope up the hill. They heard the scream about the same time he finished. The trap had presumably worked, and the knife had hit its mark. The pursuers would move slower now. Luis scurried to the backside of the peak and arranged branches and rocks so they would create noise when disturbed. When he returned, Hoshikay was gone.

Jenara was positioned by the wall with the remaining shotgun, keeping an eye on the tree break about eighteen meters away. Luis gave her a questioning look, and she only said, "Hoshikay knows things you don't." He let it go. By Luis's reckoning, there were three able-bodied attackers and an injured one. He had no doubt they would come; it was only a matter of when.

Twilight faded into darkness, and the hours ticked by. Luis studied his map again, sheltering his penlight beneath a tarp and behind the makeshift wall. If positions were reversed, he would delay attacking until the wee hours of the morning. From the map, the best lines of attack would be from the northwest, behind them, from the north immediately to his left, and from the east where they had ascended the peak. A coordinated attack from all three directions eliminated crossfire risk for the attackers and, if done correctly, would leave Jenara and him open to fire on their north flank. He quietly disassembled the mid-section of his wall and rebuilt it to partially cover the north flanks of both his and Jenara's positions.

At midnight Jenara could hear Luis rummaging around in his pack. The rock wall partially shielded him, but Jenara could see the greenish glow from his satphone. He must have gotten a weak connection because she could hear him delivering coordinates over the phone.

He returned to his watch, keeping the scope of his rifle flipped to night vision and constantly scanning the tree line. Twice Jenara heard the distant sound of dislodged rocks tumbling downhill, so they knew one of Leon's men was moving to a northwest position. Jenara stayed alert and chewed on some leaves Hoshikay had left her. She knew what to expect, and her visual acuity ratcheted up as her eyes dilated. She started to make out ghostly forms at the tree line where before, only blackness dwelt.

The attack came in a coordinated wave with simultaneous gunfire pinning both of them down from the north and the east. She counted two weapons and assumed Luis's trap had injured but not killed. The easiest position to fill by an injured man was the one to the east, where boulders provided ample cover and a wide angle of firing options. This position was about on level with her elevation, but the northern attack was coming from slightly downhill. She could already see they were badly outflanked. Two attacker positions had been revealed by the shooting, meaning two positions remained unknown.

Her drug-enhanced nocturnal vision picked up a gray blur moving along the tree line between the shooters to the east and north. The shadowy movement disappeared almost as soon as she had focused on it, and she assumed he had taken to the ground to crawl forward. Luis was preoccupied with returning occasional fire to the north and monitoring their weak northwest flank with his night scope.

Two more shots came from the east, directed at Luis' position. Jenara sighted the muzzle flashes and fired a round. She heard the sound of rocks being scrapped and battered by the pellets, but an immediate shot in her direction let her know she had done no damage. She slumped with her head below the top of the low rock wall and gave some thought to the situation. Luis was completely occupied with activity on their north and northwest flanks, and she needed a plan to take care of the two other attackers. The biggest unknown was whether they had night scopes. If they did, her options were limited because she needed the rock wall to shield her from the eastern shooter.

She knew she would have to play the odds. If the group had limited night vision equipment, then the two active shooters to the north and east would have those assets, meaning the man crawling her way was probably thwarted by darkness, just like her. The shooter to the north was slightly downhill, so she could stay out of his sights by keeping low. She started slowly crawling westward across the rock and scrubby vegetation, keeping the rock barrier between her and the eastern shooter. This opened up her range of vision to include the entire middle stretch between her and Luis. She positioned herself in what appeared to be the most favorable position to defend the gap in their wall.

The dynamics of the situation changed with a scream. Jenara focused on the eastern shooter as two more sharp cries emanated from his position. The shooting from the north stopped, and in the silence, she could make out the low snarl of a jungle cat. Luminous eyes glowed momentarily in the darkness, and she imagined she saw the cat's jaws locked around the throat of a man. For a moment, the only sound creeping through the night was the scraping of a body being dragged towards the eastern cliff edge.

Luis took advantage of the confusion and bolted westward into a stand of shrubs and small trees. Two rounds from the north chased him into the darkness. Jenara remained motionless, focused on the gap in their wall, waiting for an attack.

The minutes ticked by in silence until faint sounds from the northeast alerted her to a change in the attack pattern. The crawler was moving towards the eastern shooter's position, presumably to retrieve the weapon with a night vision scope. Jenara was about to move back to her covered position behind the rock wall when the growl of a cat floated out from among the boulders around the eastern shooter's former position. The crawler wouldn't be going there.

Luis was gone, and the crawler's only real options were to retreat or make a direct assault on Jenara's position. Jenara had fired no shots from her current position, so the odds were that he would believe she was still behind the wall. He would have to come over the wall to get her, probably using a pistol or knife. She slightly repositioned herself and waited.

Her former position was guarded by two low stone walls making an L shape. The long edge of the L was facing eastward and the short edge to the north. The attack was coordinated and started with the northern shooter placing three rounds into the north-facing wall's upper edge. The other attacker moved over the wall placing four rapid pistol rounds into the elongate shape she had made with her pack and one of the tents. This was all the opportunity she needed. Two quick rounds from the shotgun flung him backward across the wall. He was still making noise, but his chaotic retreat from the hilltop made it clear he was in trouble. Now they were down to the northern shooter and the man coming in from the northwest.

Jenara had rolled and moved as soon as she fired, but not quick enough and a bullet from the northern shooter tore through the flesh on her outer right thigh. He had changed position during the chaos and now had a direct line of fire. The next shot hit the ground a foot from her head, and she kept rolling. She knew there was no real cover at this point and started moving as erratically as possible. Two more shots missed her, but the third one ripped open her forearm. Then there was silence, and no more shots came her way.

The next shot she heard ricocheted in the forest to the northwest, and she could hear the sounds of someone scrambling downslope. She knew the northern shooter was dead, and Luis was driving off the last uninjured attacker. Daylight was not far away, and she crawled back over to her pack. Fortunately, the two wounds involved no severed arteries, and she had stemmed the bleeding by the time Luis returned. He confirmed that the two remaining attackers had retreated from the hilltop and that the group now probably numbered three, with two of those having substantial injuries. They had held the position overnight, and his best guess was Mark would reach them soon after daylight. It was not long after sunrise they spotted two choppers coming in low from the northwest.

Assembling the Extraction Party

Tom and Jillora Bindi were ensconced in their main home on the beach in Mandurah. Tom was sitting on the porch overlooking the cul-de-sac at the end of Ormsby Terrace. Tom and Jillora actually owned most of the cul-de-sac and had connected several homes, thus creating a large and functional compound. The Pacific Ocean stretched westward to the horizon. The shore break was small, but nonetheless, the breaking waves provided a pleasant background sound. A variety of shorebirds added a low cacophony. The light breeze was offshore, and the temperature was a perfect 26°C.

Tom was sipping a Calypso IPA and sharing a laugh with his old friend Croc as he told a tale of adventure on the high seas from his youth. Croc called bullshit on that one.

"You try to use my tale as your own, you old boomer? Your gray locks must have deep roots of forgetfulness!" Croc was having none of it.

"The tale is most certainly mine and not yours, you worthless old roo! I clearly recall successfully launching the life raft just before the desperately decrepit schooner took on its last pint and sank below the waves. I pulled the four other boys out of the cold drink and single-handedly rowed the dingy ashore." Tom was gazing back into the depths of time and not actually seeing much of anything. But he damn sure was not going to let on.

"Share that home-rolled with me and try to shake the cobwebs out of your age-addled brain. Before long, you'll be saying it was my fault you singed your boot so long ago in the morning coals after having too many draughts in the wee hours!" Croc brought up a well-aged argument from a time the pair was traveling and camping in their youth.

"It was your fault!" Tom shook his longish gray hair and white beard as he took a deep hit off the home-rolled homegrown. He handed the joint to Croc and they laughed the laughter of children grown old.

Jillora Bindi had been in her inner sanctum most of the day. She was still working with the Night Parrot greenery, conducting various tests and making observations that would, perhaps someday, be of use to the rest of the world. She paused to contemplate and was casually massaging her crystal between her palm and the three long fingers on her right hand. Her eyes were closed, and she roamed freely across the universe and back again.

A vague uneasiness came across her, and she envisioned a rainforest far away. There was some sort of trouble. A jaguar stood as a sentinel in the middle of a bit of bald spot on an otherwise deeply canopied hill. Such a vision has significant meaning for Ngangkari, Shaman, and the 1,111th daughter of the first Jillora Bindi. She was aware of the power of the jaguar, especially in certain parts of the world. And, more specifically, in Brazil.

She closed up shop and secured her offices. Crossing the compound, she heard the old men laughing on the ocean side of the main house, so she decided to join them. Croc jumped up and dragged another weathered wooden rocker over near Tom. Tom cracked open an IPA from the 12-pack cooler at his feet, and Jillora gladly accepted it, giving him a peck on the cheek. Croc offered the smoke, and she gave him a peck on the cheek too, but she declined the home-rolled.

"You look like something is amiss my love. Everything OK?" Jillora was Tom's entire world.

She described her vision of the rainforest. She told the men she needed to travel. She instructed Tom to get ahold of Mark and tell him to stop lollygagging and make ready for a trip; trouble was brewing, and Jenara needed help.

Anyone listening in on the conversation would have concluded that it was just about nap time at the old folks' home—or perhaps some gears had been stripped. There was no way anyone would have believed there was any validity to the statement Jillora had just made. But that anyone would have been in for a jolt.

"I'm going to skip on home and pack. I'll be ready to travel in a couple of hours. Let me know." Croc was, as always, all in. If Jillora Bindi said travel and trouble were imminent, then the logical next step was to prepare to travel and to be ready for trouble.

Tom pulled out his satphone and rang up Mark. Mark answered on the first ring, half a world away.

"Tom here, mate. I hope all is well wherever this fine day finds you!" They had developed a rare fondness for one another not too long ago doing some recycling.

"Tom, you old jack! Everything is awesome here in the Texas Hill Country! I trust all is well with you and your beautiful bride!"

"Jillora is at her best, and she is really the reason I'm calling. Do you have a minute?"

"I have until the end of time for you, my friend. Is there something I can help with?"

Tom told Mark about Jillora's vision and her intention to travel to the western reaches of Brazil.

"Interesting, because the girls and I are in the midst of planning our visit there as well. I have not been able to raise Mat, so we're trying to cover our bases. There are three airports in the northwest region, in or near the State of Acre. That is the area where we think they will be. But I'm not sure we can use any of the airports without being discovered by a nasty fellow in Rio, Carlos Mattes, who has already attacked them once. We have to presume we will be discovered. And with that presumption, we have to assume there will be fireworks."

"We're fairly certain Mattes put some of his thugs on Mat and Jenara's trail. I have not checked in with John in a while, but it's about time. Maybe he has an update on their location."

"Do that, Mark, and I'm going to make a call or two. Let's get back together in an hour. Cheers mate!" Tom rang off and scrolled his phone for a number. He had not talked to Diego Quispe in some time. Tom held tremendous sway in western Australian mining circles, and Diego was his equal in Peru. Diego was the youngest son in a wealthy family empire.

The family held interests in a number of heavy metal mines. Diego received his B.S. in Geology from North Carolina State University in 1980. He then returned home, where he stepped into the mining aspects of the family business and quickly grew the holdings into a significant operation. Over time he became well respected across the country and elsewhere around the world for his knowledge, his grace, and his ability to ride barefoot while standing atop a galloping stallion.

The story goes that when Diego was young, he was scared and refused to enter the ring with a yearling fighting bull. At the time, several family members and ranch hands were hanging around the corral. His mother scolded him and called the young Diego el coño. Everyone laughed. He climbed into the ring and vowed to himself that he would never do anything to make his mama call him el coño again. He would just as soon impale himself on a bull's horn rather than be scorned by his mama.

Tom punched in the programed number, and it was answered immediately.

"Tom, you old matador! Cómo the hell estás are you?" Diego was always enthusiastic.

"Diego, you old bull! I did not expect to reach you. I figured you would be in the arms of an old friend's wife right about now!"

"But I am my friend! But that certainly would not a be valid excuse for ignoring your ring!" Tom would never know for sure about the old friend's wife thing.

"Call me when you're free my friend." Tom clicked off. He looked at Croc and said, "five minutes."

It was actually more like ten minutes when the satphone chimed.

"I take it you required a smoke afterward, eh? I do too!" Tom laughed as he said that.

"So how are you? Keeping out of trouble or causing it." They sometimes attended mining conferences and such around the world and, on occasion, had fared the worse for wear.

"I am doing much better than I deserve to be! Let me ask you something. Are you still running the Antamina Mine?" Tom was fishing.

"No. I was fortunate enough to find a young engineer intelligent enough to find the place, so I turned it over to him. Actually, I've turned over all my direct responsibilities to Roberto, my oldest son. He oversees the entire operation now. I'm available as a troubleshooter, of course, but lately, I'm experimenting with new ways to lose golf balls. I'm becoming quite proficient!"

"Ah, but I ramble. I suspect you did not call me just to hear about my latest escapades. Can I help with anything?"

Tom gave him the facts and a supposition or two. Mainly he was trying to find a way in and out of Acre from Peru—without getting held up at the border and without getting shot out of the sky. Google Earth made it abundantly clear that his Land Cruiser would be useless where they were headed.

"So, at some point in the not-too-distant future you want to hop across the border from Peru into Acre, snatch your friends from the jaws of death and live to lie about it to your grandkids. Correct?" Diego was good at distilling information.

"Check." Tom could be succinct.

"Pulcallpa. Home of the Instituto Superior Bilingue Yarinacocha. Our family has donated millions to education all over the country for many years. The Instituto is currently undergoing a significant, campus-wide renovation. It is scheduled to reopen in about three months. I was just over there, and the work on the main dorm is complete. Plenty of rooms with bunk beds and a full cafeteria. I can have staff available to cook and clean."

"The Instituto sits on the banks of the Rio Ucayali. There is a high brick wall enclosing an over-sized soccer field. You can park a squadron of choppers there. There is exactly nothing but rainforest between the Instituto and the border of Acre. About 80 klicks to the east. If your friends manage to come within 100 klicks of the border, I imagine we can get them out."

"We?" Tom asked.

"But of course, you're my friend. Don't think for a moment you and your friends are going to visit my most excellent country and avoid me? I would not miss this big adventure for anything. Pack up your gear and fly into PCL. Also known as FAP Captain David Abensur Rengifo International Airport. The fuckers who name these places suffer from grandiose illusions. Like the Republicans up in the U.S.! Nonetheless, the 2,800-meter-long runway is about twice what you need to land a C-130. I'm guessing your American friends will arrive in a C-130 or similar. Enough plane for a chopper or two?" Diego had a knack for seeing into the future. "How about you. How will you arrive from Down Under?"

"I'll let you know as soon as I know. How can I repay you for your kindness?"

"I imagine we'll figure something out—perhaps a bottle of scotch! Let me know once your plans are firmed up. I will be there to meet you with the Customs Officer. He is one of my dear young cousins. Cheers!" Diego rang off and Tom punched in Mark.

Mark tied John in for logistics and additional security. Amber Lee and Sirocco listened in. Tom gave the essence of his conversation with Diego.

"Excellent news, Tom. Diego thinks we can be somewhat stealthy, I take it?"

"Yes. And we can arrive there as soon as we are ready. The accommodations will be a bit spartan but completely functional for our purposes. He'll troubleshoot, and I'm certain he will be a valuable asset."

"John, Sirocco here. Please line us up a ride from Lackland to PCL."

"With Croc, Tom, and Jillora Bindi, I think we'll have enough boots on the ground. I'm thinking of having Joe and Hunter put my new truck through its paces. See what its capabilities are. We may need it once we're back stateside. Thoughts?" Mark had chimed in.

Affirmatives from everyone sealed that deal.

"John, both Tom and Jillora can fly a chopper. Have a second one put onboard the transport. We may need it. Tom mentioned a jaguar. I don't know the importance, but since it came from Jillora, I suspect it is non-trivial." Mark was trying to cover the bases.

John indicated he was on it and asked if armament was necessary for the second chopper. All agreed military-grade would be best—a Blackhawk or similar with no markings.

"I have been speaking with Tom, and I have arranged transport for him, Croc, and Ms. Jillora Bindi. They leave in less than one day and will travel approximately 20 hours total." The computer was having two conversations at once. Mark wanted to shoot something but decided against it.

I think we're all set for now. Let's reconvene in twenty-four hours." Mark said, and they clicked off.

Mark called Joe, and Joe answered on the first ring with music and laughter in the background. Mark relayed all that was going on. Naturally, Joe and Hunter wanted to head down to Peru.

"We have plenty of hands for down south. I need ya'll to rent a car one way to Dallas. Pick up my new toy and put it through its paces. Take it out past the other side of beyond and see what it will and won't do. My gut tells me we may need its capabilities in the States after this current South American shit show is over. If the ride fucks up, call Lefty. AAA won't be much help. Be back in Dallas in six days."

"Understood. We'll keep in touch." Joe and Hunter, two big kids at heart, were going to have immense fun.

Mark, Sirocco, and Amber Lee spent some time totally unpacking the chopper. It was a mess because of the recent quick scamper out of Brazil, so each weapon was cleaned, checked, and stowed back in its place. All packs and webbing were set to go. Joe's and Hunter's gear was readied since it would probably be useful to Tom and Croc. Diego had indicated he would be prepared.

Mat's original plan called for an outing of approximately seven days. Mark had no way of knowing if the timing remained the same or not. Therefore, they decided to arrive in Peru on the sixth day from Mat and Jenara's start date. They figured there was no way their trek through the rainforest would be finished any earlier. The timeframe gave them a couple of days of R&R. One thing for sure was that the Hill Country was an excellent place for that.

Mark had occasionally visited Amber Lee at her Pawpaw and MeeMee's ranch over the years. They had all developed a hard and fast relationship. The ranch was located a couple of miles west of Leakey, Texas. It sprawled from there westward, encompassing a broad-to-narrow valley surrounded by mesas. It was a fairly typical Hill Country ranch from all appearances. There were cattle, horses, ranch-hands, fences, and scattered trees in the valley. The mesas were fairly steep-walled but climbable. There were fish in the ponds on the ranch but Mark had also developed a fondness for wading the Frio River in search of bass and bream. He felt at home when they arrived on the property.

Mark borrowed Pawpaw's ultra-lite fishing gear and waded the Frio River for a few hours. He caught and released several respectable largemouths and a bunch of bream. He had fished these very same waters many years ago in another lifetime.

Amber Lee talked Sirocco and Mark into a hike up the canyon and onward to the top of the mesa overlooking the Frio River valley. The weather was perfect, and the hiking was refreshing. They traversed sage, mesquite, prickly pear, and cholla. Creosote bushes, purple threeawn grass, and buffalograss were underfoot.

The Hill Country limestone is riddled with caverns. Near the top of the mesa Amber Lee cut through some fairly rough undergrowth. Mark and Sirocco followed. They came to a small open area. There was a two-foot-wide hole in the ground. They stood over it and were cooled by the breeze coming from the cavern below. The opening was too small to climb down into, but it nonetheless gave them a sense of the wonders below their feet.

They headed back toward the house. Ascending a steep part of the mesa, Mark unknowingly pissed off a Western Diamondback resting under a narrow ledge at ankle height. The five-foot snake tried to sink its fangs into his left boot. It was not the first time this had happened, but the reaction was the same as years before. He set a new world record for the backward standing broad jump. Extracting him from the prickly pear cactus he landed in required the assistance of both Sirocco and Amber Lee. The women laughed until they cried.

They knew MeeMee was preparing dinner, so the snake got to live another day. Fried rattlesnake is excellent, by the way. Later, MeeMee used oversize tweezers to extract several cactus spines from various points on Mark's anatomy. She used lots of alcohol. The faces he made elicited new peels of laughter. He whined, and MeeMee called him el coño. Now that hurt.

All in all, the few days passed tranquilly. So everyone was well rested in case things got hairy in Brazil.

Crossing the Styx

Jillora Bindi, Tom, and Croc descended from 10,000 meters into Captain David Abensur Rengifo International Airport (PCL). Diego stood at the foot of the airstairs waiting for them to disembark. His nephew, aka the Custom's man, waved at the plane, turned, and left.

When Jillora came through the doorway and descended, Diego shouted, "Ms. Bindi! I am honored to have your presence here in my magnificent country!" He took her outstretched hand and gently kissed it.

"Aahhhh, I am honored to meet you! You are even more lovely and enchanting than the Cantua buxifolia, more commonly known as the sacred flower of the Incas! Also known as the magic tree. Perhaps more fitting. I presume these two ruffians accompanying you are the hired help?"

Tom crushed Diego in a brief bear hug. Croc then received a stout handshake and a brief hug—warriors all, after a fashion.

"Come, let's ride to the Instituto Superior Bilingue Yarinacocha." Diego gestured to follow him. The walk was only to the edge of the tarmac.

"I just got myself a new toy!" Diego grinned. They climbed into the black Ford F-150 Raptor. Croc rode shotgun. "SuperCrew cab, enough room in the back even for a man of Tom's size. Four hundred and fifty horses, 4x4, off-road package, full leather plus electronics on the dash I'll never figure out!" He laughed, cranked the beast, and they were off.

Jillora Bindi poked Tom and laughed, "You men and your toys!"

"Ah, my love, you know boys just get bigger after age 13! Men are all 13-year-old boys at heart." Tom's world was sitting beside him.

"True words! Look at me. I am now devoting much of my time chasing a little white ball around with a stick!" Diego laughed as he accelerated into a curve in the road leading to the college.

Mark, Sirocco, and Amber Lee had arrived several hours earlier. Their seven-hour flight from San Antonio was uneventful. They helped offload their gear and the two birds. Thirty minutes later, they had landed on the soccer field, stowed their gear in their suites, and were out on the field prepping Sirocco's chopper and the one John had provided. It was a green and black Bell 206. A third chopper, an Airbus H155, was there as well.

Diego waved at the guard at the gate, and they were admitted into the massive courtyard masquerading as a soccer field.

"Yours?" Croc, a man of many words, glanced at the third bird and then at Diego as they pulled to a stop.

"Ah yes, another one of my boy toys. It gets me around to the various mines. Up and over the hills, you know?" Croc was taking a liking to Diego and his affinity for toys.

There were greetings all around, then Diego led Tom and Jillora to their quarters. The one-bedroom suite would have reminded Joe of his stay on the 32nd floor at the Beau Rivage in Biloxi, Mississippi. The accommodations were quite an upgrade from what they expected in a college dorm.

"VIP quarters for you and the others, of course. Can't have you thinking my humble country lacks style!" Diego exuded pure class in all things. Not bad for an old hard-rock geologist and renowned bullfighter. "Anything you need, just pick up the phone. I've brought in a full staff. They are here for the duration of our little adventure. Anything at all, just ask. Otherwise, there is a full bar, and you will find an array of food and cold beer, water, and soft drinks in the refrigerator and cabinets. Now I'll make my exit. I look forward to seeing you at the choppers once you have freshened up."

After the exfiltration from Rio, Sirocco thought about how close she came to losing the boys during the extraction from the overlook at Mirante do Leblon. The rope ladder was a particular worry. She did not want anyone falling off.

She found Falltech full-body harnesses and accessories on the internet that would suit her purposes. She ordered six XL and two S. The smalls were for Amber Lee and Jenara. Each assembly consisted of an adjustable harness, a two-foot-long lanyard, and a rope grab. One end of the lanyard attached to the back D-ring on the harness, the other to the rope grab. The rope grab was attached to either the left or right vertical rope on the ladder. Double-locking snap-hooks made all of the connections.

Tom, Croc, Mark, and Amber Lee practiced getting into the harnesses and latching off to the rope grabs. Proficiency could be the difference between a successful extraction or not. Diego was going to hang behind and act as the coordinator from the ground.

They decided Jillora, Tom and Mark would ride in the Ranger, with Jillora acting as pilot and Tom riding shotgun. Sirocco would pilot her bird with Amber Lee riding shotgun, and Croc would ride in the back.

Sirocco's bird was armed essentially the same as for the Rio event. The same was fitted on the borrowed Ranger when they were finished. They hoped the extraction would be stealthy and without incident. But they had been around long enough to know that success was often the outcome of preparing for the worst. Anything better than the worst was a winner.

Late in the afternoon, they all cleaned up and had a lite, early dinner at an intimate table in a long hall built to accommodate probably 300 people at a time. There was Lomo Saltado, Cerviche, and Rocoto Relleno and for dessert Crema Volteada rounded out the simple but amazing meal. While they dined, they discussed logistics, potential flight paths, infiltration, and possible exfiltration routes. Since they were in a holding pattern and they did not know when the call might come in, both nighttime and daylight issues were discussed and worked out.

Tomorrow marked seven days since Mat, Jenara and company headed out. Mark figured this was the earliest they might be needed. They also knew the wait could stretch out a number of days.

Jillora Bindi excused herself and walked to the bank of the Rio Ucayali. She pulled her marble-sized crystal from its nest and held it in her palm. She gently massaged it to and fro and gazed up at the star-studded sky. She was always amazed when she considered the provenance of the amazing charm she held in her hand. She slipped into the semi-trance where she often went to extend her senses beyond the horizon. What she felt made her scurry back to the others.

"What is it my love?" Tom had jumped up as she hustled into the hall.

"I am concerned. It's hard to explain, but I suggest we need to be ready to mobilize from here with five minutes' notice. I do not know when we will be needed, only that we will be needed immediately upon request." Jillora was all business. Anyone from outside of the current circle of folks would have rolled their eyes and shook their head in disbelief.

"So be it." Mark took command. They went back to the birds and triple-checked everything. Weapons were locked and loaded. Fuel tanks were topped off. "I suggest we wear our tactical gear, even to bed, until this caper is over."

Mark rang up John. John answered on the first ring. "I have you on speaker John."

"Yes sir, I know." Mark considered shooting out the lights but came back with "Any word from Mat?"

"No sir, no word, and I'm frustrated because I cannot raise them, and I cannot find them via any eye in the sky. The world's military leaders do not have much use for the vast, mostly uninhabited rain forests of western Brazil. Hence there is virtually no satellite coverage that I can tap into. I can only keep all of my lines open and wait. But I will tell you that the optimal time to receive a call will be between 12:00 and 2:00 am based on satellite positioning." A frustrated computer. What's next thought Mark?

"We're bedding down for the evening. Tie all of our sat phones in together. Chime in with even the faintest hint of any comms from Mat. We're on a five-minute travel alert."

"Yes sir. Anything else?"

"John, Tom here. Cheers. Are you able to detect any movement, from near or afar, of the nefarious ne'er-do-wells from the coast?"

"There was the initial dust kicked up when Mat departed, and Sirocco and company created that bit of a disturbance over at the Leblon. After that, only mumbles came across the airwaves, sir. There has been nothing of substance. I will alert everyone the instant anything changes." John clicked off.

"I suggest we get some rest." Sirocco looked around and they all pushed back from the table. Amber Lee started to stack dishes. Diego gently shooed her away.

"Ah, but you are a most beautiful and gracious lady! In reality, we are a very poor country. I have probably triple the staff we need here, and I am paying them double-time. They would be insulted if we cleaned up! The extra wages help them, and it also buys us some loyalty. I have a lot of eyes to the four points of the compass, both here in the compound and outside. I'm not bragging, but bad hombres cower back to their holes when my name is mentioned. I guess it has to do with my golf game!" Diego grinned, and they all headed off to their quarters.

At the crack of dawn, Diego found the others doing another check of the choppers.

"Ah my friends, I suspected I'd find you here. Breakfast is in fifteen minutes if anyone is hungry." Diego was hungry. Everyone else said they'd be there.

They gathered around the same table as the night before.

"We're having a traditional breakfast. Here is Butifarra. Simply a French roll with Jamon del Pais, seasoned ham, topped with Salsa Criolla, basically onion relish. Here we have Humitas. A corn husk filled with cooked ground corn, lightly fried. The rings there are Picarones, essentially sweet potato and squash donuts. Add a little maple syrup as a topping. They are addicting! Dig in and cajita Feliz!" Diego gave the go-ahead to chow down.

Silence reigned as they ate. There is no greater compliment to the chef than silence. It means the food is too good to waste time talking. The third plate of

Picarones had just arrived when all seven phones rang at once. They all clicked in on the first ring.

"John here. I have received a message from Luis and Ms. Jenara . I recommend you ready your birds and head north-northeast. I will load coordinates into your systems as soon as you spark off the engines, and I will call back in a few minutes." John clicked off.

"Grab the donuts!" Croc was the planner now.

The two birds cleared the perimeter wall four minutes later. They crossed the Rio Ucayali, some agricultural plots, the main course of the meandering Rio Ucayali, and continued on their north-northeast flight path.

John rang in again and said, "This morning, I managed to pry open a new satellite in the area, and I retrieved a call placed at midnight by Luis. He sent me coordinates. He and Jenara were on a hilltop expecting an attack on their east and north flanks from four of Mattes' men. He thinks they can probably hold off any attack in a stalemate. They had to leave Mr. Mat hidden away on another hilltop with injuries, about three km south of their current position. I have approximate coordinates."

"They decoyed Carlos' men into following them away from Mr. Mat. I loaded GPS coordinates for Ms. Jenara and Mr. Luis, -7.133135, -73.77710, into your nav equipment. I also loaded my estimated coordinates for Mr. Mat, -7.158299, -73.762581, as well. From the point of departure to Ms. Jenara, I estimate the distance at 128 km. Mr. Mat's position should be about the same distance, just south and slightly east by approximately 3 km." John said.

"John, can you patch us back in with Luis and Jenara?" Mark wanted direct contact for tactical and logistical purposes.

"I'm trying, but I get no signal. Perhaps a weak battery. I will keep trying." John clicked off.

Sirocco chimed in, "Clock shows we're twenty minutes out from Jenara. I recommend I pick up Jenara and Luis." Sirocco definitely had superior firepower.

"Roger that. I suspect Ms. Jillora has a role in getting us on top of Mat anyway." Mark pulled on his harness and tightened the chest and leg straps. He attached another harness to his and used small bungee cords to strap it out of his way. He double-checked the rope grabs were secure about six feet up either side of the rope ladder.

Tom readied two Wilson Ultralite Ranger .243's. He laid one near the side door and had the other in the ready position. He had extra clips Velcro'd to his forearms for quick reloading. Mark strapped on two Glock 19 Gen 5 G34 pistols, one on each side of his tactical belt. His U.S. Marine K-Bar was snuggled in beside the left-hand pistol. They were as ready as possible. Now to find Mat.

These preparations were accomplished as Sirocco pushed her bird hard. A large harness was attached to one rope grab and a small harness to the other one. Hopefully, Croc could stay in the bird and provide cover fire if necessary. He would reel the ladder down as far as necessary.

Both birds flew at treetop level and stayed inside Peruvian airspace until the last couple of kilometers. Jillora veered off to the right and crossed the border into Brazil first. She estimated being at her coordinates in two minutes. Sirocco made the same maneuver one minute later and two km north.

"There they are." Croc caught a glimpse of Jenara and Luis on the low hilltop. He almost caught a bullet too. "We are taking fire from down the slope below our packages." Croc unwound from his seat and ducked into the rear compartment. He slid open the side door and immediately raked the area just below the hilltop tree line with his Wilson Ultralite Ranger .243. As Sirocco passed over the hilltop Amber Lee tossed several grenades and flashbangs into the canopy below. Croc continued firing, ejecting clips, inserting new clips, and firing some more.

"Ms. Sirocco, please be kind enough to stand off to the west and lower your ladder. I'll only need a minute or so." Diego came in over the comms.

"10-4. Northwest bound, slowing, lowering ladder." Sirocco showed no surprise that Diego showed up.

Diego and his pilot had taken off in the Airbus H155 before the other two choppers cleared the college walls. The pilot followed the same course north northeast, but a km or two to the west. Diego readied the M61 Vulcan Gatling gun. The six-barrel rotary cannon fired 20mm rounds at a rate of up to 6,000 rounds per minute. He set the selector to 100 rounds. This meant when he pulled the trigger, 100 rounds were going into the rainforest. Another pull, another 100 rounds expended. Each burst lasted around one second. He opened the opposite door and rigged the cartridge deflector so the expended shells would fly out of the door instead of through the front windscreen.

"Flare north and hold over the hilltop," Diego spoke to his pilot and old friend Tomas. In less than a minute the east side of the hill down to the creek bed resembled a freshly mowed lawn. However, instead of blades of grass, the residual was toppled trees.

"All yours. We're moving upward and northward." Diego was grinning from ear to ear. The gun was borrowed from friends in the military. It was more amazing than he could have ever dreamed of.

"Please stand by and be my eyes." A double-click in her ears and Sirocco came in fast and low. Croc and Amber Lee watched as Luis grabbed the second rung and helped Jenara grab the first rung. Amber Lee could see the fresh but bloody bandages on Jenara's leg and arm and let Sirocco know. Sirocco steadily lowered the bird directly over Luis and Jenara. This was the only hilltop in the area without a canopy, so she wouldn't cut down any trees. Getting low avoided the need for the harnesses.

"Come in lower. Lower, we're retrieving ladder. Lower, lower, we have two passengers on board." Croc called the descent. "All secured."

Sirocco flared right, and they were clear of the area in seconds. Her route took her towards Mat's apparent location. Diego and Tomas tagged along a bit above and a bit behind.

Tom, Mark, and Jillora all had eyes open for Mat. Mark was in his harness and hooked off to the rope grab on the ladder. He intended to ride the ladder down.

"Suppose Mat is incapacitated and not visible from the air?" Amber Lee asked the obvious question.

"If that is the case, there will be a sign." Jillora Bindi whispered into her mic.

"Any idea what the sign will be?" Tom asked.

A few seconds passed, and Amber Lee said, "A jaguar perhaps? Like the one pacing around the edge of the clearing?"

Jillora flared the bird toward the small clearing and said, "Go Mark."

Mark was out the door, onto the skid, and airborne downward in a second. The ladder unspooled and Tom braked the descent, so Mark stood when he landed. He unhooked from the ladder and prepared to wrestle with the jaguar. But the mystical creature was gone, vanishing into thin air, by the time he looked around.

Mat was lying in a three-sided stone hut on the edge of the clearing. "Hello, old friend. Give me a hand. I think I can walk." Mark extended his left hand and pulled Mat up into a standing position. He was weak and limping badly.

"Where is the jaguar?" Mark did not want to be dinner.

"Here and gone, buddy—if it was ever here at all." Mat tried to look around at the eastern edge of the clearing but collapsed onto Mark. Mark lowered him to the ground.

"Jillora, we've got your six and twelve." She double-clicked. She had picked up on the fact that Diego was out there too.

"I need a hand, Tom." Mark didn't think he could carry Mat into the center of the clearing. Dragging him might cause more harm than good. Tom was there in less than a minute. They got Mat strapped into the harness and carried him into the clearing. Jillora came back in as low as she dared. There was extra rope on the ground.

"Good. Hold." Tom to Jillora.

Mark opened the rope grab and repositioned it above the sixth rung. They hooked Mat to the mechanism.

"Take the top, Tom, winch us up. I'll just hang around here with Mat." Mark grinned and gave a thumbs-up sign. Tom, Mat, and Mark were all inside and secured in another minute.

"Homeward bound," Jillora said. Double clicks acknowledged, and the three birds flew the outbound route in reverse.

"Can you get a doctor on the ground for us Diego?" Mark asked. "Mat definitely can't walk, and he seems delirious. He keeps mumbling something about a plague."

"Full medical staff is on the field and standing by my friend. I hoped for the best but planned for not so much as you Americans say. Ms. Jenara and Mr. Luis, they are OK?" Diego was being kind, but he also needed to alert the medical staff.

On the ground, after Mat was carted off and Jenara tended to, they had a short debrief. Tomas was introduced, and they all agreed having him and Diego there probably saved the day.

"A fucking Vulcan? Damn, I gotta get me one of those!" Tom was impressed.

"Definitely." Croc chimed in.

"Sorry I did not tell you my plans, but you all seemed to be completely capable, and I feared we would be a distraction during the planning stage. So Tomas and I just tailed along like old dogs. Trimming the trees, and perhaps a bandido or two, was a bonus." Diego grinned.

Later, they were gathered around the table in the hall for a late lunch. Mat was in bed, sedated, and under the watchful eyes of two nurses.

"This is Dr. Ricardo Medrano." Diego introduced everyone else.

"Excellent to meet you all. Mr. Dover is under sedation. Overall, he is in fairly good shape externally. I cleaned up and bandaged a bad wound and infection on his leg. Whoever treated him in the jungle probably kept him alive, but I am still worried about sepsis, even though he is showing no immediate signs of it. His stupor could be caused by any number of maladies found out there. Unfortunately, I do not have the facilities available to make clear determinations. And to be honest, I do not have the expertise. I recommend you exfiltrate as soon as possible back to the States."

"Thank you so much Doctor Medrano, for all you have done." Jenara was a little subdued after what they had been through.

"Please, dear lady, I am Ricardo to my friends."

"Now, my friends, let me have some food laid out for us." Diego snapped his fingers, and several staff members rolled carts out. "Please, tell us what you have for our dining pleasure."

"Senoritas and hombres, it is my pleasure to present today's lunch. This is Lomo Saltado. You sampled this last night. It is a classic Peruvian dish of stir-fried beef and potatoes. We also have Arroz con Pollo, a wonderful and simple mixture of rice and chicken. If you want something spicy, try the Aji de Gallina. It consists of chicken in a spicy aji amarillo sauce. We also prepared Churrasco de Res, which is thinly sliced beef steak served over rice. And, of course, Cerviche. Disfrute de su comida my honored guests!" The staff retreated as everyone dug in.

"This is amazing! I'm actually glad our flight won't arrive for a few more hours. But I'm also glad you had John summon the pilots this morning Amber Lee. We need to get Mat into a hospital. Thank you again Ricardo, and what can I say Diego? You are the best!" Jenara was feeling a bit better about everything. In a few hours, they would be outbound back to the States.

Time Zero

Janju lived on the eastern border of Nigeria, where the Akwayafe River separates the country from Cameroon. She did not always live there and was born in Mbenmong, a poverty-stricken village on the Cameroon side of the river. Both she and her sister fled the village after their mother died. They crossed the river on a skiff to Nigeria, landing just north of the small port town of Ikang. She had remained there, eking out a living and eventually giving birth to Crayse, her only daughter. Her sister stayed several years then crossed the country, traversing the 400 plus miles to the metropolis of Lagos, where she settled and married.

But now, Lagos was where Janju and Crayse were headed. It was not a pleasant journey under the best of circumstances, and Janju's limited funds meant walking, riding in the back of trucks of all sorts, and even the occasional cab when all else failed. She had sold what little they owned and taken her meager savings to finance the journey. Her hasty departure from Ikang was driven by fear. A type of fear preying on both rational and irrational thoughts.

Only two days before they left, she and Crayse had visited her birth village. An annual trip to see her childhood friend Kuba, now married with three children of her own. Kuba had whispered hushed words that plunged a spike of dread deep into Janju's soul.

In a village slightly to the east of Mbenmong, whispered rumors claimed the killer had returned. She still remembered her mother's vomiting, diarrhea, and bleeding eyes as Ebola took her life. Now, the threat was close by again. Kuba had not seen it with her own eyes when she traveled there the week before, but the rumors were thick. Janju and Crayse left the next morning, and within twenty-four hours of returning, they were on the road to Lagos. The city had effectively contained the last Ebola outbreak, and Janju wanted to keep her daughter safe. She had never erased the image of her mother's wasted, hemorrhaging body. It haunted her dreams and preyed on her mind daily.

The trip to Lagos took them four days, but they arrived without meeting any violence or being robbed. Sange, her sister, took them in and rearranged the small apartment to make a tiny, curtained-off sleeping area for Janju and Crayse. Space had already been tight with Sange, her husband, and their two children. Now it was even more cramped, but Sange still adored her older sister and never considered turning her out. Her husband Denjay was kind and didn't complain about the closer quarters or the extra mouths to feed. He had a decent job and a generous spirit.

Denjay worked at the prestigious Balmoral Convention Center on Victoria Island. He worked in their hospitality department, often coordinating the service staff for large meals. They were currently planning for a meeting of international energy financiers. Future business opportunities for oil, gas, wind power, and solar energy were all up for discussion at the three-day meeting.

Sange, Denjay, Janju, and the children spent several days adjusting to the new living situation, although Denjay was at work most days. Change carries its own anxiety, and by Saturday Janju was exhausted to the point where she slept until mid-morning. Even when she awoke, she felt fatigued.

Monday was the first day of the conference, and Denjay arose early for the one-hour-plus journey across town. The conference's opening-day lunch was a grand affair, with the Nigerian Energy Minister delivering a keynote speech. Denjay was unusually tired and chalked it up to stress on the home front. To his dismay when he arrived at work, two of his servers had not reported in. He had plans in place to work around the absence of one server but missing two of them would require that he help work the floor at lunch. It had happened before, though, so he wasn't overly perturbed.

Lunch started smoothly, and Denjay served the four tables in the front of the room, closest to the speaking podium. These were where the VIPs were seated, and each of the round tables held a group of eight. Midway through the meal, one dropped tray near the rear tables created some commotion, but there were no other incidents. Denjay was sweating by the time desserts were served and made a note to check with maintenance about the thermostat settings.

By day-end, Denjay was exhausted and fell asleep on the Danfo ride home. The Danfos, or Yellow Buses, were his usual mode of daily transport, but the new driver didn't know him, so he missed his stop and had to walk the half-mile back to his apartment. He hadn't stopped sweating after lunch and was soaked when he arrived home. Janju was tired and preparing for bed, but Sange warmed up some dinner and sat with him at the table.

As Janju fell asleep, she thought of her friend Kuba and wondered how she was doing. She had no way to know that Kuba was violently sick and would be dead in three days.

While Denjay collapsed into a restless sleep, Mat was lounging on the east-facing balcony of Sirocco's penthouse, enjoying the mid-day sun in Dallas. The trip out of Brazil had been uneventful, and his recovery was progressing well. The sepsis initially feared in the early prognosis never materialized, and his leg wound was healing nicely. He used Sirocco's gym for several hours each morning with a full set of stretching, strength, and cardio routines. The days were improving, but the nights remained sketchy.

He couldn't shake the specter of his dream. Some part of the vision seemed to return each night, haunting him with perfect clarity and creating a restless sleep. He had not discussed the dream with anyone. Although he tried to broach the subject with Jenara, but she placed a finger on his lips and told him whatever he saw was his alone. "Hoshikay didn't take you to that hilltop by chance, and the concoction she gave you is used by Shamans when they are on a vision quest. It's true she treated your body and probably saved your life, but she also infused your mind with information that you alone are responsible for."

"What about seeing her face as the jaguar departed?" Mat had asked.

"You saw what you saw, and only you can decide how to interpret it," was the only reply he got.

Since they arrived in Dallas, Jenara, Jillora, and Amber Lee stayed holed up every day in a newly constructed lab two floors down from the penthouse. They wouldn't discuss what they were doing, and Mark was no wiser than he was. If Sirocco knew anything, she wasn't talking. The only two things he knew for sure were that the golden seeds Hoshikay collected and some type of herb or plant Jillora had collected from Australia were at the heart of their mysterious work. The only request he had gotten was to obtain the latest analytical data and reports on the bizarre, preserved DNA he encountered several months ago.

Mat had the right contacts since his shell company, Hadean Enterprises, was the patent holder for the original genetic material. He had coaxed enough information from two separate labs to keep the ladies happy. His best guess was they were sequencing the two plants' genomes to take a peek at what made them special.

He was not a medical expert by any means, but he had read enough to understand the basics of bio-farmed viral vaccines, monoclonal antibodies, and mRNA. He was also aware of the age-old battle between humans and viruses. All indications were that viruses had a history on Earth as long as that of cellular life. So, despite what humans thought about viruses, they had a proven track record of survival. Mat understood why we needed to respect their tenacity if we wanted to learn how to defeat them.

After all, each lowly virus is just another species trying to survive like the rest of life on planet Earth. However, viruses occupy a fuzzy space on the edges of life. Their rules are different than the rules for the rest of us. They are sometimes referred to as pseudo-living organisms because viruses don't have cells as their fundamental building blocks.

Almost all plant and animal life around us is cellular. Some organisms like bacteria are single-cell creatures, but others like humans are multi-cellular, containing trillions of individual cells. Whether an organism is single-celled or multi-celled, it still reproduces by cellular division. Animal cells have the metabolic machinery to create new cells. Viruses, however, lack any metabolism and must reproduce by hijacking the cellular machinery of another organism. They can't do it on their own.

Yet, a virus has aspects of cellular life. It possesses genetic material, reproduces, and evolves by natural selection. In these respects, it seems alive. Some viruses have DNA as their genetic material, but others stick with RNA. The simple but essential physical characteristics of a virus are nucleic acid (DNA or RNA) wrapped in a protein shell. Some viruses also have fatty materials called lipids in their outer shell.

Reproduction is the essence of species survival. Viruses can't reproduce independently, but they have a highly successful strategy for overcoming this deficiency. Step one in the virus survival strategy occurs when it attaches itself to a host cell. Then, step two requires the virus to place its genetic material into the host cell. Injecting the material through the cell wall is a popular option. However, those viruses with lipids mixed into their protein shells can sometimes pass directly through the host cell's membrane.

Once inside the cell, the viruses' genetic material issues instructions for the host cell machinery to produce more individual virus particles. When the cell is loaded with newly minted virus particles, they burst free, and each of them proceeds to find another host cell.

Viral attacks occur in two stages. Once a virus is under our skin, we are infected. If that infection starts disrupting our normal body functions, then we move from infection to stage two—disease.

Most people think in terms of the virus making them sick. But, in reality, it is the body's own immune system causing much of the damage. The body's immune system is a highly efficient seek-and-destroy machine preventing foreign objects from invading beneath our skin. But the immune response system needs to know when a problem arises. One class of molecules used by humans to scout out viruses is cytokines. These molecules act as an early warning system. They are the chemical alarm bells calling in an army of defensive cells and molecules when the need arises.

The body's immune response focuses its defenses on areas where cytokines detect invaders. The immune system then sends aid to vanquish the intruders. But as immune defenses collect in a local area, they cause inflammation, redness, and swelling. So, the signs of sickness, which most people recognize, are more about our immune system's reaction to a virus than the virus itself.

Cytokine storms are a classic form of body malfunction leading to sickness and disease. Normally when a threat is neutralized, the cytokines will cease sending out alarm signals. But sometimes, things go wrong. When the cytokines should pack-up and go home, they stay and continue sending alerts to the rest of the immune system. Under these circumstances, the immune system keeps pumping defensive cells and molecules to the cytokine's location. Thus, turning the body into a chaotic battlefield with a psychopathic commander in charge.

This immune-system attack results in blood vessels filling with unneeded defensive cells and molecules, all of which are trying to attack a non-existent enemy. These excess cells start crowding out other vital cells, therefore starving the body of oxygen and nutrients. The rogue immune molecules are powerful destroyers intended to work within the circulatory system. However, during cytokine storms, they flood through the body, and they can leak out of the circulatory system, where they start attacking healthy cells.

If left unchecked, cytokine storms inflict organ damage and possibly death. The patient then dies from a malfunctioning immune system, not the virus. Of course, the virus triggers the initial cytokine response, but the direct cause of death is a malfunctioning cytokine alarm system.

The classic, modern route of dealing with viral infections is to treat them with an appropriate vaccine. The development of vaccines involves finding a compound that teaches your body to recognize a specific virus. Its ultimate goal is to either eliminate or control the virus, thereby preventing the infection or keeping it from developing into the disease stage.

The key to fighting a virus is to stop it in the infection stage before it transitions into a disease. This objective has traditionally been accomplished by having the immune system produce the correct antibodies. These antibodies are Y-shaped proteins that latch on to the virus and tag it as an intruder, marking it for attack by the rest of the immune system's defenses. Some antibodies can even bind to a virus and subsequently prevent it from entering a person's cells. Thus, they neutralize the virus and stop and the infection in its tracks.

Traditional vaccines focus on educating our bodies. The vaccine tries to train our body to recognize the virus in question and produce the appropriate antibodies, so when the real thing appears, we are ready and primed to defend against the infection. Sometimes this process involves injecting a living but weakened version of the virus into our arms. But why not simply mass-produce antibodies and use them directly, as opposed to waiting for our body to educate itself and start manufacturing its own tiny Y-shaped proteins?

Smart people have already thought of this and developed the science of monoclonal antibodies. The process first locates naturally occurring antibodies in a person after they have been vaccinated or infected — but not just any antibodies, only those with high efficacy and the ability to neutralize the virus before it enters any cells. Once located, the antibodies are then reproduced in laboratories and injected into the patient. The downside is these lab-produced monoclonal antibodies don't stay with you for long. Naturally produced antibodies can last for years, but the monoclonal antibodies disappear after several months.

As far as Mat could tell, the most promising technology on the healthcare stage was the mRNA vaccine. This acronym stands for messenger Ribonucleic acid. It holds advantages over traditional vaccines by being easier and quicker to develop and produce than conventional vaccines. The mRNA vaccines use strands of messenger RNA wrapped in protective coatings. The RNA contains a code instructing the cell to make a piece of spike protein specific to the virus. The spike protein subsequently tricks the immune system into producing antibodies specific to the virus in question. These antibodies then vanquish the virus as soon as it appears.

Mat knew that viruses were here to stay, and humanity could never stop them from evolving. Viruses had been in the survival game for billions of years, and they were good at it. The answer had to lie in our ability to rapidly develop and distribute vaccines, stopping infection and disease in the early stages before a pandemic brought our society to its knees.

Mat tipped back his head and thought about his experience with Ebola years ago. Events unfolding over the past several weeks convinced him that the herbal medicine provided by Jenara before his trip to Africa years ago was based on the same golden seeds they had retrieved in Brazil with Hoshikay's help. If he was correct, something in the seeds either primed his system to produce needed antibodies or contained a kill-toxin to wipe out any infection as soon as it entered his body.

Both mechanisms were possible, but both also had severe problems explaining how seeds from Brazil could produce either Ebola antibodies or kill molecules for a specific virus halfway around the world. He also realized the truth was probably weirder than anything he could possibly think up. He also realized that even if the women could isolate the active compounds and understand their functional pathways in the body, there was a very limited supply of these rare seeds and herbs. Anything they developed would have to be mass-produced in laboratories. Researching this part of the equation was probably the way he could best help.

Mat swiped on his phone and checked the calendar. He had a Three Rock, Inc. board meeting in Boston next Monday. The meeting would provide a great opportunity to meet with Dan Rohden and see how his work was progressing. Mat was still convinced that undeciphered data on the crystal lattice sphere in Dan's possession contained advanced medical technology.

He had another thought and placed a call to Kristen, one of his portfolio managers in Houston. She answered on the first ring.

"Kristen, how are you doing today?"

"Mat, I haven't heard from you for a while. In fact, I tried to reach you about a week ago but could only ascertain that you were out of the country."

"A week ago, I was lying half-dead on a jungle floor in South America," he replied.

"If I didn't know you better, I would take that as a joke and laugh. But, at any rate, it's good to hear from you. I hope you are safe, sound, and recovering."

"Yes to all, Kristen, but that's not why I am calling. I need you and Jagat to look into a potential investment for me. I am interested in small companies at the leading edge of developing advanced mRNA delivery systems. Specifically, I want someone heavy on research but also with solid production line capabilities. I am interested in a venture capital investment, and I will want a seat on the Board."

"It's a hot area, Mat." She paused then continued, "how much are you looking to invest?"

"Up to a billion, if necessary, but I would prefer to keep it under five-hundred million if possible."

He could hear the click of Kristen's keyboard in the ensuing silence. "It's doable, but from a purely investing standpoint, it puts a lot of eggs in one basket. Ultimately you could absorb the loss if it goes belly up, but it wouldn't be pretty."

"That's why you and Jagat are going to find me something solid. Think of it as protecting me from myself."

She laughed and replied, "the Three Rocks investment seems to have worked out okay. You are up two-hundred million in less than six months, on paper at least. Jagat and I will start on it today. What's your time frame?"

"Let's connect next Wednesday and see where you are. I have a Three Rocks Board meeting on Monday, and discussions in Boston may influence my thinking. Talk to you then."

He clicked off his phone and was about to go inside when a notification popped up on the phone—a news article directed his way from a set of filters he put in place two days ago. The article was from a somewhat obscure medical site, which specialized in monitoring world health news and teasing out significant trends in their early stages of development. This one looked interesting, so he leaned back in his chair and pulled up the article.

New Hemorrhagic Fever Variant Detected in Cameroon

Medical workers in Northwestern Cameroon, along the Nigerian border, recently reported a local outbreak of hemorrhagic fever. Dr. Nigel Oso from the World Health Organization said preliminary laboratory analysis indicates the strain is a new Ebola virus variant.

The data is sparse, but medical workers on the ground believe the new variant is transmissible through respiratory droplets. If true, this development is alarming since past Ebola outbreaks have relied on transmission via contact with body fluids.

Adding to Dr. Oso's worries are reports that the virus is actively transmitted for up to two weeks before significant symptoms develop. This long period of asymptomatic transmission complicates both containment efforts and contact-tracing.

No statistics are yet available on infection and mortality rates. However, during past outbreaks of Ebola virus disease, mortality rates have averaged 50% but ranged as high as 90% in some outbreaks.

There are currently no known cases outside of a cluster of northwestern Cameroon States on the Nigerian border. Nigerian officials are actively monitoring the border cities and report no cases in Lagos, the country's largest city with a population of nine million people.

Mat thought about the numbers. If transmissibility is high through the respiratory vector, and each person contacting the virus infects three new people each day, then roughly 5 million will be infected before anyone becomes symptomatic. If each person infected four new people each day, then the number of infections in the first fourteen days rises to over 250 million. Exponential spread is a bitch.

While Mat sat in the warm Texas sun fretting over the news, Denjay was asleep in Lagos, tossing and turning from a bad night sweat. In two more days, thirty-two executives from twenty different countries would return home from the Energy Finance meeting. All of them sat at the VIP tables for Monday's lunch, and all had been served by Denjay.

Boston (Mat)

My flight into Boston for the Three Rocks Board meeting was uneventful. The original plan had included a nonstop flight on American Airlines, but Marcelle contacted me two days before departure and advised against the public travel. She had followed up on the break-in at Jenara's office, and the news wasn't good. After tracing the intrusion back to Donald Faillen, she continued digging. She uncovered reservations made for one of his people on the same flight I had originally booked. Suspiciously, the flight was booked the day after my original trip was arranged. I had her send a crew to Jennifer's office, where they uncovered some fairly sophisticated malware designed to passively monitor Jennifer's computers. For the time being, the software remained in place. Marcelle temporarily took over my travel plans and put me on a private jet there and back. Jennifer used her compromised system to keep up a false narrative about my trip.

The Board meeting was scheduled at the Boston Harbor Hotel, and the working assumption was that Faillen's people also knew my room reservations. So, Marcelle's team booked me into a second room under her company's name, and Jennifer kept my original room reservations open. At my request, they contacted Eva to provide security services in Boston. She was booked on the American Airlines flight I originally intended to take. No one would realize I was not taking that flight since my reservations remained open.

Eva was an old flame of mine from before I met Jenara. I met her via Mark, so her business was tied into the shadows. Even after an intimate relationship, I still only knew her as Eva, no last name. She topped out at 5 foot 8 inches and 140 pounds. For all practical purposes, she was the perfect combination of muscle, brains, and street smarts. Add in good looks and the ability to read people, and she was perfect for her job. But that job was hard to precisely describe since she worked as a bodyguard, private security consultant, freelance "problem solver," and several other odd jobs. Eva was good at all of her jobs and charged a base fee of $8000 per day. She also had a good reputation and found herself turning away jobs or sending them on to other colleagues for a finder's fee cut. She had recently helped me during the retrieval of the crystal matrix memory spheres, and I was glad when she accepted the current job.

The new travel arrangements put me in Boston a day earlier than originally expected, so I arranged to visit the Three Rocks Lab and have a conversation with the lead researcher working to decipher the stored data on one of these spheres. Carl Jennings, the CEO, made the arrangements. I arrived early Saturday morning and had my driver deliver me to the main offices. Security was waiting for me at the front door and escorted me up to the sixteenth floor, where Dan Rohden kept his lab.

We exited the elevator onto a plush, deep-red carpet with elaborate gold and blue geometric designs woven into the borders. A single door was to our left, the only exit point from the elevator foyer. Despite checkpoints on the ground floor and my security escort, another permanent security station was at the end of the short hallway. One guard sat behind a desk just to the left of the door, and another one stood about six feet away on the opposite side of the door. Two scanning devices occupied the right-hand side of the desk, forcing a visitor to turn his back on the second guard when verifying his or her identity. The guard at the desk took a palm print reading from my right hand and then had me look into a state-of-the-art retinal scanner. I remembered providing both palm and retinal records when I had joined the Board of Directors. Both guards were wearing suits, and slight bulges beneath their jackets indicated they were armed. I was caught slightly off balance by the heavy security but realized, upon reflection, why the tasks being undertaken on the sixteenth floor required absolute security.

Once I was registered and ushered through the door, Dan and Jack were waiting on the other side. Jack was the head of Technology for Three Rocks, and Dan was the lead researcher for decrypting the data stores I was interested in.

"Jack, good to see you again," I said, reaching out my hand, "and this time, it's not the middle of the night."

He smiled and gave me a warm and vigorous handshake. "It's great to see you again, Mat. I'm so glad you could take time from your schedule to visit before the board meeting. This is Dan," he said, gesturing to a thin but fit-looking young man with shoulder-length brown hair neatly tied back in a ponytail. "I believe you two have already spoken on the phone before."

"We have," I replied as I turned to Dan and shook his hand. "It's a pleasure to meet you in person."

"The pleasure is mine, Mr. Dover."

"Please, call me Mat. I work with grad students and professors all over the country, and none of them call me Mr. Dover after the first meeting."

He smiled and nodded, "Will do."

Jack motioned us down the hall towards the south side of the building. "You're limping a bit, Mat. I hope you haven't injured yourself."

"Just an unfortunate accident during an uneventful trip to Brazil a week or two ago. But the leg is healing nicely. It just takes a bit longer than when I was a young man like Dan."

Dan flashed a smile before commenting. "Two years ago, I spent several months limping around after a skiing accident. So, it's not all peaches and roses for us younger guys either."

We passed by several sets of glass-walled lab spaces before getting to a door mounted in a wall of frosty glass. I assumed it was smart glass using electro-chromatic technology to control opacity. A good method of altering visibility as needed. On the other side of the door was a single workspace occupying the entire south side of the sixteenth floor.

"Is this where the magic takes place?" I asked. There were various machines scattered across the lab, some of which I recognized, but most I didn't. Of course, crystal lattice memory storage was not really my thing.

I turned to Dan. "So Jack tells me you are a whiz at linear algebra, among other things. Educate me on how that relates to deciphering information on the crystal sphere."

Dan collected his thoughts for a moment before speaking. "When Jack first looked at the data storage, he could see that some of the data was stored in binary code, but four of the eight quadrants were holding information he suspected was related to quantum computing output. Now, linear algebra is a vital connection because it is basically the language of quantum computing. Combining linear algebra with probability theory lets us model and predict what a quantum computer will do in response to a set of instructions. Linear algebra is also used in cryptography because it allows the simultaneous manipulation of multiple variables to create unique and reversible output."

My face must not have lit up with understanding because he continued. "What we have encoded on the crystal sphere is either raw code or output. Understanding it requires we first deconstruct the information to find its original intent. The good news is we are making progress. I'm convinced that the first quadrant we are currently working on is devoted to genetics or genetic sequencing."

"Do you mean DNA-related analysis?" I asked.

There was a long pause before Dan answered. "Perhaps, but if I had to place my bets, it's more about RNA than DNA. If my analysis from last week is correct, then I believe we are beginning to recognize the basic chemical symbols for various nucleotides. A lot of the data strings contain a reference to what I believe is a $C_4H_6N_2O_2$ component. If I am right, and that's still a big if, this is a reference to Uracil. The significance is, DNA had a thymine nucleotide, but uracil replaces thymine in the RNA code. So, we may be dealing with a trove of information on RNA."

His comments piqued my interest. "Dan, I'm sure you have seen the animated message Jack pulled off the sphere." He nodded his head, affirming my statement. "You know that whoever these beings were, their civilization developed advanced medical technology after a plague wiped out seventy percent of their population. I am hoping there is information stored in the crystal lattice memory about this technology."

"I'm onboard, Mat, and that is the angle I am pursuing. I am sticking my head way out with what I'm about to say, but this is my hunch based on what I currently know. Viruses are primarily genetic material wrapped into a protein shell. Their genetic material is primarily RNA, but some rare viruses also use DNA. Viruses infect us to use our cellular machinery for reproduction. The issue is they need our DNA for replication."

"Now, our body's immune system tries to defend us in several ways. It can produce antibodies, which are essentially protein markers that attach to the virus shell on the spike protein and identify it as an intruder. Once marked with the antibody, the immune system will attack and kill the virus before it enters a cell. Once a virus is inside a cell, the body can also produce a hormone called interferon that stops the virus from replicating and identifies the cell for destruction."

"Imagine now a third way to defeat a virus; I call it a Trojan-Interceptor defense. Suppose I could engineer DNA with the single primary function of virus replication. So, when a virus enters a cell by injecting its genetic payload, the Interceptor DNA interacts with the viral RNA to replicate and reproduce. But in the process of replication, the virus's shell is infused with a universal antibody protein. So the new virus has an antibody built into its spike protein. This process effectively intercepts the virus, and each replicated particle is like a trojan horse with a hidden component. When the cell bursts and the newly replicated virus particles enter the bloodstream, they are immediately devoured by the immune system. The virus can never get a foothold."

I held my hand up palm outward to pause him. "Firstly, I love hunches. We wouldn't be here even having this discussion if I hadn't followed my hunches last summer. But I do have a concern. Would the body be able to react fast enough to the initial flood of a new infection, marked or not, to keep the virus at bay? Also, how would you get the DNA into every possible cell the virus will target?"

"Questions I can't answer at this point," replied Dan. "But my guess is that messenger RNA technology is the starting point for developing a delivery mechanism to get the Trojan-Interceptor DNA into cells. Assuming what I suggest is doable, my two main concerns are: locating or developing the replicator DNA, and the possibility of permanent genetic modification."

I must have conveyed a questioning look because he continued.

"Mat, if my hunch is right, then the introduction of DNA to the cells means it may become incorporated with nucleic DNA." He let the thought hang in the air for a moment.

"A permanent alteration to the human genome," I remarked. "Alterations we pass on to our children—alterations that may destroy viruses both good and bad. We would be artificially changing the human genetic makeup, for better or worse."

Dan simply nodded. My head was spinning with the ramifications of what Dan had proposed. I made a mental note to push Kristen on finding mRNA investment options.

Eva

Eva departed Dallas-Fort Worth at 2:55 pm Sunday on an American Airlines flight directly to Boston. She had an aisle seat at the rear of the first-class section, with a clear view of all passengers entering the plane. Her location on the port side of the cabin was three rows behind Mat's original window seat and next to the aisle. If she were trailing Mat, her pick of seats would have been the starboard aisle seat in the first-class cabin's rear row. This position allowed for observation during the flight and immediate access to trailing him upon deboarding.

Eva was wearing a padded outfit that made her look overweight, and she sported long black hair from a wig. Her nose profile was slightly altered with makeup putty, and her cheeks puffed out a bit due to inserts. Overall, she looked like a plain, overweight, unfit woman in her late forties. She was one of the first to board, and she pulled out a glamour magazine once seated so she could read and casually observe the passengers. Arrangements had been previously made for Mat's seat to be left empty even if there was a waiting list.

During the boarding, she scanned every passenger entering the plane. Two men occupied the window and aisle seats to her right, and through her peripheral vision, she got the impression they were familiar with each other. The aisle man was obviously observing passengers as they boarded, and he kept casting glances at Mat's empty seat. He conversed with the window guy several times, but she couldn't hear the conversation. Once the cabin door closed, and it was clear Mat was not on the flight, window-man sent out a series of text messages.

Certainty was rare in Eva's world, but her instincts told her the starboard-side passengers were her targets. There was only one other person, seated on the starboard aisle three rows back in economy, who raised her suspicions. She was a Hispanic woman in her early thirties—fit and muscular with a military bearing. Her jet-black hair was neatly tied back into a tight bun, and she wore an outfit that caused the men across the aisle from Eva to both look over their shoulders as she passed. There was no sign of familiarity in their eyes, only a biological longing.

The three-hour and forty-five-minute trip to Boston passed quickly, and as the plane landed, Eva ran through her deboarding plan. Once the seat belt sign was off, Eva timed herself to rise and step into the aisle at the same time as the man to her right. She overreached her right foot into the aisle and gave an extra push with her left hand on the seat arm-rest. The momentum of this move let her body-check the other guy and throw him slightly off balance. She grabbed his jacket sleeve with her right hand to steady him, and as she started apologizing, her left hand slipped a minute tracking device into his jacket pocket. She did not forget about the possible huntress behind her and used her body to block the view of her left hand.

Her target was slightly annoyed but simply mumbled, "Don't worry about it." Eva sat back down once she retrieved her carry-on and rummaged through her oversized pocketbook, eventually producing a phone. She popped in some earbuds and started an imaginary conversation in low tones. She also activated an app, which turned on her phone's front camera into movie mode but left her home screen on display. She let the two targets depart and angled the camera to catch a movie of the huntress exiting the plane. Eva packed her phone back in the pocketbook and dragged her rolling carry-on behind her as she followed five passengers behind the huntress. Her tracker would let her know if the targets traveled to Mat's hotel, but for now, she wanted to quell her suspicions about the woman. She trailed her to the arrivals exit and watched from inside as her targets procured a cab and the huntress slipped into the next cab in line.

Eva made her way to the public restroom and locked herself into a handicapped booth where she took off her fat outfit, removed a new set of clothes from the carry-on, and then stuffed the discarded outfit back into the small suitcase along with her wig and pieces of makeup putty. She exited the stall wearing a pair of tight black slacks and a turquoise blue, long-sleeved blouse under a black satin vest. Her natural auburn hair flowed out from below a black fedora. After several minutes of redoing her makeup, Eva returned to arrivals and caught a bus to the car rental lot, where she picked up a maroon, full-sized SUV.

She pulled into the Boston Harbor Hotel about an hour after picking up the car and turned it over to the valet. The drive from the airport was only about fifteen minutes, but she stopped at the Wynn Collection shop in the Encore Boston Harbor Resort Hotel to pick up some clothing and dispose of her carry-on in a dumpster nearby. At the check-in desk, she presented her credentials as Janet

Franklin and picked up a card key to a room down the hall from Mat's original reservation. She saw no sign of her targets or the huntress.

She received the call, as expected, about twenty minutes later and went down to the lobby to pick up a suitcase from a specialized delivery service. She inspected it briefly in her room to ensure everything was in order and then headed down to the bar. She wasn't surprised to see her targets sitting together having a beer. The tracker had told her at least one of them was at the hotel.

The Rowes Wharf Bar had a dark, seductive atmosphere with red cherry wood paneling and discrete seating. Eva slipped in, unseen by the targets, and settled into a two-seat corner table where she could keep an eye on all the activity. She ordered a bottle of Oregon Arterberry Maresh Chardonnay. This particular wine was from the winery's Maresh Vinyard. It was an elegant wine she loved but often had a hard time securing.

The winery is just on the east side of Dundee in the Willamette Valley, off of Worden Hill Road. It is the fifth oldest vineyard in the state and has been passed down through several generations. She and Mat visited their Red Barn tasting room several times when she was seeing him, and Mat always kept some of this chardonnay on hand at his penthouse.

She sent a text to Mat instructing him to come down to the bar and make a brief appearance. She could see the targets move to high alert as Mat entered the bar and ordered an IPA. He found a table at the rear of the bar, pulled out a Three Rocks management report, and read through it for about half an hour while he sipped on the pint. He then packed up and left.

Eva observed the targets for a few more minutes and was about to depart when the huntress strolled through the door. Neither the huntress nor the targets paid any attention to her lurking in the shadows, so she settled back into her seat, wondering what would unfold. It quickly became obvious that the huntress and the targets were strangers, with the exception of them eying her ass as she boarded the plane. She passed by their table and took up a seat several tables down. Eva immediately knew one of them would take the bait, but she guessed wrong on which one. It turns out the one with the wedding ring made a move. His buddy gracefully exited from the bar and married-man walked over to introduce himself and sat down with the huntress. Eva sipped her chardonnay and wondered how this woman fit into the picture.

Eva's original plan had focused on a single man from Faillen's operation trailing Mat to Boston. Marcelle laid the groundwork by carefully feeding some misinformation to Faillen through Jennifer's computer. The misleading email implied Mat was taking samples of the golden seeds with him to Boston for delivery and testing at the Three Rocks Lab after the board meeting. So while Mat was at the Board meeting, the samples would be with his luggage in his room. The fact there were now two of Faillen's people on the job didn't bother her too much. But she didn't like having a third player involved. It complicated her plans. She pulled up the video from the plane, isolated the best picture of the woman, and sent it to Marcelle with a request for identification.

Eva was into her second glass of wine when the couple rose from their table and left the bar. She let them pass then followed at a distance. They were the only two getting on the elevator, so she could easily see their exit floor. Fortunately, married-man was the one with a tracker in his pocket. She waited for five minutes, then caught the elevator to their floor. With her locator in proximity mode, she had no trouble finding the room. Eva's best guess was the room belonged to the huntress since she would want to maintain control of the situation.

She could only think of two reasons for the huntress to be involved: observation or theft. Either someone was keeping tabs on Faillen, or they knew about his plans to steal the seeds and wanted this particular prize for themselves. Eva thought about how she would approach the job if she was the huntress. One way would be to let the two men secure the golden seeds from Mat's room and then take the product from them. But there were a number of ways that plan could go wrong. The cleanest way would be to take the two men out of action, then break into Mat's room and take the product for herself.

She returned to her room and texted Mat, telling him to stay clear of his original room and spend the entire Monday at the Board meeting, with no wandering around the hotel. She then opened her package from the delivery earlier in the evening. She broke down the pistol, reassembled it, inspected the ammo, and pushed the magazine clip into place. She then did the same for the second weapon.

On Monday morning the Board meeting started at nine, but Eva let herself into Mat's decoy room at seven and rearranged it to her satisfaction, including a hotel wheelchair she secured from their supply room. At nine-thirty Eva could hear the slight scraping sound of the door lock being forced. The room was large and accommodated her rearrangement, so she was positioned just outside the peripheral vision of someone passing from the small entranceway into the main room. She was dressed in black with a balaclava covering her face.

The huntress was good, though, and she was in the process of turning towards Eva and drawing her weapon when the first dart hit her in the neck. She kept turning, clawing at the dart with her left hand and pulling out a pistol with her right. But she froze and dropped her weapon as Eva came into sight. Eva was still sitting in a plush leather chair. Her right hand held the dart gun, elbow on the chair arm and the gun pointed up at the ceiling. Her left hand held a Glock 19 leveled directly at the huntress. They both silently stared at each other until the huntress dropped to the ground unconscious.

The sedative was designed to keep her unconscious for at least an hour, but Eva always needed a plan B, so she zip-tied the woman's wrist and ankles, gagged her, and left her lying on her right side. There was no identification, but she did recover a room key. She tidied up the room, retrieved her dart, and placed the woman's weapon in a bedside drawer.

Her next stop was the huntress's room. She donned a blond wig, a baggy coat, and applied some strategic makeup before heading down to the next floor. The room had a "Do Not Disturb" sign hanging on the handle. Eva paused, put on a pair of oversized sunglasses, and entered the room with her Glock drawn. But it turned out her efforts were overkill.

The two original targets squirmed a bit, but they were both tied to chairs, gagged and blindfolded. Eva had only heard the huntress speak once when she stopped by the bar last evening to order a drink before sitting at her table. Her accent had been neutral, but her voice was lower than Eva's. Eva pitched her tone as best she could and said, "I'm pleased to see you boys are still here." One of them grunted a bit, and she could see a nasty bruise on his left cheek.

She pulled a table in front of the two men and placed a vial halfway filled with golden seeds in the middle of the table. Her wig and glasses were removed and stored in her baggy jacket's inner pocket, and she slipped the balaclava back over her head. She stood behind the two men and removed the blindfold from married-man, reminding him to keep his eyes front and center.

"I believe this is what you are looking for," she said as the man's eyes adjusted to the light.

"Fresh from Brazil, the jungle remedy Mr. Faillen is searching for. You were so close," she continued. "Unfortunately for you, and fortunately for me, I will be leaving presently with the prize. But I'm a reasonable person, and if Mr. Faillen wants these medicinal seeds, I'm sure we can reach some sort of financial arrangement. Tell him Jackie will be in touch soon."

She put the blindfold back on married-man and said, "I will be back in five minutes and get you out of this mess you're in. Stay put, gentlemen." She removed the balaclava and put the wig and glasses back on.

Back in Mat's room, the huntress was starting to show some early signs of coming back to consciousness, so Eva gave her another shot of sedative. She cut the zips, removed the gag, and hefted her into the wheelchair. She also returned the woman's pistol to its holster. With one last check of the room, she pushed the chair into the hallway, leaving it in front of the room two doors down.

She returned to the huntress' room and removed the "Do Not Disturb" sign from the door handle. The boys were sitting and fidgeting in their chairs just as she had left them. Eva said nothing to them but simply placed a call to housekeeping, requesting an immediate cleaning of the room. The next call was to the front desk complaining about a woman carrying a weapon and sitting in a wheelchair outside of room 305.

With the calls complete, Eva removed the wig, glasses, and baggy jacket, placing them all in a small roller suitcase, and headed out to the elevator and down to the lobby. As she checked out under Janet Franklin's name, she heard the lobby day manager mention to one of the desk clerks that the security cameras had been sorted and just returned to live feed. Two police cars pulled up as she handed her ticket to the valet. She gave them a nod and a smile. While waiting for the car, she texted Mat, "Cleanup finished. Depart as soon as possible. Let Michelle know if you require additional security."

Gangue de Motocicletas Treze

Mark and Tom rode the elevator down shortly after Joe. They said good morning to Tommy, who was sitting behind the main lobby reception and security desk. He had his clock cleaned by some bad guys not too long ago but seemed to have recovered nicely.

"How are you, Tommy?" Mark asked.

"I'm excellent Mr. Mark. Thanks for asking, and you?"

"Excellent as well."

"And I hope you are enjoying your vacation here in the States, Mr. Tom."

"Having a splendid time if I do say so. Wonderful place you have here!"

"You look like you've bulked up a bit Tommy. Looking good, my friend."

Mark knew that Sirocco had helped oversee Tommy's recovery from the vicious attack on him a few months ago. The attackers had paid dearly for the transgression. She also provided Tommy prepaid and unlimited access to her trainer. Itsuki Hiroto was almost mystical in his abilities. He was a master of the mind as well as the body. His training included nutrition, aerobics, light weights, several different far eastern self-defense arts, and some simple but effective ways to permanently disable opponents in the wink of an eye.

"Thank you, sir. I used to think I was pretty good until I found out I was not good enough. Now, under the tutelage of Master Hiroto, I have more confidence in my abilities to watch over Ms. Sirocco and her friends. I hope you and Mr. Tom enjoy your time with the new beast." Tommy surmised that was their current mission.

"I'll be happy to give you a tour when you're free from your current duties." With that, Mark and Tom headed to the interior overhang where the rig was

126

parked. Mud was the first thing they noticed. Mud on the wheels. Mud on the doors. Mud on the windscreen. Probably mud on the roof. The cable on the forward winch was overlapped rather than smoothly respooled. The rear one was the same. Tug on overlapped cable, and you lose as much as 50% of its strength.

So, the Ouachita River crossing was probably not the first. Oh, to have seen where they had to back out of. A fairly large limb of what appeared to be mesquite dangled over the side from the roof rack. So they had been west before they headed east. There was an impressive dent just in front of the right rear wheel assembly. All of this was taken in during a brief walkaround.

"Looks like the boys enjoyed their time in the outback!" Tom chuckled and grinned at Mark.

"From what we saw from the satellite, this big buck will take just about whatever you toss at it."

"Good to know, eh?" Mark grimaced but realized he had put his old Land Cruiser through much of the same many times. That was why he needed a new ride in the first place. Undoubtedly, he would do even more with this new beast once things settled down here in Dallas. Alaska came to mind.

"Think I'll ring up Lefty and have him give the rig a look-see. Make sure nothing in the undercarriage is dinged or broken. You up for a road trip?" Mark asked.

"Give me a few minutes to pack my kit and kiss my beautiful bride goodbye. Then we can be off!" Tom loved to trek off into the unknown. He had done so across much of Western Australia. Conditions there were much harsher and forbidding than a short jaunt into New Mexico on the pavement—probably.

Lefty answered on the first ring and said come ahead.

There was a very loud rumble out on the street and then the unmistakable deepthroated revving of a big bike. It continued, evidently overstaying the green light. Mark and Tom walked out onto the sidewalk instead of using the side entrance that led back to Tommy's desk. There was a guy in black leathers and Harley-Davidson Darren boots sitting on what was probably an '83 Harley-Davidson XR-1000. His helmet was black, and the face shield was opaque. He looked at Tom and Mark as he revved his engine.

The hackles came up on both of their necks at the same time. Instinctively they both took several strides toward the biker. He revved again, dumped the clutch, and ran the red light. There was no early morning traffic, and the biker didn't really flee. He was just moving on, apparently.

"I think his colors read Treze. Sounds like an expensive Mexican restaurant. Ever find decent food at an expensive Mexican restaurant?" Mark looked at Tom.

"Not much experience on the subject, but I suspect they are mutually exclusive. It means thirteen, in Portuguese, if I'm correct. Interestingly, he seemed to have his eyes on you. No explaining his lack of good taste." Tom patted Mark on the back.

"Yea, and I noticed a 13 patch on his bicep. I suspect the ladies will have a perspective on the number thirteen."

"Undoubtedly. What say we head back upstairs and prepare for our big adventure out to Ghost Ranch. I look forward to seeing the famed red rock!" Tom said as they turned back to the building.

Before packing, they stopped by the laboratory where the ladies were working and asked if they had heard the motorcycle. Amber Lee stared at them for a moment before speaking. "Let's see, we are twenty-one floors above the street in a hermetically sealed laboratory. Nope, we didn't hear it."

"Someone has been working a little too hard," said Mark. Tom had the good sense to stay quite.

"Sorry," Amber Lee said. "We've been at it all night, and I think we are getting close to isolating some unusual genes in these plants." She put her head down and went back to work.

"We met a burly-looking lad on a big Harley, but he took off before we could introduce ourselves." Tom volunteered this before they went on to tell what they saw, including the Treze colors on the guy's back.

This cascaded into a discussion concerning the various pros and cons of the number 13 found in cultures all around the world. The depth and breadth of knowledge was not a surprise, and Tom and Mark seemed to enjoy the back and forth for the better part of five minutes. Then Mark looked at Tom, tilted his head and raised his left eyebrow. Tom gave him a thumbs-up, and they split to pack and get on the road. They could both be sure that the conversation would continue just fine in their absence.

Mark and Tom made their exit and headed down to the truck. Mark climbed into the driver's cockpit, and Tom took up the shotgun position. Mark brought the monster to life. A soft alarm started chirping almost immediately. Mark glanced at the dash and eased out from under the canopy and turned right. The phone rang, and Mark said, "answer call."

"Mark, John here. You have a bug on your rig."

"Yea, we noticed the pinging. Thoughts?"

"Good day Mr. Tom! The bug must have been planted overnight. I had no indication during Mr. Joe's excursion. I suggest you continue your trip to New Mexico and let me look into it."

"Will do. While you are doing that, please do the multitasking thing and look into a motorcycle gang going by the name Treze."

"I presume there is more here than a passing curiosity, sir?"

"Correct." Mark said and ended the call.

They eased past Hooter's and merged up onto I-35E, then took the State Route 114 exit and drove all the way to Seymore. SR 82 took them to Lubbock. From there, SR 84 took them through Texaco, and SR 60 took them to Fort Sumner. They took turns driving the somewhat scenic 600 miles just for the hell of it. Tom's keen eyes spotted the first small herd of pronghorn just before Muleshoe. Mark told Tom some of his stories from his West Texas days in the oil patch.

John had gotten back to them. The bug was a common tracking device available on the internet and in the big box stores. Due to the simplicity of the bug and its low cost, determining provenance was impossible. He could detect thousands of similar devices in and around Dallas. Wives checking on husbands, husbands checking on wives, and so it goes.

"As for the Treze I have more information than I have regarding the bug. I'll call them Thirteen for short since treze is thirteen in Portuguese. They are fairly new as motorcycle gangs go and are based in Houston, Texas."

"They are closely associated with Abtre's Motor Cycle Club. Abtre's MC is based in São Paulo and was formed in 1989. They, Thirteen, may also be loosely associated with the Outlaws. The Thirteen probably stands for the thirteenth letter of the alphabet, M. Possibly M stands for marijuana or meth. Most of these and similar gangs around the world have one thing in common—they deal in contraband, primarily drugs and guns. They also deal in protection to a lesser degree.

"I need to think now, but I'll call you later. When I do, I'd like to know about motorcycles and, in particular, Harley-Davidson motorcycles." Mark said end call.

"Tell me Tom, did the hackles come up on the back of your neck this morning when you saw the guy on the scooter?"

"Absolutely. That's why I tried to get my hands on him—so I could crush his windpipe. I always trust my instincts, and he was evil. How about you?"

"Same."

"I've seen some of the work of the Bandidos, Vargos, and, of course, the Hells Angels back home. I'm not a big fan."

"So, we're tagged. Believing in coincidence is a losing hand, so I assume the biker or a friend of his tagged us. If these guys are Brazilian like John suspects, then there is probably a direct link to Carlos Mattes. We definitely have reason to believe Mr. Mattes is pissed. Further, I now suspect he has made the mathematical leap of 1+1=me. If so, we'll probably hit a bump or two in the road up ahead. I think we should head back to Dallas so I can let you out of this."

"You've lost your feeble mind my friend! The chances of me missing out on seeing the Sangre de Cristo, Jemez, and Sandia Mountains because of some joey on a fucking motorbike are zero. Drive on driver!"

Mark pulled off SR 60 just after they crossed the Pecos River past Fort Sumner. The river looked fairly clear, so he took a right on a dirt track that led to the river about half a mile north, and just below, the Fort Sumner Railroad Bridge.

"Wanna catch a fish or two?" Mark tried not to pass up a chance to fish the small streams and rivers along the way. Besides, there was no hurry.

"First and biggest of each species a hundred American apiece? What am I going to catch by the way?" Tom also loved to fish. Betting made it even better.

"Probably bass and bream."

They climbed out, down, and back up into the living area through the rear doors. Mark opened a storage drawer. Inside was an array of ultralight spinning rod/reel combos and multi-piece fly rod/reel combos. Several plastic pocket-sized compartmented boxes full of lures were there as well.

"Looks like we can both be outfitted the same. If so, that will make it even easier for me to take your money." Tom was twelve years old again and the competition was on.

"Let's use Zebco 33 Gold Micro closed-face reels strapped to the 4'10" two-piece Eagle Claw Feather Light rods. They are filled with 4lb-test mono. I'm tying on a #0 gold bucktail Mepp. Take this pocket tackle box. There is a micro multitool in there with pliers."

"Bet you a hundred I beat you on the first cast!" Tom hobbled toward the river with Mark hobbling right behind him. Two teenagers laughing at the wind. Again.

Tom won the first hundred with his successful cast. His Mepp landed in two inches of water one foot beyond the water's edge at the end of a thirty-yard toss on the run. They fished, caught, and released a handful of largemouth bass and small bream for the next hour or so. They were even on the money. Tom wanted a beer, so they walked back to the truck. On the way, they heard motorcycles off in the distance. The sounds came from town and then they watched six very loud bikes cross the bridge and continue westward around the bend on SR 60. The obnoxious sound faded.

"You reckon that was our welcoming party?" Mark grinned at Tom.

"Probably." Tom suggested they let Lefty know he may need a vacation. It wasn't a closely held secret that Lefty had upfitted the Land Cruiser. The provenance of the new rig was no big secret either. There was no reason for it. Their destination was pretty obvious.

"Someone else must be watching our progress besides those guys. They'll probably get a call sooner rather than later. It may not make a difference since they probably know our destination anyway.

Mark rang up Lefty to let him know about potential company. Lefty said cool, but he was tied up and they would talk later.

Mark rang up John and gave him the latest. John suggested it was time to dispose of the bug and to reroute themselves up to Lefty's. He said he would try to find a satellite and locate the bikers. They found the bug up in the front right wheel well. Mark drove into town and pulled into the dirt parking beside Sadie's Frontier restaurant. They had called ahead for food.

Tom bent down to re-lace his boot and stuck the magnetized bug under the license plate on the back of a cattle trailer full of cattle hooked to a white Freightliner. Mark went in and paid for the sack of food. Green Chili Cheeseburgers deluxe, Burrito Supremes, onion rings, and large fries to split. Total damage $38.80 plus tax. The boys were hungry from all the fishin'. Townes van Zandt was pickin' and singin' White Freightliner Blues back on the old jukebox. How apropos. Outside again, Mark nodded at Tom, and they climbed back into the rig. They rerouted themselves by taking SR 84 north to Santa Rosa.

Mark said to the dashboard to call John. It did, and John answered on the first ring.

"How may I help you, Mark?"

Mark said, "motorcycles."

"I have information concerning motorcycles, and in particular Harley-Davidsons. I'll keep it simple sir." Right out of the chute, the computer was talking down to Mark. Mark let it slide because he had a feeling he would get to crush something soon. "Gottlieb Daimler patented the first motorcycle in Germany in 1885. The first U.S. motorcycle was the Orient-Aster, built by Charles Metz in Waltham, Massachusetts in 1898."

"Harley-Davidson was founded in 1903 in Milwaukee, Wisconsin. It is generally accepted that the first outlaw group was formed in a Chicago bar around 1935. Probably called themselves the Outlaws. Around 1948 the Hells Angels formed in San Bernardino, California. After the end of WWII and into the '60's the biker organizations grew significantly due to the massive number of former military folks that felt left behind or otherwise wanted the comradery of fellow vets. Many if not all of these former soldiers were fervent patriots, and buying American was an absolute."

"Harley-Davidson motorcycles were American-made and relatively inexpensive. Even more enticing was the fact that the Army sold a huge number of surplus Harleys at the end of WWII. The surplus bikes were often outfitted with mounts for radios and scabbards for M-1 carbine rifles. Buyers would chop off these add-ons. Such bikes eventually became known as choppers. One last thing. Bikers in gangs are often thought of as the one-percenters. That is to say that they make up about one percent of all of the people that own motorcycles. I hope this fills in some blanks in your knowledge base sir. Questions gentlemen?"

They said no, but thanks, and Mark said end call. Tom was a sponge for information and thrived on learning. Both he and Mark agreed they had learned several things from John. They also agreed that the information would be useful in a bar discussion but would probably not add to the overall betterment of their current circumstances.

Later, Mark's phone rang through the dashboard. He answered and Lefty said, hey. They bullshitted a minute then Lefty cut to the chase. He would hear from friends and family if bikers came through Española.

"Do you want these guys taken out if they show up?" Lefty asked.

"Let's see what comes up. I'll let you know. See you soon." Mark said end call.

"Bloke was pretty casual about offing bad guys. I like him already." Tom grinned.

Mark pulled into a one-off truck stop in Santa Rosa at the I-40 interchange. He ran the rig through the truck wash, paying $20 extra for the undercarriage wash. Lefty would have an easier time seeing if Joe and Hunter had caused any damage that required fixing. They took I-40 west, then hung a right at Clines Corners on SR 285, caught I-25 into Santa Fe, then SR-84 through Española and up to Abiquiu.

John rang back and Mark said, "answer call." John still had no luck locating the bikers. None of the big comms companies planted satellites over the desert. Neither did any of the various government agencies. There were no double-naught spy birds available.

Lefty's family owned a large swath of land on the northern side and in the middle reaches of Abiquiu Reservoir near the now sunken Arroyo del Chamiso. They were above the dam about two miles. His extended family occupied the twenty or so homes on the expansive property. A variety of outbuildings were used for farming and ranch purposes and various other enterprises. Lefty lived near SR-84 in a 5,000 square ranch house. He liked greenery around the house, and it showed. He had several outbuildings for his automotive endeavors. The main one was at the end of the gravel road near the lake. He loved fishing as much as he loved his cars.

Lefty was the head of the family and was loved by all. The current ranch and surroundings had been occupied by his ancestors and current family longer than anyone remembered. The USCOE constructed the earthen dam on the Rio Chama in 1963, effectively drowning some of their ancestral lands. The upside was that most of what was submerged was nearly vertical. The reservoir provided ample water for the sparse human population, cattle, and goats, and for irrigation for miles around.

The hydroelectric energy derived from the water-turned turbines provided an overflow of electricity for the region. Thus the lake improved life for everyone. Even though the water level was down significantly due to the extended drought, undoubtedly caused by global warming, the water was still 150 feet deep about half a mile west of Lefty's ranch house.

Historically, almost all of the men in the family had served in one branch of service or another. More recently, the young women had followed suit. Most came back home, but some didn't. They were all very proud of their country and their heritage.

Mark drove the truck to the west end of the gravel road, where a large shop overlooked the lake. Lefty greeted them with elbow bumps; then he crawled under the truck. Lefty was not much on formalities and he was not one to waste much time palavering. He laughed as he tossed out pieces of small tree limbs he pulled from some of the hard-to-get-at places. He emerged from under the massive rig ten minutes later and said everything was sound. The steel guard plates protecting sensitive places worked just fine.

"The dings and dents remind me of you, my friend. She will take what you give her and more. I promise you. Now, I sincerely wish I could extend the hospitality of my home to you but, alas, my beautiful wife has developed something in the way of the flu. I do not want to take a chance that it could spread to you old guys." Lefty grinned. Lines from an old Spirit song nagged at the back of Mark's mind. "It's nature's way of telling you somethings wrong."

"I trust she will make a swift recovery and that you, my old friend, will take care of yourself." Mark started to climb into the driver's cockpit when they all heard rumbling in the distance—coming from the north on SR 84. Harleys. Never a doubt when biker gang Harleys are on the road. It sounds pretty cool, then a bit intimating, then a lot annoying.

"They took the long way around and are coming in from the north. That explains why I did not get a call." Lefty gazed toward the noise coming from the east and north as if trying to decide what bait to put on the hook. He certainly did not seem to be intimidated.

"Saddle up Tom. Thanks Lefty, I'll try to clear your gate before the assholes make it to your driveway."

"Stand down. Wait until they make it past the fork. Then you can drive to meet them. I'll signal you. Trust me on this." Lefty turned and walked away, pulling out his cell phone as he went into his shop.

"So. We saddle up and hold." Mark walked around to the back and opened the rear doors. They climbed up and in and closed and locked the doors behind them. Mark opened a sliding drawer, where a variety of handguns were available. He opened a vertical cabinet and showed Tom some long weapons. Tom settled for a Smith & Wesson M&P22LR semi-auto pistol with a 10-round clip. He pulled out two extra clips. Mark chose the same. They walked forward and climbed through the hatch into the rear of the crew cab and got situated in the cockpit.

They could see the dust and clearly hear the bikes as they changed direction from southbound on SR 84 to westbound on the main gravel road. Dust kicked up and their traverse was self-evident. They made the turn into Lefty's domain, slowing as they passed homes, and revving their engines as they moved at a leisurely pace toward the showdown. As expected, everyone was cowering inside their pitiful little hovels as the bikers eased by. They were obviously used to intimidating folks into submission. There was not a soul to be seen.

Lefty came walking back out of the shop. In his left hand, hanging by his side, was what looked like an S&W N-frame nickel .44 magnum six-shot revolver with a six-and one-half-inch barrel. He gave Mark the thumbs-up with his right hand.

Mark accelerated forward and settled in at 10 mph. He did not want to make too much dust as he passed the first homes. The bikes strategically stopped where two small buildings were close to the road on opposite sides. They spread across the road, effectively closing off the exit route. The truck could not pass. Nor could the truck retreat. Tom and Mark would get very wet trying to cross the lake.

Mark eased his rig to a stop, and he and Tom stared through their twin Ray Ban Aviators at the bikers. The bikers stared through the opaque visors suspended from their helmets. The guys dismounted and one of them walked to Tom's side of the truck. He climbed the running board and tapped on the side glass. Tom ignored the guy. Mark suggested that Tom answer the door. Tom laid his right forearm on the armrest and touched the control button. The window silently slid down. He reversed his hand so it was facing upward. The guy in the helmet stuck his right hand and arm through the open area and pointed a pistol at Mark.

"Get out slow and easy driver." The biker was a big guy. Tom figured 6'6", 250 lbs. Tom glanced over at Mark, then back at the guy. He grabbed the guy's wrist with his right hand and jerked it downward over the window ledge, snapping the guy's arm at the elbow. Simultaneously, he relieved the guy of his pistol with his left hand. The asshole was howling in Tom's ear. Tom looked at the pistol and handed it to Mark. Then he tugged the guy's arm down some more, making him howl even more.

"What kind of popgun is that?" Tom asked because inquiring minds want to know.

"It's a friggin' Walther PPK. And the slide cocker and the safety are engaged. So this guy points a gun at me that ain't going to go pow when he squeezes the trigger?" Mark adjusted the slide cocker, disengaged the safety, and then handed it back to Tom. "Does this asshole look like James Bond?" Mark asked.

"Nope. And you never heard Mr. Bond scream like a little child either." The guy was howling as Tom wrenched the arm further down the inside of the door frame. "Noisy and he needs to brush his teeth."

"The racket is getting on my nerves. Can you please adjust the volume?" Mark was done with the guy.

"Gladly." Tom twisted the guy's arm about 360 degrees, and Mark heard it pop as the biker passed out and dropped onto the gravel. Mark floored the accelerator and the rig kicked up dust as it pushed forward toward the bikers and the bikes.

"These assholes brought scooters to a monster truck event?" Tom grinned as the bikers dove to either side of the road. Mark drove directly over four of the bikes like they were speed bumps in a parking lot. Bullets pinged off the side of the rig as the bikers recovered some of their pride. Mark stopped and started to back up so he could get the other two. The phone rang and he said, "answer call."

"Well done. Keep going my friend! We will clean up the mess. What goes to the bottom of the lake stays at the bottom of the lake. Cheers!" Lefty was in a good mood. But it seemed Lefty was always in a good mood. Hopefully, his beautiful bride would conquer the flu.

Mark accelerated smoothly this time and maintained 15 mph. Men and women stood on either side of the road in front of their homes. There were the young and there were the old, all armed to the teeth, cordially waving as he drove the rest of the way out of the compound.

"Call John." Mark said. John answered on the first ring.

"I hope all is well with you!" John was back to doing the Aussie thing. Mark did not care. He had run over some asshole's scooters and was a happy camper.

"Excellent now that we had the chance to crush something. Send Lefty a black card, same as cash, one million on it for now. Monitor it. If there are medical expenses, up it as need be." Mark said, "end call." Tom commented on a well-done job, and they turned left on SR 84. Up ahead the sign said the Ghost Ranch Agape Center was closed due to contagion.

Tom wanted to do some stump jumping, so they took a left on Forest Road 151 and followed the Rio Chama upstream. They fished several spots along the way. They stopped and admired the Monastery of Christ in the Desert. Just up the road, they bought a case of Monk's Ale and a case of Monk's Dark Ale from Abbey Brewing Company. Seasonal selections were unavailable.

The gentleman rang them up and noticed their rig through the window. The three of them went outside and Mark gave the guy the nickel tour. Tom mentioned his desire to see what the off-road capabilities were. The young man obliged by giving them the verbal nickel tour of the mesa to the north.

"See that trail just up the road on the right. Follow it up and to the left all the way to the top. Make sure to stay left, so you make it up all the way up the canyon. Don't want you rolling down the hill because you tried the vertical approach! You will be traveling essentially due north. Once you are on top of the mesa, just pick your way around. FR 145 can be accessed to the east and to the northeast when you decide to quit rock hoppin'. Careful when you head over to FR 145. You can drive right off the mesa and land on your nose a hundred feet below. There are several canyons cutting down the other side. I recommend you check them out on foot first. Things sometimes change due to gravity and the rare downpour. Sure wish I could join you gents but work calls. Cheers!"

Tom and Mark climbed back into the rig and headed up the trail as directed by the young man at the Abbey Brewing Company. Trail was an overstatement from the outset and it diminished quickly into 'between those boulders looks good.' They climbed upward along a dry wash. That seemed to be the best bet. The rig's high clearance and underbody plating allowed Mark to maneuver without having to worry about leaving the oil pan hanging off of a rock.

The steepness and ruggedness of the terrain was not for the faint of heart. Mark and Tom paid that aspect of the adventure no mind. They were both lifelong off-the-road drivers, and this was just the latest few lines in the current chapter in their book of life.

"My mind was on the bikers when we came up the mountain. I wonder if we've seen the last of them." Tom mused.

"I doubt it. If Carlos Mattes is behind this, then we can expect to see reinforcements. Obviously, they know where Sirocco lives. So we'll need to be vigilant. I suspect we have a few days before other members of the gang figure it out." Mark replied.

"Presumably, they will be of a higher caliber than buzzard breath back there. A fucking Walther PPK. You know what? I'll bet it was stolen from a collector. Certainly a piece to have in the collection. So you can say here is my Bond James Bond gun. Certainly not the piece to point at someone. Too damn complicated!" Tom obviously was not a fan.

"I failed to appreciate the stunning vistas and amazing color of the rocks I find myself amongst. Are you familiar with this area?" Tom, like Mark, was an avid fan of the -ologies. Way back when, Mat had once described his undergraduate studies as an orgy of the -ologies. Avid fans of the -ologies suited the entire bunch, including everyone back in Dallas.

"I am, generally speaking, familiar with the area. It happens to be one of my favorite parts of the country. Definitely one of the most stark and beautiful areas I have ever had the pleasure of traipsing through. The elevation of Abiquiu Reservoir is about 6,400 feet. We climbed maybe 100 feet or so, fishing upriver to the Brewery. We probably have another 1200-1500 feet to go to the top of the mesa."

"Along the river we were in the 215-million-year-old Triassic rock known as the Chinle Group. Probably more famous in Arizona, where it is exposed and known as the Petrified Forest. It is the quite distinctive red-maroon-green silt and mudstone we just left down the hill. We could bang around a bit with a rock hammer and perhaps come up with some bits and pieces of Coelophysis. This guy was a small carnivore dinosaur, and it is also the State fossil. Phytosaurs, 20-foot crocodile-like critters, also abounded during that time around here."

"That would have fit in well with the monster Krystyna' Krys' Pawlowski shot on the McCarther Bank in the Norman River, Queensland, back in 1957. It was 8.6-meters long, weighing in at perhaps a ton and a half. A massive beast even in the eyes of my old mate Croc!" Tom grinned, thinking about Croc meeting up with a Phytosaur.

Mark brought the rig to a halt after another half-hour of bouncing up the erosion feature. One last ledge to clear, a scraping sound, and a few minutes later, they were at the top of the mesa. They climbed down from the rig, grabbed two of the newly acquired beverages from the small fridge, and walked a bit.

"I want to go see that last bump. Sounded like we lost something. Hope it wasn't important." Mark grinned. AAA was not going to make a house call up here.

They side-stepped big sagebrush, rabbit bush, and broom snakeweed, making their way the hundred yards back downhill. The sky was brilliant blue, the air was dry, cool and carried the scent of the piñon and stunted juniper trees dotting their surroundings. A jackrabbit burst up from under a patch of brush and skedaddled across the way to the right. Tom swung up his left hand and pointed an imaginary pistol toward the rapidly escaping hare before it vanished from sight.

"At eight pounds and two feet long, the Lepus townsendii can push upwards of 40 mph. That is hauling ass for a waskilly wabbit!" Mark tried for Elmer Fudd but missed it by a bit. Same as Tom missed with his finger bullet.

"About the same speed as a red roo!" Tom was seeing a place in the outback in his mind.

"How big are red roos?" Mark didn't have much time for extracurricular activities during his visit to southwest Australia a few months back. Too busy recycling and such.

"A meter and a half and 80 kilos or so. Years ago, Croc and I were sharing a pint or three driving down a dirt track when we happened on a mob, with a few boomers and more jills. Croc got out of the Rover and decided to try to run them down on foot. A huge old boomer turned around and got in Croc's face. Croc punched the roo square on the jaw. The red seemed surprised for a moment. Then it reared back on its enormous tail and kicked Croc airborne all the way across the road. I pissed myself laughing! To this day, he will still wrestle a crocodile but is scared shitless of roos!" Tom chuckled at the memory.

They both laughed, tapped bottles together, and trekked a few more yards around yucca and cholla cactus to the large yellowish sandstone outcrop. On the lower face was a bent handlebar, a motorcycle handlebar.

"You did hear something. You lost your motorcycle handlebar!" Tom sat down on the rock and laughed until he was wiping tears from his cheeks. "I wonder if the guy is missing it?" More peals of laughter from both men. Acting like thirteen-year-olds. Again.

The light breeze was blowing Mark's gray locks across his shoulders. The faded blue bandana across his forehead and tied in the back kept the hair off of his Ray Bans and out of his eyes. Those steely, blue-gray timeless old eyes. Tom's close-cut grayness did not require the bandana. Tom was taller and broader, but otherwise they closely resembled brothers. And that is exactly what they were, brothers in arms.

"So start back down by the river where you can see that clump of cottonwoods. That is the Chinle Group. The Entrada Sandstone, 200 million years old or so, is a collection of fossil dunes. Next up is the Todilto Formation, Jurassic in age at 160 million years is that grayish layer. It consists of limestone and gypsum."

"Above that, the multi-color green, red, purple, and gray Jurassic Morrison and Summerville Formations reside. Coming in at 155-145 million years old, they are fossil-rich sand and siltstone. I have some excellent petrified wood and other plants from a few miles west of here. There are also fish, Allosaurus, and other dinosaurs represented. The yellowish cap, basically from here up to the truck, is Cretaceous 100-million-year-old Dakota Sandstone." Mark, the semi-scientist was done.

"Mat would probably have spent the better part of forever describing depositional environments; porosity and permeability; acre-feet of hydrocarbon; huge, shallow, inland seas; salinity; aeolian sand dunes; erosion; bio-diversity and the like." But Mark was done.

"Yea. This old hard rock geologist will leave all that to the oil and water guys. My specialty is smelling out gold and other valuables hidden at and below the surface." Tom was in agreement.

"Wonderful and beautiful and many other descriptive adjectives that escape me do not thoroughly describe this vista. And to think this is all youthful compared to the 3.5-billion-year-old stromatolites and such in my neck of the woods. Not to mention the crystals." Like all true outdoorsmen, Tom appreciated all that was around him. Mark retrieved the handlebar and together walked back up to the rig.

"If you grab a torch for me, I'll see if we have any other residual clutter from the speedbump." Mark did, and Tom crawled under the rig and inspected the undercarriage.

"Nothing else man-made lurking there in the dark. Just bits and pieces of the local foliage."

They set up camp as the sun dropped beyond the Navajo Nation. They built a fire using bits and pieces of dead juniper branches in a slight depression that had probably held a fire before. YETI Hondo Basecamp chairs, separated by a Coleman compact aluminum table, were set on the east side. Mark gutted and headed the handful of Brown and Rainbow Trout and one Rio Grande Cutthroat they caught below the Abbey. Two big Idaho potatoes were wrapped in foil and buried under the makings of the fire. They would be nicely done in an hour or so. The fish went into the fridge, out came some beers.

Mark scrounged up his old clay peace pipe, a relic from a cave in Wyoming dating back several thousand years. He tapped down some dirt weed he had picked up somewhere along the way. He ignited a Diamond Strike Anywhere Match with his fingernail and took a small hit from the pipe. Tom did the same.

The last vestiges of gold and magenta receded into the gray-blueness of night. Coyotes started yipping and a light breeze brought high desert night smells across the mesa. They were enjoying the world as others had done before them here and in the surrounding area. Mark talked about walking areas further to the west and finding hints of Clovis civilization dating back around 11,000 years ago to somewhat more recent Ancestral Puebloans, Mogollon, Comanche, and Utes, dating back several thousand years.

The third-quarter moon eased up the horizon. Stars, galaxies, and planets popped into view based on their apparent magnitude. Perseus, Aries, and Andromeda stood out, much as they had for many millennia.

"Fascinating. I can feel the presence of ancestral folks here. Same as I have in other wild places around the world but especially in certain grottos in the outback. Sometimes I have felt welcome, others I decided to move on from—just that sixth sense thing. I feel we are welcome here. There is a certain symmetry and harmony in the surroundings that I cannot explain." Tom waxed poetically. "Besides jackrabbits and that little roo over there, what else resides in the neighborhood?"

Marked laughed. "That little roo is a kangaroo rat. He's probably thinking dinner will be free tonight. From here north we may encounter cougars, black bear, pronghorn, deer, elk, javelina, wild turkey, bobcats, and western rattlers. Watch where you step when you go to take a leak. We saw a belted kingfisher back and forth earlier along the river. Turkey vultures, mountain bluebirds, scrub jays, and a variety of Buteos and Accipiter's all occupy a niche in the sky. Road-runners are around here too. They seldom fly but can scoot along at 20 mph.

"We might see three or four species of bats this evening. A couple of hundred miles south and a touch east lies a place called Carlsbad Caverns. Millions of Brazilian free-tailed bats come out of the cave at dusk from spring into late fall. It is an amazing experience."

Later, Tom dug the tators out of the coals with the 11.5-inch blade on the end of his stainless-steel United Cutlery Marine Force Recon knife. They felt done, so he dropped them on the camp table. Mark put his old black cast skillet on rocks set on the edge of the fire to get hot for that purpose. He poured in a bit of Borges Extra Virgin olive oil into the pan. He lightly patted the fish with some dry Zataraine's Wonderful cornmeal and magic. In a few minutes a touch of beer flicked from his fingers sizzled, so in went the fish. As they fried, the air was filled with campfire-cooked fish. You either know that smell, or you should.

While they ate, they pondered what the women and Mat were up to in the lab with the Night Parrot greenery and the golden seeds. Their understanding was that the team was trying to cobble together a framework using RNA to snuff out viruses. Trojan horse was a term Mat had used. It seemed like a tall order since viruses had survived for virtually the entirety of Earth's existence. They decided they would leave the heavy mental lifting to those capable of such feats.

A bleary-eyed Tom mumbled, "Let's leave the heavy mental lifting to those capable of such feats!"

They both burst into renewed laughter. Mark repacked the pipe, and Tom fetched more beer. Two kids communing with mother nature. Much later, after hours of philosophizing, Mark said he'd sleep right where he was in the camp chair. He would dream of a grizzly bear. Tom ambled inside and crawled into the suspended bed. They came to about the same time, just shy of the sun creeping into the sky east of Taos.

Tom found some coals still glowing under the gray ash and turned them into a small fire again with the help of some dry juniper, piñon pine, and broom snakeweed. Mark threw a rasher of thick-sliced hickory-smoked bacon in the cast skillet and started a pot of Death Wish coffee. They would need the caffeine.

Tom toasted some hunks of French bread on the rocks. He reversed the direction of the table and chairs. Mark dumped the cooked bacon onto two Stansport stainless steel plates. He cracked a dozen eggs into the hot bacon grease, flipped them once and quickly slid them onto the two plates. Tom put the bread on the table and they had a most amazing sunrise for breakfast.

"Mat has mentioned a guy in Houston named Faillen in connection with Carlos Mattes. Perhaps there is a connection between Faillen and Thirteen also. Probably so. Seems a good bet. Joe and Hunter want to go back to Brazil and hunt down Mattes. I think that's a loser. Better to let Mattes come to us. We have much more control over the real estate here. Maybe we can somehow bait him." Mark was hunting.

"Do you know any bikers?" Tom joined in the hunt.

"Nope. I wonder if Hunter does?" Getting the hunter involved was probably a good decision. Mark fetched his satphone from the rig and punched up Hunter. It took four rings before he answered.

"I spilled barbeque sauce all over me while reaching for the phone. Hold a minute." They could hear water running, Hunter cussing, and the unbridled laughter of a female. "OK, what's up?" Hunter did not seem in the best of moods.

"Just checking in to see if you can still walk and chew gum!" Tom spoke to the speaker.

"Tom you grizzled old bastard. How the hell are you!"

"Excellent! And bathing in bacon grease instead of barbeque sauce."

"Are you in Saline County?" Mark spoke.

"Yup."

"Hey, Carolina! How are you?" Mark queried.

"I'm just peachy! I hope ya'll are too!"

"So, everyone is caught up. What's up?" Hunter really was cranky. "If you must know, I blew a head gasket on the pony car this morning. I've got John hunting down a mechanic capable of allowing me to let him touch my ride."

"Sorry. You know any bikers in Houston?" Mark didn't really display any sorry emotion in his tone of voice.

"Run of the mill or one-percenters?" Hunter was starting to hunt.

"One-percenters."

"Yup."

Mark covered the subject quickly, starting with the encounter in Dallas, the speedbump and the possible Houston connections.

"I'll need a rental."

"Use the black card. Get anything else you need as well. Touch base with Mat. He needs to be in the loop. He'll have insight into what may need to occur."

"Ten-four." Hunter rang off.

"Sirocco seemed a little harried when we spoke yesterday. I think there may be more brewing than just a little Covid 19. What say we push over to Forest Road 145? We'll catch SR 84 down to I-40 from there." Mark was on the move.

Tom poured water on the coals, stirred them with his knife, poured more water, and stirred again. Smoky Bear would have been proud. Tom had experienced the devastating fires back home, so he took no chances. Mark rang up Sirocco and let her know they would be rolling in early in the evening. They discussed several things then rang off. Tom spoke with Jillora Binda for a while, mainly pining to be back in her loving arms. The trip out of the mountains was most pleasant.

An hour or so outside of Dallas Tom's satphone rang. The screen showed Unknown Caller. There were only a handful of people with his satphone number. They were all currently in Texas except for Croc. The phone scrolled and displayed incoming from cell. So, the call was to his cell phone, the one sitting on his dresser in Perth. It was tied into the satphone.

He clicked speaker then answer. "Hello."

"Tom Bindi?" The voice was vaguely Hispanic or similar.

"Speaking. With whom do I have the pleasure?" Tom being his nice self.

"My name is of no consequence. I have a message for you." The voice contained a bit of menace. Mark hit the recessed red button on his dash-mounted satphone. John answered immediately and neither he nor Mark spoke. The red button meant trouble. The predetermined plan was for John to assess the trouble and find a solution.

The voice from Tom's phone continued, "We have your daughter. We picked her up a little while ago in Austin. We wish to make a trade. If you cooperate, then everything will be fine."

"Everything will be fine anyway. Except for your health." Tom was determined but also dragging it out.

"Ah, Mr. Bindi, the deadline for my demands will be long past by the time you can arrange to even get out of, uh, Perth, is it? Dialing code +61 8. Western Australia. I'll be long gone before you can even start to plan such a trip. I require certain plant material from your friends in Dallas. I know you will be more than willing to help me with this endeavor in exchange for your precious bambino."

"You are a dead man walking. I will cut out your heart and place it in your trembling hands and watch you die." Mark glanced over at Tom's eyes and therein saw the truth. The fucker on the other end of the line was a dead man walking.

"Such emotion. This is purely a business transaction. I will follow up a bit later. The exchange will happen in Houston, Texas in approximately twenty-four hours." The phone clicked off.

"Well damn, that blows the Jacuzzi fantasy I had brewing at the back of my mind." Mark was always a step ahead.

"John, I want a picture of the asshole who just called so I can show it to him at the same time I hand him his heart." Tom brought Mark back to the present.

Mark chimed in, saying, "John, I'll need a ride waiting for me at Sirocco's. F-150 crew cab or similar. My rig is too big for a crowded place like Houston. We are about an hour out."

"Yes sir, I'm aware of your position. A driver will have the pickup there in thirty minutes or less. I will have information on the caller soon. Anything else for now?" Two no's, and John clicked off.

Tom punched in Jillora and gave her the story. She was stoic and resolved herself to the fact that the only thing she could do was to continue with the fever-pitched activity going on around her by those in search of a cure for the virus that was consuming the entire planet.

"We're on speakerphone." Jenara came on, saying, "I'll meet you downstairs at your rental with a package. You cannot come inside the building. Things have changed, and we did not want to alarm you. We're ensconced in the labs. Mark is in Sirocco's quarters. He is carrying the virus but is apparently immune. It is probable he can transmit it though, so we're keeping him isolated for now. See you in a little while." They rang off.

Tom rang up Croc. "Where are you lad?"

"I can't tell you exactly. Word might leak back to the young lasses' husband!" Croc let out a laugh. "And how are you and the missus faring up in Yankland?"

"A bit off plumb." Tom gave Croc an update.

"Damn! I wish I could be there to watch the bushranger die. What can I do to help, mate?" Croc would gladly die for Tom and his wonderful family.

"Can you do a watch-see around my place for a day or two? I doubt anyone is doing a walkabout thereabouts, but I would like to be sure."

"Done. Shall I bag any linger-ons?"

"Yup. Cheers!" They rang off.

"Tom, can you climb in the back and pack overnight bags for both of us. Plus backpacks with sidearms, ammo, and cutlery as appropriate. I anticipate nominal resistance, perhaps six to ten guys, more or less." Mark said.

Jenara was standing in the high ceiling entryway as Mark pulled the rig in and parked. She placed a small canvas bag on the hood of the F-150. Then she sprayed it with something in the bottle she held in her left hand.

"I didn't want Jillora to come down, and you two exchange a kiss. It could be lethal, so we're not taking chances. Each of you need to drink a vial of liquid from the bag. Give one to Hunter and one to Jillora when you get her. There are two extra just in case."

"Ya'll take care upstairs, and we'll do the same in Houston. Cheers!"

Mark and Tom loaded the F-150, and Mark was cranking it when Tom said damn, jumped out and grabbed a twelve-pack cooler from an outside slider on the big rig.

"Almost forgot the beer!" Tom was a most thoughtful man.

The Captive

Hunter rented the only ride available nearby. It was a brand-new gray Dodge Ram 2500 Mega Cab. The Laramie configuration came with a 6.4L V-8. The back seat would hold three or four trussed-up Trezes if necessary. Hunter only needed one. He managed to link the sat phone to the truck. Carolina tucked a sack of barbeque and some water bottles onto the shotgun seat where Hunter could reach them. He tossed his worn and spartan overnight bag in the floorboard below the barbeque. Carolina grabbed Hunter's butt, snagged a quick kiss, and shoved him into the cab.

On his way out of the Saline County Regional Airport, Hunter made a call to Houston that lasted several minutes. He was almost to Texarkana when John rang in. "Mr. Hunter, I trust all is well?"

"Yes sir, Mr. John, and you?" Hunter asked the computer how it was doing. Mark would have shot something if he had heard.

"Excellent, sir, and thank you for asking! Not everyone is as polite as you! Do you have a minute to chat?"

"Absolutely. I just turned south on SR 59, headed toward Marshall. What's up?"

"I presume you will be on I-69 for the last leg of your trip into Houston?"

"That's my plan."

"Excellent. Take exit 152, stay on the southbound service road to Kingwood Drive, turn left then right at the Wendy's. There is a UPS store behind the Wendy's. There is a package for you at the counter, and inside is a micro-tracking device. It is snuggled into the ends of a very long, very fine set of tweezers. Please be careful not to drop it because you may never find the tracker again.

There are also some small syringes loaded with Pentazocine. It is fairly mild but will knock a person out for an hour or so."

"Suggestions where I should attach the tracker on the Treze guy?"

"It would be best if you could push it an inch or two into an existing cut with the tweezers. Just turn the small knob on the handle end of the tweezers to release the device."

"Suppose there is no existing cut?"

"I leave that to your imagination, sir." The computer sounded like it was cringing.

Hunter said, "got it," rang off, and then said, "call Scooter." Hunter had talked to Scooter just after he left Carolina.

"You're in luck. A friend of mine just spotted two of the clowns at Twin Peaks. It's the one just south of the I-10, about a mile west of the Sam Houston Tollway. Out toward Katy. He says they are usually there." Scooter was quite capable.

"Does your friend wear colors?" Hunter had been planning while he drove.

"Nope. Leathers but no colors, same as me. Unaffiliated, so to speak." Scooter rode a 2009 Harley-Davidson Night Train. He actually owned two bad-ass scooters. Hunter would ride the second one for part of the upcoming adventure.

"Can he lend a hand? It will be easier if there are three of us to pull this off." A third voice would make the deception more realistic.

"He's all in. He said he'd bitch slap one of the guys for free, so the $10k you offered each of us is just icing on the cake."

"I'll be in Houston in about five hours. Make it three o'clock or so. Where do you want to meet?"

"Come to my house. I'm only fifteen minutes west of Twin Peaks. I found a warehouse that will be perfect down on SR 359 about five miles west and south from my house. It's a plumbing supply business, but it's closed weekends." Many years ago, Hunter had thrown Scooter over his shoulder and gotten the two of them out of a somewhat sticky situation. Sticky, meaning they would have been dead in a matter of minutes. A typical shady government SNAFU shit show. They had been through several more adventures together since then.

Hunter made good time and pulled into Scooter's driveway in the exclusive Parklake Village neighborhood at 2:30. He and Scooter hugged and back slapped. Scooter introduced Hunter to Nada. When Nada was born, his papa said he looked like a little nothing. His mama promptly named him Nada. Nada sported a semi-kempt black beard and below-the-shoulders thick black hair.

Hunter looked up at him a bit. Nada stood around 6'5" and looked to weigh perhaps two-fifty. Most of which appeared to be muscle. They shook hands firmly, and both recognized the slightly distant look in the eyes of the other. Slightly distant, being the look that only a few folks ever achieved. Fucking with these guys would not end well for the uninitiated.

They stood in the hot sun and talked for a few minutes. The humidity, as always in greater metropolitan Houston, was approximately 100%. So, they sweated. None of them seemed to notice. They were preparing to do what they had all trained to do many long years ago and continued to do because retirement was for others.

Nada described the interior layout of Twin Peaks. He said there was an exit door just past the Men's room with an alarm on it. The hallway was fairly narrow and the door exited on the backside of the building. Hunter would time it so he pulled his Dodge Ram right beside the door when Scooter and Nada came out with the Treze.

"Shall we?" Hunter was ready to hunt.

"Lemme make a call." The result of the call was that one asshole had left, one remained. Nada asked the young lady on the other end of the line to make sure the guy stayed.

"My son Algo will take my other bike to the warehouse. He'll drive your truck back here." Nada had the details covered. He also insisted on naming his son something.

"Let's rock." Nada cranked his 2013 Sportster 48. Hunter climbed into the Dodge. Scooter led the way on his Night Train. Hunter brought up the rear.

The plan was, keep it simple stupid. Hunter would park where he could pull up to the exit door quickly. Scooter and Nada would grab beers and wait until the 13 moved toward the bathroom. As soon as he walked through the door, Nada would go and put his back to the exit door. Hunter would greet the asshole as he came out.

Scooter and Nada parked off to the side, near some other bikes. They walked in and went to the bar. Scooter ordered up two bottles of Lone Pint Yellow Rose, an outstanding local IPA. There were some colors displayed, but everyone seemed to be playing nice; well, almost everyone. The Treze guy was being somewhat of an asshole. Actually, he was being a major asshole.

He called his waitress a stupid bitch and ambled back toward the bathroom. She told the bartender she was going to have a smoke out back. She went through the kitchen and ended up about ten feet from the fire door exit.

Scooter called Hunter on his sat phone and said, "go." The Treze disappeared through the bathroom door labeled Hombres. Nada positioned himself with his back to the exit door. The sign on the door said Do Not Open, Alarm Will Sound. Scooter stood where the asshole could take exactly one step out of the bathroom.

The Treze came out and immediately looked into Scooter's chest. He said, "out of my way, asshole." Nada quietly said, "hey." The guy turned his head to look behind him. Nada hit the shithead with a short, left uppercut that would have pulverized a cinderblock. The timing couldn't have been better because Pat Travers was belting out Boom Boom (Out Go the Lights) on the jukebox. The guy would remember a chest and spectacular fireworks going off in his head.

Hunter pulled the truck up to the door and jumped out. He pulled a hundred out of his wallet, hoping the waitress didn't go ballistic. He opened the rear driver's side door. The waitress looked at him without much curiosity in her eyes. He raised his finger to his lips and held up the hundred. At the same time, Nada pushed his back into the panic bar on the exit door. The heavy door exploded outward. Nada came through backward, holding 13 by his shoulders. Scooter had his feet. The alarm did not go off. Same as everywhere, it was not armed.

Nada shoved the guy onto the back seat. His legs dangled with his riding boots almost touching the pavement. Scooter went around to the other side to drag him across the seat. The waitress said, "wait." She walked over and planted her left foot, clad in a size 8.5 pink Lucchese cowgirl boot, square in the guy's nuts. She took the hundred and walked away a bit to finish her smoke—shades of Amber Lee. Texas girls are tough.

They pulled the guy's arms behind his back and zip-tied them. Tight. They also zip-tied his ankles. Tight. Nada tied a bandana over Treze's eyes and cinched it behind his head—hogtied and blindfolded. Hunter jabbed the guy in the ass with a dose of Pentazocine. He pulled away in the Dodge. Nada and Scooter were not too far behind him.

They got back on the I-10, exited on SR 359, and, thirty minutes all told, they pulled through the gate and stopped in between the main building and a large storage building. Algo had opened the Master lock on the main gate chain with a 3210 key. Everybody uses a 3210.

One of the rollup doors on the storage building was wide open. They carried the Treze inside and dumped him in a corner near some PVC fittings and pipe. He'd come to in a little while. They swapped lies until the captive started groaning and then came fully awake. Algo had already driven off in the Dodge Ram, leaving the other Night Train for Hunter.

"What the fuck is going on! I'll kill whoever the fuck you are! My goddamn balls are broken! You bastards!" Treze did not seem to be having a good day.

"Not having a good day, eh?" Scooter spoke softly with an easy grin showing his laugh lines. "I'll hold the water bottle, you sip." The guy sipped some water, took a ragged breath then sipped some more water. He finally finished off the 16.9 ounces and laid his head back.

"Thanks. I still have to kill you, you know?" Feisty bastard.

"Sure. There will be plenty of time for that. Now, we know you work for a guy named Mattes. Where is he?"

"I don't know nobody with that name." He was a stubborn bastard too. Hunter jabbed the tweezers into the guy's thigh and released the tracker.

"AAHHH!!!" Treze also made a lot of noise.

Hunter jabbed the guy in his other thigh. He had decided the easiest way to get away with the tracking device deception was to just jab the guy a few times with the tweezers.

"Where is he? I can jab you until you bleed to death, or just tell me where I can find Mattes, and you can die quickly. Matters not to me, asshole." Hunter could be quite patient.

He had once sweated under cover of leaves and lichen on some hill above some jungle somewhere far away for three days before he squeezed off a round from a single shot bolt action Russian-made Lobaev Arms SVLK-14S. The .408 caliber projectile, weighing 305 grains, left the muzzle traveling approximately 3,500 feet per second.

It was still supersonic when it hit the target some 1,900 yards away. Not the longest kill by any means, but still respectable. The target, an especially nasty example of humanities' worst spore, caught the projectile in his sternum. He was instantly reduced to a puddle of goo laying in the middle of the dirt road that trailed through a village over a mile away.

"We need to talk." Scooter was following the script. "But outside." He nodded at the gravel parking lot.

"No need to stand in the sun. The asshole just drank a mickey. He'll be out in another minute." Hunter jabbed the tweezers into the guy's forearm and elicited a response. In a minute or two, the guy started snoring softly. Not bad acting since there were no drugs in the water bottle. The plan might actually work.

"OK. Let's talk." Hunter winked at Scooter. Nada remained silent. The Treze guy had only heard Nada say one word. Hey. Just before the lights went out.

"A deal has been set up to trade the seeds with Faillen directly. Mattes has been cut out of the action." Hunter continued the charade. "From my perspective, that may bring Mattes out of the jungle and up here to Houston. Killing that asshole would be the bright spot of my week—any week."

"I would not want to be this guy Faillen if what I've heard about Mattes is true. He sounds like one bad hombre. I want to take a peek at your bike. We'll give 13 one last chance, then kill him." They walked around the parking lot for a while, quietly talking about fishing, drinking, and rabble-rousing. After a while they all three walked back into the warehouse.

Hunter kicked 13 in the boot. "You awake asshole?"

"You are going to die gringo." The guy was still feisty.

"Yup. Now, where is Mattes? One last time. You can answer, and it will save one of your brothers from the same fate awaiting you." Hunter said the words as though they were discussing holding or folding a hand on one of the three-card tables at the Beau.

"Fuck you." It makes one wonder what hold Mattes had on these guys; possibly kidnapped kinfolk?

"No thanks. Adios." Meaning forever. "Darren, finish off this asshole after we're gone." Hunter nodded at Nada. Nada nodded back.

Hunter and Scooter went out, saddled up, and pulled out of the lot and back onto SR 359. Distinctly, two bikes growled northward. Nada quietly walked over to 13 and kicked him in the head.

"That was for yelling at the waitress. Now. Give me one phone number. I'd love to kill you, but fortunately for you, I'm undercover DEA. My oath does not allow me to dispose of the trash. One number, then I'm out of here. I'll call whoever and tell them where to find you." Nada's voice was more of a hiss than his normal deep-throated growl.

Amazingly, the guy mumbled ten digits. Nada punched them into Hunter's sat phone. It rang a while before a guy answered.

"One of your asshole buddies is located at the plumbing supply on SR 359, three miles south of the I-10." He clicked off.

"You know we will track you down Darren using your phone number and I will personally cut you into bait-sized chunks." The guy was begging for another boot to the head. He got his wish. Nada walked out, cranked the Sportster 48, rolled through the gate, dismounted, loosely fastened the chain on the gate, and roared up SR 359. Three bikes had left the scene and vanished. A hundred supercomputers could not track down Hunter's sat phone in a hundred years.

Back at Scooters, they found a courier had dropped off three envelopes. The third one had a thousand in it for Algo. Mark was always appreciative of those who do good deeds. An hour later, Hunter called John. John answered on the first ring.

"Mr. Hunter, the implant seems to be working out just fine. The tracker is just now on the move. Mr. Mark and the others can follow progress on Ms. Scirocco's TV."

"Good." Hunter rang off. He called Mark.

"Success. You want me to hole up here in Houston?" Hunter had actually spoken more words in the last few hours than he would typically say in a month.

"Yea. Give it a day or two. I'll let you know." Mark rang off.

Hunter pulled out and meandered his way the hundred or so miles to his little place on the Gulf of Mexico just south of Matagorda.

Week Six

Stan Kenwick died alone in New York. His warped view of a white, sterile hospital room, seen through sheets of enclosing plastic curtains, was not the last view of this mortal world he had hoped for. A figure hovered outside the plastic, checking monitors and adjusting a morphine feed. At first, Stan thought he was seeing an astronaut, but it turned out to be a nurse dressed in full medical hazmat gear. He stared at the faceplate but couldn't determine if the person inside was a man or a woman. His pillow was stained with blood, hemorrhaging from his eyes. His particular situation was not the ideal way to pass from this world, but the morphine drip eased the pain.

In those last few minutes, he reflected on what money can't buy. He was worth billions of dollars, but money couldn't buy him more life. He was one of the most prominent brokers in global energy-related finance, and fate took him to Lagos on business six weeks ago. The annual meeting of international energy financiers was a prestigious affair—one he religiously attended each year. The prominence of West African oil in the energy markets provided Nigeria with the clout to host the last meeting. At the convention, he sat at the VIP table, arranging meetings and potential financial deals between the courses of the opening day lunch. Denjay had served him his meal. Stan had inquired about the man's name and complimented him on the arrangements.

Unfortunately, Stan was not the only VIP attendee at the table, and now he was not the only VIP passing into the void. The worldwide fallout was severe, and the World Health Organization, working with the Nigerian Health Ministry, recently completed their work tracing the source of this new Ebola variant. Denjay's body was long since cremated, but his name would live on as the point of origin for the plague. This assessment was not technically accurate, but it turned out Denjay was a super-spreader. The medical reasons behind his extraordinary ability to transmit the virus were not fully known. However, contact tracing demonstrated that over ninety percent of the people Denjay came in contact with over the last three weeks of his life developed the disease.

Under usual circumstances, contact spread rate was only about twenty to thirty percent. The fact that Denjay was a super-spreader and actively transmitted the virus at the Legos convention created a reversal of the normal course for this new pandemic. Usually, the working masses provide the first pathways for the virus to spread. Daily contact on the busy streets and crowded restaurants where they eat their lunches and dinners creates a large nursey for the virus to seek new victims in its exponential rise. Viruses are like any other species; they are genetically programmed to survive. The virus doesn't care whether you are rich or poor. It only wants a warm body in which to reproduce and spread.

When a virus gains its foothold in the low end of the socio-economic spectrum, the unwashed masses act as shock troops for the rest of society, taking the first wave of the attack. Viruses with high mortality rates cause the bodies of the poor to pile up as a warning sign to those at the top of the heap. But fate took a different view of the world in Lagos. The virus gained its first major foothold in the upper echelons, where the rich and powerful congregate. It spread at expensive business dinners and around the conference tables where deals worth billions of dollars were hammered out.

The Nigerian Energy Minister passed away several days before Stan, and two members of the US President's cabinet were isolated in hospital wards. Statistics said one of them would leave the hospital in a body bag. Panic set in several weeks ago, but by the time national health organizations developed a grip on the extent of the threat, the virus had worked its way down the socio-economic chain. In first-world nations, the middle class and the poor were flooding into hospitals where doctors and nurses didn't have enough equipment or people to care for them. In third-world countries, hospitals were simply shutting their doors.

Governments took desperate measures to stem the transmission of the virus. But such measures only proved successful in slowing the spread, not stopping it. As a result, many of the world's one percent were locked down in nameless, unidentifiable bunkers explicitly designed for global disasters. But even with the best defenses money could buy, the disease wormed its way into some safe houses, wiping out entire families.

Governments fortunate enough to have money and resources were engaged in a mad scramble to find a vaccine, but the virus was moving much faster than the research meant to stop it.

Stan attended ten separate conferences or meetings during the three weeks after his Legos trip. For two of those weeks, he was infectious. By the time his first definitive symptoms were diagnosed, he had met with over 200 people. Contact tracing started immediately, but that was still too late for many. One of his meetings had been with a group of wealth management firms seeking energy investments for their clients. Marcos Kohlfer attended that meeting and then had dinner with Stan and three other longtime associates.

On the other side of the country in Los Angeles, Marcos was also staring through plastic walls in his medical isolation chamber. Marcos was an infinitely practical man who spent a lifetime dealing with facts and making risk-weighted decisions. Yet, he was also a man who knew his own body and its limitations. He could feel the cold wind of death blowing on the back of his neck, and he knew in his heart of hearts that he was on his last earthly journey.

He refused the morphine drip and had a computer monitor beside his bed where he was in hour three of a meeting with his company's legal team and his personal lawyer. He was making his limited time count, wrapping up loose ends where possible, and arranging for orderly transfers of money and power. Marcos flatlined thirty minutes after the meeting was over.

His death triggered a series of phone and video calls. One of these calls was to Kristin Duncan at DoubleSource Investments in Houston Texas.

Ten minutes after Kristin received her call, she was on the phone with Mat. He picked up the call from the east deck of Sirocco's penthouse in Dallas. Mat was alone. Mark was off with his crew, and Jenara, Jillora, and Amber Lee were working in the lab several floors down. It had been three days since they last contacted him, but Mat knew they had isolated an unknown gene shared by the DNA of both the golden seeds and the plant from the night parrot feces. They disappeared after that, working, sleeping, and eating in a lab where no one else had access.

Only a few people had access to his encrypted sat-phone. He could see the call was from Houston and suspected Kristin was on the other end of the line when he accepted the call.

"Mat, this is Kristin."

"I suspected as much," he replied.

Just three weeks earlier, Kristin and her firm brokered a deal that cost him $800 million but gave him a stake in a startup mRNA company and put him on their board of directors. Shen Wu, the company founder, was intrigued by Mat's insights and his odd connection with cutting-edge information from the Three Rock corporation. Mat had remained silent on the original information source, but Shen took his own guesses and was willing to move forward on a joint project.

Shen had been in the business of genetics and viral delivery systems for decades and knew the information provided by Mat was far beyond anything else in the field. He also recognized the inherent danger of using this information from an unknown source. But he was a risk-taker, and the offer was too sweet to turn down. So they cut the deal, and work started before the full scope of the Ebola pandemic took form. Because Shen's business required precise control of genetic material and viruses, he was uniquely prepared to continue operations in spite of the current panic.

Mat was already suspicious the pandemic was developing when the deal closed, and all his communications with Shen and Three Rock had been virtual since that point in time. But as the pandemic deepened, Mat analyzed his contact history and recognized a weak point in the chain. He suspected Kristin was about to confirm his fears. He had figured it out about ten days ago and cut off all person-to-person contact with the rest of his group. He remained couped up on the twenty-sixth floor, and all communications were virtual.

In-building communications were via a one hundred percent hardened internal coms system, and external contacts occurred over heavily encrypted networks. Mat let Kristin deliver the message.

"Marcos died four hours ago from the Ebola virus. Because of the nature of your meeting with him three weeks ago, you were not on any official contact tracing list, so he wanted this message delivered to you in confidence. I'm sorry to be the messenger of bad news."

"It's okay, Kristin. I suspected I was at high risk and have been isolated for ten days. I have access to testing to confirm or deny an infection, so I will find out by day's end. I have been exposed to Ebola before, many years ago, and it's unknown if my body will still generate antibodies. Thanks for personally contacting me, and, by the way, I really appreciate your work on the DSM Research deal with Shen. I suspect you didn't sleep much while putting that deal together on short notice.

"Mat, I know you are a survivor, but take care of yourself anyway. I'm here if you need me."

The line clicked off, and Mat reached into the small refrigerator beside him and opened a cold beer.

Vanished (Mat)

I poured my pFriem IPA into a cold mug and sat back, thinking about the conversation with Kristin. I had largely recovered from the incident in Brazil and now trained in Sirocco's penthouse gym for several hours each day. Her line of business required top-notch physical fitness, so the gym was spacious and well equipped. The setup also included a large training floor for various martial arts. I trained on a full spectrum—cardio, weights, flexibility, Aikido, and an aggressive branch of Karate. My gut told me some tough challenges were coming our way, and I wanted to be physically and mentally ready.

Marco's demise was not a shock since I knew from another source that he was infected and hospitalized. I didn't tell Kristin, but I already knew I was carrying the virus, but my body was also producing antibodies keeping it at bay. Jenara and the others were aware, and I kept isolated because there was uncertainty about whether I was transmitting the virus. Most of the evidence indicated I probably was.

The women several floors down were currently using samples of my blood to understand if my antibodies were related to the golden seeds or my previous bout with Ebola. It was a toss-up, but my observation was that avoiding the disease several years ago was probably due to the herbal medicine Jenara administered before my trip to West Africa. She had recently confirmed, the infusion she gave me used a batch of ground golden seeds from her stores, and the break-in at her office was probably a search for those seeds.

This line of thought brought my thoughts back to Donald Faillen. He was almost certainly behind the break-in, and Marcelle provided me with clear evidence he worked directly with Carlos Mattes. Both of them were dangerous, but Mattes was a full-blown psychopath and needed to be dealt with. Faillen would probably avoid outright violence if possible, and he would certainly lean towards saving his own skin as his top priority.

I ruminated over my options for several hours, but the information I received from Eva the day before sealed my forward plan. The call had been brief and over lines with hardened encryption. Even then, she had first texted me with a code phrase to use the burner phone provided after the Boston incident. It turned out the woman she had duped and drugged at the hotel was a deep-cover federal agent. The government was following the same trail as Donald Faillen, and that trail led them to my figurative doorstep. They still weren't sure of my actual doorstep, but Eva indicated they were close and may pay me a visit soon.

The last time federal agents traced me to Sirocco's building, when we were chasing the crystal orb, was a disaster for them, and bridges with the Dallas Police department were burned in the process. They would err on the side of caution this time. But I didn't kid myself. The situation was getting desperate, especially for those politicians and power brokers at the top of the heap. Agents would come. Eva was convinced from her information that I was the target, and they were only marginally aware of how Mark's crew and Jenara may be involved. This blind spot of theirs was an opportunity for me. If I vanished, leaving a breadcrumb trail, then they would follow.

I pulled out another burner phone and dialed a second number for Eva. She picked up on the third ring. She said nothing, so I spoke. "Eva, can you locate where Faillen has stashed himself."

"Affirmative," was the only reply.

"I will be in Houston tomorrow night. I need a safe house, and I need you to disarm Faillen's security system by 2:00 a.m. Send me his location, and I will take it from there. I am probably contagious, so deep clean the safe house when I leave and keep your distance if you see me."

"Done. Anything else?"

"That's it. Take care."

The phone clicked off. I checked my stopwatch, and only thirty seconds had elapsed, well under the sixty-second limit Eva had specified for any call. I destroyed the phone in a custom shredder Sirocco kept in her main office. Now I had to get my ducks in a row and arrange for a discrete set of video surveillance breadcrumbs.

I got Jenara on the internal building coms and explained what I was doing. She was unhappy about the plan but couldn't see any other path forward. So, I started making online arrangements that would be traced back to a dead-end near Love Airport. Jenara let me know when she left the sealed spray container I requested outside their lab for me to collect.

I packed a travel bag and a lightweight, compartmentalized, black backpack, and at 11:00 p.m. I took Sirocco's private elevator to the subbasement garage. There were three access points in the garage, but only two were visible—reinforced steel doors on the east side and the elevator door I was exiting from on the opposite wall. I headed to the south wall, and behind a worn, black SUV was a locked steel panel. I had a key to unlock it, and I placed my palm on the scanner inside. Once the light turned green. I extracted a short crowbar from beside the scanner. Its metal clips snapped as I pulled the bar out.

After relocking the panel, I walked around to the east side of the SUV where a sewage manhole cover was set into the cement floor. The cover, which also unlocked with my palm scan, popped off with some help from the crowbar, and a flashlight beam confirmed the sparse rebar ladder on the south side of the hole. I descended slowly into the darkness, leaving the manhole cover beside the entrance. Someone would be along at 11:30 to replace it. Once replaced, the cover would lock in place and only be accessible via scanner authorization.

I descended to a concrete tunnel, which was one of Sirocco's escape holes. The space was cramped but large enough for me to walk stooped over and not have to crawl. The gray concrete sides glistened with moisture here and there, but otherwise, the tunnel was in good condition. It ran straight for about four hundred yards and terminated in another round utility hole with a rebar ladder, just like the one I entered on. Three meters above me, I exited by removing a cover with a mechanical inside lock and climbed through into a small utility room. Brooms were hanging on the back wall, and shelves of various cleaning supplies occupied the west wall. I exited the closet into another parking structure. Only three cars were visible, and I headed to a dark red SUV with its doors unlocked and keys under the driver's seat.

The garage exit was through a flimsy, rollup, steel grate, and I could see traffic headlights passing by at street level. My convoluted exit from Sirocco's building was driven by my concerns that the feds were already surveilling the entrances and exits. I needed them to know I was on the move, but not quite yet.

A remote on the dashboard raised the garage door, and I merged with the traffic on the street. From there, the drive across Dallas was smooth. I picked up Interstate 45 and headed south, exiting on SR 31 in Corsicana. The road turned into 7th Street as I headed westward into town. One block after a righthand turn on South Beaton street, I took another right on East 6th and then a left on South 10th. I left the car parked across the street from an Italian restaurant and walked a block and a half to the Chase Bank ATM at the corner of Beaton and Collin. A total of three hundred dollars was withdrawn from one of my accounts, letting the cameras capture video of me. Any interested parties could verify when I was at that particular spot.

My car, however, had avoided all cameras in a sixteen-block area. Beyond that, I was most certainly captured on video, but the dark tinted windows were specifically designed to impede visual verification of the driver. The feds were bound to have a lock on all of my banking activity or at least all of it they could trace, and my presence in Corsicana would trigger an alert. I couldn't be directly tracked, but my inferred destination, Houston, would be the logical guess for anyone working the case, and I needed my pursuers in Houston.

I was in Houston before sunrise, and Eva sent me an encrypted text with the safe house location. The northern suburbs of Houston encompass a neighborhood called The Woodlands, and my destination was an upscale home on the banks of Lake Woodlands. I pulled a second remote from the glovebox and quietly eased into one of the four garage bays. The bay door closed behind me.

A breakfast of scrambled eggs and juice was taken on a patio overlooking the lake. The cool of the morning created a thin mist across the lake, and not much was stirring that early. An inspection of the kayaks in the home's private dock assured me I had what I needed. By the time the neighborhood woke up and things started buzzing, I was headed to bed with an alarm set for 3:00 p.m.

At 4:00 p.m. I took one of the kayaks for a spin northward on the lake to the Lake Edge Boat House. The half-mile trip took a little over ten minutes at a quick but not too strenuous pace. Once I returned, I immediately took another short kayak and put it in the back of the Red SUV. From the house, I drove back to the shopping center behind the Lake Edge Boat House and parked in a secluded area at the far end of the lot. I removed the kayak and locked the car, sealing the key in a magnetic, fingerprint-keyed lockbox under the front fender. From there, I carried the kayak up the road for several blocks before cutting back to the lake. My path avoided all security cameras.

It was a ten-minute paddle back to the safe house. When I returned, I had a bite to eat by the lake and started packing gear in my backpack. I packed, disassembled, and repacked. In addition to my SUV, the garage had two other cars: a black RAV4 and a white Ford F250 pickup. The RAV4 had a peppy six-cylinder engine and fit my needs best, so I put on latex gloves and loaded my gear into its trunk. Then it was just a waiting game.

Eva's text providing the location of Faillen's bolt hole arrived at 6:45 p.m. She included some brief notes about access to Faillen along with a warning that he could have a bodyguard with him. Once I located the address on a map, I realized he was hidden away in an unregistered condo just two blocks from his company's offices in the Galleria area.

I set my alarm for another two-hour nap but was woken up at 8:00 p.m. with a call on my sat-phone, number untraceable. Mark was on the other end with Tom and Hunter, and the three of them were headed to Houston.

"We have a situation, Mat. Tom's daughter was taken from the UT Austin campus this morning. She has been there for several months on an exchange program. There is no question that Mattes and the Treze gang are behind this. They have already contacted Tom and are using his daughter for bait. Do you have any leads about where they operate from in Houston?"

The universe has a weird way of making unexpected connections. I can't account for it, and neither can anyone else. Karma? Mark would have no idea about my location because no one but Eva knew. Jenara didn't even know all the details.

"First, there are two things you need to know, my friend. I'm in Houston as we speak, and I'm infected with the Ebola virus. So if we meet, don't give me a hug. As always, your timing is impeccable. Now, I presume you are not coming to Houston to negotiate, and to answer your question, I believe I can get you to the Treze compound by tomorrow morning. But first, I have to pay someone a visit and persuade them to help me."

"We won't arrive until after midnight, but we may have a lead also from a tracker that Hunter planted in one of their bikers." Tom commented from the background.

"My bait will be carrying a tracker also." I said.

Mark cut back in, "Do you have some backup for this evening?"

"I am afraid it's just me and myself. But I'm sending you two tracker ID's. One is an SOS switch. If you start picking up that signal, it means I have failed. The second is a subcutaneous tracker. If that activates, then my bait is in action and moving towards Mattes. There is one unfortunate but very important thing you need to know. When you arrive at the compound, it will probably be crawling with Ebola virus. Tom, I can't protect your daughter from this. Hopefully she will be isolated in another part of the building."

Tom kicked into the conversation again. "I'm carrying something that Jillora thinks can help keep her baby girl safe. I only have one goal, to get to my daughter."

Hunter's voice sounded slightly faint but clear. "I don't personally give a flying fuck about the virus. Mattes is going to pay."

He will pay in many ways, I thought. "My advice from afar, for all of you, is to get in and out quickly with the girl. I will probably be in federal custody by the time you get there, and the Feds will be descending on Mattes and the Treze like a shit storm from hell. They will hold me for a while without any probable cause, and I will tell them Mattes has the cure they are looking for. This tactic will buy the ladies in Dallas more time. Too much is a stake for me to wander farther from my original plan."

I rounded off the call. "Tracker IDs are on their way. Good luck and God-speed, my friends."

The phone clicked off, and I made my third boat trip up the lake and withdrew another $300 from a local ATM in the shopping center behind the Boat House. An hour later, I was on Interstate 45 again, headed South into Houston. I connected up with the I-610 loop and took it west, then south into the center of the Galleria area, parking in a large open lot off of Westheimer, near Morton's Steakhouse. From there, I spent the next two hours casing the neighborhood, making several layers of plans for exiting Faillen's place and setting a trap for Mattes.

At midnight I moved my car to a street location near Faillen's condo and waited. A bit before 2:00 a.m. I walked a block to a sheltered spot where I could observe the back service entrance to the condo building and remain unseen. Eva stepped through the door at 1:55, paused, and looked around. She tapped on her phone a bit, looked directly at me, waved, and disappeared.

She basically told me in the text that I was crap at hiding, and everything I needed was in a bag to my right as I entered. Damn, how does she do that, I wondered. The bag had a single key and a handwritten note with some instructions. So, I climbed nine flights of service stairs and exited into a warmly lit hallway with plush blue and tan carpeting. I slipped the key into a lock three doors down from the service entrance and slid through the door into a completely empty condo.

The entrance foyer had polished wood floors, and a relatively large kitchen lay off to my right. The foyer and kitchen opened onto a large living room with sliding patio doors on the far side. I checked the door leading off the right side of the living room and confirmed it opened into the master bedroom. The bedroom also accessed the same outside balcony as the living room. Faillen's apartment was a duplicate immediately above me.

I moved onto the balcony and inspected the layout and the railings. As Eva had written, there was already a rope ladder outside the bedroom hanging from the balcony above. I grabbed one of the rungs and tugged, testing the strength. I then took a last look around and ensured I had the key in a zipped pocket on my pants before swinging onto the ladder and scrambling up to Faillen's balcony.

I walked over to the living room patio doors, where the blinds were open, and inspected the room's layout, noting where the dining area chairs were located. After pulling off my backpack, I extracted a gas mask and a set of night vision goggles from the top of the pack. I then proceeded to unpack a small case with a roll of plastic explosive putty and a timer, a pistol, and two small gas containers, one with red tape around the cylinder and the other with blue tape.

There was a re-inspection of the room once I slipped on my gas mask and goggles, then I moved on to the master bedroom doors. There, a long strip of putty was pressed onto the glass around the edges of the sliding door. The timer was inserted into the putty and set for eight seconds before I backed away about twelve feet with my pistol in one hand and the red stripe container in the other.

The crack sounded like an automobile accident on the street below, and glass from the door disintegrated into tinkling rain on the deck's concrete surface. I twisted the top nozzle of the canister and tossed it through the gaping hole that was once a door, and immediately followed with my pistol raised.

Faillen was floundering at the edge of his bed with his left hand covering his eyes and his right hand groping in the drawer of the nightstand, presumably searching for a weapon. I fired, and the dart caught him in his right shoulder. He jerked around trying to look in my direction, but I was already moving towards the bedroom door. As I looked out the bedroom door, I could hear the apartment's front door opening. As soon as it shut, I tossed the blue canister into the living room.

At the sound of a body dropping, I shut the bedroom door and walked over to the bodyguard. His gun was on the floor beside him, so I emptied the chamber and extracted the ammo clip, placing it in my pocket. He would be out cold for at least six hours. He was a big guy, so zip-tying him to one of the dining room chairs took a while. I grabbed a second chair on my way back to the bedroom.

Faillen was still out from the tranquilizer dart, and I zip-tied him to the second chair. Two hypodermic needle devices came out of the left-side pocket of the backpack. The first one was used to inject a subcutaneous tracker into Faillen's left shoulder, and the second pumped a stimulant into his veins, bringing him back to consciousness. He was an unhappy man. His eyes were streaming tears, his throat was on fire, and both hands and legs were immobilized. I stood just at the edge of his peripheral vision.

"Easy, Donald, and quit trying to thrash around. It will just make things worse. Oh, and your bodyguard is not coming."

"What do you want?" was the only raspy reply that came from his mouth.

"It's not what I want, Donald. It's about what you want. You see, my employers were quite upset when you tried to interfere with their agent in Boston. You're messing with the wrong people. St. Petersburg originally tasked me with killing you until your relationship with Carlos Mattes came to light. The only thing they hate more than interference is when someone steals from them. They think you can lead us to Mattes."

He retorted with a denial, "I don't know Mattes."

"But you do, Donald, so let's not waste time hashing through that issue. More importantly, you are going to lead us to him. You might ask me why you would do that, and I will give you two reasons. Life and money."

My right leg twisted up and around, driving the heel of my shoe into his solar plexus. The air emptied out of his lungs, and as he gasped to fill them back up, I sprayed contents from the container Jenara had given me into his mouth. He choked as the viral-laden liquid entered his lungs.

"What the hell was that for?" He asked as his breath returned.

"Life, my friend. You just sucked down a concentrated dose of the Ebola virus."

He gave a halfhearted laugh. "I don't believe you because you would also be exposed."

"Oh, I was, Donald. But you see, I am already infected. The difference between you and me is that my blood is chocked full of antibodies from our first experimental treatments." This wasn't true, but I needed him to believe it. "Your early instincts were right about the herbal seeds you were chasing. They are a pharmaceutical wonder when properly processed. So, we come to the first part of the agreement. Help us locate Mattes, and we will provide you with the experimental treatment."

He was very still. I had his attention and followed on with, "additionally, we are prepared to deposit one million US dollars in your Cayman account ending in 7793."

I knew the hook was set. "On your bed stand is a vial with the seeds you and Mattes so desperately want. They are the real thing. You are going to deliver them to Mattes in five hours, at 8:00 a.m. this morning, as per your previous agreements with him. Every breath you take in his presence will spew out the virus, so be sure to breathe heavily. When the task is done, and we will know if you don't perform, then, and only then, call the only number programmed into the burner phone beside the vial. You will get instructions on where to collect the virus treatment, but only when you finish with Mattes. I know you think you can't trust me, but you really have no choice. Go alone to see Mattes. You are fortunate. My employers don't usually give anyone a second chance."

"I'm leaving you with one last gift, the blue pill beside the vial. Take it, and in twenty minutes, you will be puking your guts out. After you deliver the vial to Mattes, tell him you have been feeling ill and need to leave. Pandemic panic will set in once you heave onto his floor."

I stepped out onto the balcony, detached the rope ladder, and rolled it up. When I returned Faillen's hand ties were cut off, but his feet were left strapped to the chair. I also left my pocketknife on a dresser table where it would take him five to ten minutes to retrieve.

"I'm leaving through your front door, Donald. But you may want to stay here for at least an hour since the residual nerve gas used on your bodyguard is still in the living room."

I was gone, out the door, down the stairs, and through the ground floor service door. The RAV4 was a one-block walk, and my trip back to The Woodlands was uneventful. Several hours were spent wiping down the safe house and the car.

In a utility room, off the garage, I found a plastic barrel and gently removed the top. The acid was about two feet deep in the bottom. In went backpack, weapons, canisters, pants, shirts, and shoes. Within two hours, there would be nothing left.

I called Eva on my burner phone and confirmed that Faillen was headed towards West Houston and asked her to notify Joseph and text Faillen's final location to my personal phone. Lastly, I injected a tracker under the skin of my thigh, then dropped the phone and syringe into the vat.

At 7:00 a.m. I put on latex gloves and a fresh change of clothes, being careful to wipe and clean as I exited the house. The ten-minute paddle northward to the Boat House was refreshing, and I left the kayak on the dock. The local coffee shop in the shopping center seemed the best place to finish this bit of business. Masked and gloved, I got a large Americano and claimed one of the outside tables. As expected, Texas had made the call that fear of the virus was overblown and ignoring it was the best solution, so my mask was not completely necessary.

When the clock in the coffee shop hit seven-thirty, I switched on my phone, put in some earbuds, and hooked into the shop's internet. I let some Pearl Jam and Pink Floyd roll around in my head while I caught up on the news. Most of it was pandemic related. It took a full twenty minutes, but Eva's text popped up from an unknown number about the same time three black SUVs pulled over beside the parking lot curb. Two men in suits got out and sat on either side of me without saying a word. Then a third more familiar face emerged and sat across from me.

"Mr. Dover, we meet again under strained circumstances," he said.

I only knew him as Jeff Smith since he never used his real name. "Mr. Smith, what brings you to my table? Oh, before I forget, I'm infected, so you may want to keep your distance. I'm double-masked with an N95, but still better to be safe than sorry." There was silence as the men on either side of me slid their chairs away. Mr. Smith didn't budge.

"Clearly your phone brought me here. We are playing your game for now, but you probably know what we are looking for."

"I suspect you are looking for some herbal seeds, and I am prepared to tell you where they are. Sources tell me they are in the possession of a one Carlos Mattes at an industrial park in Pearland. Your crew in the Galleria area is probably closer. The whole affair appears to be moving very quickly, so you may want to get them moving." As I spoke, I held my phone up for him to see the address.

Mr. Smith got out of his seat and stood at a distance by the cars talking on his phone, before returning to the table. "How did you happen to come into this information?"

"Like you, I have been making inquiries. Interestingly I also found out that Mattes' compound is crawling with Ebola."

He was up for a second time making another call. When he returned, he simply said, "You're coming with us. Stand Up."

I was wearing a tee-shirt and jeans with sandals and no socks. He put on a heavy-duty respirator and gloves before patting me down. Then I was ushered into the back of the front vehicle. "It is a negative pressure isolation chamber for everyone's safety," he said as I looked at a compartment more akin to a hospital ward than the back seat of an SUV.

He got into the front seat, flipped a switch, and said, "The line is open if you want to talk."

"Thanks, Jeff, but I might just take a nap since I am feeling a little tired."

In truth, I was exhausted and drifted off with no problem.

But I didn't get much of a nap and woke up to Mr. Smith knocking on the glass divider and sending a sealed bag with my phone through an exchange slot between the front and back compartments. The call was from Mark, but there wasn't much I could say under the circumstances, so I told him I was busy and hung up. I think Mr. Smith had hoped for more.

We ended up at an unidentifiable building near Tomball, where I was hustled into an isolation room and finally got my nap. About three hours later, Mr. Smith and another agent came in dressed in hazmat suits and ran a scanner all over me until it beeped at my right thigh. Mr. Smith feigned a frown, but I detected a faint smile behind his face shield as he spoke.

"Your friend Mr. Sebastiao and his lawyer just arrived at our front door demanding your release, unless you were being charged with something. You are free to go, Mr. Dover. By the way, your tip was good, and we managed to take one Carlos Mattes into custody. A man who has been on our wish list for quite a while. The materials we wanted were there also, as you promised. Unfortunately, we arrived after some sort of attack on the compound. Do you know anything about that?"

"It's a mystery to me. After all, I have been in your company for the past several hours."

I departed with Joseph, and the lawyer looked at me like I was a leper before taking a separate car.

Shattered Mind

"How was the fishin'?" Mark always had a lure in the air in the back of his mind.

"Good. Nothing like fresh specs cooked in a black skillet over a fire on the beach." Hunter could fish too. "Plan?" Now he was back to matters at hand.

Tom, Hunter, and Mark were standing outside the front entrance of the Crown Plaza in Houston. There is no better way to casually catch suspicious eyes than to look like typical patrons having a smoke out front.

"John has nailed down the location of the Treze with the tracker I implanted in his ass, and he said Mat's tracker is headed in that direction about forty minutes out." Mark was itching to move. Tom showed no nerves, just the slight look into the distance marking his intent.

"Let's grab a shower and meet back here in thirty minutes. We'll have our answer by then." Mark grabbed a quick cold shower to get the blood flowing and called Sirocco.

She mentioned Mat's vanishing act via her last-resort escape hatch and suggested they head towards Leakey once they collected Tom's daughter.

Mark placed his next call to Mat. He knew something was amiss when the sat phone call routed back through Mat's personal phone. But he knew John would be covering their digital tracks, "You doing okay my friend?"

"Well, not exactly. I'm actually tied up at the moment." Mat's voice was neutral, and based on a lifetime of knowing Mat, he gathered that Mat could not speak freely. Nothing he could immediately fix, so he filed it into the pending box in his mind for later.

Back outside, they climbed into the F-150. Tom rode shotgun, and Hunter stretched across the back bench seat. Hunter doubled-checked the three packs Tom had stashed there during the vehicle trade at Sirocco's. There was a Glock 19 Gen 5 G34 in each pack, four clips, tactical webbing, and a Ka-bar. Tom also had his United Cutlery Marine Force Recon knife on him. Good for pulling baked potatoes out of the fire and such.

Hunter called Scooter and gave them the address. They'd meet on the west side of Love's Truckstop, just north of Thirteen Modular Scaffolding. The location was on the north side of the Pasadena Freeway, off the Frontage Road, on the northwest corner of Battleground Road, in Deer Park.

"We're about an hour out."

"Same here. See you in a little while." They rang off.

Mark said to Hunter and Tom, "There are two entrances, both gated. South is the office-looking entrance, and the north entrance goes into the equipment yard. Satellite images show it to look deceptively like a bona fide business.

"Typical." Hunter spoke. "Most gangs are run as a business these days. The warehouse has probably been renovated into living quarters, a recreation area, and shop space for bike maintenance."

"Recreation area?" Tom pondered.

"A pool table or two, self-serve bar, and common kitchen. Probably a widescreen TV or two and a sound system. Laundry room." Hunter had first-hand knowledge of such places, obviously. "My guess is that your daughter is being held in one of the adjoining living quarters. Typically arranged like a suite at a Holiday Inn. The suites are not dedicated, so the doors are usually left open unless it is occupied. Once we're in, a quick scan may tell us what we need to know."

Mark cut back in. "The gate at the office end is close to the front doors. The rear entrance is close to the street and away from the building. We will use it. We'll have Scooter and Nada approach the office gate and make a bit of noise with their bikes. Under cover of their racket, I'll run us through the gate to the rear entrance. I hope John got me the full insurance coverage package on the truck." He grinned a bit at his levity. Hunter and Tom did not. "We'll play it by ear from there."

"Don't worry, Tom. We'll get her out safe and sound." Hunter was unusually talkative.

"No worries, mate. Just ready to make it happen."

Mark drove on I-65 south to I-610 east and took the Pasadena Freeway to Battleground Road. He turned left, and the three of them eyed Thirteen Modular Scaffolding as they drove by. He pulled into the west end of the Love's parking lot. Scooter and Nada were standing beside their bikes, talking. They both wore jeans and white tee shirts. Tom, Mark, and Hunter bailed out of the

F-150, and Tom got a bear hug from Scooter and Nada—mutual admiration club and a show of absolute solidarity.

"Plan?" Scooter was ready to reunite father and daughter.

"Ya'll pull to the front of the building and rev it up a bit. It should at least make the occupants curious. We crash the rear gate, hit the rear doors, make the rescue, head out toward elsewhere." Mark was succinct.

"Keep your fire directed away from the front area, and we'll do the same in reverse." Nada, a man of many words.

"Great plan," Scooter said, "but Nada and I knock on the front door. We'll definitely be a diversion then." Scooter and Nada did not ride across Houston to be bystanders. "Google Maps shows a gap between the righthand turnstile gate and the building. We'll park at the gap and hit the front doors. We'll knock, then enter. Just don't shoot anyone in a white tee shirt."

"We'll be fifteen seconds behind you," Mark retorted. "The gate-crashing will be your cue we're in. Let's do it." Mark, Tom, and Hunter got back into the F-150. Scooter and Nada saddled up, drove the hundred and fifty yards, quickly reversed their bikes in, kickstands down, and headed to the front door.

Mark drove a hundred yards south, turned right, accelerated, and crashed through the gates about the same time the gunfire started out front. He fishtailed the F-150 and braked, so the rear end was facing the back doors of the building. They all three bailed out on the run.

Scooter and Nada shot up the front steel and glass doors with twin 9mm Gen 5 Glock 19's and pushed their way in. They both fired into glass and sheetrock partitions on the left. These actions made a lot of noise. They dropped their empty clips, shoved new fifteen-round clips into the receivers. They slowed their rate of fire and punched a few holes high into the sheetrock walls and 2'x4' ceiling tiles into the warehouse area. They purposely kept these rounds high.

Simultaneously with the frontal assault, the rear door blew inward off its hinges, and Tom was the first one through. He recognized the biker scrambling to his feet and pinned him against the wall with his right hand wrapped around the guy's throat. His United Cutlery Marine Force Recon knife came up low from the left and quickly made three angular movements.

Hold this Tom whispered as the dead man's head hit the concrete floor with a thud. He waved his satphone with a picture of the biker in front of the lifeless eyes. "Sorry, I had wanted to show you this first before I handed you your heart."

They made their way fifteen feet ahead and turned right into a hallway. There were eight rooms off to the right and center. One door was closed.

Tom looked at Hunter and said, "I'll take out the door; you take out whoever is in the way."

Hunter nodded and ran after Tom. Seven massive strides, and Tom went left shoulder straight through the door, tumbled and rolled. Hunter was a step behind. He pulled up short when he saw what looked like a Heckler & Koch HK 45 being held to Jillora's pillowcase-wrapped head. Her hands and ankles were zip-tied. Hunter's gun was level and shoulder-high. He squeezed off a round into the biker's forehead. His mind was shattered.

Tom caught Jillora Bindi before she hit the rug. He pulled her over his shoulder and sprinted back out the door, crossed the recreation area, and headed out the door with the Exit sign above it. Mark covered him, and Hunter had Tom's back. Mark motioned Hunter out, and he followed backward and kicked the door shut. Mark aimed into the air and expended three evenly spaced rounds. That was the prearranged done signal to Scooter and Nada.

Tom pushed Jillora into the rear seat and pulled the pillowcase off of her head. He grabbed a vial and gently said, "drink this." She did.

"Shit. It tastes like cat piss puked out by a buzzard!" was her only remark—a spunky lass, just like her mom.

"Tell yer Mum. It's something she, Sirocco, and Amber Lee concocted. He strapped her in and cut the zip ties just as Mark kicked up a cloud of gravel and dust and accelerated through the gate. Mark turned right on the service road and was up on the Pasadena Freeway westbound in a matter of seconds. Scooter and Nada were fifty yards behind and maintained the distance, just in case.

Mark told the dashboard to call Sirocco. She answered on the first ring.

"We're on speaker," she said.

"The cocktail you cooked up tastes like cat piss puked out by a buzzard!" Everyone burst into laughter. The world would continue to spin around the sun.

"Have you heard from Mat?" Jenara asked.

"Not since he confirmed the Treze location. He seemed a bit circumspect during that conversation. Thoughts?"

"Yea. You, Tom, and Jillora head to Leakey. Hunter, can you stay with Scooter for a bit? Just in case Mat needs a hand?" Hunter answered in the affirmative. "We'll talk in an hour or so." They rang off. Hunter punched up Scooter and told him the plan. Scooter and Nada pulled ahead, and two bikes and an F-150 pulled into Scooter's driveway an hour later, where goodbyes were exchanged, and Mark, Tom, and Jillora Bindi 1,112 headed westbound on the I-10.

The Houston ABC TV affiliate, KTRK-TV, later described the chaos as a brutal fight between two rival biker gangs, with a side note that unidentified federal agents swarmed the Treze clubhouse soon thereafter and took everyone alive into custody. A Brazilian organized crime boss named Mattes and an unnamed Houston businessman were also found on the premises and arrested. An unidentified source described the Treze gang as heartless bastards.

Week Twelve

Frank Johnson used his right index finger to peel back the light blue, flower-bordered curtains of his living room window. The window faced directly onto Wingate Drive, where the view took in his sidewalk, the street, and all or part of three homes across the road from his house. He thought he heard people outside talking and tilted his head to peer through a three-inch gap between the boards he had fastened to the outside window frame just last week. He didn't see anybody but still gave a nervous glance to his right, checking on the shotgun beside the front door as he let the curtains fall back in place.

He could hear Maureen in the kitchen preparing some of the food they received three days ago. Food prices were skyrocketing during the crisis. But he had a reasonable nest egg, and his other usual expenses like gasoline and an occasional dinner out had fallen by the wayside, so covering the extra cost was not a problem yet. The weekly food delivery was carried out as usual yesterday, with four boxes delivered to his driveway—one clearly labeled 'freezer.' He had sprayed them down with a Clorox solution and sat in his garage guarding the packages for an hour while the Clorox did its work. After that, the boxes were unpacked, then every container and package was sprayed again. The freezer food got packed away, and the rest sat on the garage floor for two more days before he allowed the containers into the house.

General panic over the Ebola virus set in several weeks ago as the extent of the threat became apparent. Frank had assumed it was another fake virus at first, ignoring the news until his brother passed away. Jim was isolated in the hospital for the five days between when he entered with a mild fever and cough, and when he died. Frank couldn't visit with him, but even after Jim passed, he was suspicious of the hospital's claim that the Ebola virus had taken his brother. He was only convinced when his pastor called and told him he had been allowed to see Jim through the window of his isolation cubical to pray for him. Frank still got a bit nauseous when he thought about the pastor's description of Jim's condition several hours before he died. The pastor hadn't wanted to talk about it, but Frank had pressed him.

Frank now believed the virus was probably real. Some of the internet groups he followed claimed it was from Africa and transmitted by black people. The whole issue was confusing because some of his favorite talk show hosts still claimed the virus was a hoax by the government to take away citizen's rights. Maureen believed the virus was real, but she was an anti-vaxxer and firmly held that God would see the righteous through this crisis—faith in Him was better than any vaccination. Frank wasn't so sure since Jim had been a devoted church member for all his life. But when he discussed the topic with Maureen, she was unbudging.

"Well, Jim must have been one of those Sunday Christians. Something was going on we didn't know about. I remember when Sue suspected him of having an affair. She was probably right. It's the road to hell, and the fact that God didn't protect him is pretty good evidence that something was up."

Frank cringed inside, and his guilt from a three-day affair he had on a business trip some twenty years ago surfaced in the back of his mind like a dark cloud. He knew the guilt would never disappear, but he was also damn sure that Jim never had an affair. Sue was a paranoid wreck of a wife, and she was constantly suspecting him of one thing or another. Frank and Jim had been tight, and when Frank revealed his affair, Jim was the supporting shoulder he leaned on. He would have shared with Frank if he had done the same. Now Jim had taken Frank's secret to his grave.

He thought he heard voices outside again and took a second peek out of the window. Two people were walking on the sidewalk in front of his house. They were both staring towards him as he tracked their progress through the three-inch gap between the boards. He muttered to himself, "move on, move on," when one of them stopped and pointed at the boards over his windows.

Frank's mind was in bunker mode, and keeping people, both friends and strangers, away from his house was a priority. He hadn't discussed the vaccine subject again with Maureen since her unfounded indictment of Jim. Frank kept his thoughts to himself, but he was leaning towards taking a vaccine when one appeared.

The government claimed progress was being made on the vaccine front, but details were sketchy, at best. Evidently, immunization technology developed during the COVID pandemic a number of years ago was helping speed up the process. But Frank wondered if the Ebola virus might be a byproduct of all the unsettling genetic work. Perhaps there were mistakes made, and something escaped. It made him angry that scientists were messing with human genetics. It wasn't right. Why would people interfere with God's greatest creation? But still, what was done, was done, and maybe God was testing His people, and the vaccine was part of the grand plan. He considered how he was not as harsh as Maureen in his expectations of religious purity. This thought made him think about the bottle of bourbon stashed away in his basement workshop. He had been down there more than once in the past week for a nip.

Frank checked for the third time that day if the shotgun by the front door was fully loaded. He needed something to divert his attention, so Frank retired to his desk in the corner of their bedroom and switched on his computer after checking on Maureen.

He let the computer boot up and logged on to the American Truth site. The site had gained a reputation in Waco for its cutting-edge reporting. They were the ones who first made the connection between virus transmission and African-Americans. The more liberal news media claimed this wasn't true, but Frank had stopped trusting what they said many years ago. Blacks accounted for 25% of Waco's population, and he was taking no chances.

The headlines weren't encouraging, and he focused in on an article entitled "Frankenstein Vaccine Under Development by Government." Part of his hope faded as he read.

"Sources at the highest levels of government revealed today that research programs for an Ebola-Nano vaccine are hiding facts related to dangerous DNA side effects. The vaccines may alter an individual's DNA, so they aren't really human anymore.

"Previously developed vaccines are only effective in treating four of the known Ebola species (Ebola, Sudan, Taï Forest, and Bundibugyo). The current virus devastating the world was unknown until about three months ago, and it has been designated Ebola-Nano due to its unusually small size. Its small size allows the virus to spread via airborne transmission.

"Previous Ebola vaccines used tested and proven live vaccine technology, but the current research into Ebola-Nano is focused on RNA and DNA technologies where vaccines insert genetic material into human cells.

"The mRNA technology developed during the first COVID pandemic is still considered risky and unproven by most scientists. But now, reckless researchers at government-controlled labs are developing ways to insert new DNA into human cells. Once this DNA makes its way into a cell's nucleus, it can combine with human DNA to change a person's genetic makeup. Even worse, humans may be able to pass this foreign DNA on to their offspring.

"According to a separate source, the Frankenstein DNA is altered in a way which allows the government to track people and even selectively kill those who oppose the government on key issues."

Frank switched off the computer and lowered his head, resting it on his forearm. He was so very tired, feeling the mental strain of coping with the virus, like a heavy weight on his back. And now, the one ray of hope he had been nursing vanished like smoke in the air. He would rather take his chances with death than change into a zombie human being and risk eternal salvation.

Halfway across the continent, on the West Coast, Pastor Quince was deep into his morning reflections in the empty chapel of his San Diego church. Some of his congregation called this ritual his morning meditations, but he didn't like the term. Meditation implied some pseudo transcendental state and didn't adequately describe what he was doing each day. He was truly reflecting on the world around him and probing his position in the kinetic landscape of human activities.

He was the pastor for the Church of Holy Evolution. Quince had often considered how the fragmentation of the Christian Church was an inevitable byproduct of social evolution. God did not make a static universe, and time did not run backward. The dynamic nature of life itself forced change, and at any given time, the church was merely a work in progress. He knew his church was on the fringe of Christendom, and that knowledge provided him with the excitement and enthusiasm to tackle each day as another step on the road of holy evolution.

His core beliefs originated in verse 27 of the first chapter of Genesis: "*So God created man in his own image, in the image of God he created him; male and female he created them.*" This verse forced consideration of two possibilities. One possible interpretation was that the word 'image' referred to a physical resemblance, meaning God exists in human form. Quince fully accepted the universe as being 13.8 billion years old and some 93 billion light-years in diameter. Given this vast expanse of time and space, he felt it unlikely that God, who existed before the universe formed, actually looked like Homo sapiens.

Possibility two seemed more likely—the word "image" referred to a spiritual likeness, meaning humans have a divine spark within. The implications of this interpretation were staggering. Each person has a bit of the divine in their soul; we are each Christ-like. Quince knew this thinking bordered on heresy, but he couldn't ignore it, so he started his own church ten years ago. He now had over 400 people in his congregation, but the church structure was different, and he ran it more like a business dedicated to community improvement.

This morning he was again thinking about the Ebola-nano virus and its impact on the local community. Several of his congregation had died from the disease, and the number of local infections was climbing. Church resources were devoted solely to the crisis at this point. Heavy-duty N95 masks were distributed for free, and the church had about a hundred web-connected computers on loan to people for shopping and video conferencing. Everything was rapidly shifting online, including shopping for food and home supplies, routine healthcare needs, group support meetings, and more.

Quince held support meetings twice daily. The morning meeting was for helping people with the physical aspects of daily survival and the afternoon meeting focused on emotional support. These daily events were helping to keep his congregation tight and spreading a lot of aid to the rest of the local community. Every morning before his reflection time, he scanned the internet for news of a vaccine. The only article he found this morning was published on the racist American Truth network, but he read it anyway.

He was loath to believe anything they published, but nevertheless, here he was contemplating a vaccine that worked by altering Human DNA. He was unexpectedly excited by the whole concept. His vision of a physical evolutionary step occurring in his lifetime was enthralling, but above and beyond his logical thoughts on the subject, he sensed a future pregnant with the potential for a step-change in Christian evolution. He felt an exuberant ray of hope welling up from within.

Frank and Quince were both at a critical crossroads, each eying a different path forward. But eastward from both of them, a third person in Washington DC was considering the future. Representative Gratas from Florida was sweating as he weighed his options. He had narrowly won his seat last election by taking hardline positions on several issues that drove his party's reliance on single-issue voters. One of them was mandatory vaccines. Anti-vaxxers were up in arms about the vaccine passports recently proposed in Congress. He had run on a platform stating most vaccines were unnecessary, and the dangerous side effects of many were poorly understood. He knew facts and robust statistics didn't support this position, but the anti-vaxxers were a force to be reckoned with, and they carried a lot of sway with other groups under his party's tent.

He won the election by supporting three positions: unfettered access to assault weapons, total bans on abortion, and outlawing the use of vaccinations as criteria for entry into shops, businesses, government buildings, public spaces, and public transportation. Now stark reality reared its ugly head, and with forty to fifty percent mortality rates, the death tolls would be catastrophic unless an effective vaccine could intervene. Experts estimated that the national mortality rate would reach over a million people a day within the next sixty days.

He understood the coming storm when the public learned that the only effective vaccine available altered their DNA. He didn't doubt what he heard at the secret briefing yesterday. His dilemma was, many of the people who elected him would resist the vaccine, but most who voted for his opponent would welcome it. He could lose up to forty percent of his voters if to the virus on the one hand, but if he changed his position and supported mandatory vaccinations, he could also lose forty percent. Why does this shit always happen to me, he thought?

Gratas was pragmatic and had no compunction about lying if it got him where he wanted to go. But now, he was trapped in a cage of his own making, damned if he did and damned if he didn't. What he really hated was showing any weakness or admitting an error. But as he pondered his situation, a path forward took shape in his mind. His plans had always been grander than securing a place in the House of Representatives, and there was a gubernatorial election coming up soon enough. Perhaps there was an opportunity for him to use this crisis for some personal gain.

He would put out a public statement about the dangers of vaccines and their threat to human health. This statement would be followed by a leak to major news channels about the DNA issues with the new vaccines. He could then become the face of a movement to defend our humanity from the Frankenstein vaccine. His colleagues would, of course, sensibly pass legislation allowing or even mandating the vaccines since there were no other options. He could take the vaccine in secret but rail against it publicly.

He smiled to himself at the simplicity of the plan. He would be the darling of the far-right and could probably carry the vote at a state-wide level, even if the disease took a significant number of his supporters.

He called in his staffers and gave them their marching orders to craft a strong public statement. After they left, he made a single phone call.

The phone picked up, but no one spoke from the other end, as usual, so he laid out his request. "I need a major leak. I will provide the encrypted documentation at the usual drop. But I need it this week."

After a long pause, the reply came back with a slight Russian accent. "It will cost you, but the payment won't be monetary."

"Agreed." He hung up.

Ignorance and Fear (Mat)

The west-looking view from the ranch house front porch was expansive, and from where I sat, I could see the occasional car appear and then disappear in a small gap between two hills. A light snow had fallen in the early morning, and now the landscape sparkled with an icy white glazing. A large cup of coffee kept my hands warm. The night before, I was up until after midnight on a conference call with Carl and Shen discussing their recent debriefing with Congress. The politicians had not taken the news very well—excitement about the vaccine effectively counterbalanced dismay over its potential to alter human DNA.

Of course, this wasn't a statistically proven side effect since Shen, Dan Rohden, and I were supposedly the only ones who had received the vaccine, and technically I didn't count for statistical analysis since I had consumed the original infused tea remedy with the golden seeds. The ladies had cracked open the DNA secrets of the night parrot and golden seeds to identify a common gene, which appeared to be doing the work of stimulating antibodies to the virus. We had passed this genetic data on to Shen's lab.

At the other end of the equation, Dan's work resulted in the decryption of the medical data from the crystal matrix memory. His work uncovered an entire process for producing a trojan DNA delivery system. Shen's lab had coupled the two pieces together and rapidly produced a trial vaccine. Even with the mRNA technology at their fingertips, the development timeframe was unbelievably short, to the point where most experts were describing the situation as impossible. This skepticism is why the three of us had taken an early version of the vaccine.

All of us had proven to be immune to the Ebola-nano virus, but two days ago, an analysis showed the gene had inserted itself into my nuclear DNA.

Shen and Dan were still being tested. A further complication was the depleted supply of night parrot and golden seed material. We used it all between the lab research and the medicinal infusions we produced to protect ourselves during the past six weeks. But the depleted supplies were a moot point from a practical standpoint. The supply of these materials was so limited that only a handful of people in the world could be treated with raw materials. The only real path forward was replicating and using the genomic materials Amber Lee, Jenara, and Jillora had isolated.

In principle, the government had some raw material they recovered from Faillen during their raid on the Trezes' compound. Mattes and half his men were dead from the virus, but Faillen was alive from a small amount of the medicinal infusion I injected into him when I forced his help in locating the Trezes. He was in Federal custody, but the money I promised was in his accounts, not that he would be able to use it now.

Mark and his crew faded into the woodwork, and Jenara, Joseph, and I were holed up on a ranch he owned outside of Bend, Oregon. We could do nothing more to hasten a vaccine, and I had turned my attention to the social and political issues surrounding its distribution. But none of these things were on my mind this morning.

Last night, Jenara told me she was about seven weeks pregnant. She was convinced it was a girl, even though she had no way to know for sure. My anxiety level peaked when she also informed me she had taken the experimental vaccine just a week ago. She didn't address the unanswered question lurking in the back of my mind. Did the drug alter the baby's DNA? She would have vaccinated herself several days before testing confirmed that my DNA was altered as a result of the vaccine. When I quizzed her on the reasons for taking that risk, she had no answer, but she also seemed to have no anxiety over her decision, so I let the matter be. What was done was done.

Joseph came out of the front door and took a seat beside me in another rocking chair. "Beautiful, is it not?" he commented while taking in the morning scenery.

"Quite the place you have here," I replied.

"Yes, but I can never seem to spend enough time enjoying the views." He handed me his phone, and I read the article on the fascist American Truth site.

"It's going to get worse, Mat. One of my contacts in Russia tells me a massive news leak will hit tomorrow exposing the DNA issues with the vaccine, and it's also naming Shen's and Carl's companies as the primary research facilities."

"It's got to be one of those narcissistic assholes in DC behind it," I remarked. "They just had a briefing yesterday and are the only ones besides us who know about the problems. I need to let Shen and Carl know. This news will draw all sorts of loonies out from under the rocks. Nothing gets their adrenaline going more than ignorance and fear. Physical security may also become a major task. On top of that, every government hacking team around the world will be probing both company's computing systems looking for a way in."

"We need to think about ourselves too, Mat. We are okay here for a while, but eventually, people will trace you to this ranch."

"Any suggestions?" I asked.

"Let me think about it. I will come up with something. Any idea where Mark is?"

"Probably in Leakey. He scooped up a dozen of the experimental vaccine doses when he split and said something about a defendable hole in the wall."

"One last thing, Mat. My source said Jenara was mentioned in the leaked documents. He doesn't know whether his boss will put her name into the final materials." Joseph sat back in his chair and returned to sipping his coffee and gazing at the view.

I sipped my coffee too, but my stomach was crawling. I needed a plan that gave maximum protection to Jenara and the baby. There was a partially formed plan drifting around in the back of my mind. Like looking at trees through a morning mist, I could only glimpse small pieces at a time. I stuffed the fog-laced plan back into my subconscious where it could ferment and develop, and I focused on the situation with Carl and Shen. I was on the boards of both companies, a fact that would quickly surface once the news media got a hold on this story. I needed to talk with my business partners.

My first phone call to Carl was straightforward. His operation was already geared up for high-level security. The entire computing complex for the crystal matrix research was sandboxed, isolated from the internet with strictly controlled data-in and data-out gateways. But Shen was another matter. His company's internal controls on physical access and material containment were excellent due to the type of viral material they handled. But I was uncertain about their capabilities for dealing with external threats, and I felt the cybersecurity was good, but probably not good enough.

Shen answered on the first ring, and I laid out what we knew about the pending leak. "I'm pissed at those bastards in Washington, Mat. You've seen how this whole pandemic is bringing the crazy ones out of hiding. Armed groups are forming in some areas, vowing to shoot on sight if anyone comes near their territory. For the survivalist and religious fanatics, news of the DNA problem will be like waving a red flag in front of a bull. There will be a subset, probably armed, who will want to physically eliminate the vaccine threat."

"I don't doubt you are right, Shen. I already briefed the CEO of a security firm I have used for years. Marcelle's group is one of the best in the business. She can provide you with both physical security and cybersecurity, but doing it on short notice, particularly on the cyber side, may cause some disruptions. I know you already have some security people employed but give Marcelle a call and listen to what she has to say."

"We can handle some disruption," he replied. "Thanks to the connection with Carl, we are miles ahead of where we should rightfully be. To be honest, the issue, in my opinion, is more about ramping up production and not the basic immunization platform we have developed. But I'm worried about the safety of my employees."

His words struck home with me as my thoughts returned to Jenara and the baby. If things got crazy, there were a lot of innocent people who would be in jeopardy. Thoughts, which were fermenting in my subconscious, popped into view, and I could see a plan forming, like pieces of a jigsaw puzzle self-connecting. The biggest physical threats we faced were going to be poorly organized, self-styled home militias—gun nuts with lots of firepower and ammunition, but very little in the way of brains. However, they would see themselves as highly trained special forces. There was no question they were dangerous, but critical thinking was a weak spot we could take advantage of. Like a pack of dogs, they would chase the first moving target they could see. So let's give them a target.

"Shen, I am sending you Marcelle's phone number as soon as I hang up, but I need you to do something for me immediately. We have to get ahead of this leak." Joseph was still sitting on the front porch beside me, and he raised his eyebrows with a "here we go again" look. "On the public pages of your website, I need you to place a section called New Immunization Technologies. Make it look good and legit, but somewhere in there, talk about exciting new DNA research. Then I want you to name me as both a company director and head of the Immunization Technologies research. Also, mention that the research is being conducted at facilities in Portland, Oregon."

"Mat, we don't have any facilities in Portland."

"True, but by the end of the day, it will appear that we do. You just need to make the web information convincing and easy to find for an average person looking at your company. Just make sure the posting looks like it was created a month or two ago. The key point is, I have to be the key player in the DNA alteration research. They need to believe they can stop the project by cutting off the head. You set the bait, and I will set the trap. We will draw attention away from your people and some of the people close to me."

There was a very long pause before I got an "Okay."

After I hung up and sent Marcelle's number to Shen, Joseph looked my way and said, "you just can't keep yourself out of the flame, can you my friend? We had better start working if we are going to keep you in one piece."

The next twenty-four hours were solid work. Joseph and Jenara departed the next morning for Leakey, Texas via a private plane. He would deliver her and return to Portland. I took his SUV and headed westward for a several-hour drive to Portland.

Homo Novus

Sirocco settled the bird down where Pa had done the X marks the spot thing. Jillora Bindi, Joe, and Amber Lee grabbed their gear and climbed out. Sirocco spooled down the rotors and finished the post-flight checklist. Tom had pulled up in a '78 Dodge D-100 pick-up. One of Pa's older models. It was only a hundred yards to the main house but there was enough stuff in the bird to make the walk a bit cumbersome. He got a big hug from Jillora Bindi and she wanted to know where her baby girl was. She climbed into the shotgun seat. The gear was stowed in the bed and the others rode with their legs dangling from the tailgate. Joe kicked up his heels and dropped them again over and over. They were all laughing. Oh, for some pink fuzzy dice dangling from the rearview mirror.

"Reminds me of long ago and far away up in the Blue Ridge mountains." Joe grinned like he was a little kid again. Old fart. And not a bad distraction if there were any nerves among the others. MeeMee got the latest arrivals settled into their quarters. The plan was for everyone to get together on the front porch a bit later in the day.

Pa, Joe, Tom, and Mark had strolled down to the pond. Pa was giving up some local history and stretching the truth a bit about the size of a catfish he caught. Mark's sat phone rang and he answered it on the first ring. After all there were only a handful of people with the encrypted number. People he knew and trusted.

"Mark, Joseph here. I hope you are well and perhaps you have a minute."

"All the time in the world for you, my friend. I'm excellent and hope you are too. What's up?"

"Mat felt like Jenara needed a change of scenery. More importantly, he felt she needed to get lost and resituated in a more secure environment. He was cryptic, as usual, but did mention something about it raining shit in Portland. Amber Lee said come on down. So, we're airborne, an hour out of Portland, headed your way. We have about another three hours to go."

"Flying into San Antone?" Mark asked.

"Leakey if you think we can pull it off. I see the 'airport' is officially closed but the runway still looks to be functional. I chartered a Swiss-made Pilatus PC-24 to bring in Jenara. It is an eight-seat jet with a 2,200-mile range. The owner/pilot describes it as rugged and was specifically designed for small, rough runways. Even dirt. It can land and take off in less than 3,000 feet. The Frio River Landing runway is approximately 3,200 feet long. He is comfortable with it but requests you put your eyes on the pavement since the sat photo is probably a bit aged. Kerrville is the alternative."

"Hold a second. Pa, do you know who owns Rio Frio Landing? Trying to get Jenara here safe and sound. The runway is just long enough." Mark said.

"Old friends of ours. I'll ring them up. ETA?" Pa was on it.

"Also, Mat wants me to personally give you a message if possible." Joseph made it interesting. Sometimes Mat did not trust even the most secure communication systems.

"OK. And Pa is nodding at me so we're good to go at Rio Frio Landing. I'll be there a couple of hours early and drive the runway. If it's a go we're good. If not, it gives me time to get to Kerrville before ya'll land." Mark finalized the simple, impromptu plan.

"If anyone asks, Old Charlie will say the jet was a special delivery for his wife's insulin since the mail has slowed down so much." Pa was on it.

Mark ran the blacktop runway end to end in the F-150 and found it to be clear and sound. He called Joseph and let him know. He was excited that the runway was functional. It gave him some free time. He parked in front of the now-abandoned Quonset hut hangar and the adjacent old ranch house. He crossed the barbed-wire fence and walked east a couple hundred yards then dropped down into the mostly dry bed of the West Frio River. The river was intermittent, mostly running underground at the moment, but he could see one pool from where he was. He walked north up the dry bed, watching for fossils and possibly a chert tool or two until he reached the pool.

He slowed his pace and walked beside the pool. It was perhaps three hundred feet long and thirty feet at its widest. The pool was crystal clear, even in the deeper section. He felt he could read the date on a Mercury dime if it was laying on the bottom. There, in the deepest section, perhaps four feet of water, he watched several small Guadalupe and largemouth bass and sunfish, a foot-long channel catfish, lots of tadpoles, and there was even a blotched water snake sunning along the rock ledge on the west side. A variety of moss and small aquatic plants rounded out the amazingly beautiful miniature ecosystem.

He had traveled far and wide in search of whereabouts unknown most of his life and his favorite place always seemed to be the next discovery like this one. He soaked in the artistry of the light and shadows in the water thrown by the sun and a sunken Bald Cypress branch. Minnows, perhaps endangered Darters, played tag with each other and tried not to become a meal. The warm dry air had a subtle scent of sage and about a hundred other things he perhaps, once upon a time, knew the names of but had forgotten. He checked his 360 and saw the tail end of three Rio Grande turkey hens crossing the dry bed a hundred yards above him. A Golden-cheeked warbler in the brush provided an amazing array of background music.

Near the upper end of the pool, he found a hand-sized tannish-gray chert multi-tool near the water. There were perhaps fifty or sixty individual facets chipped on both sides of the tool. It could have served a variety of purposes, from cutting to chopping to crushing. It was a natural and man-made work of art. Not for the first time in his life did he think to himself, man, it don't get no better than this.

Joseph rang in just as Mark was back at the F-150. "The old windsock is almost limp and shows what wind there is out of southwest. Come straight in north to south, touching down above the 15. I'll park the F-150 on the dirt road adjacent to the runway on the south end just past 33. Have the pilot stop parallel to me. Note the runway is perhaps 50 feet wide. Recommend we talk outside." Mark rang off and drove to the south end of the runway. Moments later a dot in the sky became an aircraft clearing the trees and dropping onto the runway just past the arrow. The pilot pulled up tight on the right edge at 33 and stopped. The side door popped open, the stairs folded down and Jenara then Joseph climbed down and out. Each had travel bags in both hands. They walked across the rest of the tarmac and then some short grass to where Mark was waiting. He helped place the four bags in the bed.

Jenara gave Mark a big hug, Joseph shook his hand and said, "You look well my friend! Excellent to see you. I'll be brief. Mat says the government appears reluctant to share our technology with the rest of the world. Fuck them, his words. He thinks it is time to see if perhaps the Sentinel can help us. This is about the survival of humanity, not just some bureaucrats. Thoughts?" Joseph was brief.

"I agree. Sounds like the former guy. Probably the likes of Gratas and his fucking asshole buddies too. Sell their souls and their entire families for fifty cents. I'll ask John to ring up the Sentinel as soon as I get Jenara situated. Cheers my friend!" Mark helped Jenara into the shotgun seat. They watched through

Jenara's side window as Joseph climbed back aboard the jet and the door sealed. Mark texted Mat that Jenara was safe and sound. The pilot pivoted on a dime, stood on the brake, and pushed the throttles to the stops. The small jet trembled slightly like a cheetah ready to pounce. The pilot dumped the brake and in moments the tiny jet was 300 feet above the north end of the runway and climbing. They would refuel at Midland-Odessa International Air and Space Port. Diego, down in Peru, would get a good laugh out of the ostentatious name. Joseph would be back in Portland in time for a sip or two.

Jenara and Mark chatted along the way until Pa clicked them through the gate. Mark paused and watched the gate close in his mirrors, then proceeded to the main house. MeeMee greeted Jenara warmly and got her settled into her quarters.

Pa pulled out his iPhone and told Mark, "I saw you wait until the gate closed. I presume you know I have cameras at the gate and up and down the road. And elsewhere on the ranch. I just pop them up on my phone."

"Yup. I figured you did. That or a magnet in the road." Mark replied.

"Got magnetic sensors buried below the gravel, center of the road, on both sides of the gate as well. But, as you know, a tire tool tossed over the gate to the correct spot will trigger the gate. I figure I ought to let you know I also have some C-4 planted under the road in a sealed off culvert pipe about fifty yards past the gate toward town. I did that after Amber Lee told me all that was going on and ya'll were going to park here for a while in the valley. Based on what I know it's a good bet someone is gonna be pissed off and looking for one or more of you. If we blow the road my backhoe and Mark's Benz will be the only thing in or out unless it's a dirt bike or similar." Pa nodded.

"I always knew there was more to you than that Texas-sized smile." Mark said. "Excuse me, I need to make a call."

Mark walked down to the pond and rang up John.

"Hello Mr. Mark. I hope all is well on the ranch." John said. Mark wanted to shoot something but refrained. Fucking computer knew, of course, exactly where he was. Mark understood how important that could be, with still being alive as one of the main attributes of the system. Still it pissed him off in an apparently non-sensible way to the uninitiated. He muttered, again, even after all the years that had floated under the bridge since college, "fuck Fortran."

"It's time to contact the Sentinel. How do we proceed?" Mark was to the point.

"I will attempt to make contact and then let you know. It could be a while. Sometimes the Sentinel, as you have chosen to name the person, is unavailable. Somewhat like you Mr. Mark. Anything else sir?" Mark said no and thanks, and rang off.

182

Everyone convened on the hand-hewn floorboard and Bald Cypress-pillared front porch of the main house. The pillars were over two feet in diameter and sat nicely on two-foot-tall square-cut limestone bases. A variety of antique rockers, straight-back chairs, and drink tables were scattered across the twenty-foot wide by hundred-foot-long porch. Several Hunter Cassius fans suspended from the twelve-foot ceiling were turning to the right. A massive free-standing stone fireplace occupied a space on the edge of the porch two-thirds of the way to the north end. Everyone had a drink in their hand because it was five o'clock somewhere.

"Pa and I are so happy everyone can be here. I toast all of you!" MeeMee being the perfect hostess, as always.

Everyone said cheers and turned up a beverage. "I thank you, my generous hosts, for allowing us the comfort of your most amazing home!" Tom doing the Aussie thing. More cheers followed and more than a few tales were spun.

Off to the side was an impressive grill. The metal nameplate on the front said Texas Bar-B.Q. Pits. Pa got up and started the ritual. Hunter and Joe joined him. In reply to Hunter's question Pa said, "The Luling Loaded model. The company is actually based in Baton Rouge. I like it because it maintains the temperature I want. And it's big enough to cook a sheep or small deer on. I'm going to throw a variety of meats on for tonight. Venison, mutton, cow, and wild turkey."

"Sounds excellent. How can we help?" Hunter and Joe could manage a grill in their own right.

"We'll manage the whole thing together if you like." So, they did.

Pa placed a few stubs of lighter wood into the fire box. On top of those, he placed some small, cut-up mesquite branches. He used a wooden white and red tipped Diamond Strike Anywhere Match to get the lighter wood going. Hunter fetched some more mesquite from the neatly stacked selection off to the side. In a few minutes he put some small branches then some larger cut-up branches, perhaps two inches by twelve inches, on top of the tiny conflagration. Later they would add slightly larger split pieces of trunk and thicker limbs. In a couple of hours, the grill would be ready to use.

Carrying on from several previous conversations Jenara summarized things, "It appears that the Trojan-Interceptor DNA may cause permanent genetic modification. It may permanently alter the human genome. Mat says it's possible we can pass the alterations on to our children. Alterations that may destroy viruses both good and bad. We would be artificially changing the human genetic makeup, for better or worse."

"The human genome is specific to Homo sapiens?" MeeMee brought herself into the conversation.

"Correct. It is specific to our species. Neanderthals, Homo neanderthalensis, had a neanderthalensis genome. The same is true for other hominids. Chimpanzees, Pan troglodytes, our closest living relatives, have almost 99% of our DNA. The same is true for essentially all living things." Amber Lee and MeeMee often had long discussions. Sometimes it was hard to tell the two apart unless you were watching them.

"About 3.7 to 3.2 million years ago Australopithecus afarensis roamed around East Africa from Ethiopia to Tanzania. Mary Leakey made the first discovery about fifty years ago or so, followed shortly thereafter by Donald Johanson and Tom Gray. Everyone has heard of the famous skeleton named Lucy, one of our early upright-walking ancestors. So, there was an Australopithecus afarensis genome. Point being that the evolution train is always moving. And has been since the orbs full of DNA were dropped off on Earth four billion years ago. Change seems to be the only constant." The young Jillora Bindi was a new-comer here but was obviously well-versed and certainly not shy. MeeMee had taken to calling her J.B. so as to not confuse her with her mom.

"Is Leakey named after Mary Leakey by chance?" Joe joined in.

"Good question. No. The town is actually named after John Leakey. He settled on the Frio River in 1856. MeeMee's relatives and mine were among some of the other folks that settled here around the same time. Mary's name is pronounced Leek-ey and John's was and still is pronounced Lake-ey." Pa loved his heritage and was a fountain of information. "We've been told that the gene pool is a bit shallow around here since the population has never been much more than a thousand folks!" Pa got a laugh. "It's down to four hundred or so now."

"Well, it sure is beautiful!" Carolina was sitting next to Hunter with her hand on his left knee. "I'd like to hike some if it's OK."

Pa said, "Of course you can. Just watch for snakes. You could run into a western diamondback rattler climbing the mesas."

MeeMee, Amber Lee and Sirocco burst out laughing. Pa joined in and Amber Lee told the tale. Mark was, naturally, the center of attention. During a hike up the mesa he performed a record-breaking backward broad-jump into a prickly pear cactus. He had become a local legend. All because of a little ole rattlesnake buzzing a bit. MeeMee performed an epic cactus spine removal procedure. All the while Sirocco and Amber Lee cackled. Everyone got a laugh out of it. Mark took the ribbing well and said that he may need to go play with his Desert Eagle.

Once the melee settled down Pa continued, "We see a few copperheads here in the valley. Around the ponds there are a few banded and blotched water snakes and maybe a moccasin. A good rule is to leave them alone and they will do the same. The rattlers will be nestled deep under ledges out of the sun, so I doubt you'll run into any. Just don't stick your hands where you can't see."

Drinks were replenished and a breeze cooled things off as the day waned. MeeMee asked who would like to help with the dinner preparations. The ladies jumped up and they all headed inside. Tom looked at Mark and grinned.

"First, most, and largest, $25 bucks per category. Pa, Hunter, Joe, ya'll want in on the action?" They declined and seemed content to get the grill ready for corn, tators, and some meat. Doing the grill thing stretched back to a time when their ancient ancestors found something grilled by a fire caused by a lightning strike. Probably. Archeological evidence points to the use of actual firepits dating back more than a million years. Harnessing fire as a tool was perhaps the single most important event in the history of man. It sparked everything thereafter. Mark felt the second most important event in the history of man was the invention of Scotch. This occurred in 1495 in Scotland.

Mark and Tom pulled their usual ultra-lite tackle out of the back of Mark's rig and ran down to the pond like little kids. Little sixty-something year old kids. Mark's #0 gold buck-tailed Mepp hit the water an instant before Tom landed his near some brush in the water. One up for Mark. Instantly Tom was hooked up. He soon released a one pound largemouth. All tied up. And, so it went as they worked their around the pond in opposite directions.

When they met at the upper end of the pond Tom pulled out a worn silver flask. Inside was 15-year-old Balvenie Single Barrel. Mark did the same. His was inscribed with Tears of My Enemies. Inside was 16-year-old Lagavulin. They tapped the flasks together. Tom said, "Cheers mate!" Mark said, "Speedbumps my friend!" They both laughed and continued in opposite directions, ending back at the dock. Tom won according to Tom. Mark won according to Mark. They bumped flasks and declared their efforts a tie. All the fish lived to fight another day.

They all had supper sitting in a rough circle on the porch. Everything was amazing according to everyone and there was more than plenty to go around. MeeMee had also invited Mária Elana and Juan, the ranch hands living in the last bunkhouse up the valley. Earlier, Juan had delivered the fresh meat to Pa. The conversation led to hunting laws as they ate fresh-killed venison and wild turkey.

"The game warden comes over occasionally to replenish his freezer. We only take what we eat and we're keenly aware of wild game populations. Right now, there is an abundance of whitetail deer and Rio Grande turkey. We also have a lot of bobwhite quail and even few blue quail. Juan, Mária, and the other ranch hands supplement ours and many others' diets in a responsible manner. Believe it or not there are plenty of poor and hungry folks living close by. We help out because we're lucky enough to be able to. The warden also makes a few deliveries to the more unfortunate ones and to some elderly folks that can't get out.

We also allow some of the needy to hunt in-season. We pitch in on a local level, same as ya'll helping a lot of folks all over the world with your philanthropy."

Everyone nodded and agreed that helping others was a noble cause. Another toast went out to Pa and MeeMee.

"We also can a lot of meat, vegetables, and fruit on the ranch. We raise some of the fruit and vegetables and buy the rest from local growers. We store much of it in the cavern. Tomorrow I want to show it to everyone. It has been a fairly closely-held secret but there are things in there worth being aware of, including the entrance location." Pa made tomorrow worth waiting for.

Everyone had been so engrossed with the food, drink, and amazing conversations that they seemed to forget their surroundings. J.B. was the first to notice and said, "Look at all the deer and turkeys!" The fields to the south suddenly looked like a menagerie. The longhorns were greatly outnumbered.

"They come out late in the day and early in the morning. Keep watching and you may see axis deer or some Thompson's gazelle. Hell, sometimes a zebra or two will show up. The exotics from other countries are escapees from the large pay-to-kill ranches." MeeMee said with a bit of a scowl. "I'm not particularly fond of those folks."

The conversation turned back to the pandemic sweeping the globe. Sirocco had given enough of the remaining vaccine to MeeMee for the ranch hands. The few remaining vials would be selectively distributed.

"We appreciate you giving us the vaccine. We hear that there is much death spreading across the land back home around Matamoros and beyond. Hopefully soon there will be enough vaccine for people in Mexico and all around the world." Mária Elana joined in. "I wish there was something we could do to help."

As if coincidence is normal, Mark's sat phone chirped quietly in the pocket of his old Columbia fishing shirt. The chirp took him by surprise. It was a sound he had never heard from the small and very sophisticated instrument. The screen displayed the word Sentinel. He answered before a second chirp could be emitted, gave a slight wave, and walked off the porch and headed toward the pond.

"Mark here."

"Mark, you have given me a nick name. Sentinel. It is perhaps more apt than you can know. I understand you wish to speak with me." The voice was neutral, neither male nor female, and there was no particular accent or inflection. It was soft, clear, and concise. Probably filtered through a computer program.

"Yes. Thank you for calling. I suspect John's security is acceptable to you since you have indeed called me."

There was a brief chuckle. "Yes, as John is prone to say the call is being transferred around various top secret satellites every split second or so and there is no chance of being detected, much less actually being overheard. I'm comfortable to chat. I understand that you and another individual named Mat are the focus of our conversation."

Mark concurred and gave a brief synopsis of the issue at hand. The U.S. government was using national interest as an excuse for not sharing the vaccine technology with the rest of the world.

"I had heard rumors to that effect. Now I know it for a fact. Of course, there are many other governments around the world that would use the same ploy given the opportunity. Still, it is relatively onerous for the U.S. or any other government to act in such an uncivilized manner. Naturally it is self-serving politicians leading the way down this pathway to destruction. Sorry, I digress. Politicians are not among my favorite forms of pond scum. Yes. I can help with the distribution of the information globally. We have manufacturing and distribution capabilities, but ultimately we can only lessen the blow. Please know this is not just me, but a consortium of like-minded people from around the world will be involved. Collectively we have considerable power, resources, and the shared desire to work for a common good. We can help many, but ultimately we can't avert the catastrophe descending upon humanity."

Mark was silent for a long moment. "Any help you can give is appreciated. The planning may take a few days. That ball is in Mat's court. Either he or I will be in contact with the details for transferring the information into your hands as soon as possible."

Mark said cheers and rang off. He came back to the porch, nodded at Jenara, and helped everyone else with the cleanup. It was done quite efficiently, and the evening respite was rejoined on the porch.

"As I was saying corn, a specialized maize that started out as the plant teosinte, was first cultivated around 9,000 years ago, in central Mexico. Folks realized they could save the largest kernels, dry them, and then plant them. Subsequent plants were more robust and yielded larger kernels. Plants that had both larger and more kernels were even more prized. Hybridization had begun. The best genes were perpetuated. Not long after that it some of it showed up around here." Pa was on a roll.

"Archeologists have studied numerous sites within a hundred miles or so. Including on our ranch and a significant stretch of the Frio and West Frio, where you were walking. Their discoveries bear this out, among other things. Tomorrow I will show you a bit of such history. So, what started as a two-to-three-inch-long plant with perhaps ten tiny kernels is now a twelve-inch ear with five hundred or more kernels."

Daylight had faded into twilight. Pa, with Hunter and Joe helping, had built a roaring fire in the massive free-standing stone fireplace perched on the edge of the deck. Everyone had pushed or pulled their chairs and tables closer to it.

It was a primal thing. No zebras appeared before it got took dark to see across the fields. But the opportunity to see so many wild things made everyone happy.

"Mark, you've been your usual reticent self today. Any thoughts?" Amber Lee usually tried to draw the normally quiet Mark into the conversation.

"Well, first off, the call I received was mixed news. I can't say more about it, at least not now. Because I won't know anything else until Mat frees himself up. Now, I have listened to all of you talk about history, from the deposition of DNA in the orbs four billion years ago here on Earth, to the present. I think those ancestors of ours, making the attempt to survive so many billions of years ago, were DNA-driven to extend their survival beyond the life of their failing, last gasp civilization on planet faraway. They were obviously successful. If success can be gaged by mankind as it exists today."

"And I believe they had no choice in the matter. The rise and fall of species over millennia is obvious to all of us. From the great dinosaurs to the tiniest plankton, Darwin's notion of survival of the fittest has displayed itself. The fittest, of course, being those species capable of adapting to changes in their circumstances, changes in their environment. Lucy and her kin managed to survive by getting up off of all fours and walking bipedally. And so on until the story of our evolution brings us to the present."

Mark continued, "Jillora Bindi's ancestors discovered the night parrot green-ery. The last of it corralled in the ancient bone container still held the scent that allowed her to chase down perhaps the very last remnants on earth. In the wilds of the outback. In the middle of the night. In a nest of the reportedly extinct Night Parrot. Jenara's shaman mentor introduced her to the equally rare Golden Seeds. Some of these same seeds were fetched by Jenara, Mat and company. That adventure was a near thing for Amber Lee, Jenara, and Mat."

"Then an extraordinary scientific team came together in Dallas. The team was able to isolate genes that are apparently effective against this newest plague. Others figured how to convert this genetic discovery into a vaccine and mass-pro-duce it. Now groups are working to figure out the logistics of global distribution. These things did not happen in a vacuum. These things did not happen by chance or coincidence. These things happened because our DNA required us to search for the means to survive."

"Will the cure change our genetic make-up? Perhaps. Will we survive? Time will tell. There is one certainty. And that certainty is that change happens. Our genome is significantly different from even our recent ancestors. Our children's children's genome will be different from ours. The genetic make-up will change with or without our consent. Change, by its very nature, is required."

"Finally, the question of whether or not to take the vaccine is not a valid question. Of course, we will take the vaccine. Our DNA demands it of us. The question of whether or not the vaccine will change our genome is not a valid question. It matters not because our DNA requires us to do our best to survive. The vaccine appears to be the best bet. Therefore, it is our destiny to take the vaccine and hopefully survive to fight another day. This may or may not be the first time a conscious decision had been made to alter our genome. That may have been done by our ancestors all those billions of years ago on planet faraway."

"There will be those on the left that will disagree or agree, same as on the right. There will be far right extremists saying you can stick a needle in my cold dead arm. There will be those also on the far right thinking what a great way to recreate the Aryan race. All of these folks will flap their gums and shake feathers from their wings. Some will bring out their AR's and pretend to be warriors for a cause. None of it really matters. We sit here enjoying this magnificent evening and are both party to and witness to some non-trivial change."

"Lastly, if it comes to pass that the vaccine indeed changes our DNA, I suggest future generations be called Homo novus." Mark seemed spent.

"Ms. MeeMee, I greatly appreciate the room but now that my new home has arrived, I intend to occupy it. I do hope, however, to continue to be allowed to take advantage of the board. I am tired and am going to retire for the evening."

"Your boots will always be welcome under my table Mark!" MeeMee beamed.

"Good night all. I'll see you in the morning. Pa, I look forward to discovering the many mysteries held in the cavern and elsewhere." Mark stepped off the expansive porch and made his way to his Benz.

Those gathered on the porch sipped their chosen beverages for several minutes without so much as an utterance. Finally, Joe said, "I'll be damn. That's probably more words than that old cowboy ever strung together. Ever."

"Probably," said Sirocco. "And he's right." There was assent across the board.

"Anyone know what novus means?" Juan asked.

"Latin for new." Amber Lee said.

"I think I'll go tell him I agree with his assessment." Sirocco added.

Amber Lee said, "Mind if I tag along?"

"I hoped you might want to. Good night everyone! See ya'll tomorrow!"

Hill Country Ready

The next morning, they all engaged in the act of destroying an epic Hill Country breakfast on the front porch. They were all there. MeeMee, Pa, Amber Lee, Sirocco, Mark, Jenara, Joe, Hunter, Carolina, Tom, Jillora Bindi, and J.B. There were eggs, bacon, sausage, country ham, gravy, fried potatoes, grits, biscuits, fresh fruit and more.

"This is amazing! Excellent food, excellent hosts, and excellent company as well!" Jillora Bindi was radiant in the early morning sun. The air was crisp, dry, fresh, and full of pleasant scents and sounds. Deer and a few turkeys were fading off into the distance and up onto the sides of the mesas. There was more small talk and tall tales until they had all gotten their fill and the kitchen was cleaned up. Back outside there was a bit of excitement in the air.

Pa said, "Like I said last night, we're going to show ya'll a place that only a few folks are aware of. My grandfather made the discovery when he blew out a bit of the mesa for some reason that has been lost in time. Probably to settle some of the rocks that had broken off and fallen to the foot of the mesa. I do that occasionally to prevent getting crushed by rolling boulders."

"When the dust cleared, Grandpa could see a door-sized hole in the rocks leading into the foot of the mesa. Now there are many caves and caverns throughout the area, so he apparently was not totally surprised. After all the vent up near the top of the mesa where Mark met the rattler has been known for generations. There are other ones further to the west on the ranch as well. The tale is he took a torch and headed in. The room opened up almost immediately ahead, to his left and right. Looking back, he saw that the original entrance, probably fifty feet wide, had been closed off by previous rockslides. The roof tapered up and away into the darkness. At his feet was a hearth. It was not alone. There were actually several, each separated from the others by perhaps twenty feet or so."

"Who made the hearths was unknown, but the hearths were obviously very old. When he was a child, he had developed a certain reverence for the old folks as he called them. Ya'll have seen the many artifacts around the house. He started the collection. Everything you see is from the ranch. As time allowed, he explored more of the cavern. There were many artifacts in addition to the hearths. There were even paintings and etchings on the walls. It seemed there were probably burial spots as well. He decided to leave everything inside the cavern where it was. And he decided to keep it a secret."

"Grandpa built a rough shed up against the ledge with the door hidden behind junk he stacked there. Over the years he and Grandma spent considerable time putting in simple wooden walkways and stairs deeper into the cavern, allowing them to explore ever further under the mesa. They ran electric lines and positioned lights as they ventured deeper and deeper into the cavern. My father and his brothers and sisters followed suit until most of the cavern was explored. That is to say most of what could be safely accessed. There are actually several chambers to the west and northwest. We can walk in almost a mile."

"Oh my gosh! I can't wait to see it!" Jillora exclaimed.

"Follow me!" exclaimed Pa.

They walked uphill from the main house and stopped at a weathered pole barn, measuring perhaps thirty feet by thirty feet, nestled on the left up against the foot of the mesa. The upper pond, much smaller than the one downhill, was off to the right.

"MeeMee and I replaced the old shed thirty or forty years ago. Come on in." He swung the two doors wide open, and they all walked in. There were farm implements, sacks of this and that, and a long work bench sporting a variety of tools, both hand and electric. At the back he touched a place on the apparently solid wooden wall, and it slid open sideways at the central vertical seam. They walked through and immediately issued a collective gasp.

The cavern spread out before them in the distance. Columns and stalagmites and stalactites and glimmering pools were artfully bathed in muted lighting. To the right were rows of stout wooden shelving stocked like a grocery.

"There wasn't any obvious reason not to put the wooden storage units in that area near the collapsed rocks. It's a constant 70°F year-round inside the cavern. The Mason jars full of canned meats, vegetables, fruits, jams, and other similar items will probably keep here for years. However, what we don't eat we rotate out annually and give to those less fortunate than us." MeeMee informed the gathering. "Watch your step and careful not to slip on the boards. The high humidity and drips from the ceiling make the boards constantly wet."

"The water trickles outside through several springs and keeps the ponds full. The water is potable, so we always have aplenty by pumping it from a dedicated spring to the house and most of the outbuildings." Pa explained how they got by without wells like many ranches had.

"A friend of mine, Jenni, is a professor of archeology at UT Austin. She has been conducting several different simultaneous studies here for several years. There is painstaking documentation required of the art and etchings on the walls, digs to determine the age and extent of occupation and the cataloging of, so far, over a thousand artifacts. Recently others at UT have dated an area north of Austin as having been occupied as long as twenty thousand years ago. My friend thinks this cavern may have been occupied even longer. I help her when I'm in town. She also has grad students help. Pa shows them the stores the first time they enter. One jar of meat is labeled Talkative Grad Student." Amber Lee garnered a laugh. "They get the message."

Tom, Jillora Bindi, and their daughter were enthralled as they explored the cavern for most of the rest of the day with the others. "On our property in the Outback we have found evidence of habitation going back at least seventy thousand years. It is incredibly humbling to visit somewhere halfway across the globe to where folks established themselves before the advent of the friggin' telephone!" Tom laughed and smiled his smile.

"You can see the various excavations marked off with yellow tape on the ground. Jenni thinks an area between those two columns over there is a burial site. Another six months or so of excavation should tell the tale. Removing dirt carefully a teaspoon at a time can take a while, but that is her methodology." Amber Lee explained even though she knew that just about everyone was cognizant of the scientific methods employed by archeologists. They all continued talking excitedly about their day and the magnificence of the cavern all through another amazing supper and into the growing darkness.

Mark aka Mr. Talkative said, "I suggest that tomorrow we begin to develop a long-range plan of survival in what has become a rapidly deteriorating state of affairs across the globe according to my recent brief conversations. John says the fifty percent mortality rate is taking a toll in boardrooms, factories, schools, office buildings, and just about everywhere else where people congregate. Mass transite, including air, rail, and buses, may grind to a screeching halt."

The following morning, they cleaned up after breakfast and reconvened on the front porch. Sirocco, Amber Lee, Jenara, Jillora Bindi, and young Jillora decided to set up the lab equipment brought down from Dallas. There was still vital work that needed to be done. MeeMee and Pa wanted to close down and secure their store in town. Carolina asked if they needed help. "Absolutely dear!"

MeeMee was definitely happy to have the extra set of hands. She wanted to be done and back on the ranch as soon as possible.

That left Mark, Joe, Hunter, and Tom the opportunity to decide how to best secure the ranch from government and criminal groups, and potential common outlaws. The Boy Scouts of America have a motto; be prepared. Any practitioner in the arts of survival uses the same philosophy. So, they planned to be prepared.

"Any word from Mat?" Hunter asked Mark.

"Nope. I've texted, called, used mental telepathy, and am considering sending smoke signals. I called John this morning and was told to hold my horses, quote unquote. Fucking computer. Actually, it's a positive sign because apparently the computer knows something we don't. Meaning Mat is still among the living. Hopefully we will hear from him soon. My fear is that some rogue branch of darkness within the blackest regions of our government has him. If so, hopefully he can bullshit his way out. He's a pretty good bullshitter." Mark said. "If not I'm gonna clean out his bar on the way to my next adventure out to whereabouts unknown. Alaska I'm thinking.

"That Mat is a pretty good bullshitter is an understatement." Hunter agreed.

Mark laid a 1:24,000 Leakey Quadrangle Texas topo map, aka a 7.5-minute map, out on the serving table near the grill. Pa had a drawer full of maps covering the region. Produced by the USGS, each map typically covers from 49 to 64 square miles. The ranch was in the upper central area of the map they were looking at. "We're here." Hunter pointed. "We need to consider defense first, then offense. From my perspective we're in the best shape possible from a defensive perspective. I want to traverse the four points of the compass using the tracks on the map just to be sure." Hunter was hunting. "I like the paper USGS maps better than any electronic version. They gives us the best possible perspective."

"We can split up and use the ATV's. I'm sure Mária Elana and Juan can point us in the right direction regarding places we may miss. I suspect that they and the hands on the western edge of the ranch are going to be important assets. Doing our due diligence is important but having been here for a couple of days, I think the front gate and the sky are our weak points. I also think they are both defensible. Further, with Mark's truck, his armory, Sirocco's chopper, and the impressive array of weaponry on hand in the main house, I believe we can mount a crushing offensive thrust if necessary." Hunter putting it together.

"By the way Pa has magnetic sensors buried below the gravel, center of the road, on both sides of the gate. He also has some C-4 planted under the road in a sealed-off culvert pipe about fifty yards past the gate toward town. He can set off the C-4 from his phone." Mark tossed that card on the table.

"I knew there was more to Pa than his sunny disposition and brilliant smile." Joe offered. "He reminds me more and more of, well, us."

"Let's see if Mária Elana and Juan are home. We'll decide how to divvy up the tracks from there." Using the number he got the night before, Mark called Juan. Juan answered on the first ring. He was tending some horses. He'd meet them on the porch of the main house in twenty minutes.

"I want to see exactly what Pa and MeeMee have in the way of shooters. Let's take a walk around the house and create an inventory. Also, let's remember to get Pa to show us the rest of his toys. The hidden ones. There are bound to be hidden ones." Hunter said, and the four of them walked inside. Without being too invasive or trespassing into Pa and MeeMee's inner sanctum, it appeared they had enough pistols, rifles, and shotguns to overthrow most small countries. Then there was Mark's inventory.

Juan arrived on a chestnut quarter horse. He dismounted and whispered to the mare to wait. She milled around a little and waited. Quarter horses are the classic ranch workhorses. Juan provided them with very detailed information on the various tracks up and down the mesas and across the length and breadth of the ranch. "This is washed out completely, that is totally overgrown, this is the route we use to get to the western edge of the ranch." Juan seemed to know the ranch as well or better than Pa and MeeMee used to know it in their early days. "I discovered a female cougar with cubs. Their den is about here at 2,100 feet along the lower rim of this part of the mesa. She is la perra. Scared the shit out of me a few days ago when I was chasing some blue quail over there. I tell you do not fuck with her." They all laughed at the face Juan made. He seemed like a good hand.

Tom traveled due north then west, basically along the property line track. Hunter went northwest then west, taking a north central line. Joe took the southwest then west track. Mark went due south then west along the southern property line. The routes sounded simple except for the fact that there weren't really any straight tracks up the mesas and through the canyons. The five hundred to six hundred foot elevation changes were a bitch. They all made it to the bunkhouse on the west-central edge of the ranch just after noon. Scratched up and bleeding. Aching. Bitching. Mark wanted to sit down and whine, but he knew that the young lady who greeted them, Rosa, would just say grow a pair, so he sucked it up.

"Let's get Sirocco to fly over and pick us up," said Joe, being Joe.

"Great idea!" Tom was onboard with a short hop in the chopper.

"Rosa, can you get us home using the easiest route?" Hunter the hunter.

She nodded, saddled up with Hunter, and they were back at the main house in a little over two hours. MeeMee, Pa and Carolina were back from securing the

194

store and barn. MeeMee laughed when she saw the great explorers. The others heard the laughter and came out and laughed with MeeMee. Joe, Hunter, Mark, and Tom failed to see the humor. There was nothing funny about having your rugged clothing shredded by the myriad thorn-laden plants they encountered every foot of the way. Because virtually everything growing in this neck of the woods has thorns. Everything.

"I have been there, done that, and returned many times in my life. But I swear that if some bad guys manage to attack us from the west, I'm gonna roll up in a ball on the ground in front of them and kiss my ass goodbye." Mark was not happy. The guy who was friends with a grizzly bear. The guy who had a bull elk essentially laugh in his face. The guy collecting bullet holes in an airplane flying out of a jungle shitshow just in the nick of time. Not to mention speedbumps and the like.

Sirocco hugged him and said it would be okay, using that momma will take care of the poor baby tone. Naturally this brought new peals of laughter from the gallery. Mark walked away and down to the dock at the pond. He unlaced his roughout boots, pulled off his old, and now torn and bloody fishing shirt, then dove into the pond. Tom, Joe, and Hunter were right behind him. Juan said he had work to do so he was off on the quarter horse. Before long MeeMee was the only one not in the pond. The respite was good for everyone since they were all feeling the growing pressure exerted by the occurrences happening elsewhere and beyond their control.

Carolina joined the others in the newly established lab. Pa showed the rest of the guys his various weapons around the main house. They had already seen most of them.

"So, if there is a ground attack, I think we have the advantage. Tom, I take it you found the perches above the gate and road? If we use the C-4 then anyone or anything on the road will be like fish in a barrel. If forces make it from the west, then I'm on the ground beside Mark kissing my old ass goodbye. That leaves us thinking about the air. Follow me. They went into the library. The room looked to be probably fifteen by thirty feet. The shelving and molding were made from rich hardwood. Hundreds of books lined the shelves, from the floor to the ten-foot-ceiling. Tom pulled on the top of Tolstoy's War and Peace. The book tilted forward. A ten-foot-long section of the bookshelf moved forward off of the wall and slid to the right, leaving a recessed area ten foot by ten foot. The wall was covered with an array of sophisticated weaponry.

"Amazing what you can find at estate sales!" Pa grinned and poked Tom with his elbow.

"Well done my friend. You are a credit to species! I will toast you later this evening." Tom was obviously impressed. Hunter was obviously impressed. Joe was obviously impressed.

It became obvious what stood out to Mark. "MISTRAL MANPADS?" Mark whispered. "I'm impressed."

"Man-portable air defense systems, very short range, manufactured by MBDA Missile Systems. It has a 97% proven engagement rate. The man-portable system weighs just 19.7kg. The MANPADS uses a MISTRAL fire-and-forget missile, which integrates a homing head that holds a 3kg warhead." Hunter pulled that information out of his head.

"Looks like we have the air angle covered as well. Shoot from the shoulder and forget rounds and Sirocco's hardened chopper offer me relief." Mark said. "Now, where the hell is Mat?"

Well-trained, well-equipped, and with a well-thought-out plan, they were ready. Hill Country ready.

Point Counterpoint

Rain and cold drenched the Portland area for three days straight. Tommy Grove and a dozen other members of the Tennessee Defense were holed up in a clean but worn roadside motel in Gresham just off Interstate 84. Another eight men from Iowa and two guys from a relatively unknown militia in upstate Minnesota filled out the team. Chuck, one of the founders of the Tennessee Defense militia, was commanding the operation, and Tommy was excited to be a designated squad leader. His mind reeled from the honor of defending his country against those responsible for the virus and its ungodly cure.

The heavily armed group kept a low profile with weapons and tactical gear always stashed out of sight. Everyone was fully tested and virus-free. Tommy felt his many weekends of militia training were finally paying off, and he was overly confident in his ability to lead his squad. When he looked into a mirror, he failed to notice a slightly bulging belly stretching his shirt around the waist until the buttons were taut.

Tommy's mind conflated his weekend training with movies he once watched about Navy SEAL Teams and their exploits on international missions. The fact that neither he nor most of his squad could run a full mile in hilly terrain was obscured by his vision of how the Tennessee Defense would save his country.

Chuck had initially spotted reports on the America First site about government leaks around the Ebola vaccine development effort. The government's plot to dehumanize Americans quickly became clear to anyone paying attention. The little-known ViruVentures Corporation played a key role in developing the vaccine, and the company owner and CEO was a guy named Shen Wu. Tommy became agitated when people failed to understand how the last name of Wu meant the company was almost certainly a front for foreigners wanting to destroy the country. The development and distribution of a zombie vaccine was an attack on unsuspecting American citizens and weakened the country's defenses.

Tommy didn't hesitate to join Chuck when he proposed a team to hunt down the perpetrators of this vaccine attack. He and Chuck were able to do some deep investigating and determined the key figure in this unholy vaccine development plot was a shadowy figure named Mat Dover. He ran a set of hidden laboratories in the Portland area where the company was trying to implement the vaccine attack.

Dover was evasive, but now, thanks to the two Minnesota Militia members, they had latched on to Dover's trail. He and his comrades were close. The Minnesota guys wouldn't say exactly where they obtained their data, but the implication was it came from sources at the heart of the government. The most vocal congressman campaigning to stop the Frankenstein vaccine was Representative Gratas. Tommy heard the guy speak on several occasions, and his patriotism was impressive. He was tuned into the threat and actively worked to prevent the attack. He wouldn't be surprised if Gratas was helping the militias. In one statement, Congressman Gratas said the nature of the attack was such that the military was not up to the task of defending against it. But the Tennessee Defense Militia read between the lines and heard the message loud and clear. *"Patriots, now is the time to rise in defense of your country."* Tommy was determined to do his part.

Their work tied Dover to three possible locations in the metro area. Chuck split the men into three teams, with each team assigned to one location. His squad had already done multiple dry runs to their assigned location, and they had worked through several days of tactical scenarios at an abandoned warehouse Chuck secured for training. Tommy was confident Squad B could handle anything Dover threw at them.

Now, Chuck possessed the last bit of information they needed; Dover's guaranteed presence at one of the three possible locations. A message went out for everyone to go to the meeting room. The mission was going live.

Tommy and his squad filed through the door of an extra-large motel suite used specifically for meetings and tactical coordination. Pinned to the wall just to the right of the room's door was a large map of the city. Three large red thumbtacks poked through the paper map showing the locations of Dover's labs. Primary entry routes stood out as green lines with yellow, orange, and red tracings highlighting possible exit and escape paths.

The beds from the suite were pushed to the back wall on Tommy's left as he entered. They served as bench seating for some of the men, and the rest of the troops seated themselves in folding chairs. The motel's color motif used a pale, pastel green for the walls with a carpet containing a gray and dark green woven pattern. The swirling, floral pattern of the bead spreads used a green and blue patterning with occasional small strokes of a subdued orange. It all reminded Tommy of something his wife Sally would like.

Squad B and one of the Minnnesotans sat along the edges of the beds against the back wall, and the other men occupied the folding chairs. Chuck and the second Minnesotan were in front of the room, and behind them was the city map along with three sets of blueprints—one for each lab.

"Soldiers," said Chuck, "Operation Vac-One has commenced. You all need to hear this." He placed a smartphone on the white folding table to his right and pushed the play button.

A female voice echoed out. "Mr. Dover, we have reports of armed, trained military squads preparing to take down our three labs. I have already initiated a breakdown and evacuation of the labs to our secondary locations. What do you want me to do with the latest test data and analyses in our central safe?"

"Thanks for getting the process started, Rosa. When will the labs be fully cleaned?" The male voice was soft and had a faint southern lilt. Tommy connected this lilt with what they already knew about Dover.

"By five this evening, there won't even be dust left in the labs, and the alarm systems will be dismantled."

"Good," Dover continued. "I want to personally inspect one of the facilities with you, and I will collect the hard drive with our critical data at the inspection. It's crucial we don't leave any traces, and I want to see the quality of the cleanout for myself. I will call you at six once I decide which building to spot check, and I want you to meet me there at seven sharp." There was a pause, and then Tommy heard footsteps and the sound of a door opening and slamming shut.

"We picked this up two hours ago thanks to the good infiltration work from each of the squads," said Chuck. "It's taken since then to verify the information, but we have the green light. It's 4:00 now, and we know that Dover will be at one of the labs in three hours. Unfortunately, we couldn't narrow it down to which location. But with three squads, we are covered."

Chuck paused and then continued. "The three quads will be synchronized to arrive simultaneously at the labs. As soon as one team confirms contact, the other two will converge on their location. The first contact team will lock down the location and restrain Dover and his assistant. I'm only going to say this once—we need him alive. If Dover has the hard drive, great, but if not, simply hold him until the full team has reassembled. He may be the key to recovering the data, and we need that information."

He paused again and let his eyes scan each of the men. "Squad leaders, do you understand."

An instant "Yes Sir" reverberated from Tommy and the two other squad leaders.

"Good," Chuck exclaimed. "We have exactly ninety minutes to suit up—full tactical gear but with side arms only for everyone except the squad sergeants. Sergeants will carry assault rifles. Remember, we are professionals. We are not here to shoot anyone or anything unless necessary. As planned, Squad A goes to the north location, Squad B to the central lab, and Squad C to the larger southern facility."

One floor up and four doors down, a smile came to Eva's lips when she heard the word professionals. It certainly would not be the word she would use to describe the motley group of overweight and undertrained men on the screen in front of her. She had spent most of the past week monitoring this group and two other similar sets of amateurs. This one had managed to get the farthest along in their investigation, and she was interested in the two Minnesota members. The group's training center was also bugged, but with cameras only. Still, she could see there was more to this pair than they let on to their other militia buds. Some discrete questioning of either one might yield helpful results.

Her instincts and surveillance observations told her the Minnesotans deliberately positioned themselves in Squad C, probably thinking the largest facility was the highest value target. After consideration, she picked the central location, Squad B's target, for phase one. She sent a simple text for Mat, "We're on for Delta Lab."

The faked phone call between Eva, acting as Rosa, and Mat was surprisingly easy to arrange. All of the mock lab locations, Alpha, Delta, and Tango, had convincing reception areas. Each reception area was staffed during working hours and housed security guards at night. The setup also used a steady flow of people in and out of the labs, with higher influxes near the beginning and end of each workday. Three days ago, one of Chuck's men had wandered into Tango's reception pretending to be lost. He 'accidentally' knocked some business cards off the receptionist's desk and planted a bug under the desk when he dropped to his left knee to help pick them up. The ploy appeared successful to the militia, so the next day the same routine was used at Alpha and Delta.

She placed a call to her cleanup team, instructing them to clear out all of her equipment and bugs from the motel and training warehouse as soon as the militia left the area at 5:30. A second crew was to leave a block of C-4 plastic explosives under Chuck's bed, note the rooms with arms or military gear, and pass the room list on to her. She did a final check, put her gear in a backpack, donned her wig and glasses, and walked past several militia members on her way to the parking lot. She and Mat had some work to do at the Delta location.

Mat was waiting for her when she arrived. They stripped down the reception area leaving only an empty desk and the receptionist's chair. From reception, they took the door to the rear of the building and entered into a large forty-foot by fifty-foot space with concrete floors and a twelve-foot-high ceiling.

The central portion of the room was well lit with a single bank of overhead lights, but the edges and corners faded into dim lighting and even darkness in some areas. They took eight sturdy, metal-framed office chairs and stacked them into two groups of four near the rear of the room. Behind the chairs, obscured in the darkness, was scaffolding with a plywood platform eight feet off the ground.

Eva and Mat laid some specialized floor panels into a twenty-foot by twenty-foot square in the center of the room and connected the overhead lighting to a pressure switch in the center panel on the side of the square opposite the door. She tested it with the ball of her foot several times to ensure all was in working order.

After the central portion of the room was prepared, Eva and Mat retreated to the raised platform in the darkened back of the room. The lower portions of the scaffolding were dimly visible when the lights were on, but the upper platform was completely obscured. Nestled on top of the platform was a black tent structure with two areas. There wasn't enough room between the platform and the ceiling to stand, but a person could sit comfortably or lay down. One tent partition contained a monitor with views from hidden security cameras in reception and on the front street. The second one had a six-foot-long foam pad lying on the platform plywood and a rifle rest at the end facing the main room. A small cutout in the tent wall allowed for a rifle barrel and scope to poke out.

Eva inserted a communication earbud in her left ear, and they tested it before she left and took her position on the flooring they had just rigged. Mat kept an eye on the cameras, and at 7:05, a black van pulled up in front of the building. "We're on Eva," was all he relayed to her.

Eva turned her back to the door and waited. Mat tracked the progress of the militia squad as they picked the front door lock and entered the reception area. They thought they were moving quietly, but Eva could hear them from the next room.

The door from reception burst open, and Eva swirled around with a surprised look on her face. The first man into the room had an assault rifle trained on her, but the others kept their sidearms holstered. She modulated her voice to project fear and indignation. "Who the hell are you, and why are you in my building?"

She immediately recognized Tommy as he took command. "Stay where you are, keep your hands visible, and everything will be okay." He was proud of the way he kept a cool and professional demeanor.

Eva held her open hands at shoulder level as the group quickly crossed the floor and formed a semicircle around her. Tommy took a position directly in front of her, and the sergeant with the rifle stood beside him. But the barrel was now angled towards the floor and not towards her. When two of the squad took positions on the 180's of the semicircle, she gave an internal sigh. There was nothing she could do about that bit of stupidity other than letting it play out.

Tommy spoke up again. "We are looking for Mat Dover. We know you work for him and are meeting him here tonight."

Eva feigned a look of surprise and stuttered a bit. "He... he's running ten minutes late."

Tommy checked his watch. He then pressed a button on the side of his coms earpiece and said, "Squad B has made contact. Confirm." After a pause, he looked back at Eva. "Stay calm, Rosa, and no one will get hurt." The sergeant's rifle was again leveled at her.

She leaned her upper body slightly forward. "How can I be calm when you burst in here and point guns at me." As she spoke, her right foot slid forward until the ball was on the pressure switch.

Tommy signaled the sergeant, and he raised his gun towards the ceiling.

Eva's right knee bent slightly as she pushed most of her body weight forward in a smooth motion. The pressure flipped the switch, and the room went black as she somersaulted forward and rose up just below the sergeant. She heard his wrist snap as she wrenched the gun from him and continued moving forward into a second roll, taking her another eight feet beyond Squad B. A shot was fired behind her as she rolled. It was answered with a grunt and a scream.

Four seconds after the lights switched off; they automatically flipped back on. Eva was in a kneeling position with the rifle trained on the squad. The guy who had been on her left was holding a pistol and had it pointed at his buddy, who was originally on her right. The man to the right held his hand over a bleeding leg wound.

"No one moves, and you drop your gun," she said to the shooter with her barrel looking straight into his eyes. He complied. "It's called crossfire, gentlemen, and you foolishly set yourselves up for it. You, with the leg wound, stop moaning and stay on the ground. It looks like Mr. Dover has arrived, she said as Mat emerged from the darkness at the rear of the room and disarmed the team. Weapons were unloaded, and ammunition was tossed through a slot in the top of a steel lockbox in the back corner.

Mat came back and tossed them each a zip tie to bind their own hands. The sergeant was having trouble from his broken wrist, so Mat yanked the loop tight. The man winced, but to his credit, didn't cry out.

Next, he took the eight chairs and started placing them in a large semicircle facing the door. While he was working, Eva kept a tight watch on the group and finally spoke. "Tommy ... yes, I know your name. And Carl," she said to the sergeant, "shouldn't you be at home with your wife Anne and that new baby. As for the rest of you, what would your wives and daughters think about you picking on a helpless woman like myself? Also, what would they think about the fact that dealing with you has actually been the easiest part of my day?"

Once Mat had the last chair in place, the men were hauled into the seats. Legs were strapped to the chair and hands behind the chair tied off to their legs. They were not going anywhere. Eva stood in the middle of the half-circle of chairs, relaxed but alert, holding the rifle like it was a permanent part of her anatomy.

"Well, you boys have gotten yourself into quite a mess here. You are playing at being soldiers when you should be home with your families. Yes, we know your other squads are on their way over. You will all get to sleep for a bit, and when you awake, your buddies will be here. Before the morning, you all might be able to have a little reunion and discuss the things that went wrong."

While she was talking, Mat dressed the gunshot wound from the crossfire incident. He checked his watch. They still had fifteen minutes. He stood up and said, "Well, guys, you came here to find me; what did you want to ask?"

Tommy spoke up with some righteous indignation in his voice. "Why are you trying to poison us with this vaccine of yours?"

"Tommy, you misunderstand me. I don't give a rat's ass whether you take the vaccine or not. I've taken it. Rosa has taken it. Humanity is heading for a breakpoint, and there will be those who want to live and those who don't. That decision is entirely up to you. I'm not pissed off that a dumbass like you doesn't want the vaccine. I'm just pissed you want to take it away from the smart ones. But we are wasting time here, and some preparations are still needed."

Mat and Eva slipped on gas masks, and Mat took out a large aerosol can and started spraying. "Pleasant dreams, gentlemen." They would all be out for at least sixty minutes.

Phase two kicked in, and Mat re-jigged the front door locks while Eva set the reception room gas canisters in place. The two retreated into the main warehouse space with about five minutes left, and took up their respective positions on the back-wall platform. Mat operated the surveillance cameras and lock switch. Eva took the shooter's pad with two rifles ready for action.

Two vans pulled up, and the men piled out onto the street. Chuck tried the front door, and it was open. He posted guards, and then the men cautiously filed into the reception area. Mat watched closely, and as soon as the second Minnesotan entered, he pressed a button, and the front door slammed shut. Simultaneously the gas canisters began injecting a foggy cloud into the room. Men started falling, but as Eva predicted, the two Minnesotans were the first through the door to the back room. They tried to react to the sight of Squad B slumped over in a half-circle of chairs, but they were too late. Eva pumped tranquilizer darts into each of them before they could find cover in the poorly lit corners. Several more men staggered through the door, some collapsing on their own from the reception area gassing, and two needing some additional help from Eva to drift off to sleep.

Mat and Eva scrambled down and dragged one of the Minnesotans to a chair where he was strapped in with zip ties. He was the only one Eva had secured a positive ID on. A bright light was placed in front of him, with Mat and Eva standing off to the side while she gave him a stimulant injection in his right arm. It took him a minute to start coming around and another two minutes before he was alert enough to speak.

"Ivan, you are a long way from Belarus, and you seem to have gotten yourself into a jam. Now be a good boy and give me your phone password," Eva whispered in a seductive voice.

Ivan remained silent but tried to cut his eye to the right and see Eva. With her gas mask still on, there wasn't much he could see.

"Look in front of you, Ivan," she continued. When his gaze was on the small table, she continued. "You see the syringe Ivan, but you don't know what's in there. Let me enlighten you. It's full of live Ebola virus. You probably know that the current experimental vaccine only works if you are not infected. The good news is that even if you were injected with the virus, you still have about a fifty percent chance of survival." Ivan was staring intently at the syringe.

"We have a way out for you, Ivan. Unlock your phone and tell us who you are working for. No one will be the wiser. We will put you back on the floor with your buddies and even let you wake up a bit early. The mission will be deemed unsuccessful, and everyone can go home happy."

There was a long pause before he muttered, "Gratas, there is a direct voice message, 26458."

Eva opened the phone, searched the voice mail, and listened. "Very good, Ivan. Back to dreamland for you."

They dragged his limp body back to where it had originally fallen. Mat checked his watch and went back to the cameras, confirming the six men who were out front, locked out of the building, were waiting in their vans. They wiped everything down, fried the electronics, and exited from a small door in the rear of the building, taking their weapons with them.

Eva dropped Mat off at NW Everett and NW 3rd Ave beside the Lan Su Chinese garden. She disappeared into traffic, and a dark blue SUV immediately pulled up. Mat hopped into the back seat where Michelle was waiting. His seat was separated from Marcelle and the driver by a transparent barrier for virus protection.

"It's time to give the police a call and let them know about the problem they have in Gresham," he said.

She placed the call and then collected the Minnesotan's phone from him. "The phone has information linking Representative Gratas to a Russian mercenary group. Eva will be sending you a file on the mercenary. Strip down the phone and collect any info of value, but hold onto it for now. With a word from either Mark or me, leak it to as many national media outlets as possible. Gratas is essentially a traitor; make it visible."

"I will take care of it, Mat. Also, I have hardened the physical security around your penthouse and have a team stationed in your lower floor guest suite for the next several days. There are still several other groups rummaging around Portland looking for you, and your residence is not hard to locate, even for these lowlifes."

"Thanks, Michelle. I am out of here tomorrow with Joseph."

She dropped Mat off at reception, where he was met by one of her people. On the elevator ride up, he opened a recent text from Mark confirming Jenara was safe and sound in Leakey.

His mind had turned to distribution by the time he sank onto his couch with a cold beer. The speaking heads in Washington were still yammering on about the vaccine, but two things were clear to him. One, the government would authorize the use of the vaccine, albeit under emergency powers, and two, no one was too keen on immediately sharing the lifesaving medicine with the rest of the world. The most common phrase to describe it was "National Security Asset."

He knew it was not enough to have driven the development of the vaccine; it needed to get into people's arms. He was tired, but people were dying, and he couldn't stop. He would contact the Sentinel in the morning. Mat rested his head on the couch pillow and drifted off into a restless sleep.

Two hours after he drifted off, Chuck, Tommy, and the rest of the militia boys rolled into the motel parking lot in three vans. Glory had evaporated before their eyes, and now, licking their wounds, the plan was to retreat back to their respective lives and pretend the whole thing never happened.

A dozen police cars surrounded the vans before a single door opened. Slowly, one by one, they exited the vans into the care of an FBI Terrorist Threat unit. Tommy could only think about an old police show he once watched. It ended with the detective cuffing the perps, looking the leader in the eye, and saying, "Point, counterpoint."

World on Fire

The guys were sitting on the front porch finalizing plans for just in case. Contingency plans included a sneak-attack frontal ground assault; a mass frontal ground assault; the highly unlikely ground assaults from the west, north, or south; and an air assault. They decided an air assault, if it occurred, would be by helicopter.

"If it's government, the flight will probably be coming in from Lackland in San Antonio. If it's some of the mega-church crazies, Houston or Dallas. If it's some of the paramilitary crazies, then who the hell knows where they may be coming from. I doubt it will be from the air though. Day laborers typically don't have the resources to put a bird in the air." Hunter leading the way.

"The reports I read this morning indicate there are more of the paramilitary-types coming out of the woodwork. Anti-vaxers and the like trying to force their way into the diminishing mainstream. If they show up it will be on the ground. They'll have long guns and sidearms and be ready to fight right up until we kill a few of them. Then the rest will start crying and run away. Bullies always cave at the first hint of real resistance." Mark the reader and philosopher.

"The mega-churches are trying to assert themselves into the don't get vaccinated, God will protect you realm. These people can be very dangerous to Mat, and to us, in that they have gazillions of dollars in their accounts and entire congregations they could bring to bear." Joe said, sliding into the conversation. "Nagging at the back of my mind are the Treze assholes. We could presume they are all dead but that might just be wishful thinking. I think we need to at least have a plan on how to deal with them."

"Speedbumps mate!" Tom laughed and everyone else did too. "Speedbumps and a toothbrush!"

"When do ya'll think they'll come if they do." Mark flipping another card on the table.

"If it's one of the black ops double naught government superspy agencies, it'll be at the crack of dawn, probably by air. Paramilitary crazies—any time of the day. Just whenever they manage to figure out where we are. Megachurches the same as the crazies unless its Sunday. Sunday it will be after 1pm, just like their alcohol rules. Gotta go to church before you can buy a drink or kill someone." Mark was obviously not a big fan of the Kool-Aid people.

The conversation drifted into other areas. They were all set on roles and responsibilities in the event bad guys showed up. They'd discuss it with everyone once lunch time rolled around.

"I guess, with everything ya'll have seen, you must think MeeMee and I are some of those crazy survivalists you read about in the news. We're not. Hell, we've been what I'd call independent around here for generations. There are everyday things we appreciate as much as the next folks. You can look around and see that for yourselves. But, if those things cease to exist, we won't miss them. Who really needs TVs and such when we have the turkeys, deer, livestock, mesas, the caverns, the Milky Way and each other?" Pa's way of looking at the world. Mark was most appreciative of the attitude since he was prone to head off to whereabouts unknown most any time.

"We've always had shotguns, rifles, and pistols for hunting and plinking. Most of what you see, including the library fittings, literally came to us from estate sales, auctions, folks pawning them to us at the store, and certain odds and ends from a few gray, grizzled dropouts working things under the table just to survive. The old saying is that what happens on the ranch stays on the ranch." Pa knew a good expression when he stole it.

"Pa, I hope you kind folks can come see us in Western Australia. You would feel right at home!" Tom laughed. "We have a hidey-hole or two ourselves. Filled with knickknacks similar to yours. I must admit though that I'm jealous of the ground-to-air stuff. Not sure if I'd ever use it but there are some assholes flying around that I might take a shot at!"

Pa, Hunter, Mark, and Joe laughed. They all knew an asshole or two that could use some help reaching the other side. "Mark's arsenal is full of big boy toys too. He never knows when a chipmunk or woodpecker might attack him!" Joe getting into the action. "And Hunter recognized the modified bazookas. You ever capped a mosquito, Hunter?"

"I could tell you, but you know the old saying. I'd have to kill you. A secret is a secret only if one person knows it. And you seem to have forgotten the times you and I were forced to swat a bug or two out of the air hauling ass out of one shithole or another. Alzheimer's getting' ya?" Hunter getting his licks in. "Yea, both Joe and I have squeezed a trigger or two trying to help a bird experience abrupt altitude loss."

MeeMee, Jenara, Amber Lee, Sirocco, Jillora Bindi, and Jillora returned from the lab to fix themselves some lunch. Mark asked Jenara if she had any update from Mat. "No. I'm getting a bit worried. He usually updates me on his status."

"I'm worried about Mat and the labs. Hopefully they contacted the Sentinel and were able to get the vaccine data off to the rest of the world." Tom was thinking of Croc and the rest of the good folks back in Western Australia.

"I hope we can return home soon, although I don't know exactly how or when that can happen. And I wish we could take a bunch of vaccine with us. Not to say we don't appreciate the amazing hospitality and company!" There was a slight tautness in Jillora Bindi's voice. She had significant responsibilities, both at home and all across Australia.

"Maybe there is a way to get ya'll home. Let's see if we can get an update from John." Mark pulled out his sat phone and rang up John. John did not answer. "Shit, John does not pick up. That's a first. Where does a computer go and hide when things go to hell?" The rhetorical question was ominous in its implications. John was a whole lot more than just Mark's travel agent and eye-in-the-sky. A whole lot more. "I'll try later. What we don't know we don't know." Everyone went silent at the news that John could not be reached. They all had been positively impacted by John in one way or the other.

"So, let's do something positive. Anyone hungry?" MeeMee pulled everyone out of their momentary reticence.

"I'm starved but I need to start being careful about what I eat. I have a little one to consider." Jenara pulled the pin and dropped that grenade amongst everyone's feet. And it went off. They all jumped and laughed and shouted congratulations and I can't believe it and this is so exciting, and a lot more. There were hugs all around, especially for the mother-to-be.

"This is so awesome! Crap, does Mat know?" Amber Lee asked.

"Yes. I think it's why he insisted on me disappearing." Jenara grew thoughtful. "I'm sure we'll hear from him soon. And I'm sure I'm still hungry!"

"Then there is no time to lose. Let's get into the kitchen and see what kind of healthy things we can muster. Hurry before starvation sets in!" MeeMee was beside herself to have a mom-to-be to care for. "After that you are to get off your feet and rest." MeeMee being MeeMee.

While they all ate a lite and healthy lunch, in deference to Jenara, the guys spelled out the what ifs and who would do whats in the event of X, Y and Z. Joe and Hunter had both used the ground-to-air ordinance so they were it. Everyone else was comfortable with everything available in Sirocco's bird, Mark's truck, and the ordinance in cabinets, in corners, and on shelves scattered throughout the house.

There was a huge old dinner bell hanging from the eves of the front porch. A faded braided cowhide cord hung down from it. They decided one ring meant a ground assault at the front gate, two rings meant a ground assault from the west, three and four rings for ground assaults from the north or south, and five rings if an attack came from the air. Not quite Longfellow's Old North Church version but it was functional.

It was intuitive that they would probably hear the approach, especially from the air. However, they had eyes and ears three miles to the west. Pa had also notified folks near and far that they expected trouble and to get on the horn soonest if strangers happened by. Even though they were surrounded by hundreds of mostly empty square miles it was a relatively small, close-knit community. The Hill Country was like that.

Sirocco's chopper was parked in the landing zone closest to the house. A sparse but adequate number of cottonwood and oak trees just happened to block a helicopter from landing in any of the other fields nearby. The closest clear area was to the north of the bunk house occupied by Mária Elana and Juan. Over a quarter of a mile. Pa rang up Juan and asked him to park the backhoe and a few other implements there to dissuade any aliens from landing. He wanted it to be a no alien landing zone.

"If it's an airborne threat I'll jump in my chopper. Even if I can't get airborne, we may need air-to-air comms." Sirocco lined herself out. Hard to yell at people in a bird hovering a few hundred feet off the ground.

That evening they all hung out on the front porch after another great dinner. Amber Lee convinced Mark to drag out his old Yairi Alvarez guitar. He picked a bit then did Leavin' Texas, the old Jerry Jeff Walker standard. He picked, and Sirocco and Amber Lee sang Love at the Five and Dime, a tribute to another late, great Texan, Nanci Griffith. Naturally they did London Homesick Blues, the tune by an Okie named Gary P. Nunn. The song is, of course, universally acknowledged as the national anthem of Texas.

MeeMee asked for Keep on the Sunny Side, a song written in 1899 by Ada Blenkhorn and J. Howard Entwisle. It was a nod to the Grand Ole Opry. Everyone sang along and MeeMee made Mark do it again. The fire in the massive fireplace crackled and a light breeze and the ceiling fans made it comfortable. The dimming of the day saw the last of the turkeys and deer fade into the mesas. Like every other true guitar picker, Mark played until his fingers bled. Then he played some more.

Finally MeeMee shooed Jenara off to bed. "The little one needs her rest!" She exclaimed.

"Her?" Mark arched his eye.

"Of course her! Can't you tell by the way Jenara looks? You guys are all alike thinking a baby has to be a boy." MeeMee brushed the men aside with the remark, took Jenara's hand and they walked inside. Silly boys. Soon thereafter everyone called it a night.

The next morning, around 7am, Tom was standing alone on the dock when he got a call from an old friend. An old friend who just happened to be the first Indigenous Australian Consul-General assigned to the Australian consulate located in Houston. "Tom you old roo, how the hell are you this evening? Is the tide in or out?" Benji presumed Tom was at home.

"Benji you cobber! What's up?" They had not spoken in a while but had known each other almost forever, so time had no meaning.

"I'd like to come see you and Jillora Bindi very soon. Is that OK? I'm leaving Houston late this afternoon, final destination Perth." Benji made it sound somewhat serious.

"We'd love to see you but we're actually out west of you in Leakey as we speak. J.B. is also with us. Visiting with old friends. Can you postpone your trip and come see us? Or we can probably hitch a ride and come see you."

"Would you consider cutting your visit short? I'm flying a dedicated diplomatic flight and there is plenty of room for the three of you. I can't discuss the why over this open line but I assure it is important enough for me to beg you to consider." Benji begging. What the fuck Tom thought.

"Can I call you back at this number? I need to clear it with the boss." Tom was on the hook.

"I'll only answer your call. The flight leaves around 7pm from IAH." Benji rang off.

Tom went and found Jillora Bindi in the lab. Amber Lee, J.B., Carolina, and Sirocco were there also. He told them about the call from Benji. "There's your ticket home." Sirocco said. "Ya'll pack and I'll get my chopper prepped. We'll leave when you're ready. It's about 270 miles to IAH. Two and a half hours or so."

"But…"

"No buts except get your butts moving." Amber Lee was already hustling them out the door. Whatever Benji needed from them was obviously important. MeeMee and Pa said they'd miss them but it was obviously for the best. They were needed back home. So be it. Mark, Joe, and Hunter agreed. "I wish there was room in the bird for me too." Mark was thinking about the added security for Sirocco.

"We'll be fine. I'll refuel there and be back here by supper time." Sirocco was used to doing things on her own effectively and efficiently. This would be a cake flight, so to speak.

"We'll be ready in less than one hour. I need to get some things from the lab, then I'll pack the few things I brought with me. Tom? J.B.?" Jillora Bindi looked at the two. Both said they'd be ready in no time and would help her get ready to depart.

"Hunter, please fetch the last package I gave you in Dallas." Sirocco was on a mission. He was back in a few minutes. Sirocco gave it to Jillora Bindi, who gave Sirocco an appreciative nod and packed it away without opening it.

"Benji, Tom. We're coming with you. Arrival by helicopter. ETA for us is around 11:30am."

"Perfect! Thank you! I'll arrange for a car to pick you up at the heliport and bring you to our jet. I'm also going to see if we can depart early. No need to make you linger at the smelly old Houston airport any longer than necessary. See you in a little while."

The flight to Houston went without a hitch. Benji met them at the heliport in a black Excursion. They were offloaded from the chopper, loaded into the Excursion, and gone in less than five minutes, including hugs. Sirocco refueled and was back at the ranch by 4pm.

"Houston seemed desolate. The news says the governor and half of his staff are dead from the virus. The same is happening across the country and many places across the globe. Top people and minions seem to be taking the brunt of the disease. Probably because of the way it was initially transmitted across the top tier businesspeople and waitstaff." Sirocco was a bit down. "On the bright side things may be looking up for Australia. I sure hope so."

The front porch was somewhat subdued that evening. Pa had cooked thick, fresh steaks on the grill. MeeMee had invited Mária Elana and Juan to join them. They were a delightful young couple full of themselves and so grateful to be a part of the current events on the ranch. They brought a huge, fresh, homemade apple pie from home. It was a hit. Everyone helped with the cleanup and they all decided to retire early.

Several days passed uneventfully. Mark and Jenara had been unsuccessful in reaching either Mat or John. The stress on Jenara was beginning to show. Mee-Mee and the other ladies did their best to keep her occupied, both in the lab and the kitchen. For a change of pace, they explored the caverns. They marveled at the amazing architecture rendered by the mineral-rich water that trickled from myriad sources on the ceiling, walls, and floor throughout the extensive grottos.

Joe and Hunter decided to find the mountain lion and cubs so off they went. Sirocco and Amber Lee were busy in the lab. MeeMee, Jenara, and Carolina were back in the caverns searching for Mexican blindcats. Pa and MeeMee had seen them occasionally in various pools. Seeing the extremely rare three inch long eyeless, albino catfish was a major treat. They had never been reported this far north. And still weren't. They also looked for Texas blind salamanders.

They came out late in the day and headed back to the house. There was no cell signal inside the cavern so Jenara missed the call from Mat. There was a message. "Hey beautiful girl! Joseph and I will be at the ranch a little before midnight, hopefully. We're driving. Be ready to leave immediately. I'll explain then." Mat clicked off. She hit call but it went to voicemail. Mat's voicemail was actually a deliberate dead-end.

Joe and Hunter successfully viewed the big cats. They also succeeded in getting scratched and bloody from just about every sticky thing between the house to the ledge and back to the house. Their condition was promptly ignored when Jenara and Mark started talking.

Jenara had found Mark and played the message for him. They gathered everyone together so the matter could be discussed. "I imagine he feels flames licking at his ass. I just wish I knew the source of the heat." Hunter was succinct and probably right. "We need to be ready in case the hounds are too close to the hares when they arrive."

"I agree. After Wood Hollow Drive, Patterson Creek Road is it. There is no other way in or out. Unless he seriously trespasses, cutting padlocks off of gates and such." Pa was quick on the uptake.

"Yea, he'll use Patterson Creek Road. I want to park my ass well before the gate to make sure he doesn't have any fleas." Hunter starting to hunt. "Joe, I suggest you put your butt on the ledge above the gate, just in case."

"I'll stay with Jenara and hand her off. Whatever has spooked Mat is bound to be close behind. We have to presume he has a plan. The best we can do is to make sure he gets in and out of here cleanly. After that he will ask for help or not." Mark was finalizing their plan.

"I'll stay on top of the cameras. I'll also be ready to blow the road if ya'll decide we need to." Pa put the period at the end of the plan. "MeeMee can cover the front yard from inside."

Mark's sat phone chirped, indicating John was calling. "John, I've been worried about you. You're on speaker."

"Hello Mr. Mark, hello all. I'm so glad you are OK. I'll explain my situation. My system was compromised. As soon as I realized it, I cut all outside ties, hoping to keep you and the rest of my clients from being compromised. I think whoever or whatever it was was partially successful during the incursion. It took a massive amount of time, relatively speaking for me, to isolate the infiltration pathway and neutralize it."

"Did you determine the source?" Mark was doing the Hunter thing.

"Sir, all I can tell you is that, ultimately, it simply felt like a specter of evil. I realize those words were used by Ms. Jillora Bindi. They also apply in my circumstances. For the life of me I cannot determine the source of the intrusion." John the computer uttered for the life of me. Mark let it slide. John, the AI computer to end all AI computers, could not determine the source of his own potential demise.

"I am back to being one hundred percent secure. I just spoke with Mr. Mat. He and Mr. Joseph should be arriving at the ranch a little before midnight, departure is planned immediately with Ms. Jenara in tow. He has plans after that but was kind enough not to share. I wish I knew so I could watch over his shoulder but it is not to be. At least not for now."

"Many of the satellites I typically use are now non-responsive. It's seems the operations people are on break or perhaps dead. I obviously have you on sat phone but I can't see you. The satphone satellites are low-tech and don't require handlers."

"We'll get him in and out of the ranch safely. After that it's up to him. He'll divulge his plans or not. I'm glad you're back up John." Mark rang off.

"I have a confession to make. I didn't think it was important to share with the group at the time but maybe it is. Probably about the time John went down I had that same specter of evil feeling Jillora described she had back home. It emanated from the crystal. I wish I had spoken then." Jenara said. "Jillora Bindi told me the same thing happened to her again. At the same time it happened to me. Similar to the incursion at my office."

"No way for ya'll to equate those disparate events." Hunter immediately let her off the hook. "There is certainly a lot happening well above my pay grade too. Too damn many pieces to this ever-evolving puzzle."

"When the going gets tough the tough get to the dinner table!" MeeMee the forever cheerful person. "I'm whipping up something healthy. We'll eat on the porch in one hour." Carolina and Jenara joined MeeMee in the kitchen.

"Let's take a walk out to my truck." Mark wanted to gear up for the evening. Hunter and Joe followed Mark across the yard. Pa said he would gather up his own gear from inside the house. Mark opened the twin rear doors and they climbed aboard. He opened the appropriate cabinets. All three strapped on a Ka-Bar KA1214 BRK USA Fighting Knife. It was a simple choice so they each strapped on a Glock 19 Gen 5 G34 Competition 9x19mm pistol as well. They inserted 17 shot magazines and locked. Extra mags were strapped to the tactical webbing/holsters, just in case.

Joe and Hunter also picked up Wilson Ultralite Ranger .243's fitted with Ranger 1-8x24i Rifle Scopes. The scope's night feature would come in handy later tonight. They returned and Pa was just starting the evening fire. Hunter fetched extra wood.

"I called the western crew. Two of the boys are driving over, be here in about two hours. I want them just up the trail where the yard meets the woods. If for some reason the gate is breached without my consent, they'll be the next line of defense." Pa clearly had certain experiences under his belt that he had not discussed with the present company. Good. "Mária Elana and Juan will be hanging out as well. By the way MeeMee and Mária Elana can probably outshoot any of us." That was a handy thing to know. Don't piss off MeeMee or Mária Elana.

"Can I take the '67 Chevy pickup?" Hunter asked Pa. "That old Dark Green from PPG will help me blend in with the night."

"Good choice. There are several large cedars along that stretch, big enough to park behind and still see the road. Remember it's three on the column!" Pa grinned.

The ranch hands from the western edge of the ranch arrived and took up their station. Hunter dropped Joe off at the gate. He would climb up to a perch about 30 feet above the road. Hunter snugged the old Chevy tight against the west side of a large cedar just past the Wood Hollow Drive intersection on the south side. The thick branches draped all the way to the ground. He was essentially invisible to westbound traffic on the wide gravel road.

One by one they clicked on the comms indicating they were in place. Mark had said it was all probably overkill but they all agreed to overkill. Their collective experience told them that overkill was a much better selection than being killed.

The third quarter moon cast a peaceful glow across the landscape. Out where Mark was parked there was minor light pollution in the distance from some of the homes on the outskirts of Leakey. He had rolled both windows down. There was the faint smell of wood smoke on the light southwest breeze. Probably the remnants of Pa's fire. Approaching midnight there was no traffic anywhere near. After all, ranchers and farmers are early to bed, early to rise. Then there was a pair of headlights cutting through the air as the vehicle veered off of RR 337 onto Patterson Creek Road. The lights' intensity grew and bounced a little as the vehicle hit minor potholes. It passed Hunter in less than a minute.

"Car. It's a new Caddy Escalade." Hunter broadcast.

"Mat wouldn't rent a Caddy if it was the only thing on the lot." Mark interjected.

"Glassing it, dark tinted windows. Hold. Shit, there is a third person, apparently in the back. I'm rolling, lights off. Joe, you're on deck. You got a clear shot at the road?" Joe clicked affirmative. "Pa, bullshit them out of the car." Pa clicked affirmative. "I'm in their dust so I doubt I'll be seen." About two minutes later Hunter pulled up sideways across the road, effectively blocking ingress and egress. He was about a hundred yards east of the gate. He climbed out and took up station at the tailgate.

The Caddy pulled up to the gate. Mat rolled down his driver-side window and pressed the call button on the keypad. Joseph was riding shotgun. An asshole with no name was in the middle backseat with his pistol trained on the back of Mat's head. The gun was being held in a very steady hand. Pa could have answered immediately but he waited a minute or so.

"Who is it?" Pa used a sleepy and tenuous tone of voice.

"Pa, it's Mat."

"Mat? Uh. Mat? Oh, Amber Lee's friend. That Mat? From Oregon?" A bit of wonder had crept into Pa's voice. "What in tarnation brings you way down here? And it being midnight and all?"

"Pa, I'm hoping to see Amber Lee. I left something with her that I need. Is she here?"

"Mat, my cameras aren't the greatest in the world. And they are up on the gate posts. I can't see you through that dark windshield. Can you step out. You probably know its usually just MeeMee and I here. We're a bit wary of folks, especially unexpected guests who come aknockin' at midnight." Pa had tossed the lure near the submerged brush before.

The asshole in the back whispered take it easy getting out. "Joseph is with me too. This is kinda weird Pa, you not letting us in right away."

"Sorry, but I'm just a skittish ole bronco here. Let me get a look at you." Pa breathed loudly and watched the two men climb out of the Caddy. "Why it sure looks like you! I reckon I'll meet the Joseph feller shortly. Say, hang on a minute. I see a shadow. Is there somebody else with you?"

The asshole climbed out and wrapped his left arm around Mat's throat and stuck the pistol into Mat's right cheek. "Open the fucking gate or your friend Mat dies. Then your new friend dies. Then I'm going to come through the gate and you and your woman and daughter are going to die." The asshole hissed. The gun was very steady on the side of Mat's throat. "I just want the one named Jenara. I know she is there with you."

Joe pulled the asshole in on the nightscope until the guy's right earhole loomed large from about fifty feet away. He had a downward angle. He briefly pondered the damage he was about to do based on that angle.

"Mister, ain't no one else here. But if you promise not to hurt anyone, I'll open the gate and let you take a look around. It would help my frame of mind if you could point yer pistol somewhere besides Mat's head. I'm clicking you in now." The gates started to swing in silently on the massive and well-lubricated support pins. The asshole loosened his grip on Mat and said "get in and drive."

216

The gun came down. Joe exhaled slowly, held it halfway out, squeezed the trigger, double-tapping. Both rounds entered the bad guy's right ear at supersonic speed.

The guy dropped hard to the ground, dead before impact. The swiftness of the fall must have been due to the second round hanging up somewhere inside the left shoulder. Forcing the dead guy down. Maybe the first round opened up a path, Joe speculated briefly, before clicking in and saying, "Asshole down."

"Drive through, I'll catch a ride with Hunter." Joe spoke loud enough for Mat to hear and acknowledge. "We'll take out the trash."

Unmarked Graves

Hunter pulled up to Joe and the dead guy. Joe handed Hunter a pistol and said, "Look at this." Hunter held it in the light from the interior of the truck.

"Damn." He clicked his phone. "Mark, guy had a Desert Eagle Mark XIX, black, .44 cal., one chambered, seven in the magazine."

"Damn. Bring the guy in." Hunter and Joe tossed the trash into the bed of the '67, came through the gate and stopped. They both watched the gate until it was closed. Then Hunter drove to the front of the house. Mat was hugging Jenara and she was hugging him back. Everyone else was close by. Mark and Joe climbed out. Mark fist bumped Mat. "Fucker had a Desert Eagle. Two thousand dollars' worth of custom hardware. He ain't military and he sure as hell ain't militia."

"Yea, I think he was one Donald Faillen's acquaintances." Mat said. "He was quiet and had a steady hand. A steady hand holding a five-pound pistol. Government keeps sending cars full of guys or a bird. The militias send vans full of guys. So, that pretty much narrows it down to the religious guys. They knew Joseph and I were on the move. I do not know how. Maybe had to do with the breach in John's system. The asshole probably killed our original driver. Got the jump on us cleanly. MeeMee and Pa, I'm sorry for bringing this on you, but Jenara and I have some business we need to finish up with Mark's aquaintance, the Sentinel. I have to impose on you to borrow a vehicle and Jenara, Joseph, and I will be out of you hair."

"Let's load the F-150. The Caddy probably has a beacon attached somewhere. No time to try to find it. I'll just deal with it later. The F-150 is a rental of course. Leave it wherever. Want help or an extra rider?" Mark ready to rock.

"No, but thanks. I'll let you know where we are when I know it's safe. We gotta go." Mark turned toward the F-150.

Mark put Jenara's bags in the rear crew seat. Hunter handed over three of his Glock 19 Gen 5 G34's and a small gear bag with nine extra clips. The weapons were loaded and locked. Just in case. MeeMee handed them an old milk crate loaded with food. Quick goodbyes and Mat climbed into the F-150 driver side, Jenara rode shotgun and Joseph took the left rear crew seat. Mat left the lights off and pulled out. The two western hands had walked up the road to just inside the gate. They briefly waved as the F-150 went by, then waited until the gate was closed.

Pa had the boys put the dead guy in the trunk of the Caddy. "Juan, please park the Caddy near the backhoe." Pa was thinking ahead.

The next morning after breakfast Pa got on a golf cart and rode to the Kubota M62 backhoe. He started excavating a hole. The hole grew as he continued his efforts. The soil was rich and deep, having been deposited over the years by the meandering ways of Patterson Creek. Mária Elana drove a big Cat from the large pole barn near her bunkhouse. Pa's hole was easily 15' x 10' x 10' when she brought the tracked earthmover to a halt near the Caddy.

Pa pointed at the wreckage, then the hole. Mária Elana positioned the Cat's front 10'3" blade at ground level and pushed the car to the bottom of the hole. Pa used the inverted bucket on the backhoe like a sledgehammer, packing the remains into the hole. Then Mária Elana backed off and scraped a few inches of soil from twenty or thirty feet away. She essentially made spokes on a wheel with the hub being Pa's now full hole in the ground. In thirty minutes, no trace remained of the Caddy or the trespasser. Who knows how many unmarked graves there are in Texas?

Later Pa, Mária Elana, and Juan rode horseback a few hundred yards across the valley to one of the large cattle lots. They drove around thirty head of cattle back to the site of the grave. Hoof prints and cow shit would seal the deal so to speak.

Everyone stayed alert the rest of the day but there were no further incursions onto the ranch. Pa built a fire in the fireplace and the grill. Joe and Hunter helped, naturally. Juan brought a big load of cut mesquite he'd placed in the trailer behind his ATV. Mark went fishing. He slowly circled the pond, catching and releasing a bunch of bass and bream. At the upper end he tipped his silver flask to the sky and whispered cheers. In his mind he said cheers to speedbumps. Cheers to the sun and the moon and the stars and the rest of the universe. Cheers to the ranch and everyone around him. Cheers to life. Cheers to Homo novus.

MeeMee, Sirocco, Amber Lee, Carolina, and Mária Elana whipped up some first class grub in the kitchen. The gents barbequed cow and the porch was filled with warmth and soft laughter. Every single one of them had seen and done much more than the morning's events. They all had the ability to put such events into a mental box. The box could be opened and the contents examined later. If anyone actually cared to examine the contents later.

They remained vigilant in the days and weeks to come but apparently there would be no more unwanted visitors. The news of the world became more and more grim. The death toll had risen astronomically. A massive power outage had taken out the entire grid feeding most of the Dallas-Fort Worth region. North Texas had gone dark. This was nothing new because of the stupid way most of Texas managed the utility through politics rather than through technical competence. And it was creating havoc. The grid had also dumped the ranch several days before. Pa simply switched to the solar arrays placed strategically around the ranch. Several generators and ample fuel stored in multiple tanks could also be brought into play if need be. As a last resort the cavern would provide year-round climate-controlled quarters.

"The roof-top solar array will provide plenty of power to my building but now there is no electricity for the city to pump water. The reports say this could be an indefinite development. I'm going to fly home, get some essentials and additional equipment from the lab, then come back here. I'd like to stick around the ranch if it's OK." Sirocco said late one evening. MeeMee and Pa said absolutely. "None of you have to ask. Ya'll are always welcome and this is your home for as long as you like."

"I'd like to retrieve my pony car from your garage. May Carolina and I join you?" Hunter was hunting again. "From there I think we'll head down to my place on Matagorda Beach. That's where I started this part of my current big adventure. The house is totally self-sufficient. I designed and built it to be off the grid. You wanna get back to some salt water fishin' Joe?"

So, Sirocco, Hunter, and Carolina decided to fly to Dallas early the following morning. Pa told Joe he could have the '67 pickup. Nothing could have made Joe happier. Pa threw in an old horse trailer. They'd stock it up with provisions so there would be food and other necessities that would last a while on the Gulf coast. Hunter and Carolina would help Sirocco pack what she needed into her chopper, then head to Matagorda in the Mustang. Ultimately, Sirocco was back at the ranch mid-afternoon. Joe made it to Matagorda Beach about the same time. Hunter and Carolina arrived there later in the evening.

Pa and MeeMee reverted to their ranching routine except they did not re-open the store in town. Sirocco and Amber Lee spent their days in the lab. They stayed in touch with their scientific contacts worldwide as best as they could. Mark had enjoyed being around so many people just about as much as he could handle. The fish in the pond started to ignore his tosses. He walked the mesas until he grew weary of walking mesas. Even the rattlers ignored him.

One night at dinner on the porch MeeMee said, "Mark, you are surrounded by some of the most beautiful offerings that exist in the Hill Country. You have two of the most intelligent and beautiful women in the world sitting here with you. You have the best MeeMee and Pa that a man could ask for. And, in spite of these things, you are beginning to look like a most miserable soul. What can we do to help?"

"I apologize for my downtrodden appearance. No doubt I am the luckiest man on the planet. It's just that I'm not used to being around people for so long. I think it is time for me to head out for whereabouts unknown. North this time. Alaska. That's what I got the rig for. It can straddle bigger rocks and fallen trees, and ford wider and deeper rivers. I appreciate ya'll's hospitality more than you can know but it is time for me to find some solitude. Just last night I put my finger on the map. It landed on a place called Mayo, in the Canadian Yukon. It's about 3,600 miles as the crow flies. It will be a bit further I'm sure since I'm not a crow!"

Sirocco and Amber Lee dragged Mark into the Jacuzzi that night and in the morning they, MeeMee and Pa waved as he drove his rig out of the yard and through the trees. Pa clicked him through the gate. Mark watched the gates close in his rearview mirror, then he headed for Leakey. He turned left on SR 83 and headed for Mayo.

Mayo

It had been a week or so since Sirocco and Amber Lee had climbed on board the Embraer KC-390 and headed back to Dallas. They had flown the rough and rugged jet into Mayo (YMA), Yukon, YT, Canada, and landed with plenty of room to spare on the 4,843 foot long gravel runway.

Mark was resting comfortably in the Jacuzzi, gazing into the infinity called space. The Jacuzzi had been part of the equipment Sirocco and Amber Lee brought with them. It was the only thing Mark had requested. They had set it up on the sturdy, fifteen-foot-high log frame in the open space between the main house and several outbuildings on the Alkanair property. The property was located on the Stewart River just east of Mayo. And just about 3,500 miles north northwest of Dallas, Texas.

The view was an unimpeded 360°, and the ephemeral pastel palette called the aurora borealis was shimmering in the midnight twilight. Mark packed the ancient peace pipe with some homegrown, took a toke, and whispered peace. He took a sip of Lagavulin 16 and closed his eyes for a bit, letting the blend of homegrown and bottled smoke infuse into his soul. He thought about when things in Texas were settled enough that no one would miss him terribly.

The ride up from Dallas had taken the better part of two months since there was no hurry to get to whereabouts unknown. Mark wasn't sure of his destination until a few hours after crossing the old thru-truss bridge across the Stewart River on Route 2, the Klondike Highway, just above Stewart Crossing. Stewart Crossing consisted of a trading post, a Canadian Highway works facility, and a few homes scattered across the woodlands.

Mark stopped there to top off his tanks. Unfortunately, there was no one around, like several such stops earlier in his jaunt. He stumbled onto the animal-ravaged remains of two different people, but that was all. The virus had apparently invaded this most distant area on the North American continent. He suspected the fuel, food, and material haulers had been the culprit. The two-to-three-week incubation time was probably an exacerbating factor. Drivers naturally interacted with their customers. Much more so in the wilderness.

Standing around a stove, drinking a cup of coffee and shooting the shit came naturally. Then head to the next stop. The cramped quarters of most such stops were ideal for spreading the airborne disease. Locals would also stop by, and, in the end, most everyone became infected. With a mortality rate of fifty percent or so, half of the folks were dead within a few weeks. Another percentage became too sick to make a run for it to a city and perished from any number of things, including starvation and exposure. They were, in essence, too sick to care for themselves.

Those who managed to make a run for it probably spread the ravage at each stop along the way. So it goes.

Mark used his siphon to draw fuel directly from the underground tanks into his rig. He put a case each of Yukon Brewing Company Ice Fog, Yukon Gold, Lead Dog Ale, and Conspiracy IPA in the crew area of his rig. He also found the four-ounce stash secreted under the counter. He would add it to his own stash. He stocked up on canned goods, flour, olive oil, and the like. He left a sticky note on the register counter with a handwritten IOU on it. Contact me, and I'll pay for the fuel, beer, food, and the homegrown.

He crossed the Stewart River and stopped at the stop sign. Left would take him into Alaska, another hundred miles or so northwest. Instead, he turned right on the unpaved road identified on the sign as Silver Trail. He ended up at the Mayo Airport about an hour later. He was greeted by the same eerie stillness as had been the norm for the last thousand miles or so. The valley was pristine.

Noticeably absent was the smell of wood smoke from chimneys. There were no sounds at all except the whisper of the breeze and the caw of a raven traversing the eastern end of the runway—no motors, no voices, no man-generated sounds. As he turned his gaze back toward town, the air was crystal clear. Not a hint of humanity existed other than the obviousness of the tiny airport complex.

He explored the small terminal and found no one. He did, however, find something that could prove useful. A bill of lading. From a fuel hauler. It indicated that the tanks had all been topped off less than three months ago. The fairly new tanks included jet-A1, 100LL avgas, home heating oil, unleaded gasoline, and ultra-low sulfur diesel. Total storage capacity showed 270,000 liters (71,000 gallons).

There was a relatively new Airbus AS350-B3e in the 70' x 70' Quonset hut. The rugged helicopter was the perfect machine for high-altitude rescue. Anything else, such as moving equipment around or day fishing trips, was a breeze. A Roadpro 32-Series snowplow attachment was off to the side. It could be attached to the massive front bumper of his Mercedes' Zetros if need be. It was big enough to plow the gravel runway.

He backtracked and drove into Mayo. The little green information sign said Welcome To Mayo. Population 496. He slowly zigzagged the entire town, starting at Fourth Avenue. He went north up to Seventh Avenue, then south all the way to First Avenue. The Stewart River ran parallel to First Avenue for about a quarter-mile. That was it—a quarter-mile square village. The largest grouping of structures was the Mayo Members Municipal Council. It consisted of several buildings. There were several offices, a large shop for trucks and maintenance equipment, and smaller garages. All-in-all, around twelve thousand square feet under roof. There was also the swimming pool building.

A grocery store, Mayo Foods Ltd., faced the river on First Avenue. Most of the perishables had perished, but it was stocked with Yukon life's necessities. There was also a walk-in freezer. There was no power on anywhere, but he could figure that out later.

St. Mark's Anglican Church sat on the southward bend of the river. Maybe fifty small houses in all. Not a lot to see. Circling back, he continued to scan his surroundings for human lifeforms. He found no one alive but scattered evidence that scavengers had cleaned the bones of at least several different individuals.

The breeze picked up a bit, and he caught movement from the corner of his right eye through the shotgun window. There, on a porch. Two dogs. The breeze had fluffed the coat of one of them. He climbed down from his rig and very slowly approached the porch from thirty yards away. They looked like wolves, but he decided they were Malamutes. He talked calmly and quietly during his approach. He stopped when he reached the three-stair climb onto the porch.

One dog tried to stand but gave out. The other one simply lay there limp. Mark went back to the Benz and dug out cans of chicken and beef. He used his Freek pocketknife to open the cans. He jabbed the locked blade into the top, and the serrated rear edge of the four-inch blade cut a ragged circle in the top of the can. He would never tell Mat he used the dinky little thing.

He dumped the meat onto two plates and took them straight to the dogs, placing one in front of each. He fetched two bowls of water also. He realized there was a male and a female. The male tried to eat and drink some water. The female did not. Mark sat on the porch floorboards and pulled the female onto his lap. He crushed some beef in his palm and hand-fed her the gruel.

Slowly she responded and ate more. She spilled water on Mark's lap, making him laugh softly. The dogs would probably live.

He had ignored the male. It barked softly. His plate was empty. Another can was emptied onto the plate and almost instantly disappeared.

"What is your name beautiful girl?" Mark ruffled some fur and teased her a bit. She looked at him but did not answer. The male softly barked again. He wanted some attention too.

"Very well boy. I shall call you Mala and your girlfriend is Mute." There was probably some subliminal message about the female being silent, but he would never let the thought make it to his mouth. He knocked on the front door. It was unlocked, so he called out and entered. There were obvious signs of habitancy but no habitants. Perhaps the loyal dogs were awaiting an event not likely to ever occur.

Mark picked up the female. She probably weighed sixty-five or seventy pounds. He walked to the back of the Benz, opened the duel doors, and laid her on the all-weather carpet. He turned to fetch Mala only to almost trip over him. Mala tried to jump into the rig but was apparently too weak. Mark gently picked up the ninety-pound critter and laid him beside Mute. He brought the dinnerware back and tossed the plates and bowls into the sink.

Mark headed east of First Avenue to where it intersected Duncan Avenue. He turned right onto Duncan. A quarter-mile later, he reached Hilder Avenue. A sign read Alkanair, and an arrow pointed the way. He drove through the woods consisting of a mix of spruce, aspen, pine, birch, poplar, willow, and cottonwoods. The Mercedes rolled into Alkanair compound a mile down the road.

Mark parked the rig and helped Mala and Mute to the ground. He called out to the owner's home. No one answered. He walked around to several small rustic outbuildings, quietly calling hello as he did. Mala followed him around. Mute seemed content to rest. They walked down to the dock. A plane and a boat were tied up in their slips. They appeared to be ready for work.

The plane was a workhorse Cessna 206, resting on Wipline floats. He knew the floats also housed traditional landing gear. The boat was a 2470 SJX Jet Boat. Perhaps the best 24-foot aluminum tunnel-hull jet-powered boat around. It had a rollbar package w/ canvas cocoon. Undoubtedly there was an onboard heater.

He and Mala walked back to the main house. The front door was unlocked. He called, but there was nobody home. He told Mala to sit. Mala sat. Mark did a brief walkthrough. By all appearances, five people lived in the thirty-five hundred square foot home. The clothes indicated an adult male, an adult female, two girls, and a boy. They became, in Marks' mind, Mama Bear, Papa Bear, and the three little Bears.

Back outside he determined that a small stone outbuilding housed a generator. More specifically, a Generac 22,000-watt, air-cooled generator. More than enough power to operate the home and outbuildings. There was a manual in a ziplock bag hanging on a cut nail driven into a mortar seam. A quick perusal showed that the generator was hard-wired to the house. Check the fuel and the flip of a switch would light up the night.

In a larger shed, perhaps thirty by forty feet, he found, to his delight, a Shaman All-Terrain Vehicle. It was essentially a one-third-size replica of his Mercedes. A Lotpro snowplow attachment sat nearby. It would easily attach onto the front bumper. Ideal for a run up the roads or a few days out in the bush. It required a lot less horizontal and vertical clearance than the Mercedes.

There were four Ski-Doo Freeride snowmobiles arranged neatly along the wall. A DR Versa-Trailer, looking like it could hold a thousand pounds or so, was parked on the back wall. The Husqvarna 545 Mark II 20" chainsaw sitting in the trailer was a clear clue as to how firewood arrived. Hand and power tools spoke to the fact that a significant amount of self-reliance was required to live in these environs.

Flyrods and spin casting equipment hung like fine art on pegboards above wooden work benches affixed to the walls. Fly tying vices, feathers, thread, and other necessities took up a ten-foot section. Tackle boxes were neatly tucked underneath.

The owners of Alkanair were perfectly outfitted to provide their clients with the ultimate Yukon experience. Mark hoped against hope he could meet them someday.

He decided to live out of both the home and the Mercedes. He plugged the Mercedes into the home for power from the generator. He adapted the office on the main floor of the home to his own purposes. His old Yairi Alverez guitar, mike and amp were set up with a barstool from the kitchen for butt support. He plugged up his MacBook Air and laid it out on the desk.

He tried to call John several times, but apparently, the world-wide communications issues caused by the virus included the upper reaches of northwestern Canada. He finally got a patch through, and John answered.

"Greetings Mr. Mark! I was afraid you had met your demise through an encounter with a wild beaver or some such. It is truly good to hear your voice! I lost your tracker several days ago and just regained your location." Emotions. From a computer. Mark needed the smartass computer. Otherwise, he might have shot the sat phone.

"Likewise. How do I run my computer communications through the sat phone?" Mark got directly to the point in case he lost the connection. He had forgotten how to make the connection. John gave him the simple numeric instructions and he was hooked up.

"Thanks, John. Anything I need to know about since I've been incommunicado for the last month?"

"Sir, if you can, please try to contact Ms. Sirocco. She and Ms. Amber Lee have expressed concern about you."

"OK. Can you try to patch me through?" John was able to secure the connection from Mayo to Dallas through a top-secret Arctic fly-over satellite dedicated to disrupting Russian government intelligence. An obvious oxymoron for any government intelligence agency.

Sirocco picked up on the first ring. "Mark we're glad to hear from you! You're on speaker."

"Hey, handsome! We miss you!" Amber Lee was all smiles.

"Where is whereabouts unknown this time?" Inquisitive minds wanted to know.

Mark told them where he was, what he had experienced along the northern trek, and his current circumstances. He used enough detail to give the ladies an idea. He told them he had decided to winter over so he'd be there at least six months or more, depending on his mood. He could hear the ladies go back-and-forth a bit, then Sirocco said "We'll see you in a week or two! We love you! Bye!"

"Wait!" Mark had an idea.

"What?"

"Bring me a Jacuzzi, please."

"Of course! It is on the list we're already making." The ladies clicked off.

Well damn, Mark thought. Later, when he had given it more thought, he considered packing up and heading for a different whereabouts unknown. Because, sure as shit, the ladies had something up their sleeves. Instead, he cut firewood for the fireplace and the freestanding Buck wood stove. He cut and notched logs for the Jacuzzi platform. He used ropes and the front winch on the Benz to erect the notched logs into the fifteen-foot-high platform for the Jacuzzi. He made the platform essentially bear-proof. Nothing like having a grizzly join you in the hot tub! Access was via an extension ladder secured vertically from the ground to an improvised landing.

He thought of Bear down on the Yak and wished her well. He spent the next few days running the boat up and down the river, pushing the plane into the sky for a few hours and making sure the chopper was operable. Mala and Mute made a quick recovery from their hunger and dehydration. They stayed underfoot like puppies even they were probably two or three years old. Mark was normally averse to constant companionship, but he quickly grew to appreciate their presence.

He caught chinook salmon and some rainbow trout. There would be time to catch several more species. Beaver lodges and dams were abundant and obvious from the air. There were small herds of elk and whitetail deer nearby. He spotted a black bear mama with two cubs. He cruised near a ragged old male grizzly bear fishing near some rocks in the river. A variety of hawks and songbirds made themselves known. Bald and golden eagles fished and scavenged along the abundant lakes and the river.

He was settled in and had established a flexible routine by the time he heard the KC-390 in the distance. It was the first man-made sound, other than his electronics, that he had heard in a while. He loaded Mala and Mute into the Shaman and drove up to the airport. Sirocco was doing the shutdown checklist and Amber Lee had dropped the rear cargo ramp. She leaped into his arms and smothered him with kisses. Sirocco joined them shortly and did the same thing. Then they saw Mala and Mute. So much for that Mark thought. The ladies and the dogs instantly bonded, and joy was boundless.

Eventually, Mark surveyed the interior of the cargo hold. It was completely stuffed with a variety of what looked like scientific equipment. And the Jacuzzi.

"Where are ya'll taking all of that equipment?" Mark asked.

"Here, of course!" Amber Lee was obviously excited, and Mark could not quite figure out why. He'd learn soon enough. He left the dogs with the ladies and drove back to the Municipal Council. He traded out the Shaman for a slat-railed twenty-four-foot flatbed truck. Like so many places he had been, the keys were above the sun visor. He returned to the airport. It took two trips, but they were able to get all of the equipment from the no-frills cargo jet to the municipal buildings.

"We're putting your ass to work handsome!" The ladies were having fun. It had been a long time since Mark had seen both of them in their old carefree mode. "We, being our collective organizations, have established scientific monitoring stations across the globe. In spite of the recent downward turn of events for mankind, we still believe there is time to rehabilitate humans into stewards of the environment. You are now a far north monitoring station!" Sirocco was emphatic and enthusiastic.

"Does this mean I am on the payroll?" Mark was less than humored by this turn of events.

"Actually, you are an investor. John made payment on your behalf through one of your business investments. The total cost was a modest one-point-two million." Amber Lee mostly disarmed him with her infectious grin.

"So, I'm in the hole for a million, and I have to work? Do I at least get a title?" Mark was slipping into his 'I'm fucked' state of mind.

"Absolutely. Mark Baret, Semi-Scientist!" Mark realized that the Temporary Technician title was probably already taken.

"So be it. For the next few months, I will address all of my correspondence accordingly."

Sirocco and Amber Lee traded off responsibilities for several weeks until they were satisfied with the placement of field instrumentation and two-way communication back to Mayo. Mark was the hired hand, strong back, and weak mind, as he so elegantly expressed his lot in life. They set up an extensive lab in the office spaces at the Municipal facility; Gas chromatographs, a small TEM, a variety of mono- and binocular microscopes. Other instruments would come into play over time.

"We need to continue air quality monitoring for carbon dioxide, etc. as well as small and very small particulate. We set up TSP, PM-10 and PM-2.5 monitors and other atmospheric monitoring devices for these purposes."

Altogether a dozen sites had been established within two hundred miles. There was one at the airport, and the others were scattered to the four winds from Tombstone Territorial Park northwest to the Nahanni National Park Reserve to the east and south. The mountains in the area went as high as 2640 meters in the Ragged Range in the park's northwest region. This elevation was near the upper end of the chopper's capabilities.

Mark would periodically visit each site to make sure the instruments were unimpeded by fallen trees, snow, and animals. Certain techniques required individual sample collection and transport back to the lab. He would perform various microscopic and benchtop chemical analyses for things like micro-plastics and heavy metals such as arsenic and lead.

The job required he keep meticulous notes on everything he did, including sightings of wildlife, fish caught, and a number of other standard field observations. Mark strongly suspected that he would fall down on the meticulous notes aspect of his newly minted Semi-Scientist job. He was a lifelong generalist and probably would not undergo metamorphosis from a caterpillar into a butterfly. The ladies were under no illusions either but were truly excited to at least gather some data and at the same time hear from Mark periodically.

He had been known to slip off to whereabouts unknown for a year or more at a time. At least the loves of his life would know where he was using science as a deflection.

Mark drifted back to the present. He casually ran his hand over the grips of the Desert Eagle resting on the shelf he installed on the edge of the Jacuzzi. The .50 caliber monster would do the trick on a grizzly at close range. He had no desire to do such a thing, but shit happens. Besides, Mala and Mute were standing guard at the base of the platform—well, sleeping anyway.

His scraggly white beard was lying down on his chest, and his long white hair was wet from a dunking. It was in disarray. He conjured up visions of the three of them in the Jacuzzi, spent and totally content, after a few hours enshrouded in the aurora borealis and the vastness above them. The memories would suffice until their next trip up to whereabouts known.

Another sip of scotch and another hit from the peace pipe, combined with the soft music the Stewart River was making, and a particular but nondescript flavor in the air, sent him back to 1964 or so. He and Mat were wading and fishing amongst the granite boulders, gravel, and sand near Little Sandy on the James River, just below the Trestle. The night before, Mark had heard a song on the white plastic AM radio beside his bed.

It was called My Girl. Smokey Robinson and Ronald White wrote it, and The Temptations crooned it. Mark hummed it to himself and perhaps sang out loud a bit, changing only one thing. He added an 's' to girl.

"Well, I guess you could say

What can make me feel this way?

My girls….".

And so it goes.

Week 54

Gusts of wind slapped cold, morning rain against the floor-to-ceiling windows of Doug Kryzinsky's tenth-floor corner office. He was oblivious, sitting in his leather office chair and slumped over a mahogany desk with his head resting on his right forearm. He had fallen asleep somewhere around 3:00 am, and twirling spirals of color danced across his computer screen, controlled by the machine's screen saver program. He would have continued sleeping, but his cellphone rang, startling him from a disturbing dream.

His left eye was dry from hours of staring at his computer screen last night. It stung as he lifted his head from a sweaty arm and saw a puddle of drool on the desk where his head had been. His right hand floundered around, trying to locate the phone while his eyes struggled to focus. He could feel a migraine forming in the center of his forehead, slightly over his left eye.

He swiped the phone as the third ring started and noted the time as quarter after seven. The caller, Jean, was his primary contact with the government task force driving vaccine production. His company was just one of the cogs in the supply chain. Still, it was deemed a critical asset and therefore subject to the good and the bad of temporary government control. The US Defense Production Act had been in force for six months now.

He glanced out the east-facing window as he moved the phone to his ear. He could see the outline of a furniture factory about a quarter of a mile south of his complex. The early morning light was enough to silhouette the charcoal gray outline of the several small towers and one six-story office building. Not a single light was on in the factory. No warm lights twinkled from the darkened windows of the office building. The rolling blackouts would give them six to eight hours of power each day, but only if they were lucky. Doug's business had enjoyed around-the-clock power since being designated as a critical asset. His company's status also provided him with an emergency cell tower.

The guaranteed communication links were a blessing and a curse. Now, as the phone reached the corner of his mouth, it seemed a curse.

"Jean, this is an early call."

"I figured you were probably sleeping at your desk again after yesterday's fiasco." She certainly got that right, he thought to himself.

"I might have a workaround. But without new chips for the two synthesizers, it's only a temporary solution. I can probably keep up deliveries at ninety percent for the next four days, but after that, the output will drop to fifty percent." He was being optimistic but staying within the bounds of realism.

"Do you know what the problem is with the chip delivery?" she asked.

"In one word, pilots." Doug shifted in his seat. He could feel the migraine growing. "Over twenty-five percent of the world's trained pilots have been taken out by the virus. I know the military is doing what it can, but it's not enough. There is no one to fly the plane. I was told a pilot should be available by the end of the week. So, in the best-case scenario, we will be at fifty percent output for three days. But if things continue to deteriorate, three days could turn into three weeks. I have a team of engineers looking at other alternatives, but they haven't come up with any workable solution yet."

"Look, Doug, I understand the problem, but you need to sort something out. You are one of only three operations that can produce the carrier solutions, and the other two operations are already at eighty percent production."

Doug's right elbow was on the desk, and his hand cupped his forehead. His eyes were shut tight as he thought about a potential solution. Silently, he shook his head as Jean continued.

"Can we run the synthesis process by hand?" She asked.

"We can, but the quality of the product degrades, and the final solution usually falls outside of acceptable safety boundaries. We know from the early tests that the deaths from the anaphylactic shock will more than quadruple if we use an out-of-spec carrier solution. Jean, global supply chains are collapsing. There are not enough living, healthy people to keep the supply lines going. We knew it was a possibility. Now it's a reality."

"It's not as bad as you imagine, Doug. We have things under control." Doug listened but knew she was lying. "I will speak with the military liaison and see if we can do a special run for the chips." Maybe, thought Doug.

Doug thought about the state of affairs around the globe. The last time the world's population declined was during the Black Plague, some seven hundred years ago. Then, about a quarter of the Eurasian population fell to the disease.

Today, mortality rates in first-world countries were holding at about twenty-five percent, but only because vaccines were helping stem the slaughter. With the most recent advent of the lambda variant, some third-world countries watched while over fifty percent of their people perished. The sad truth was that the vaccine couldn't be produced fast enough to outrun the virus.

In first-world countries, the situation was made worse by large pockets of the population who refused the cure. Once the virus took hold in these areas, it spread like wildfire. The only mercy, if you could call it that, was the lambda variant usually killed within five days of the first symptoms. Long, lingering deaths were not an issue. If you survived past the fifth day, you were on the road to recovery and life. Mortality rates for this variant hovered just below sixty percent for the unvaccinated populations. Infection rates for the vaccinated hovered slightly below one percent, and mortality rates in this group were negligible. Still, large groups of people refused the vaccine preferring to take their chances.

The situation in some areas was out of hand. Recently a truck full of vaccines was attacked and burned outside of a community in Idaho. Parts of rural America were effectively a collection of small fortress communities where vigilantes were the law, and any unauthorized intrusion into the community was a death sentence. Killing people was easy compared to stopping the virus. It didn't care about borders, politics, religion, or race. The virus didn't think; it only acted—relentlessly probing any and all defenses until a weak point burst, and microscopic messengers of death surged through, bringing another wave of destruction.

Doug's company produced a specialized solution used in the vaccine injection. The fluid was chemically balanced and designed to accomplish two tasks: preserve the Trojan DNA and provide a protein coating allowing the DNA to slip through cell membranes. The problem Doug faced sprung from the delicate chemical balance required in the solution. Out-of-balance carrier fluids quickly became toxic to humans, and the cure became more dangerous than the disease. His operation achieved quality control through their synthesizers, where cutting-edge computer technology managed the final preparation of the carrier solution. Essentially this allowed every single dose to undergo rigorous quality checks before being sent out.

Even with the best computer controls, only sixty percent of the dosses passed the final inspection. If he reverted to manual control of the synthesis process, the final products were almost guaranteed to contain four toxic dosses out of each ten produced.

Doug stood up from his desk and walked across the office to get a cup of coffee from his Nespresso machine. He usually limited himself to one capsule, but he made a double this morning. His coffee drawer was down to a hundred and fifteen capsules, and once they were gone, hopes of refilling his supplies were dim. Supply chains for critical assets were shaky, but it was worse for everyday products. Most big cities were reporting that grocery stores and supermarkets were empty more often than they were full.

Crops rotted on the stalk because fuel shortages left the harvesting machines standing silent in the fields. Even if farmers could produce a harvest, getting it to market was a purely hit-and-miss affair. But the pain wasn't distributed evenly. Vaccination rates in politically left-leaning communities were significantly higher than in right-leaning areas. Consequentially, the more politically conservative the region, the more severe its virus-related problems.

Lost in the fog of its perpetual hypocrisy, the US Congress could not pass vaccine mandates but would not let anyone into its Washington DC isolation sector without proof of vaccination. The task force ordered Doug to require proof of vaccination for anyone working in his manufacturing complex. But he had to proclaim this was his corporate order and had nothing to do with the Federal Government.

Doug returned to his desk with a large, hot cup of coffee and started his morning news scan. The headlines still focused on Representative Gratas from Florida. He vehemently fought against vaccine mandates for most of the year, playing to his rightwing base and leveraging himself onto the national stage. Initially, he was frequently mentioned as a potential presidential candidate in the next election. But about a month ago, his operation started to fray around the edges as reports surfaced of alleged involvement with Russia's FSB. Multiple national security leaks were quickly attributed to Gratas. It also emerged he received the vaccine as soon as it was available, despite encouraging his base to resist taking it. While not illegal, it certainly didn't increase his popularity.

The nail in the coffin came several days ago when an anonymous source came forward with a recorded call between Gratas and the FSB. They agreed to help him with his presidential campaign in exchange for access to the computer records of the US Virus Task Force. Gratas was now under house arrest, but more evidence of his complicity in treason was now coming forward.

There is a silver lining in every cloud, and the silver lining in the Gratas affair was a classic case of removing the head of the snake. He was the de facto leader for some of the most virulent anti-vaccine groups. The entire movement was now in disarray, and its members were starting to turn towards the vaccine out of desperation. For many, it was too late.

Doug noted a reluctance in the daily news to touch on the largest issue looming around the virus—population decline. Perhaps people had not yet put the pieces together. But he was close to the vaccination pipeline and understood a basic truth. Vaccine production could not outrun the virus. Yes, it would save millions of lives, but the world's human population was taking a mighty blow. Three days before, he was privy to a mistakenly circulated report from the US Virus Task Force. It was only available for fifteen minutes and quickly retracted. But he was online and actively catching up on his email when it hit. Somehow, CEOs in critical assets were mistakenly added to the mailing list.

The report was bleak. Population reduction in many developing countries was projected to top sixty percent. Even in developed countries, where vaccines were available, population losses of twenty to thirty percent were expected. Of the 8.5 billion souls on the planet, 3 billion would perish from the virus. Another 3.5 billion would succumb to starvation or murder during the ensuing chaos. Earth's human population was on a trajectory to return to levels not seen since the early part of the 1900s.

Manufacturing was already crumbling, but without a consumer base, it made little difference. Global supply chains were severed and collapsing. Sealed borders rapidly became fortified. Doug knew that most of the available vaccines in the USA initially went to the military and the political class, as defense of the country's borders rose to the number one spot on a long list of concerns.

The future looked bleak, with developed countries becoming havens of technology and undeveloped nations collapsing into chaos and anarchy. Collapsed governments would be replaced with tribal and gang factions, fighting for the scarce resources available.

There was little Doug could do other than work to get as many people as possible vaccinated. He turned his eyes back to his computer and started working on reviving his supply line.

As Doug returned to his problems, Carl Jennings sat in his CEO office on Three Rock's Boston Campus. He was absorbed in a report Dan Rhoden sent last night. Dan's new position as Head of Research at their latest spinoff company was already paying off. While the rest of the world was falling to Ebola, Dan buried his head in decoding the crystal matrix sphere. His latest breakthrough, four months ago, unlocked vast stores of medical information. Buried within the data were unexpected insights into advanced bioengineering and nano-robotics.

Carl operated on a series of basic principles. Included in his philosophy was a bit on social direction. His observation as an entrepreneur who built a major corporation was that people split into three categories regarding their visions for the future. The best vision of the future many people could muster was a retreat to the past. This group lacked the vision to see a future different from the past. They lamented about the "good old days" when life ran without significant problems. Returning to those days was the best future they could imagine.

The second group lacked the insight to develop any vision for the future. The past was not particularly attractive, and their apathy robbed them of the creativity to envision a future materially different than their present situation. It's not that they didn't dream of winning the lottery. They could see themselves being rich, but only in a version of the present-day culture. They would change, but the world around them would remain static and stagnant, perpetually looking like the present moment.

The anti-vaxxers, for the most part, appeared to be composed of these two groups of people, living in a mental fog with so much fear of the future they would rather perish than move forward. But Carl understood the kinetic nature of existence. Time only moves in one direction, and retreating backward was not an option. He sensed humanity was perched on the precipice of monumental change. Human evolution had reached a fulcrum, and Homo sapiens would either move into a radically different future or perish.

Evidence at hand suggested those who could not or would not adapt were destined for the fossil record. The world economy was taking a blow as billions of humans fell to the virus. If the survivors only recreated a future mimicking the past, humanity was destined to repeat the current devastation. But there was a better way, and Carl was inextricably bound to a new vision of the future he had forged during conversations with Mat and Dan. The information uncovered by Dan offered a path towards the genetic modification of humans so the species could avoid future plagues. Even more exciting was the possibility of integrating bio-engineered technology into the human system. Nanosystems designed to expand human computational capabilities, self-repairing organs extending human life spans, and clean energy systems allowing people to live in closer harmony with the rest of the biosphere.

Carl was part of the third group of people, those who embraced change and envisioned a future where humanity could thrive and grow. The future was in front of them, not behind. The new spinoff where Dan worked was the first step towards this new vision.

Raw information extracted from the crystal matrix memory might allow humanity to leapfrog into a new future where the concept of a technological singularity could become a reality. The brilliant mathematician John von Neumann was one of the earliest thinkers to formulate the singularity concept, and it was later popularized by the mathematics professor and science fiction writer Vernor Vinge.

Humans with integrated biotechnology and altered by DNA enhancements would essentially represent a new evolutionary step, with technology and biology fusing together. Technology, which had demonstrably shown exponential improvements over time, would drive rapid changes in human evolution.

His company was dipping its corporate toe into the waters of the future with their new spinoff. But Carl knew the uphill battle they faced. Many politicians viewed human evolution as an existential threat. Carl viewed them in the same light as one might observe a child becoming an adult. Geological history was littered with examples of species unable to meet the challenge of the future. Change or perish into the void of extinction was the only message they left. Humans would go the same path without radical change. The degree of Anthropocene damage done to the planet over a mere 150 years was terrifying. The plague was a human disaster, but one largely of their own making.

Carl had committed his company to this vision of the future. Mat infused the new venture with most of his personal fortune, and Dan held the technical expertise to manage their path forward. Not too many generations from now, the world would be unrecognizable from pre-pandemic Earth.

Four Years On

Dappled sunlight played across the worn dirt surface at the edge of the forest. Mat sat in the entrance of their hut and watched as Maria played with her friends. She was turning from a toddler to a young child and growing taller each day. Her Rohodi friends were the only ones she had ever known. He smiled and went back to reviewing the latest report from Carl. It was the most encouraging one so far.

The world would never return to the way it was, but new pathways were opening. The best estimates available placed the world's population slightly over two billion, about equivalent to the planet's population in 1900. Over three billion perished from the Ebola-nano pandemic, and the other three billion disappeared in the ensuing chaos as agricultural and industrial ventures ground to a halt, supply chains collapsed, and starvation ravaged the globe. Earth was littered with the bones of the dead. Virtually everyone left was either vaccinated or had inherited the new human genome.

Information gained from the crystal memory spheres was transforming technology, but adjustments to life's new realities were difficult for most people. Local economies gained momentum, but long-distance supply chains remained largely unworkable due to the lack of people to run them. Self-dependence was the rule of the day, causing local agriculture to carry the heavy load in providing needed food for urban centers. Solar, wind, and hydroelectric power quickly replaced fossil fuels in most regions as oil and gas transportation systems faltered.

Humans are a species of adaptors, and new realities called for new social structures. Supplies of raw resources far exceeded population demands, driving the price of commodities down and taking away some of the classic reasons for aggression and war. Conflicts occasionally arose, but most nations were too busy rebuilding to pour money into useless fighting. Nuclear threats still existed, but diplomacy was far more useful than war, and more warheads had been destroyed than produced over the past four years.

The general consensus among nations was that future pandemics must be avoided at all costs. Medical technology and medical access quickly became the focus of international cooperation. Currently, not enough was known about the long-term effects of the genomic changes wrought by the vaccine, but Mat was convinced the changes offered an improvement in human survival.

At Jenara's insistence, she and Mat vanished into the western jungles of Brazil after his work to distribute the vaccine as widely as possible. He worked with a global coalition, but they were not enough to stem the catastrophe, even with their extensive resources. However, they did play a critical role in preserving core areas of civilization on all continents. They prevented governments from using the vaccine as a weapon to further their own narrow interests.

Maria, named after her great grandmother, was one of the first children in the world born with an inherited, vaccine-altered, genome. She needed no booster against the virus; it was built into her DNA from birth. Jenara would not have her child be a medical guinea pig, and for the time being, she chose a life as far from medical researchers as possible. Mat happily followed. The western jungle was far from prying eyes, and the need for rebuilding in the east of the country meant few outsiders ever visited the Rohodi lands. Demand for rainforest lumber ceased as economies emerged from the pandemic. An overabundance of cheaper and closer lumber kept people's eyes off the Rohodi homeland.

Mat still left the jungle several times a year to tend to his investments and business obligations at one of the most powerful companies on Earth, Three Rock Corp. The company's technologies, developed from the trove of data in the crystal matrix memory core, were revolutionizing the new norms of the future. Robotics and nanotechnologies took unbelievable leaps forward, providing the world with the tools it needed for civilization to advance in a world depleted of humans.

Social norms were changing also. Eliminating food, shelter, and medical insecurity within communities took top priority in most nations. Technology that would have made Three Rock the wealthiest entity on the planet before the pandemic still generated wealth for its owners and employees. But not the winner-take-all wealth that existed before.

But life in the western jungles of Brazil seemingly went on as it had for centuries before. Plants needed gathering each day, and the men hunted so that the tribe could eat. Below the surface, though, changes were stirring. Advanced medical supplies, arrayed on shelves in the back of Mat and Jenara's hut, kept the sick alive. Solar arrays blended in with the village surroundings, hardly noticeable but providing a stream of electricity, which powered satellite communications with the world outside.

Hoshikay was aging, and over the past several years, Jenara took on more of her tribal responsibilities. But she and Mat knew they would eventually return to their own world. Maria needed an education, as would her sister, even though she was still in Jenara's expanding belly. Jenara took a girl of Hoshikay's choosing under her wing. The tribe would need their shaman when Jenara and Hoshikay were no longer there.

The world would never be the same, and Mat was irrevocably changed. He could not stop the dreams, where he roamed the jungles and more in the guise of spirit animals. Under Hoshikay's watchful eye, his visions of the future grew sharper. He, more than anyone else, saw the coming future of evolutionary change. The genetic technologies decrypted in the Boston labs of Three Rock left no doubt in his mind that humans were on a path where genetics, robotics, and nanomechanics would craft a new species of sentient beings.

About the Authors

Rand Soler - Writer, environmentalist, and geologist living in the Pacific North-west. His writing follows his travels around the globe, investigating the science and mystery of the world around us.

Y.A. Picker - Author, fisherman, player of the guitar and harmonica, lover of the outdoors, life-long member of the orgy-of-the-ologies club, all-around ne'er-do-well. Chaser of the crooked roads and the ancient ones.

www.ingramcontent.com/pod-product-compliance
Lightning Source LLC
Chambersburg PA
CBHW071131200626
46817CB00018B/2693